A ROGUE AT THE HIGHLAND COURT

THE HIGHLAND LADIES BOOK THREE

CELESTE BARCLAY

OLIVER HEBER BOOKS
GNARLY WOOL PUBLISHING
EST 1961

 Created with Vellum

"I may be a real bad boy
But baby I'm a real good man."
~Tim McGraw, "Real Bad Boy, Real Good Man"

Perhaps a rogue can be reformed.

Happy reading, y'all,
Celeste

SUBSCRIBE TO CELESTE'S NEWSLETTER

THE HIGHLAND LADIES

A Spinster at the Highland Court

A Spy at the Highland Court

A Wallflower at the Highland Court

A Rogue at the Highland Court

A Rake at the Highland Court

An Enemy at the Highland Court

A Saint at the Highland Court

A Beauty at the Highland Court

A Sinner at the Highland Court

A Hellion at the Highland Court

An Angel at the Highland Court

A Harlot at the Highland Court

The Highland Ladies follows the lives and loves of the ladies-in-waiting at King Robert the Bruce's court. If you are a fan of Highlander romances, then you've surely encountered the time period that spans the Wars of Scottish Independence, along with the rise and reign of Robert the Bruce. I have taken creative license in a number of areas, especially the creation of characters such as our hero and heroine, but the events in the early portion of this story are true to history.

Without giving away too much, our heroine, Allyson Elliot, is a runaway bride from Stirling Castle. Clan Elliot land lies on the border of Scotland and England. It was once part of a larger region known as Northumbria, which stretched through both England and Scotland. Today, that land borders the English county of Northumberland. Cheviot Hills, England, which is just across the border, was the site of more than one battle during the Wars of Scottish Independence, and the land along the border changed hands numerous times. Hermitage Castle is mentioned in the novel and was a medieval keep once in the possession of William de Soulis, but when he was convicted of treason against Robert the

Bruce, his land in Liddesdale and Hermitage Castle were given to Robert Bruce, the king's illegitimate son. The land surrounding the castle was part of the Clan Elliot territory. The ruins of Hermitage Castle still exist and are a tourist site.

Chillingham Castle has an appropriate name. It was a chilling location where the events that are alluded to in this story truly took place. It is known as "England's Most Haunted Castle." Sir Thomas Grey was a vaunted English knight who worked his way through the ranks to become a trusted guardian of a border castle. He was married to Lady Agnes Grey, but not much is known about her. King Edward I visited the keep during his journey to battle William Wallace. The only chamber in the castle to have glass windows was the one in which the king stayed. During a campaign with King Edward, "The Hammer of the Scots," John Sage was injured and no longer able to serve as a knight. He begged the king to find a position for him, and so he was assigned to Chillingham Castle, where he became the king's chief torturer. He was notoriously violent and arbitrary. He spared no one, not man, woman, nor child. The events described in this story are as near to history as I could write without being too gruesome. The death of his mistress did occur as described in this book, and the woman's father, a border reiver, did seek retribution. This is as far as my story goes where Chillingham and its residents are concerned. The border reivers played a vital role in King Edward's control over that land, so he was unwilling to anger them or risk their allegiance. John Sage was convicted and given back to be hanged. He was not so fortunate; he was dismembered while alive. This castle also still remains a popular tourist site where even the dungeon is open for a tour, and people can spend the night as guests of the hotel.

Redheugh Castle was the primary stronghold of the Clan Elliot during the reign of King Robert the Bruce. The name comes from the old word for red, 'rede,' and heugh which meant 'bank.' The tower had a view of the valley that ran alongside the Hermitage Water crossing and was the first of a series of pele towers built along the border. A farmhouse and grounds now stand where the pele tower once did. It still remains in the hands of an Elliot.

I hope you enjoy *A Rogue at the Highland Court* and come to love Allyson Elliot and Ewan Gordon as much as I have.

Happy reading,
Celeste

CHAPTER ONE

The crunch of frost echoed in Stirling Castle's royal gardens as Allyson Elliot trudged along with the other ladies-in-waiting, enduring another one of the queen's morning strolls through the struggling blossoms. It was mid-March, and spring had arrived for their neighbors to the south, but Mother Nature seemed to have forgotten that Stirling wasn't truly in the Highlands. Sitting on the border between the Highlands and Lowlands, the weather in Stirling was fickle, playing both sides of the fence. Allyson puffed out a cloud of condensation as the ice crackled beneath her booted feet. She didn't mind the distance of the morning constitutional, but having been raised in the Lowlands, Allyson was still unaccustomed to the frigid temperatures of the north.

"I still can't believe he married her." Allyson caught the waspish voice of Cairstine Grant as her attention returned to the young women around her. Allyson realized Cairstine spoke of Maude Sutherland without hearing the former lady-in-waiting's name. Maude had been a shy lass from the northern Highlands, and several of the other ladies-in-waiting —Cairstine Grant included—had teased her without

1

mercy. It had come as a shock when Kieran Mac-Leod arrived at court and immediately took an interest in Maude, who the other ladies considered overweight and plain. He'd been one of the most eligible lairds, and more than one nose was out of joint when he chose a woman so many believed was beneath him.

Allyson struggled to smother her giggle as she considered just how Maude was beneath Kieran these days. Allyson arrived at court four years ago as an impressionable girl overwhelmed by the attention her fair hair and robin-egg blue eyes garnered. She soon realized she enjoyed the attention after being the youngest of her parents' six children. A few batted eyelashes and a coy smile earned her the appreciation of the young courtiers who flocked to court hoping to gain attention and favor from King Robert the Bruce. While Allyson wasn't as daring as some of her peers, she had stolen a few kisses from these men, hoping to find one who would make her his wife and take her away from both the royal court and her family. Her attempts hadn't garnered a husband, but it had resulted in a reputation as a flirt.

"Allyson. Allyson, are you listening to me?" Cairren Kennedy nudged her, and Allyson turned a blank stare at her friend before remembering that they'd been speaking about the upcoming festivities for the spring equinox. The court would celebrate the return of the sun and the forthcoming warm weather.

"I don't know that there will be much to celebrate if this cold weather persists. It's more like winter's beginning rather than spring. I'd be happy to never see snow again," Allyson grumbled.

"Not bluidy likely living in Scotland," Cairren muttered the oath. Another Lowlander, Cairren had been at court since the previous spring and was still adjusting to the harsher climate. "I'm more likely to freeze my toes than freckle. It's just an excuse to feast in the hopes of forgetting the miserable weather. Why else would the queen allow pagan celebrations?"

"She allows them because she knows no matter how Catholic we Scots are, we will always cling to tradition. It's not like we run aboot caterwauling to the old gods. We light some bonfires and drink too much whisky and ale. I don't mind encouraging spring to arrive, and I don't mind how warm a belly of whisky will make me feel. Especially since I agree that my toes are aboot to chip off." As if to convince herself that they wouldn't, Allyson wiggled her toes as they paused for Queen Elizabeth to speak to a gardener. Allyson supposed the queen was requesting the flowers that would decorate the Great Hall and instructing the man on how to care for the blooms, lest this late frost damage them. "I'm looking forward to the feast since we'll have the tedium of Lent within a week."

"I wouldn't let the queen hear you say Lent is tedious. I swear it's her favorite time of year. More hours to spend in prayer." Cairren pretended to rub her knee with a surreptitious look around. "I dread the time spent on my knees."

"Aye, but some ladies are already well versed in that," Allyson snickered.

"Shh! You'll have us be among those, and not with any pleasure. I have no desire to be trapped on the prie-dieu in the queen's solar in front of the others." Cairren failed to hide her smirk despite her censoring words.

"Very well. But you're just as aware as I am that I speak the truth," Allyson murmured, allowing the subject of the other ladies-in-waiting's less-than-ladylike behavior to drop. Neither Allyson nor Cairren should have been privy to such knowledge, but living among courtiers for more than a day gave the young women an education they never would have received at home. Allyson had mourned her loss of innocent ignorance when she first arrived, but she soon learned that women wielded power by choosing with whom they shared their favors. Allyson hadn't gone beyond a brief kiss here and there, but she wasn't averse to more sinful behavior if ever a situation where her wellbeing at court counted on it.

"Are you pleased that the Gordon twins returned in time for the feast. Which do you think is the better looking?" Cairren redirected their conversation to a safer topic. It was expected that they would gossip about eligible men.

"Can you even tell them apart? They're mirror images of one another."

"Nay. Not really. But both are handsome as the devil, and just as tempting."

"Then it's a good thing Lent is around the corner. I'll be sure to withstand that test." Allyson rolled her eyes.

"But in the meantime, we have the equinox and Shrove Tuesday to indulge."

Allyson tsked. "The only things I intend to indulge in are honey cakes and lamb stew. I shall miss meat when all I have to look forward to are potatoes and turnips."

"I can think of a few women who will miss both meat and taters," Cairren chuckled.

"You're worse than I am." Allyson didn't say any more as the group arrived at the castle doors. The queen swept in ahead of them and gave a glance that told the ladies to hurry to her salon after returning their outerwear to their chambers. Allyson and Cairren wound their way through the twisting passageways until they reached the one where the matrons and widows lived. They halted and stared as the Gordon twins emerged from Lady Bevan's chamber, both tucking their leines into their breeks. There was no way for Allyson and Cairren to misunderstand the situation. The twins turned towards them and offered remorseless grins. They strolled toward the shocked pair.

"We seem to have found two little chickadees separated from their mother hen," one of the Gordons purred. Allyson wasn't certain, but she decided that the one speaking was Ewan, who had a small scar that sliced the left side of his upper lip. His twin had no such scar, to Allyson's knowledge.

"Such a shame they should encounter two foxes in their henhouse." The other brother, who she assumed was Eoin, offered a smile that could only be described as wolfish.

"Aye, and the farmer lops off the heads of the foxes he catches. A couple clucks in the right ear ends the foxes' hunt." Allyson bristled. She'd met the twins several times during her time at court, and even enjoyed dancing with the accomplished set of brothers. But their reputations preceded them, and their arrogance rankled. This time it wasn't their reputations that spoke to their roguish behavior but the behavior itself. "I hadn't realized roosters liked to share their spent hen."

"She is most definitely spent." A dark eyebrow twitched as the man she believed was Ewan smirked.

"She would be after brooding so often." Allyson grew tired of speaking in euphemisms and analogies. "Excuse us. We have somewhere we'd rather be."

"Testy chickadee," the same brother spoke again.

"Bored," Allyson used her practiced smile, but there was no missing the derisiveness in her voice.

"We've entertained you plenty of times." Eoin matched his twin's twitching eyebrow.

"Perhaps on the dance floor. But then again, you are interchangeable." Allyson chirped. Cairren elbowed her as she gasped for at least the third time. "One is as good as the other to waste away the time."

The brothers' matching glares made Allyson laugh. She elbowed Cairren back, but this was in jest. She shook her head before composing herself enough to speak.

"Does that expression come naturally, or did you practice to ensure you match in everything you do? And you want me to believe you're not interchangeable." Allyson linked her arm through Cairren's, and the women attempted to step around the brothers. However, the closer one snagged Allyson's arm and leaned in to whisper in her ear.

"Lass, you wouldn't last five minutes if we took turns with you." Allyson froze as she turned an icy gaze upon Ewan, who still held her arm.

"Are you threatening me? Because that isn't an offer I will ever want."

"What? No." The man jerked back and shook his head. Realization of what his words would mean to an innocent dawned upon him. He softened his hold on her arm but didn't release her. Instead, he bent forward again. "Lass, my apologies. That wasn't what I intended. I took our banter too far. I didn't mean to scare you."

Allyson's pinched expression relaxed at the sincerity in his voice, which caused a shiver to run along her spine. She nodded once, and this time he released her arm when she pulled it away.

"Which one are you?" She murmured.

"Ewan, my lady." The sun streaked head bowed in a courtly presentation that would have earned the giant Highlander laughs if he were home. That meant the other man now standing in silence was Eoin, as she'd guessed.

"Good day." Allyson didn't wait to drag Cairren along as they rushed to their chamber and then to the queen's solar, all the while Cairren lamented the consequences of their tardiness. Neither could admit they'd stopped to speak to the notorious twins.

CHAPTER TWO

Allyson felt restless for the duration of the day as the scene in the passageway replayed in her mind. It wasn't that different from the countless conversations she'd had with courtiers attempting to corrupt and seduce her. However, something unsettled her about this exchange. She suspected it stemmed from the surprise of such innuendos being tossed about after she and Cairren caught the brothers leaving a woman's chambers, and how that very event led to the exchange. She'd studied the men while they stood nearer and tried to find anything that would identify the difference between the two. She hadn't lied when she said they were interchangeable; at least, that was how she'd viewed them before that day.

U-en and O-en. She sounded out in her head. *How original that their parents should give identical twins rhyming names. I wonder what tricks they got up to as weans with matching faces and similar names.* Allyson flinched as her blank gaze remained on the book in her lap. *Why do I care? Why am I even wondering that? They were both arses today. I shouldn't waste a moment of thought on them, but I can't help it. They've irked me and piqued my curiosity. This bluidy curiosity will be my downfall.*

Allyson forced herself to pay attention to the book of poetry that lay open in front of her. She inhaled, filling her lungs, before beginning the page for the third time. This attempt was a success, and she lost herself in the flowing verses until it was time to dress for the evening. She dreaded and anticipated the evening meal in equal measure. Part of her wanted to avoid the twins and the reminder of their exchange, but another part wanted a chance to have the definitive last word. "Good day" seemed weak after the inappropriate nature of the earlier conversation.

"Lady Allyson," called a page as she stepped out of the queen's solar. "Your presence has been requested in the king's Privy Council chamber." The boy of eight or nine didn't remain for a response, instead turning on his heel and dashing back the way he'd come. Allyson's gaze swept the ladies who accompanied her out of the salon, but no one seemed interested in the message delivered to her. She couldn't guess why the king would single her out and request her presence. She hurried to the doors of the king's meeting room, wiping her clammy palms on her skirts as the guard slipped inside to announce her arrival. When the door opened to admit Allyson, the first person she recognized was her father, Laird Kenneth Elliot. A sense of dread took root in the bottom of Allyson's stomach. Rarely did anything good occur when her father arrived at court. Her throat tightened at the hard edge in his eyes. He was steeling himself to deliver news she wouldn't want.

"Allyson," her father's brusque tone reached her as she approached, then dipped into a low curtsy to the king and her father. "I've made a decision that pertains to you."

Allyson blinked, but realized she failed to hide

the fear creeping over her like the cold hands of death. She nodded and opened her mouth to inquire if this had something to do with her mother and siblings, but her father's raised hand stayed her. Allyson glanced around the chamber and spotted the Gordon twins standing across the chamber with their own father, and neither appeared pleased to be there. Suspicion coursed through her as she looked between her father and the twins, shaking her head and backing away.

"This isn't a time for histrionics, lass. I can see you're deducing the reason I have summoned you. We may as well have it out and be done. I need to sign the betrothal documents and be on my way." Her father never would have survived as a courtier with his blunt manner. Allyson's chest felt like a vice was locked around her heart, and her stomach felt as though someone plowed a fist into it.

"Betrothal?" It surprised her how strong her voice sounded in spite of her shock. She turned to look at the twins, and her upper lip curled in disgust. "Which womanizing lecher have you shackled me with?"

"Shackled?" The man she recognized as Ewan lunged forward. "You should count your blessings, lass."

"So, you're the one to marry me, but which one of you will come to my bed? Or will you share me like you did Lady Bevan this morning?" Allyson snapped her mouth shut, shocked at her own runaway tongue. She grinned when both twins shifted, but there was no mirth in her expression. "Assumed I'd forgotten? Assumed I'd never speak of it?"

Allyson tossed her head and canted it before employing her repertoire of flirtations. She smiled seductively and glided toward the twins, angling her body to offer the best view of her cleavage. Hours of practice made her actions seem unintentional and natural, almost unnoticeable in their singular occurrence, but coming together to foster the image of an experienced courtier. She came to stand before the twins and their father, who was a widower. She dropped into a deep curtsy that offered the older man a view down her gown and between her breasts. She exhaled, allowing the gown to slacken and offering a hint of her chemise. Ewan growled before reaching out to grasp her arm as he had earlier that day, but she shied away. She wanted to determine if her potential father-by-marriage was as much a skirt chaser as his sons. Did she need to fear him, too?

"My father's words lead me to believe the documents haven't been signed. I don't belong to you yet, so don't touch me," she hissed before returning her attention to Laird Gordon. "My laird, it is a pleasure to see you again. Pray tell, how long have you and my father been in negotiations? From your sons' appearances, it came as a surprise to them, too. After all, what man would tease his future bride aboot bedding her the same day as she caught him coming from another woman's chamber? The day you'd announce their betrothal?"

Laird Gordon's face suffused with heat, and his ruddy complexion turned scarlet. He swung his gaze toward his sons, the accusations clear without him saying a word.

"As the chit said, I didn't know." Ewan crossed his arms and glared at Allyson. "It matters little now."

"There I disagree. It matters a great deal. You've proven to be a womanizing lecher, as I said before. You didn't deny that." Allyson looked over her shoulder to her father. "Men who go through women like him go through alcohol and money just as quickly. You intend to give my dowry, money and land from our clan, to him?" Allyson didn't say more, knowing that what she left unsaid screamed far louder than if she voiced any further opposition.

"Tread carefully, lass," Ewan hissed.

"Or what? You and your brother will take turns with me? I believe that's what you said earlier."

"What?" The two fathers roared.

"Shall I tell them, or will you?" Allyson demurred even though her posture spoke to her readiness to go into battle.

"It matters not." Kenneth stepped beside his daughter. "You're in no position to object to aught your husband does."

"That may be, but he isn't my husband yet. I intend to object." Allyson set her jaw and stared into her father's eyes. "Now and at the altar."

Allyson understood no priest in Scotland would marry her to any man without her consent. She also understood she played a dangerous game, one where her father might use a proxy to ensure the marriage went forward.

"Father," Ewan spoke up. "You want me to bring this shrew home to Huntly? You'd subject our clan to her viperous tongue?"

"I'm questioning whether I should subject the lass to you," Laird Gordan grumbled. "You denied none of what the lass said, so I take it, it's the truth. She found you leaving Lady Bevan's chamber with Eoin."

"Aye. We were. But as she also said, it was before any of us, Lady Allyson or Eoin or I, were aware of this arrangement. The lady is a widow, and Eoin and I are unwed. We did naught wrong."

"Naught wrong? You're depraved!" Allyson blurted. She spun around toward her father. "They share their women! How am I to be certain which one arrives at my chamber? How do I know they don't expect to do with me what they did with Lady Bevan? You'd force me commit adultery at their whim?"

"Allyson, you're overreacting. You're speaking as though they're lads who still play tricks," Kenneth scoffed. Allyson swung back around and shifted her eyes among the three Gordon men.

"When's the last time they swapped their positions?" she demanded. She suspected that it would vindicate her. There was something about their nonchalance and ennui that told her she wasn't far off the mark. The sheepish glance Laird Gordon exchanged with his sons was enough to answer her question, but she would have her due and hear it admitted. She crossed her arms and cocked her eyebrow.

"A fortnight ago when I sent Eoin on patrol, but he had plans with a woman in the village," Laird Gordon admitted.

Allyson's lips thinned as she glared at Ewan. She remained silent, letting the laird's last words hang in the air. When no one else spoke, she turned to her father.

"And you'd make me believe my concerns are for naught," she whispered. Frustration and fear caused tears to prick the back of her eyelids, but years of repressing public displays of emotions and pride enabled her to overcome the threat of crying.

"Lass, men must sow their wild oats before settling into marriage," Laird Gordon offered the placating words, but Ewan's grumble proved them to be an empty reassurance.

"I owe her naught, not even once she's my wife. You'd have me marry her for her dowry, just as she said. You'll get your grandson and my heir, maybe even additional sons, but other than clothes on her back, a roof over her head, and food in her belly, I owe her or any other wife naught more." Ewan spat each word at her as his temper got the better of him. He didn't mean what he said, but he was tired of being lambasted for his earlier choice, one he couldn't undo nor could he have known not to make. He realized that he'd erred when Allyson's already ramrod straight back seemed to lengthen, and a look of such loathing entered her eyes that he feared she would thrust a dirk into his chest on their wedding night.

"You intend to continue your whoring?" Allyson demanded.

"So what if I did? There is naught a wife can do to control a husband. You are to be my property, not the other way around." The remorse that tried to take hold of Ewan evaporated as he dug himself into a deeper hole.

"Will your leman live in the keep that I will run? Will she share your chamber? Will you bed her before or after you come to swive me?"

"Allyson," her father hissed, shocked that her vocabulary contained such language.

"What do you think I've learned in the years I've been here?" she threw back in his face.

Throughout the exchange, King Robert remained quiet. The Bruce was impressed with the young woman's gumption to take on four towering men with a mettle he wished more of his warriors possessed, but the time had come to draw an end to the squabbling. After all, the men were right that she had no say in the outcome of the negotiations.

"Lady Allyson," King Robert strode toward the group. "What your father and Laird Gordon failed to inform you of is that it's my wish for the two of you to marry. I've decreed the alliance."

The high color drained from her face and neck, and her ghostlike pallor caused Ewan to shift toward her, fearing she might collapse, but the scathing glare she shot him warned him away.

"Yes, Your Grace. As you wish." Allyson curtsied and lowered her gaze. She'd fought a good fight, but she realized the time to challenge the arrangement had ended. For now.

"That's a good lass." The king offered her a conciliatory smile. "We shall announce the betrothal at the feast tomorrow night, and the betrothal ceremony will take place the following morning so that it is done before Lent begins. The banns have already been posted, so you may wed here or at Huntly."

Allyson's gaze shot up, her eyes widening as she discovered they could force her to marry Ewan any day, now that the church had given its blessing. Her heart's rapid staccato slowed when she remembered that no priest would conduct the ceremony during Lent. She had at least forty days before she'd be bound to Ewan. She nodded, but refused to look anywhere but over the king's shoulder.

"Allyson," Kenneth rested his hand on her back, but when he caught the look of betrayal in his daughter's eyes, he pulled away and swallowed. He loved his children, but he barely knew his youngest. He realized he'd overlooked her far too many times, and now her inability to trust that he did this not only for their clan but for her came home to roost. "I believe you need to prepare for the evening meal. By the king's leave, return to your chamber."

"Aye, Father," Allyson murmured. The king nodded his dismissal, and Allyson slipped from the chamber like a wraith.

Once the two lairds and Ewan signed the contracts, Laird Gordon spun on his sons, his temper ready to rain down on them. "You shamed us in front of the king," he hissed. "Go directly to my chamber, both of you."

The twins bowed to the king when he offered them the same dismissing nod. When they entered the passageway, Ewan searched for Allyson, but she had disappeared faster than he expected.

"You're an arse," Eoin muttered. "You didn't mean half of what you said, but you were spiteful because she poked at your pride."

"She started it."

"And now you're a petulant child. You and I made our beds, and it's not one we want to lie in. In fact, we've done far too much in bed. You'd do well to smooth this over with her, or you'll have a long and miserable life with a woman who detests you."

"With that mouth, she'll survive just fine. So what if she detests me? I need only get a son on her and be done with her."

Eoin halted and pushed at his brother's shoulder, so they stood facing one another. "You don't mean that, and we both know it. Have you stopped to consider that she's terrified?"

"Of what?" Ewan demanded. "I never gave her the impression I would beat her."

"No. But you scared her into thinking you'd rape her and pass her off to me to finish the job. You gave her the impression that she's worthless. You gave her the impression that you will humiliate her in front of a clan that she must join and who will judge her regardless of her relationship with you. You gave everyone the impression that you, and by default me, have no honor to speak of. What mon admits that he'll commit adultery in front of his own father, the bride's father, and the bluidy King of Scotland? I hope you won't, but our reputation doesn't exactly speak otherwise."

Ewan ran his hand through his blond hair and

looked into the emerald eyes that matched his own. He saw the shame and disgust on his brother's face that he shared. He'd gone much too far in his self-defense and caused greater damage than if he'd accepted her initial accusations and kept quiet.

"What do I do now? How do I make it right without coming across as a cad who's trying to manipulate her?"

"Pray," Eoin huffed before breaking into a grin.

"You're enjoying this far too much. Wait until it's your turn."

"That shall be a long wait. I'm only your second, not our father's heir."

"You're not 'only' aught. Don't say that." Ewan was always quick to come to his brother's defense, especially when he was trying to convince Eoin that no one thought less of him for being the younger twin. More often than not, Ewan wished he could hand over the burden of becoming laird to someone else—anyone else. But he would never put it on his brother's shoulders. He struggled with the persistent fear that he would never fill his father's boots, and his behavior in the Privy Council proved he might be right to possess those concerns. Ewan recognized he hadn't behaved in a way befitting a laird. He'd been a petulant arse. "I still don't know what to do to make this right."

"I'd begin with convincing Father not to rush the marriage. You have an uphill battle ahead of you. You'd do well to come to a truce before the wedding rather than once she's convinced she's trapped. You need to court your bride."

"Court her? I'll be lucky to get within a league of her without her pulling a blade on me."

"True," Eoin admitted.

Ewan looked at Eoin and shook his head. He inhaled deeply and closed his eyes as he tried to calm his frazzled nerves. He ran his hands through his hair before scrubbing his face. He needed to devise a plan to woo Allyson without coming across as phony and conniving. He wasn't prepared to change, but he understood he'd have to be more discreet so his betrothed didn't stumble upon his liaisons again.

CHAPTER THREE

Allyson arrived at the evening meal as the servants presented the third course. She'd hurried to change, but had spent the better part of a half an hour with her head hanging over the chamber pot as she retched over and over. She failed to ease the tension between her shoulder blades. Her stomach remained in knots as fear of the unknown threatened to drown her until she soothed her frazzled nerves with several drams of whisky smuggled to her by her maid. She felt calm with a cheery warmth in her chest and belly as she approached the table where the other ladies sat. She slipped into her seat but poked at the food placed in front of her. She joined in the conversation when it became unavoidable, but she wasn't her normally talkative self. The other ladies sensed something was amiss, but no one commented on it.

The longer Allyson sat without eating, the stronger the effects of the whisky took hold. By the time the dancing began, she recognized she was tipsy and should retire for the evening, but when she caught several courtiers smiling in her direction, she stayed. Allyson became aware of the Gordon twins as soon as she entered the Great Hall, and she was aware Ewan kept looking in her direction. She didn't understand his expression—it appeared to be a combination of guilt, uncertainty, and speculation—and she wasn't interested in deciphering it. She disliked being on the receiving end.

As one man after another asked Allyson to dance, she allowed them to twirl her about the dance floor. She tipped her head back and laughed when they attempted humor, she flirted when they attempted to tease her, and she redirected their attention when they attempted to seduce her. Allyson moved from one partner to another throughout the night, but steered clear of either of the Gordon brothers. When a member of the Maxwell emissary suggested they step outside for a breath of air, she agreed. The temperature was still frigid, and she didn't have a cloak with her. She suspected the man would attempt to kiss her, and as long as they remained near the doors, she was confident that she could control the situation.

The bracing air bit into her cheeks and neck as the perspiration turned into ice water against her temples and between her breasts. She looked back at the Great Hall and decided she needed to return, lest she turn into an ice figure rather than a lady.

"It's quite a bit colder than I realized, and I didn't bring my cloak. I don't think I will last long out here. I'm sufficiently cooled, so I believe I will return."

"I'll keep you warm, lass." The young man wrapped a band of steel around her waist, and she realized she'd underestimated the man's strength. She didn't even recall his name, as the effects of the whisky had made her forgetful, but the brisk air had sobered her.

"I must return before my father wonders where

I've gone. He arrived at court today and is keeping a close eye on me."

"What I intend won't take long." He pressed a kiss against her throat. Its gentleness eased her fear, and she relented as his hand caressed her back. He pulled her closer as his lips traveled to her jaw, then cheek, before resting at the corner of her mouth. He paused for a heartbeat before pouncing. He caught Allyson off guard as he pressed his lips against hers, persistently swiping his tongue across her lips. Allyson tried to jerk away, but his steely arm had her locked in place. She grasped fistfuls of his leine as she attempted to push him away. She had no intention of allowing his tongue into her mouth, and didn't understand why he kept pressing it against her lips. When her attempts to break free failed, she reverted to what she'd done as a child when her older siblings tormented her. She grabbed a fistful of hair and yanked as hard as she could. The thwarted swain bellowed and lashed out. Allyson ducked under his hand as it swung toward where her cheek had been a moment ago. She didn't hesitate to stomp on his foot and dashed into the dark toward a door she recalled would be unlocked. She heard heavy footsteps following her, but once she reached the hidden door, she sprinted through the passageways, taking the shortest route to her chamber. She slammed the door shut behind her and leaned against it as she struggled to catch her breath. Allyson lambasted herself for being so foolish as to go out into the dark with the man. The other times she'd allowed a man to kiss her had been quick pecks in the gardens, with daylight and discovery as incentives to keep the interludes brief. She'd been a fool to take such a chance, and she admitted she'd given the man a mixed message. But she also was certain he hadn't misunderstood her when she struggled to break free. He'd disregarded her attempt to say no, and that was unforgivable to her.

Is that what it will be like once I'm married? Will Ewan force me? Will he give me a chance to say no, or will he take what he wants?

The fear from earlier in the day, both in the passageway and in the Privy Council, returned. Allyson moved to sit on the foot of her bed as she looked around her chamber. Her roommates would return that night, but she intended to be asleep, or would at least appear to be asleep, by the time they arrived. She assessed her armoire and chests, considering what lay inside. She eased off the mattress and opened one of her chests to pull out a satchel and flipped it open, looking inside for a long moment before glancing at the other contents of the chest. She retrieved a plain kirtle she hadn't touched since before she returned to court the previous year after spending Christmas with her clan. She'd worn it the last day of the journey to court and then retired it to her chest, acknowledging that it would never meet the standards of courtly attire. She ran her hand over the stitching around the hem, remembering how she'd labored over it, pulling it apart and redoing it until she was certain no one would find fault with it. Her thumbnail picked at the one tiny imperfection where the left side seam met the bottom hem. She remembered how her mother chastised her for the uneven stitching even though it was in a place no one else would notice.

Allyson heaved a deep sigh as she set the gown on the bed and pulled out two older chemises that she'd also worn while traveling. They were sturdily made, but again not the quality expected of a lady-in-waiting. She placed one on top of the kirtle and the other in the satchel, then dug through the chest, pulling out three pairs of stockings, a pair of gloves, and a scarf. These were of superior quality, but the colors were subdued, unlike what she wore in Stirling. They were the clothes of a country laird's daughter, not a courtier. They were what she preferred, what she felt most comfortable in. Once she'd placed the clothing and her Elliot plaid in the satchel, she lifted what remained in the chest and placed it on the floor beside her. She pried the false bottom from the chest and removed a pouch that filled her palm.

She'd tucked away coins for years and kept them in the suede bag. Anything she'd received for her saint's day, Christmas, Hogmanay, Beltane, or any other feast, she hoarded. While her sisters had frivolously spent their money at the markets and fairs, purchasing ribbons and sweet treats, Allyson had only bought enough to keep her family from questioning her, anticipating she would one day need the coins after leaving home. She understood as well as any woman that anything she possessed when she wed would become her husband's, but she also understood a woman should have a nest egg in case her husband failed to provide for her. She'd seen it with her oldest sister, married to a man twice her age who hoped to beget a son. He died of a heart attack in their bed, leaving her sister destitute with her new clan deep in debt. She hadn't the money to even buy food for herself or her maid on their return to Elliot land. She'd had to rely on the meager contingent of guardsmen loaned to her from her husband's garrison, and their father had to repay the men for what they'd spent on her sister and the maid. Allyson had sworn to never find herself relying on someone else for a meal and a blanket. She could always provide at least that much for herself. Now she would need the coins when she left Stirling.

Allyson considered her friend Elizabeth Fraser, who had been a lady-in-waiting before her marriage to Edward Bruce, the adopted brother, not blood brother, of King Robert. She and her husband left court and made a home at Inverlochy Castle after a threat to Edward's life nearly killed Elizabeth. *Dare I go to Elizabeth and Edward at Inverlochy? Would they take me? If I can make my way there, I think Elizabeth would allow me to stay until I can figure out what to do next.* Doubt niggled at her mind that Edward might send her straight back to Stirling once he learned that she'd disregarded Robert's order for her to marry Ewan.

I wish Isabella still lived on Dunbar land. At least I know my way around the Lowlands, even if we're from opposite sides. But she and her husband have gone to the Sinclairs. There's no way that I could travel that far north on my own. I barely know aught aboot the Highlands that border the southern portion of Scotland. I won't make it in the wilds alone. A mon or a beast is more likely to attack me than I am to survive.

Allyson remembered how to reach Elliot land from Stirling, but it would be the first place anyone searched. She might go to their neighbors, the Kerrs or the Douglases, but they would turn her over to her father. Desperation set in, but Allyson refused to allow it to dominate her. She hurried her packing and hid the satchel in her chest before undressing and crawling into bed. The candle had just finished smoking when the door creaked open and her roommates entered. They eased through the door and moved about the quiet chamber as they readied themselves for bed. Allyson forced herself to remain still and regulate her breathing despite her mind jumping from one idea to another.

Who says I have to be Allyson Elliot any longer? No one has to discover I'm a laird's daughter, nor do they need to learn I was ever a lady-in-waiting. For all anyone knows, I'm the young widow of a farmer and couldn't maintain the plot on my own. I'm a fair seamstress despite what my mother might say, and Morgana said I was a natural in the kitchen. If our clan's head cook believes that, then I must be at least decent. I don't intend to work in a tavern, but perhaps I could work for a family in Edinburgh or Glasgow. I can't remain in Stirling, but I need a city large enough to get lost in. That's what I'll do. I'll say I'm a poor widow willing to assist a shopkeeper or become a maid in exchange for room and board. I must trade my finer clothes for money and use the money to buy less questionable stockings and gloves. I can claim the cloak and scarf were wedding gifts from my husband. I never imagined I'd become a servant, but I know I can do the work. I know how to do the work. At least my mother was wise to ensure all her daughters understood the duties of every servant if we were ever to be a proper chatelaine.

I'd rather be alone than with a husband who will shame me with a mistress under my roof. I don't want to believe Ewan would ever force me, but he did little to disabuse me of the notion that he might. Some women might accept that lot, but I refuse to be overlooked and discounted any longer. It hurts too bluidy much.

Allyson slipped into slumber as she found some resolution to the quandary of how to evade her arranged marriage. She would figure out the rest when the situation demanded a solution.

CHAPTER FOUR

Ewan observed Allyson flirt with every man between the age of eight-and-ten to eighty. He ground his teeth as she glided from one partner to another, tossing her hair and dazzling the men with her smile that showcased perfectly aligned teeth. When the dancing began, he assumed she was taunting him and trying to make him jealous, so he partnered with the most beautiful widows and matrons in attendance. But he soon realized she never glanced in his direction. Although she arrived late for the meal and merely pushed her food around her trencher, Ewan noted she appeared animated and cheerful. He failed to understand how her mood changed so drastically until a man standing near he and Eoin mentioned Allyson.

"I can't be sure, but I suspect Lady Allyson's had more than a tipple of whisky this eve. She's in even better spirits than usual. I intend to test my theory."

Ewan recognized the man as one of the Maxwell clan's representatives. Before he had a chance to listen to more or even inquire about the man's plans, the Maxwell man slipped away and swept Allyson into a dance. Ewan edged around the Great Hall as he caught his intended leaning closer to hear what the man whispered in her ear. She nodded and allowed her partner to guide toward the terrace.

Like hell she's having a dalliance under my nose. I'm not taking a wife who isn't a virgin. I'll not have her bearing some mon's bastard and passing it off as mine.

Ewan recognized the hypocrisy of his thoughts, but he believed in his right to do as he pleased as a man, an unmarried man. He followed the couple onto the terrace and watched Allyson tilt her head to allow her partner to nuzzle her neck. Ewan ground his teeth as he crept forward. He would note how far she allowed the interlude to go, but he wouldn't intervene. If she allowed the man any liberties, he would gain his reason to call off the wedding. He didn't care if he destroyed her reputation. She would deserve it for being loose. He noticed Allyson grab the man's leine, but it wasn't until she yanked the insistent swain's hair that Ewan realized she'd been trying to push him away rather than pull him closer. Allyson twisted and squirmed until she had enough space between them to stomp on the man's foot and duck under his flying hand. She ran into the dark with the Maxwell clansman following her. Ewan darted forward and plowed his fist into the unsuspecting pursuer's temple and watched him crumple to the ground. He heard the click of a door closing and rushed to find the portal Allyson used to slip into the castle. Once he was inside, he looked around, but just as she had done earlier in the day, she'd already disappeared.

"Where did you go?" Eoin asked when Ewan returned to the Great Hall. Ewan's fist smarted, and the punch had split the skin over two of his knuckles. "You better not have been chasing after Lady Bevan with Father's eagle eyes on you. It's bad enough you've danced with every eligible and ineligible woman here."

"I followed Allyson onto the terrace to see how far she'd allow that Maxwell swine to go. She didn't appear at all unsettled when he kissed her neck and cheek. She didn't even shy away from him pressing his mouth to hers, but at some point, he became too insistent, and she struggled to break free. She was already running back into the keep by the time I reached the lout. I plowed my fist into his head and chased after her. She was nowhere in sight when I followed her inside."

"Are you certain that she's all right? He didn't do more than kiss her?"

"I'm sure he would have if she'd allowed him to. She must have known the message she sent by going outside with him. There is no way she couldn't after the knowledge she shared this afternoon."

"Do you think she was drunk like that Maxwell said? She's never struck me as a drinker. Why would she have tonight?"

"It's rather obvious she needed some liquid courage to face the evening meal, and I'd say that's largely, if not entirely, my fault. I'd also guess she allowed him to take her outside as a silent rebellion. She may be savvy aboot life at court, but her mind was too slow, or she's still too innocent to realize that saying no and having the mon listen to her wouldn't be as easy as she assumed."

"Ewan, don't you see how this makes everything you said earlier even worse? You left her under the impression you'd force yourself on her and then discard her like sennight-old fish. Then a mon she might have been willing to kiss tried to force her to do more. She'll never trust you now. She'll see at you as being no better than that piece of shite, and she wouldn't be wrong to do so. I might know you'd never force a woman, but she doesn't know either of us well enough to understand that. And like it or not, what she saw this afternoon entitles her to a poor opinion of both of us."

"You're not saying aught I didn't already think aboot. It might seem ridiculous to us, but I can understand how she might fear us sharing her or playing her a fool by taking turns unbeknownst to her. Rather than try to sooth her fears, I acted like the petulant child you called me. I just couldn't seem to still my tongue each time she needled me."

"Neither of us likes to fail to have the last word. This time, you lost both the battle and the war."

Ewan looked at his brother's concerned face and shook his head. The uncanny way their minds ran along the same path was a benefit that kept them alive on the battlefield, but it also meant that their consciences were never silent. Eoin spoke the doubts and regrets Ewan struggled with all evening.

"I suppose I should begin wooing her tomorrow. Though after my performance tonight, dancing with every woman in sight just to spite her, most likely didn't endear me to her any further."

"I doubt it did. Before the evening meal, I might have recommended you begin tomorrow, but now I fear you need a few days of lying low and ignoring temptation." Eoin paused for a long and assessing gaze at his brother. They were mirror images in more ways than their looks, but they didn't share the same beliefs about everything. Eoin was more romantic and believed in the sanctity and preservation of marriage, no matter why the union began. Ewan viewed marriage as a business transaction between two clans rather than two people, and as long as the parties upheld the terms of the agreement, he saw no reason to alter his life. He understood how some might view him as selfish, but he considered himself practical. He didn't expect his wife, whoever she might be, to harbor soft feelings for him, nor did he anticipate loving her in return. Except for needing an heir, he was content to allow his wife to do as she pleased. Eoin's voice broke through his thoughts. "Will you accept her taking a lover once she's bred your children?"

"What?" Ewan jerked away as his brother's questioned registered. "Of course not."

"Then you aren't as willing to allow her to do as she pleases. You've always said your wife could do what she wanted once she'd borne you an heir. What if what pleases her is a lover? You intend to keep a leman."

"It's different."

"Why? Because she's a woman? Because she might give birth to a bastard? You're just as likely to sire a bastard. If you don't believe you need a woman's love, then why keep a leman? You might enjoy bedding your wife and be satisfied there. You might marry a virgin, but then teach her all the things a more experienced woman had to learn one way or another. Why go to another woman when you can enjoy the pleasure you want with your own wife?"

"Because a mon doesn't bed his lady-wife like a whore."

"Lady Bevan was once someone's lady-wife, as you put it, and she knows more than most tavern wenches. She had to learn that somehow. Do you consider her less of a lady for it? Is the word just a title that doesn't fit its owner?" Eoin shook his head. "I think you're peeved that Father didn't consult you before this announcement, and I think you're peeved that your wings are being clipped before you wanted to settle down. You have the opportunity to take a beautiful and alluring woman to your bed every night and not spend a penny or worry aboot the pox ever again."

Ewan recognized the logic in his brother's words, and they were another example of ideas that had already occurred to him. It proved they were like-minded in more ways than not. He was angry at the king and their father along with Laird Elliot, but he'd vented his spleen at Allyson when he felt attacked. He understood she shared his sentiments, but she felt threatened while he felt inconvenienced. Rather than ease the terror, he poured oil on the fire, then grew angry when the conversation went up in flames. "I haven't shown a redeeming quality since the moment we encountered Allyson and her friend today," he admitted.

"No, you haven't." Eoin shrugged when Ewan shot him a scathing glare.

"I have a lot to make up for, and I worry she'll decide what she saw today is the real me rather than when I try to prove otherwise."

"That's because parts of the real you were on display today, too. You need to reconsider your ideas on fidelity. A woman like Allyson may not expect you to love her, but she expects and deserves you to honor her."

Ewan glanced around the Great Hall and caught sight of not only Lady Bevan, but several other women he'd bedded over the years of visiting court and attending various clan gatherings. He'd made his rounds and revisited several eager and willing bed partners. For the first time, he regretted his choices and his refusal to consider how they might affect a marriage that was inevitable. He knew plenty of men who kept mistresses, his father included, so he'd never questioned whether he should give up bedding whoever he wanted once married. His mother hadn't been able to tolerate his father, and they rarely spoke while she was still alive. She'd loathed any form of affection whether it came from her children or her husband. She'd wanted to be a nun, but she hadn't been given the choice. His mother turned a blind eye to her husband's infidelity because it meant he left her alone.

Their home hadn't been a happy one while his mother was alive, and Ewan realized now how an unwilling bride had spoiled more than just the groom's life. He didn't want to repeat his father's life as his own. Allyson had objected strenuously to his bed-hopping ways and expected he be faithful, which was the opposite of his mother. Allyson proved on the terrace that she didn't oppose physical intimacy, even if she put limits on it. He'd reacted to the news, assuming Allyson would be like his mother and reject passion and pleasure. She'd never actually objected to it; she'd objected to him sharing it with women other than her.

"I've made a right cock up of this. I jumped to the conclusion that she would be like Mother."

"Mother?" Eoin scoffed. "She's not a bit like Mother. Not even in the least. They couldn't be more unalike, and the pluck Allyson showed today proves that. Mother would never have spoken out against any mon, nor would she have cared whether her husband made his bed with another woman. She never cared. She welcomed it. Once we were born, she had no reason to allow Father ever to return to her chamber. Allyson wanted your head on a pike because she expects you'll be unfaithful. Mother and Allyson couldn't be more different than chalk and cheese."

"I realize that now, but at the time, my emotions clouded any sense of reason." Ewan rubbed the back of his neck. "Anyhow, I'll gain naught more tonight. I have no desire to continue dancing, and Allyson won't return. I shall bid you goodnight."

"Where are you going?" Eoin cast a suspicious glance at his brother.

"To bed. Alone."

"Then I shall retire, too."

The brothers quit the Great Hall without a second glance, and Ewan fell into an exhausted sleep as soon as his head touched his pillow.

CHAPTER FIVE

Allyson carried out her duties as though she hadn't been given life-altering news the day before. None of the other ladies-in-waiting noticed anything out of the ordinary about her, and she forced herself to remain patient as she went through the daily routine of Mass, meals, and mingling. She'd resolved to slip away from the keep during the equinox feast that evening, so she bribed a guardsman she knew was having an affair with another one of the queen's attendants. Allyson didn't doubt she could slip out of the castle gates with the guard and rely on him to escort her to the city gates, which he would ensure she could pass through before they were locked for the night.

"I'm glad we returned to the overheated Great Hall after our morning pilgrimage to Cairnpapple Hill." Arabella Johnstone mused. "The view at sunrise might be spectacular as the light filters among the standing stones, but I didn't appreciate the view of my breath freezing at the end of my nose."

"I wouldn't have minded the cold air if it hadn't still been dark when we departed," Cairstine Grant added.

Allyson kept her eyes on the noon meal as voices

flowed around her. She hadn't minded the morning excursion because it gave her the opportunity to scout the road north as the sun rose. She'd discovered that Elizabeth and Edward Bruce had returned to Culcreuch Castle to stay during the festivities. At an hour's ride away from Stirling, the couple preferred to be guests of the Galbraiths rather than the royal couple. Allyson intended to pull Elizabeth aside and request shelter at Culcreuch until she could decide what to do next. If her plea was answered, then she would journey to the nearby keep with Elizabeth and Edward after the feast was over. But if Elizabeth refused, then Allyson already had palms greased to facilitate her escape.

As the afternoon bled into early evening, Allyson failed to spy Elizabeth anywhere near the queen's solar. Discreet questioning allowed Allyson to discover that the couple didn't plan to attend the feast because Elizabeth wasn't feeling up to the heat and odors while she was still in the early months of her first pregnancy. She wanted to groan when she realized that traveling alone was inevitable, but at least Elizabeth wouldn't deny her request before she left the castle.

The court gathered in the Great Hall as the feast began, servants bringing laden platters of meats and pastries. Allyson pasted a smile on her face. She forced herself to appear inconspicuous, all while focusing on the exit she'd use to flee the crowd and retire to her chamber to change. She pretended a jovial disposition far from how she felt but was necessary for her ruse to succeed. When the music began, she engaged in one flirtation after another, but kept her eye on the sinking sun as it moved past the windows and doors of the Great Hall. More than once, she noticed Ewan watching her, but she turned away before their gazes could meet.

Allyson made her move when she caught sight of a man she'd flirted with earlier as he eased his way toward the exit she intended to use. She followed behind as though he led the way but hung back as he slipped out of the gathering hall. Fear of being stopped tempted her to glance back over her shoulder, but she waited until she didn't need to worry that the man would see her following him. If anyone was paying attention to her, and she hoped they were, they would assume she followed him for an assignation. She needed people to believe she was with a dalliance so no one would question why she disappeared and didn't return to the feast. Once she made it into the passageway, she lifted her skirts above her ankles and ran toward the ladies'-in-waiting chambers. She didn't pause until she reached her door, breathless but relieved.

Ewan tracked Allyson as she batted her eyelashes at each would-be suitor who approached. She didn't decline any request to dance, and she danced more than once with a couple of men. He forced himself to remain propped up against a wall as he'd sworn not to dance with any of the women who batted their own eyelashes at him. No one knew of their betrothal, and Ewan had beseeched the king to give him another day to make amends before everyone learned of their engagement. In the meantime, Allyson continued to appear like an unattached young woman, free to dance with whomever she pleased. Ewan failed to find a moment to speak to her all day. He'd attempted to ride alongside her, but she maneuvered her horse between two other ladies. He slipped between men and women at the standing stones, hoping he could approach her, but she positioned herself next to the queen. He wondered if she sensed his intention to speak to her and was avoiding him.

"Damn it," Ewan grumbled. He glanced at Eoin, who had implicitly agreed to keep him company and forego any offers from the women. "She's followed a mon out of the Great Hall again. Didn't she learn aught last night?"

Before Eoin could respond, Ewan wove his way through the crowd until he pushed through the doors he'd watched Allyson pass through only moments ago. No one was in sight, but he heard the rustling of clothes in an alcove to his left. Soft murmurs and moans carried, and Ewan felt a wave of panic that Allyson might enjoy more than a mere kiss. He might not want to marry her, but if he had to, he refused to share her. He pushed aside the voice that bellowed he was a hypocrite of the worst sort as he pulled aside the tapestry and yanked the man away. While Ewan recognized him as the man Allyson followed, the woman who screeched and scrambled to push down her skirts wasn't Allyson.

"I beg your pardon. I thought you were someone else." Ewan backed away before spinning around to search for Allyson. *Where the devil did she go? And how does she disappear in the blink of an eye?*

———

Allyson tugged at the laces of her gown, twisting and grasping to remove a kirtle that in normal circum- stances required a maid's assistance. There was no way Allyson would alert anyone to her plan or that she'd returned to her chamber. When she was free of the ornate gown, she hung it on a peg in her ar- moire, pushing it behind other gowns, then lifted the lid of her chest and withdrew the plain travel kirtle and chemise. She rushed to don the new outfit, breathing a sigh of relief that it was an easy gown that didn't require any help. Allyson lifted the satchel strap over her head and shoulders before wrapping her cloak and scarf around her, leaving enough slack to pull up over her nose and mouth. She raised the cowl and hood before peeking out of her door. When nothing stirred and no noise carried to her, she eased along the passageway, remaining in the shadows until she reached the servants' stairs. She raced down them and out to the bailey where she crept toward the postern gate. The guard she'd bribed waited for her. They didn't exchange a word as he led her away from the castle and deposited her outside the city's gates.

She hurried along the road for ten minutes until she came to an outlying village that the royal party had passed through that morning. Allyson had noticed a livery and blacksmith, which had lifted the dread of trying to escape with a horse in tow or on its back. She needed a mount, or she would never make it to Culcreuch unnoticed. As she approached the village stables, she realized it was beside a coaching inn where travelers stopped before reaching Stirling. She entered the stables, but no one greeted her. She passed along the stalls and called out for a stable hand, but there was no response.

Most of the stalls were empty, but she found a friendly but powerfully built gelding that nodded his large head in greeting. She held out her hand for him to sniff, and when he didn't nip her, she stroked between his eyes. Allyson felt around behind her for the nearby barrel and retrieved an apple, which she offered on her palm. The animal crunched through the fruit as Allyson eased into the stall. The horse swished his tail once as Allyson hurried to saddle him. She led him from the stable with coins in her hands, then knocked on the back door of the inn.

When a man answered, his eyes grew wide to find Allyson on the other side holding the reins to the massive steed. She pressed the coins into his hand, but remained silent. Before the tavern keeper questioned her, she swung into the saddle and nudged the horse forward. She'd kept her hood up and face covered with the shawl. She appeared like an elegant highwayman rather than a lady-in-waiting and laird's daughter.

Night was fully upon her when Allyson approached the gates of Culcreuch Castle. She pulled her hood down and lowered her scarf as the distance between her and the portcullis shrank. She wanted to ensure the guardsmen on the battlements could determine she was a woman and posed little threat.

"Who goes?" A voice bellowed once she was within earshot.

"Lady Allyson, friend of Lady Bruce," Allyson called back. She was unwilling to announce to all and sundry who she was. She offered enough information for the guard to pass along, and she prayed Elizabeth would recognize her name and think of her fellow attendant. She need not have feared; only moments later, Elizabeth rushed down the keep's steps with Edward gripping her elbow. Elizabeth ordered the portcullis raised and Allyson admitted.

"Allyson, what're you doing here at this hour? What's happened?" Elizabeth peered around Allyson's shoulder and frowned when she realized there was no escort waiting to follow Allyson into the bailey. "Why're you alone?"

"Could I speak with you in private?" Allyson murmured as her gaze shot between Elizabeth and Edward, and the nervousness she'd been able to control threatened to weaken her knees.

"Of course." Elizabeth led the trio to a chamber

Allyson realized was a solar the couple shared. "What's happened, Allyson? Why are you alone?"

Allyson unwrapped her scarf and loosened the cloak before she looked at Elizabeth. She took a fortifying breath before launching into her tale of woe. "Do you remember the Gordon twins?" Elizabeth nodded but looked ill at ease at the mention of the brothers who had tried to seduce her into being their mistress more than once. "Your brother-by-marriage ordered me to marry Ewan. He made his decree known only a few hours after I discovered him and Eoin leaving Lady Bevan's chambers together. Tucking in their leines and grinning. The cad taunted me in the passageway and then threatened to pass me between him and Eoin."

"They wouldn't, Allyson. They wouldn't dare," Elizabeth whispered, but her objection rang hollow in her own ears.

"Why wouldn't they? They'd just done that very thing with Lady Bevan. To make matters worse, Ewan admitted in front of the king, my father, his father, his brother, and me, not to mention the other men present in the Privy Council, that he had no qualms aboot forcing me into his bed and keeping a leman, too. None of the men seemed nonplussed by his declaration. None cared aboot the shame that would bring upon me. None cared that I— " Allyson choked out the last words as the tears she'd controlled for the past day overwhelmed her. Elizabeth pulled her friend into her arms as she looked at her husband. She and Edward knew Allyson couldn't remain. They were in no position to gainsay Edward's brother when it came to alliances the king demanded between clans. Furthermore, Culcreuch wasn't their home. They were guests with an open invitation, but that arrangement came from Robert, not the Galbraiths. They weren't at liberty to extend shelter in another laird's home.

"Allyson, did you run away?" Edward knew the answer, but he needed to be certain. He watched as his wife's friend nodded but continued to sob against Elizabeth's shoulder. He wished he could plow his fist into Ewan Gordon's face, but the young man wasn't there, and it wouldn't do Allyson any good. "Does anyone know where you've gone? A friend? Your maid?"

Allyson straightened and brushed the tears from her cheeks. "Nay. I didn't tell anyone. I don't want my maid punished for my choices, and beyond that, I don't trust anyone else."

Elizabeth exchanged a knowing glance with Edward before tucking stray hair behind Allyson's ear. She wiped a wayward tear from Allyson's chin before offering her a reassuring smile. Allyson responded with a weak smile of her own, but her sobs had subsided.

"Let's get you settled into a chamber, and in the morning, we can decide how to proceed," Elizabeth offered. Allyson stared at her for a long moment before nodding.

"You're sending me back, aren't you?" Allyson shrank into herself as the thin hope she'd pinned on making her way to Edward and Elizabeth evaporated.

"We'll discuss it in the morning. Naught's decided yet," Edward reassured.

"You haven't decided whether you're returning me personally or just sending your guard as my escort. I shouldn't have come." Allyson turned toward the door. "I shouldn't have involved you."

"Allyson, wait. Regardless of what happens tomorrow, you can't go back out in the night alone. You're tempting fate. Stay the night, rest, wake up with a clear head, and we'll decide what to do." Elizabeth squeezed her hands before leading her from the solar. The trio walked in silence until Elizabeth showed Allyson the chamber where she could pass the rest of the night.

"Should we post a guard?" Elizabeth murmured as she and Edward made their way to their chamber. "She will run again."

"How do you know?"

"Because, Eddie, it's what I would do." Elizabeth frowned as she weighed her words. Her husband was protective to a fault, and while his possessiveness never kept her from doing what she wanted, it could overwhelm anyone on the receiving end of his ire. "Both Gordon twins made offers to me over the years, and they never had aught to do with marriage. Everyone knows both men are womanizers. Laird Gordon may be a good mon and a good leader, but he hasn't done aught to hide his mistresses over the years. The apples didn't fall far from the tree. Neither Ewan nor Eoin believe in the sanctity of marriage, and while it shocks me to hear Ewan threatened to mistreat Allyson, it doesn't surprise me he did naught to hide his intention to keep a leman. Eddie, I know most women aren't as fortunate as I am to marry a mon I love and who loves me, but no woman deserves to enter a marriage where her groom will flaunt his infidelity in her face. And no woman should be forced to accept a mon who has already admitted he has little regard for her wellbeing."

"Beth, what you and Allyson have said concerns me, but neither you nor I are able to thwart Robert's plans. I'll travel back to Stirling with Allyson and speak on her behalf to my brother, but I can't promise he'll listen."

"I'm coming, too."

"Nay."

"Aye. Eddie, she's my friend. I've also experienced the Gordons' less-than-honorable advances and can speak to their behavior. She needs people on her side, and who better to accompany the king's brother than a former lady-in-waiting who also happens to be the king's sister-by-marriage?" Elizabeth placed her hands on her hips and challenged her husband to argue with her. Edward shrugged and rolled his eyes, his capitulation coming without an argument. "But you still haven't answered my question aboot whether we should post a guard. I'm afraid she'll bolt before daylight."

"She can't. None of the guards will open any of the gates to her that early. And if she tries to saddle her horse, at least one of the stable hands will notice and notify me."

Elizabeth looked doubtful, but nodded as she climbed into bed.

CHAPTER SIX

Allyson dropped the satchel on the floor beside the bed and collapsed onto it, too exhausted to do more than remove her outerwear and boots. She pulled the covers from the far side over her and wrapped herself in them like a cocoon. Her eyelids felt like they weighed a ton, and her tired eyes were dry and scratchy after crying. Despite feeling worn out, Allyson's mind wasn't as depleted as her emotions and her body. She contemplated how to slip away from Edward and Elizabeth before they arranged to return her to court. She once more considered heading toward the Sinclairs and seeking sanctuary with them through her friend Isabella Dunbar, but she remembered two factors that would prove impossible to surmount. She couldn't travel into the northern Highlands alone, and she'd made more than one inappropriate comment about Magnus and Tavish Sinclair in front of the women they married. She doubted they would receive her warmly after jesting about what laid beneath the men's plaids. Besides that, Isabella had a husband now and a baby on the way. Allyson dropped off to sleep when her mind gave up its resistance, but she had no new plan in place.

Allyson woke with a start to an owl hooting while sitting on her window ledge. The animal had moonlight behind it, and it appeared to be observing her. It was an unsettling feeling, as though the bird saw in her chamber and into her soul. Roused from slumber, Allyson lay on the bed contemplating her options. She could remain at Culcreuch until Edward escorted her back to court. Once she was there, she had the choice between running again or accepting the marriage. She refused to make that choice because she refused to return to court. This created a choice between running away from Culcreuch before everyone began waking or trying to slip away from Edward and his guards while they were on the road. She had no doubt Edward would track her and drag her back to court, kicking and screaming if he had to. As the realization that she needed to leave soon settled into her mind, she considered how she might leave the bailey wall with no one notifying Edward.

It had been dark when she arrived earlier that night, so she had no way to tell if the village outside the keep had a stable or livery. She wouldn't assume it did, which meant she needed to decide whether she would try to sneak a horse out of the bailey or leave on foot. Allyson could travel farther and faster on horseback, but she imagined she'd be more difficult to track on foot. She wouldn't be able to decide until she made it outside and surveyed the bailey.

Allyson climbed out of bed and gathered her meager belongings before opening the door a crack. She'd feared they would post a guard outside her chamber, but there was no one visible in the passageway. She slipped down the stairs to the Great Hall but avoided the main doors and entered the kitchens. She eased through the side door and looked around the bailey. There were guards on the battlements, but there was no one in sight on the ground. She hid in the shadows as she crept through the alley between the back of the outbuildings and the retaining wall. Two guards stood on the wall walk above the postern gate, both facing away from the keep. Even if she opened the gate, they would spot her as soon as she passed through it. This ended the option to take a horse through that way. She glanced toward the portcullis, but it wouldn't open for several hours, and by then, she would be too noticeable. Any attempt to leave through the main exit would draw too much attention. She looked along the side of the keep to where she glimpsed construction work being done on the retaining wall. She inched her way toward the site, praying there might be a crumbling hole in the wall that she might sneak through. She realized it was an unlikely event, but she hoped, nonetheless. While she didn't find a hole in the wall, she found a ladder propped against it. She knew that section of the wall butted up to the shore of a loch, so there were few guards in sight, and that portion of the wall would be difficult for the guards to see in the dark. Allyson saw her only option for escape.

She scaled the ladder with her skirts tucked into her waist before rolling onto the wall walk. Allyson waited for the alarm to go up or for a guard to rush toward her, but all remained quiet. She grasped the ladder and yanked as hard as she could. She was close to falling over backwards when she discovered the ladder was far lighter than she expected. She pulled it up and away from the side of the wall until she passed it along to the other side. She looked over the edge and found there was a small strip of dirt between the wall and the edge of the loch. She lowered the ladder and wiggled it several times to ensure it wouldn't shift too much. Allyson scampered down to the ground and caught her breath as she looked around. She glanced back at the ladder and winced.

She couldn't push it back up and over the edge, nor could she leave it propped against the outside of the wall. That would be an invitation for anyone to breach the keep's defenses. She tucked as much of it as she could under the foliage that grew along the shore.

I can travel southwest to Glasgow or northeast to Edinburgh. Glasgow is closer and the opposite direction from Stirling. Which way is southwest, though? The sun won't rise for a few more hours, and I have no clue how to use the stars to navigate. I admit it was a large dose of luck that got me here, but now what?

Allyson had ridden west from Stirling with no need to turn north or south, which meant the gate must face east. She walked along the length of the keep until she came to the eastern wall, and from there, she turned to face her right. She would have to travel west until she reached the far shore of the loch, but then she would adjust her course and turn south, then eventually southwest.

I just don't know how far south to go before needing to head west again. Do I point myself between what I believe is due south and due west and take that path? What will I encounter if I do that? I figure I have a full day's walk, but I've brought no food or provisions. I haven't eaten since the feast. I should have thought this through more and nabbed bread and cheese while I was in the kitchens, but I can't very well go back, so I can only go forward.

Allyson shuffled her way down the ledge to the shore of the loch. She noticed it was tidal, so she walked under the partial overhang, realizing no one on the battlements could see her. But after a few steps, she noted her footprints being left behind in the wet ground. Allyson had no way of knowing when the tide would come in and wash away the evidence. She couldn't assume it would be before sunrise. She retraced her steps and wiped them away until none remained, and she scrambled back onto the ledge. She'd lost precious time she didn't have, so she lifted her skirts and ran.

She turned south when she rounded the portion of the loch that obstructed her direct flight from the keep. She wouldn't be even a speck in the distance to the guards on the battlements, but she didn't slow until there was no trace of the castle. Winded with a stitch in her side, Allyson paused to catch her breath. Her shoes and clothes weren't designed for such vigorous activity. It wasn't long before she arrived at a village she'd heard was called Fintry. She hesitated to pass through in case someone questioned her—or worse, in case Edward questioned the villagers—but she needed food at the very least, and preferably a mount. She kept her hood up, with her shawl and scarf obscuring her face, as she entered the village. No one was stirring yet except for a few homes where the smell of baking bread wafted to her. She feared knocking on a door and asking for food, even if she paid, but she wasn't ready to steal.

"Lass?" An older woman's voice called out as Allyson drew close to the village's well. Allyson froze before turning toward the hunched over figure. "You aren't from here, and you shouldn't be skulking aboot in the dark."

"I became separated from my party when highwaymen attacked. I lost my horse and my guards." Allyson observed the woman's reaction before she continued her lies. "I hoped I might find food and a mount. I can offer some coin."

The old woman cast a speculative gaze at Allyson before responding. "Culcreuch Castle isn't far from here. The laird and lady aren't in residence, but there is another noble couple there. You look and sound like a lady. They'd offer you shelter."

"I don't doubt that they would, but that's the opposite direction from where I'm headed. I need to travel southeast to return to my clan's territory. I'm a Buchanan." It was the only clan she thought of nearby, and they were a large one. The likelihood of anyone knowing all the members, even the noble ones, was slim. She wasn't wearing her Elliot plaid, so she didn't fear her ruse being discovered.

"In that case, you aren't far from home but just far enough that you'll need some sustenance, and a horse would ease your troubles."

"Do you know of anyone who might offer me either or both?"

"Aye. I can offer you the food, lass, and my son can sell you a horse."

"Thank you, kind lady." Allyson flashed a genuine smile that earned her a toothless one in return. It was a short time later that Allyson's belly was full, she had food in her satchel, and she mounted on a horse more suited to a plow but would plod along. She'd fished out a few coins from the pouch while the old woman led Allyson to her home. Allyson wasn't wearing any jewelry, so when she proffered the coins from the hidden pocket in her skirt, it didn't appear as though she hid more money. She rode southeast until she was out of sight, then adjusted to head further west. Allyson prayed she was pointed in the right direction.

CHAPTER SEVEN

Cairren pushed past people as she dashed toward Laird Elliot, who broke his fast alongside the Gordons. She skidded to a halt when she reached their table and covered her chest with her hand as she attempted to catch her breath.

"She's gone," Cairren blurted out. "Allyson never returned to her chamber last eve and wasn't there when I went to meet her before Mass. She wasn't in the chapel either, and she's not arrived to go for our morning walk with the queen. No one's seen her since the feast."

"Perhaps she's run away," Ewan jested around a chunk of bread, but when Cairren turned a cold gaze on him, he realized it was most probable he'd guessed correct. "She followed a mon out of the Great Hall last night. I found him with another woman, but maybe she decided to break our betrothal by breaking her— Oof."

Eoin's sharp elbow bashed into Ewan's side before he could finish his insulting remark. Kenneth was on his feet and pushing the bench away from the table. He placed his meaty fists on the table and leaned over until his nose nearly touched Ewan's.

"If the king hadn't ordered my daughter to

marry you, there would be no way in hell I'd ever allow you near her, you puffed-up popinjay. This is your fault, with your crude comments and taunts. She ran to escape the hell you'll put her in. I swear by all that's holy, if she comes to harm, I will skewer your cods then lop off your head." Kenneth stormed away from the table and approached the dais. The Gordons and Cairren observed Laird Elliot's animated conversation with the king before Cairren returned her gaze to Ewan.

"He's right. You did this, and you'd best fix it before someone defiles her or kills her." Cairren glared at Ewan. "You embarrassed us both the day before yesterday, then you frightened Allyson with whatever you whispered, and now she's run away after finding out she'll be shackled to you. It's not mere disappointment that's driven her away or even pride. You've made marriage sound like a terror. She may be a flirt, but the attention she gets at court is the *only* attention she gets. You've sentenced her to a life even worse than the one she left behind to come to this godforsaken hellhole of iniquity. You may look like a mon, but it's time you grew up and acted like one."

Cairren spun on her heels and fled the Great Hall while Ewan sat stunned alongside his father and brother. He resented first Allyson, then Cairren for referring to marrying him as the same as being shackled, but then he'd felt that way about Allyson. He never imagined she would run away to avoid the marriage; he assumed she'd come around and then go quietly to Huntly, where he could leave her.

"What do you think she meant that the attention she gets here is the only attention she gets?" Eoin's question broke through Ewan's thoughts.

"I don't know. I don't care right now. I will have to help Elliot find his wayward daughter. Father, she should be committed to a nunnery, not to our clan."

Ewan grumbled as he left the table to approach the dais.

"She's been gone all night, Your Grace," Kenneth said as Ewan approached. "I need to determine where she's gone and bring her back."

"Bring her back?" The queen interjected. "Aren't you the least concerned that she was so overset by this betrothal that she ran away? Don't you care what might have befallen her along the way?"

"I am, Your Majesty, but she serves at your leisure. I assume you expect her to return to her duties."

Queen Elizabeth rose from her carved chair and peered down at Ewan and Laird Elliot. Her lip curled in disgust before she raised an eyebrow. "You'd better explain to your future son-by-marriage why Lady Allyson didn't find his jests humorous. If you don't, I will." Queen Elizabeth swept from the table and left the dais before entering the royal antechamber.

"What was the queen talking aboot?" Ewan demanded. He glanced at the king before returning his glare to the Elliot.

Kenneth Elliot closed his eyes and swallowed several times before looking at Ewan. It stunned the younger man to see sadness and a hollowness to the older man's eyes. "I arranged a marriage for Allyson's oldest sister when Allyson was still very young. The ceremony took place at our keep, and the couple remained there for their wedding night. Allyson awoke to the sound of her sister's screams while her husband forced her to consummate their marriage. A few years later, her sister returned to our home after her husband's heart gave out while he was still trying to sire a son. He left Mary destitute with no money to travel back to Elliot territory. She had to beg guardsmen to bring her home and pay for her expenses while they traveled. I reimbursed them, but it wasn't until after the men left that we discovered they demanded a different payment before they arrived at our keep."

Ewan tasted bile in the back of his throat as he listened to the tale, which explained why the suggestion that he and his brother might share Allyson had spurred such a terrified response. His words that equated her to chattel only exacerbated a problem he didn't realize existed.

"Thank you for confiding in me," Ewan whispered. "I wish I'd known this before I spoke to Allyson either time. But I know I shouldn't have said what I did regardless of your family's past. Let me gather my sword and my bedroll, and I'll be ready to ride out in a quarter hour."

"I'm not taking you. One look at you, and she'll bolt again. You've done enough." Kenneth barked and turned back to the king.

"Like it or not, Eoin and I are the best trackers you'll find here. None of these Lowlanders parading around in their silk and velvet will find her. You need men like me and my brother who are used to being outdoors, used to hunting. Rather than argue, tell me where you think she would go first."

"I don't bluidy know. She won't go to our home because she knows her mother will send her back. She might consider her friend, Isabella, but Allyson has enough sense to realize she can't travel all the way to the Sinclairs alone. I'm certain she's not in Stirling, so mayhap Glasgow or Edinburgh."

"I'd check with my brother and Lady Elizabeth at Culcreuch," King Robert offered. "The ladies are friends, and it's a short ride that she could have made with no one noticing." The Bruce paused. "Gordon, set this right, or it won't be Laird Elliot who cuts off your cods."

Ewan and Eoin charged out of the castle's bailey with Kenneth and a mixture of Elliot and Gordon warriors following them. They made good time, and when they arrived at Culcreuch, they found Edward Bruce preparing to mount his horse as they clattered into the bailey. Edward strode over to Kenneth Elliot and clasped forearms.

"She was here, but she disappeared before sunrise," Edward stated by way of a greeting. "We couldn't figure out how she disappeared until a village fisherman notified the head of the guard that he discovered a ladder hidden beneath some shrubs near the loch. We've deduced she must have scaled the ladder left propped against the western wall, then lowered it on the opposite side to make her getaway. I've already had scouts out looking along the shore and through the village. I was just aboot to ride out to Fintry, which is the closest village beyond the walls."

"We'll join you," Ewan responded. The look of revulsion that crossed Edward's face took him aback when the Earl of Badenoch and Lockerbie swung his gaze toward Ewan. "I take it she spoke of what happened when we learned of the betrothal."

"If finding her wasn't so dire, I'd challenge you right here and now," Edward spat. Ewan wisely remained quiet during the ride and while Edward questioned villagers in Fintry. They learned that a young woman claiming to be a Buchanan purchased food and a horse before sunrise and was headed southeast. Ewan and Eoin dismounted and searched for tracks that led in the direction they were told. The hoofprints were easy to find, but it wasn't long before they disappeared once they left the village behind.

"She's changed directions. Allyson has no intention of traveling to the Buchanans. She must have used their name because they're large with plenty of septs. No one would know whether she was one." Kenneth shifted in his saddle as he leaned over his horse's shoulder to catch sight of any traces of the way Allyson headed.

"She's headed southwest," Ewan announced. He'd found the hoofprints that proved she turned away from her original path and estimated where the horse would step. His search took him several yards from the others before he picked up her trail again. "She intends to go to Glasgow."

"She'll be halfway there by now," Eoin tilted his head to look toward the sun. It was midmorning, and she'd had at least a four-hour head start.

"More likely, she's already there," Kenneth muttered. He wheeled his horse around and set off, leaving the other men to catch up.

Allyson approached the Glasgow city gates just before midday. Smaller than Stirling, Allyson could weave her way through the streets until she reached the marketplace. Vendors called out their wares, and Allyson was relieved to see she arrived on market day; she'd be able to trade her finer clothes for money. The coin would replace what she'd already spent to secure two horses and some food. Allyson left her horse in the town's stable, but was careful not to allow anyone to see more than her eyes. She kept the rest of her face and her hair covered. She imagined her father had discovered her disappearance by now and Edward Bruce had informed him of her visit the night prior. She approached a haberdasher and listened as he haggled with the customer before her. She noted what he said and how he said it as she prepared for her own negotiations. When it was her turn, she approached the booth and angled her body so few people could see what she withdrew from her satchel.

"I have some fine items given to me by a lady when she and her husband sought shelter during a storm. I have no use for them." Allyson kept her voice low, hiding the noticeable refinement in her speech, and she was careful not to show the man her palms. He would see her smooth skin and realize in an instant that she wasn't a farmer's widow.

"Where did you say you were from?" The man countered.

"I don't recall that I did, but I'm from Inverlochy."

"You don't sound like a Highlander."

Allyson fought to keep from clenching her jaw. "I want to blend in. I dinna need anyone wondering what I'm aboot on account of them thinking to thieve me." She attempted to sound like Maude Sutherland and the other Highland ladies she knew, whose brogue slipped out from time to time.

"Right you are, right you are." The vendor examined the gloves and stockings Allyson placed on the counter of the stall. "These are fine quality. What do you want for them?"

"That they are. Tell me what you're willing to pay, and I'll tell you whether I'm willing to sell them to you."

"A silver groat."

Allyson laughed. "Four pence is what you'll pay? I'll be saying good day for aught under a gold quarter-noble."

"That's the real thievery. I won't pay more than a shilling, let alone a shilling and eight pence."

"Sold for a shilling!" Allyson grinned as the man

realized his error. They exchanged the goods for the coin, and Allyson tucked it away but once more didn't touch the pouch she had hidden. She pushed through the crowd until she made her way to the far end of the market, where the least profitable vendors set up their stands. She would make her money stretch since she didn't know how long she would be on her own. She found a woman selling material, but Allyson had no time or way to sew her own clothes while she was on the run. She feared there wouldn't be a merchant with premade gowns at a price she was willing to pay, but the last stall had what she needed. She purchased two more kirtles before leaving the market and moved along the streets to find the more permanent shops.

Allyson peeked through open doors, scanning the occupants for elderly shopkeepers most likely to need an assistant. She came to a bakery, where an old couple attempted to serve a line of customers while the woman shuffled back and forth between the counter and the kitchens. The smells wafting from the oven made Allyson's stomach growl, and the long line was a testament to the shop's popularity. Allyson lingered in a corner out of the way, attempting to appear inconspicuous. She was about to approach the couple as the crowd thinned when she was certain her father's voice carried through the open door. She peeked around the edge of her hood and caught sight of her father standing in the street with Ewan and Eoin. Allyson forced herself not to panic, but she slid past the counter while the couple was busy and darted through the kitchen, praying that there would be a second door that led outside from the kitchen. Otherwise, she would hide abovestairs in the couple's private residence. She breathed easier when she spotted the door and dashed toward the town stables. She hadn't expected the search party to reach

Glasgow so soon. While she was in a city, it wasn't large enough for her to go undetected her first day. Allyson would stand out as a stranger. She approached the stables but ducked around a corner when she recognized men in both the Elliot and the Gordon plaid. She cursed under her breath as she tried to figure out how she would gather her horse and escape with none of the guardsmen spying her. She made her way to the back of the stables and found a stable boy mucking out the back of a stall.

"I need your help," she whispered and waved the boy over. He couldn't have been over ten or eleven summers, but he appeared strong. "I fear those men will make shameful comments if they see me retrieving my horse. Could you bring him to me?"

The boy narrowed his eyes at her until she lowered her scarf but kept her head covered. The boy nodded his head several times, understanding the beautiful woman before him would draw unwanted attention. Allyson covered her face again and waited until the boy returned with her mount; then she slipped several pence into his hand and mounted on her own. She kept off the main thoroughfares and galloped out of Glasgow without looking back.

CHAPTER EIGHT

Ewan wanted to drive his fist into something or someone. He couldn't explain why his senses screamed that Allyson was nearby, but his temper was running thin as Kenneth continued to ignore his suggestion that they divide into smaller groups and work their way through the vendors. Ewan was certain Allyson would need less-conspicuous clothes than what she wore at court. Elizabeth informed them that Allyson was wearing a plain gown and carried one satchel, which Ewan also guessed had no food or provisions.

"Laird Elliot, even if she hasn't been visiting vendors for clothing, she will need to eat. She may have gone to buy food, and someone might recognize her description."

"The lass is more likely to wander into a tavern and order a meal there than to know how to negotiate with street merchants. She didn't go to fairs or markets often at home."

Ewan wanted to bellow that the lass hadn't lived at home in four years and demand to know why the man couldn't recognize that four years at court had changed Allyson. In Ewan's mind, they wasted precious time searching the town's taverns when he understood Allyson wouldn't be foolish enough to enter one unless it was dire. She'd realize the danger a tavern was to an unaccompanied woman, and she had to guess that her father would look there. Ewan sighed and waited until Kenneth continued the search among the permanent shops.

"The mon worries aboot his daughter; give him some credit for trying," Eoin whispered as Ewan passed him once more during his pacing.

"And the mon doesnae ken his daughter even a tad. She isnae going to give herself up so easily. She might have been foolish to run, but she isnae foolish enough to get caught this soon." Both men lapsed into their Highland burrs as they felt more themselves away from court. "What I said is true. Even if she didna go to the street vendors, she needs food and clothes. I'd venture to say she also kens she needs coin. If she hasnae already traded, then she'll have the sense to look for employment."

"Employment? What can she do? She hasnae been to any of the taverns, so where else would she ken to go?"

Ewan glared at his brother. He didn't understand why everyone underestimated Allyson after she'd escaped two well-fortified keeps, evaded detection for the most part, and remained elusive after more than a day on the run.

"She can sew at the least. She may have found a dressmaker or haberdasher where she might trade her services for a roof over her head."

Eoin paused and considered what his brother suggested before nodding his head. "Mayhap she can cook, too. Mayhap she'll hire herself out as a maid." Eoin grinned at what seemed like nonsense to him. "She's a lady-in-waiting nae some village lass. She doesnae ken how to do any of that. Nae when she's had someone to do it for her, her entire life."

Ewan's scowl darkened before turning toward Kenneth. "Laird, did Allyson spend any time in your keep's kitchens before she left for court? Does she ken how to run a household?"

"Aye, she knows because her mother taught her how to be a chatelaine. As for the kitchens, I have no idea. Perhaps."

Ewan wanted to ram his fist into the man's belly for knowing so little about his daughter. He swept his gaze up and down the street, peering into any doorway he could see. Movement across the street caught his eye. The very merchant he suggested they visit had a shop in front of him. He squinted against the daylight to glimpse the people milling about the bakery, where the scent of warm bread wafted from the doorway.

"There! She's in there. I'm certain of it." Ewan pushed his way across the street and dashed into the store, but he didn't see Allyson. He was certain he had, but instead of finding her, he heard a door slam shut. He followed the sound, disregarding the elderly couple's complaints when he entered the kitchens. He ran to the back door, but when he looked down the alleyway in each direction, there was no one to see. He ran toward the public stables. Intuition told him that if Allyson had been in the shop and feared being found, she would claim her horse and disappear from Glasgow. The streets were congested and while being a large man made it easier to see over people's heads and to intimidate them into moving aside, it left little space for him to maneuver. He slowed his pace several times before he found a stable boy mucking out stalls. Gordon and Elliot men still lingered about the front of the stables, so Ewan suspected Allyson would have found someone else to gather her horse.

"Aye, a young woman asked me to fetch her

horse. Said she feared the men out front and what'd they say. Face like an angel, ma mama would say. She gave me a few coins, and I brought her horse out. She didn't linger and spurred the beast as soon as there was room. I watched her go."

Ewan thanked the boy and ordered the guardsmen to ready all of their mounts. Ewan gave up politeness as he steered through the people milling about until he reached his brother and his potential future father-by-marriage. He wasn't sold on the idea of marrying Allyson, but he didn't want her to come to any harm, especially not after Laird Elliot explained what happened to her older sister. The story had haunted him the entire ride to Glasgow, and he felt shame now that he understood how real Allyson's fear was.

"She's run again. A stable boy just gave her back her horse and said she barreled out of the city gates. We missed her. Again."

As the day wore on and another night approached, frustration grew among all the men. Ewan wanted to throttle Allyson for sending them on the least merry chase he could imagine. He was grimy and tired, and what he wanted most was a hot meal and a pint of ale followed by several drams of whisky. For the first time in ages, a willing woman wasn't on his list.

"Allyson may have gone to the Hermitage. She doesn't know anyone there, but the keep is under our clan's protection. She would find shelter there with few people recognizing she's my daughter. I say that's where we try next."

"The Hermitage? That's barely more than a league from the border." As a Highlander, Ewan detested being in the Lowlands, but the possibility of traveling to the border was unpalatable. He had no respect for the English, and no desire to go anywhere near them.

"So is our keep on Elliot land. Allyson grew up within miles of the border and will be more comfortable in this area. While most wouldn't recognize her face, they would recognize our clan's name."

"And you assume she'd give that out. She must understand that along the border, she'd be a prize to capture. She'd be held for ransom; a ransom you couldn't pay because you're not home to receive the demand." Ewan ground his teeth as he looked south. He would shake her when he finally got his hands on her slim figure.

It was too late for them to continue riding, so they made camp. Ewan settled on his bedroll and looked at the stars. He was certain they shone brighter in the Highlands, but he picked out patterns just as he and Eoin had done countless times as children. His mind wandered to where Allyson must have been spending the night. He pushed away the guilt, reminding himself that she'd chosen to run away and not return with Edward. While he didn't want her to come to harm, he still believed it was her fault if she did.

The mixture of Gordons and Elliots rode hard until well after sunset, when they reached the Hermitage. A young man who bore a striking resemblance to the king welcomed them. There was little doubt that the Robert Bruce who stood before them was King Robert the Bruce's illegitimate son. While Kenneth and Robert spoke in hushed tones, Ewan glanced around the Great Hall and up the stairs to the family and guest chambers. He wondered if she was hiding in one of them. His frazzled nerves tempted him to bound up the stairs and tear each room apart until he either found her or was certain she wasn't in residence.

"The matter is worse than you think, Laird Elliot." Robert's words carried to Ewan, making him turn toward the young man. "We've had trouble with reivers over the past sennight. These men are more ruthless than the usual lot. They've done more than steal horses and cattle, terrorizing the local villagers. They aren't men we're familiar with, and none of our reivers know them. There're rumors that they're from Chillingham."

The group fell silent at the mention of the infamous keep where unimaginable torture was the norm. Ewan's stomach clenched as he pictured John Sage getting his hands on Allyson if these reivers got hold of her—assuming she made it there alive. His mind flashed a picture of Allyson lying on the ground, battered and defiled, dead where they left her. He glanced at Kenneth, then Eoin, and knew they imagined the same thing.

"There's naught we can do tonight. It's too dark to track them, but we leave at first light," Ewan announced. He'd deferred to Laird Elliot's leadership until that point, but he'd lost faith in the man after they missed Allyson by a hairsbreadth. His opinion on marrying her and his opinion on marriage may not have altered, but he wouldn't ignore any woman in such danger. He could admit to himself, and maybe even to Eoin, that he had liked Allyson and enjoyed her company up to the time when they discovered they were being forced to marry. He'd danced with her and shared jokes and easy conversation in the past. It was his fault things soured because he'd antagonized her in the passageway even before they'd learned of their fathers' plans. Now he needed to collect his runaway bride.

CHAPTER NINE

Allyson didn't know where to go. She considered cutting back northeast and making her way to Edinburgh. Now that she knew her father and Ewan were away from Stirling, she didn't fear them finding her on roads outside the city. She discarded the idea because she sensed her father would have guards posted around the city just in case she made that very attempt. She set off south from Glasgow, wondering if she dared go to the Kennedys and use her friendship with Cairren as an excuse to shelter there for a few days. Laird Kennedy was only an acquaintance of her father, so she didn't worry as much that the man would notify her father with haste. She glanced at the sun's position and gained her bearings before galloping further south.

The sun was setting hours after she fled Glasgow. She approached a cluster of crofts that was more of a hamlet than a village. Men were gathering their tools and making their way from the fields. She strained to see the plaid draped over many shoulders. She sucked in a breath so sharply that it whistled. The further south she traveled, the easier it became to recognize the woven patterns. These men were Crichtons; she'd been certain she'd aimed far enough west to be entering Wallace territory. The great defenders of Scotland were well-known for their loyalty to King Robert after their most famous member, William Wallace, was butchered by the English while he fought for Scotland's freedom. She thanked all the angels and saints that the Elliots had always been loyal to Robert the Bruce and not switched sides like so many other border clans. She didn't intend to announce she was an Elliot, but if she had to disclose the information, at least she didn't fear their response.

Allyson dismounted among a cluster of trees and hid in the foliage until after the sun set. She nibbled at some food she carried, but she was careful to ration it. When she saw no one who might question her, she eased away from her hiding place and guided her horse into a stable. She scanned the area and found there weren't any horses in the small building, but there was some hay that looked edible for her mount. She looped the reins around a post, then huddled in the shadows until she drifted off, but she stirred at every sound and every time her steed shifted. It was well before sun up when Allyson left the building as quietly as she entered.

While the Lowlands didn't have the same landscape obstacles as the Highlands, Allyson encountered several bodies of water that proved impossible to ford because of their size or the current's strength. It forced her to double back a few times and alter her course more and more. The sun was nearing the western horizon after another full day in the saddle when she glimpsed the top of a tower. She pushed herself and her horse a little further until the keep came into sight.

Bluidy bleeding hell! How can this be? How did I end up at bluidy Hermitage Castle? Wonderful. I do everything I can to escape my father and end up at a keep under the control of

King Robert's illegitimate son. The very mon named after him. As though that isn't bad enough, who did the king task with the keep's guardianship? My father! Bluidy sodding hell.

Allyson fumed as she realized the blunder she'd made. In her attempts to remain far from Elliot land, she'd stumbled upon it. While her family didn't reside at the Hermitage, plenty of people would recognize her. It was more because she stood out in her family than because she resembled anyone, but her blond hair and blue eyes were memorable. She'd approached their territory from a route she'd never taken, so she hadn't realized she'd brought herself so close to home. Avoiding the castle wouldn't even guarantee her freedom, since the people in Liddesdale were also likely to recognize her. She'd brought herself within five miles of the border and had nowhere safe to spend the night. Several more oaths and curses crossed her mind as she tried to decide what to do next. In the meantime, she turned her horse away from the castle and rode a short distance to ensure guards who had an elevated vantage point wouldn't spot her.

As dusk settled into night, Allyson didn't dare seek shelter anywhere near the town or the keep. She remained outside where the temperature dropped, and her teeth chattered, but exhaustion overrode the discomfort. She fell into a deeper sleep than she expected and was startled awake when someone grabbed a handful of her hair through her hood and lifted her onto her feet. Her eyes snapped open as pain ripped across her scalp. She scanned her surroundings and understood in an instant that a band of border reivers had discovered her hideout.

"Look what we have here." The clipped English tones came from behind her, and she grimaced that she hadn't had at least a little good fortune to have Scots find her. The danger she faced grew exponentially now that she was in the hands of an English group of thieves. "Why would a young woman be sleeping alone in the woods with a keep and a town so nearby? She's avoiding someone, or they've left her to struggle on her own."

"I bet she'll struggle. Struggle when she's beneath me," a deep voice boomed from somewhere to Allyson's right. She twisted one way then another as she tried to count how many men were in the party.

"Let me go and take the horse. That's all you want."

"The horse may be what I want," came the voice of her captor. "But what I need is to leave no witnesses." A blade appeared in the moonlight before it pressed against her throat. Allyson considered stating her name, hoping they might ransom her rather than kill her, but she wouldn't bring these men anywhere near her home, her family, or her clan.

"I haven't even seen any of your faces. You're English and will be back across the border before daylight. There is naught to fear from me," Allyson reasoned.

A man emerged from between two trees, tugging the reins to her horse. He took one glance at her, then paused and gave her a much longer assessing look. He stepped forward and pushed her hood all the way off her head and yanked her shawl from her head and the scarf from her face.

"Bloody hell, if it isn't Lord Elliot's daughter," the third man announced. He was the only one whose face she'd seen. And he was the one who gave away her identity.

"Elliot's daughter? What're you doing out alone?" The man who held the blade against her throat muttered. "Never mind the horse. We just gained something far more valuable."

Allyson sensed more men were in the surrounding area, but none materialized. Within moments, they bound her hands in front of her and tied her scarf as a gag. They tossed her onto her horse, and she almost sailed over the other side with her hands unable to steady her. The man who recognized her kept her reins, and while they kept the pace slow to reduce their noise and to keep her from tumbling off the horse, she had to squeeze her thighs with all her might to stop herself from sliding from one side to another. She assumed they would cross the border and arrive at a small keep, where the reivers would deposit her until someone demanded a ransom from her family. She was unprepared for hours of riding through the dark as they headed east after crossing the border. They rode parallel to her clan's land, but on the wrong side of the border. When Allyson realized they had no intention of stopping near the Hermitage, she used the dark to hide her movements. She pulled the shawl from around her neck and frayed the edges, dropping pieces of bright colored yarn on the ground. No one could see them in the dark, but in the sunlight, they would leave a trail. She prayed her father made it far enough south to return to their land. He might assume she'd gone home, and he might even look for her across the border since he knew she had a terrible sense of direction. At least she hoped he knew. She was unconvinced her father was any better acquainted with her than most strangers; he'd never taken the time to get to know her. Perhaps someone in their clan would suggest they look in England.

The sky was lightening as the air changed, and Allyson was certain it smelled like the sea. She strained her neck to look around, but she soon wished she hadn't. She recognized the enormous fortress they were approaching, and she saw stars before her eyes. They were nearing Chillingham Castle, not only home to the Greys, descendants of William the Conqueror but also home to John Sage, King Edward's chief torturer. She glanced at the men surrounding her, and several grinned at her discomfort.

"You recognize where you are," the man who woke her stated. "You know who awaits you."

"Why did we come this far? Or rather why were you reiving so far from here if the Greys support you?" Allyson yanked the gag from her mouth to question them.

"We go where the money is, and there will be plenty of money for handing you over." The man who still held her reins tossed over his shoulder.

Allyson remained silent as they arrived at the gates to one of the most notorious castles in Northumberland. King Edward, the Hammer of the Scots, had stayed in the castle on his way to fight William Wallace. He'd left behind his most trusted soldier, giving him carte blanche to rain down terror on all Scots near and far. She could only imagine the vile depravities and pain that awaited her. Marrying Ewan became more appealing by the minute. Her impetuous decision would probably get her raped and killed. Allyson entered the bailey with her hands still bound, but her shawl no longer existed. She'd dropped the remaining length when she recognized where they were taking her but before they would notice her actions. Allyson remained motionless until a guardsman pulled her from the saddle. She stumbled and pitched forward, landing hard on her knees. No one offered assistance as she struggled to get to her feet, her skirts twisted around her feet.

The massive castle doors opened and two men along with a woman emerged. The woman was stunning, willowy, with graying hair. Despite her age, she was still remarkable, and Allyson couldn't look away until movement in her periphery distracted her. She looked at the man who walked with a limp and gasped. She was watching Sir John Sage coming to greet her or, more likely, assess how he would torture her.

"Who is this?" The man who stood next to the elegant woman demanded. Allyson deduced they were Sir Thomas and Lady Agnes Grey. The older knight had an illustrious career fighting on behalf of King Edward. He'd moved through the ranks, surviving one battle after another. While John Sage might have a sadistic streak, Sir Thomas wasn't to be underestimated.

They've brought me to hell on Earth. This is where I shall breathe my last.

"One of the Elliot daughters. She hasn't said which one." Allyson wished she could stick a dirk in the man who kept announcing her identity. Lady Grey approached, and a chill ran down Allyson's spine when she noticed the gleam in the older woman's eyes. It was lascivious and calculating. The woman swept her fingers along Allyson's jaw before grasping it in a tight grip, turning her head one way then another. Allyson felt like a horse at market, waiting for Lady Grey to curl her lips back to test Allyson's gums. She braced herself not to flinch or cower. She looked over the woman's shoulder until Lady Grey curled a lock of hair around her finger and tugged to bring Allyson's head closer to her.

"You'll do well here," Lady Grey purred. Defiance crackled between Allyson and her new tormentor. "You haven't told us your name. Where are your manners?"

Allyson glanced at the woman and offered her a practiced court smile. It was coy and suggestive at the same time. "Wouldn't you like to know, my lady?" Allyson's voice matched the saccharine sweetness of Lady Grey's.

"Playing the coquette won't endear you to me, even if the men find it alluring. You need an ally here if you wish to survive, so I wouldn't piss that away." Lady Grey's jaw firmed as her eyes narrowed. "Your stay can be one where you are an untouchable and honored guest, or you can be a toy for any man interested in tupping a nobleman's daughter. Either way, Sir John will ensure you don't cause any unnecessary difficulty."

"Perhaps a tour is in order, my lady," Sir John wandered closer, and once more Allyson steeled herself not to flinch or cower. The man's reputation for sadism preceded him, and Allyson was well aware of the torture chamber that lay in the castle's dungeon. After William Wallace's attack that killed much of the surrounding village's women and children, Sir John arrived to instill fear in everyone within a day's ride of either side of the border. She'd heard his name before she left home; parents used it like the bodach—the bogeyman—to scare children into listening to them. Now she stood face-to-face with the monster of her childhood nightmares. He was an intimidating figure despite his limp, but upon first glance, no one would guess the horrors he perpetrated. There was a haunting emptiness in his eyes, as though he were devoid of a soul, and Allyson supposed that must be so, for him to be capable of the atrocities she'd heard of. She didn't want to imagine the ones she hadn't heard.

"I believe once we know this young lady's name, we'll find her more agreeable. Your reputation appears to precede you once more, Sir John. I don't expect to have many problems from her now that her memory has been jogged. I suspect she's familiar with what lies in our dungeon." Lady Grey chuckled as she glanced at her husband and Sir John.

Allyson nodded once before clearing her throat.

"Lady Allyson, my lady. My name is Allyson, and I am Laird Elliot's youngest child." She watched the looks exchanged between the lord and lady along with the ones that passed to and from the retired knight.

"I will have her shown to a chamber where she can bathe and ready for the morning meal." Lady Grey spoke to everyone and no one before turning to Allyson. "You're in time to break your fast."

Allyson followed the trio into the Great Hall and missed a step when more than a hundred pairs of male eyes turned toward her. Every guardsman and male servant at Chillingham must have been present for the morning meal. Allyson felt like the proverbial lamb to the slaughter. She kept her eyes straight ahead as a maid led her to the stairs and to a chamber where she waited for the bath to arrive. She declined the maid's offer to help her bathe because she needed time alone to assess the situation and begin planning. Allyson looked out of the window to orient herself within the castle and the surrounding land.

The chamber faced the rear of the keep, but it was too great a height for her to leap from the window and hope to survive. She crossed the chamber, and as she suspected, they'd locked the door. She placed her ear against the wood and could hear movement on the other side, even though she couldn't distinguish what it was. Allyson presumed they posted a guard lest she try to escape when the servants arrived with the tub and hot water. She rushed to lay out a fresh kirtle, chemise, and stocking before the maid returned to direct the filling of her bath. Once she was alone again, she peeled down her stockings and removed the dirks strapped to her legs. She had a knife on the inside of one thigh and the outside of another. If ever a man raised her skirts against her will, she was prepared to defend herself. Part of the reason she didn't want any help was because she had no desire for anyone to discover where she stashed her weapons. She pulled a *sgian dubh* from its sheath at her waist. It looked like an ordinary eating knife while tucked away, but it was far more deadly. The short blade was razor sharp and pointed. She'd begun carrying it soon after arriving at court and the first unwelcome suitor attempted to accost her in a darkened passageway.

Allyson resolved to bide her time, obey her captors, and tuck away any information that might aid her newest escape endeavor. In the meantime, she would do what she could to get along and be as unobtrusive as possible. She appreciated the plain kirtles she had in her satchel, as opposed to the gowns she would have donned at court.

CHAPTER TEN

The sun's first rays poked above the horizon as the Gordon twins prepared to mount alongside the other men in the search party. They would need the daylight to track Allyson. Ewan led the charge through the portcullis, but he swerved toward a copse of trees. His intuition told him Allyson must have stopped there if she hadn't approached the keep. He reined in before dismounting when he spotted the disturbed earth. He kneeled and swept his hand over a spot where several hoofprints overlapped. He looked around and noticed a spot where something squashed the grass, as though a person sat there for an extended period. Taking the reins of his horse, he followed the hoofprints that separated into individual trails but moved in the same direction.

"Either Allyson's hiding nearby from whoever came into these trees, or they've taken her." Ewan looked south toward the invisible boundary between Scotland and England.

"Ewan, come look at this," Eoin called to him. His brother had examined the same spot where the grass was disturbed but moved a few steps away from the hoofprints. When Ewan approached, Eoin pointed to a patch of dirt Ewan hadn't noticed.

"There was some struggle. Look at the footprints. Their pattern is in too much disarray to be men who stood around talking. These boot prints are smaller than the others."

"Someone's taken her then." Ewan suspected he knew who took her and feared where she was being taken.

"It's those bluidy reivers," Kenneth proclaimed. "And they've dragged her to Chillingham. If they rode through the night, then they will be there. We ride for the border and the pieces of shite who took my lass."

The party rode south the five miles that separated the Hermitage from England and crossed over. Ewan's gaze alternated sweeping the surrounding landscape and watching the trail of hoofprints. They hadn't traveled far into England before Ewan's brow furrowed when he noticed a brightly colored piece of wool beneath his horse.

"Halt!" Ewan swung down from the saddle and pulled the threads loose from where horse trampled them into the grass. "This is yarn. I can't imagine a mon wearing aught this bright a shade of green, so my guess is it came from a woman's clothing."

"Let me see," Kenneth examined the wool, then clenched it in his fist. "The last time Allyson was home, she helped die several spools of wool then began knitting a shawl that included yarn this color."

Kenneth only knew of Allyson's project because he'd had to pay for the expensive dyes and had objected, arguing it was frivolous. He'd hurt Allyson's feelings and had seen the disappointment in her eyes. She'd offered to unravel the shawl and find a better use for the wool, perhaps making something for the less-fortunate members of their clan. Kenneth had felt so guilty that he refused to allow her to destroy what he could tell she'd worked hard on.

"My laird!" A guardsman at the head of the entourage called out. "I can see another piece of wool up ahead."

Ewan jogged to where the warrior pointed and discovered several purple threads. They looked like they'd come from the frayed end of a garment, but it was another sign Allyson had passed that way.

"She wouldn't have dropped these if she wasn't leaving a trail. She knew people would follow her, but we have answered many a prayer tracking her with little difficulty," Eoin commented.

The riders pushed on, following the ongoing trail of fabric until Chillingham lay over the next rise, and the remnants of a tattered shawl lay on the ground.

Allyson forced herself to swallow another spoonful of porridge. It looked and tasted more like sludge, but she understood she needed the sustenance, or the lightheadedness she experienced as she stepped out of the tub would leave her unable to protect herself. She kept her head lowered as she ate, but her gaze shifted among the people gathered on the dais and at the tables below. The only women she noticed were the servants, and many of them looked haggard, sporting bruises on their faces, necks, and arms. Allyson could only imagine what their clothing hid. She shuddered as a warrior grabbed a young woman's arm and pulled her into his lap before squeezing her breast. Allyson saw more than heard the responding whimper, but what concerned her the most was the woman's acceptance of the poor treatment. She tolerated being manhandled even when she flinched as the man's hand wandered up her leg beneath her skirts. Allyson used all the restraint she possessed not to order the man to cease, realizing making a scene would endanger her and the servant.

"I propose that tour is in order, my lady." Allyson jumped at Sir John's menacing tones, but she could do little more than nod. She laid her spoon on the table and rose, hesitating before placing her hand in Sir John's. He guided her off the dais and toward the doors of the Great Hall, leading her outside. "You had the opportunity to see the bailey when you arrived, but there is much that lays around the keep that might hold your interest."

Allyson managed a nod while fighting a cringe as Sir John's hand clasped hers in what appeared like a lover's hold, but crushed her fingers. She held her head high and her back straight as Sir John led her from one building to another. She didn't understand his interest in showing her so many storage rooms until she realized he was offering her places to hide as he taunted her with a game of cat-and-mouse. He wanted her to attempt to flee, and he wanted to be the one to find her. They returned to the keep through a side door before Sir John pushed her toward a descending set of stairs. Allyson was certain the dungeon laid at the bottom, but Sir John crowded her, denying her any chance to turn back. Lest she tumble down the steps and injure herself, Allyson had no choice but to walk down them. When they reached the base, Sir John's breath tickled her ear as he reached past her to unlock a door. As he retracted his arm, his hand pressed against her breast before sliding down the front of her gown. Allyson could feel the metal of the keyring as Sir John used his other hand to open the door. He'd used his body to cage her in, attempting to intimidate her with his size and proximity. He intended her to understand that he remained in control, since he possessed the tool that could free her or lock her in.

Sir John was in no rush to reach their destination, making it appear as though they were strolling through a park rather than a dungeon. When they reached the end of the corridor of cells, many of which contained battered and broken men and women, the knight swung a large door open and nudged Allyson to enter the pitch-black chamber. She waited for what felt like an eternity before light flooded the room from the torch Sir John placed in a wall sconce. She recognized his tactic of trying to terrify her by leaving her alone in the unknown. Like an unpredictable wild animal, Allyson wouldn't allow him to smell her fear. She'd intuited he'd brought her to his torture chamber, but she was unprepared for all the devices intended to create pain. Her eyes traveled over whips, cat-o'-nine-tails, metal cuffs, and wooden paddles before settling on the enormous stretching rack that appeared to take pride of place in the center of the floor. Allyson smelled the stench of death as much as she noticed the blood that stained the floor, parts of the walls, and was ingrained in the wooden table.

"I conduct most of my business here. You might say it's my solar," Sir John mused as his hand rested on her lower back, precariously close to where her bottom began. "It's my favorite place within this entire castle. Lord Grey may rule the keep and surrounding land, but here, I rule the underworld."

Allyson turned her head enough to look over her shoulder at the man. His expression held pride and anticipation. Once more, Allyson reminded herself that predators pounced when they sensed their prey was most vulnerable. If she cowered or protested, it would encourage him to mistreat her. Instead, Allyson chose a different tactic and stepped away from Sir John. She wandered near a set of metal restraints that she brushed her hand over. Moving on to a set of whips, Allyson glanced at the knight, offering him a seductive but curious expression. He nodded once, and she lifted the whip with the shortest handle from the rack. She ran the leather tail through her hand before cracking it through the air. She transformed her mien into one of satisfaction before moving on to swipe her hand over a portion of stones discolored from blood that had long since dried. Every so often, she canted her head to glance at the knight who observed her with intense interest. At last, she stood at the stretching rack, running her hands over the surface and bending forward to not only extend her reach but to offer the man an enticing view of her cleavage.

"My chamber of horrors intrigues you, my lady." It was a statement, not a question.

"I've seen naught like it." Which was far from a lie. The room disgusted Allyson, but she was committed to the charade.

"The whip you selected was not only the perfect size for a woman to hold, but is the perfect size to flay a woman's bare back." The man leered at her before adding, "Or bare breasts."

"And you have someone to whom you do that?" Allyson inquired as she attempted nonchalance while she cranked the handle and watched the mechanisms separate the planks of wood.

"I do, but there is no reason for me not to find someone else."

Allyson swallowed as she noticed a bulge at the front of the torturer's breeches. She understood their visit to his dominion aroused him. She'd heard of women who enjoyed a man's dominance, but she never suspected that it could be so extreme. The knight made it obvious that he enjoyed such interludes, and Allyson grew terrified that not only would he torture her for the sake of the pain, but that he would find a different form of pleasure than she expected.

"That is a tremendous amount of power you wield over another. Power that must gratify in so many ways," she purred. She hoped her feigned interest would convince the man that she shared his desire to dominate rather than suggest she desired being dominated.

"Have you ever witnessed a lashing, my lady?" Sir John rounded the table and once more stood behind her. He stretched his arms on either side of Allyson's and ground his rod against her backside.

"Several. You cannot live at court for as many years as I have without witnessing public corporal punishment. It is a necessary evil."

"Evil? Is that what you Scots believe? There is naught evil about carrying out God's will. He would see wrongdoers punished for their transgressions, and in order for that to happen, someone must mete out those punishments. Tell me, my lady, have you ever watched a woman be whipped?" Allyson shook her head, horrified that Sir John continued to rub himself against her. She hadn't anticipated this turn of events when she attempted to gain control. She should have realized that he would always have the upper hand. His fingers trailed down her throat and over her exposed chest in a light caress before his fingers toyed with the edge of her neckline. They slid far enough beneath the material to cover his nails. "You've not watched a woman's breast bared to a crowd, then observed them jiggle and sway with each impact of leather against flesh? You haven't had the pleasure of witnessing a woman's submission? Never wondered what it would be like to have such control of a weaker yet desirable person? Perhaps you will before long."

Sir John stepped away, and Allyson's stomach

clenched from the unexpected space. It didn't feel like freedom, but another round of cat-and-mouse. The knight retreated far enough to give him room to pounce. Allyson remained silent, refusing to answer any of his questions or offer any opinions. The man limped to the wall sconce and lifted the torch before opening the door and waving a hand to indicate it was time to leave.

CHAPTER ELEVEN

"We can't besiege the castle because we don't have the men or the resources, nor can we storm it, but you heard the villager, she's in there," Kenneth huffed.

The search party turned rescue party camped in a clearing less than a quarter mile from the castle. They'd considered crossing back into Scotland, but it would take them at least two hours to ride each way. Neither of the Gordon twins nor Laird Elliot wanted to be that far from Allyson now that they'd located her. One of Laird Elliot's guards had an English mother and could adopt an accent that wouldn't make him stand out. He'd entered the village mid-morning and pretended to be a knight looking for a lord to serve. With the Elliots' Lowlander attire, he could pass for an English soldier even if he didn't have full armor. Ewan and Eoin had both changed into their plaids when they reached Culcreuch, so neither blended in. The Elliot guardsman discovered there had been a stir at the keep because a group of reivers brought in a young Scottish woman with her wrists bound and her mouth gagged. No one in the village knew who she was, but it was obvious she was a captive. The man learned both Lord and Lady

Grey were in residence, as was Sir John Sage. He dreaded passing the last piece of information to his laird.

"Eoin and I will take some of our men to scout once it grows dark. We can't approach the keep during the day, even if we don our breeks again. We need to understand the lay of the land before we make any plans to break in or be invited in."

The men spent most of the afternoon planning the scouting mission along with trying to anticipate what they might discover. They wanted several contingency plans already fleshed out, so there would be no delay once they knew how Allyson fared. Some of the guardsmen set up camp and hunted while others tended the horses. They remained hidden among the trees until the sun set and the stars appeared. Ewan and Eoin covered their faces and neck with mud, thankful for the intermittent showers that had left the ground soft enough for the hoofprints they followed to be trackable and so they had a means to camouflage their skin, which would shine in contrast to the dark night. The Gordon warriors selected for the scouting party followed their leaders, covering their faces and wearing their plaids with its muted colors. Kenneth sent his spy back into the village to learn if anyone had come or gone from the keep and seen Allyson.

"We're just going to have a look, get a lay of the land," Ewan reminded his men. "We're not engaging unless there is no other way to save our lives or if we see Lady Allyson might lose hers." Ewan grimaced at the image of the vibrant young woman's life being snuffed out so prematurely. He recalled the last time they had danced together, only three nights before their run-in outside Lady Bevan's chamber. They'd joked, and Ewan remembered enjoying the feel of Allyson's body pressed against his. He wouldn't deny he was attracted to the lady; she was beautiful, but he'd never considered more than perhaps stealing a kiss. Now he was tasked with rescuing her, so that not only would she live, but he could marry her. Part of him felt he should be furious that he had to chase after her, but he was impressed with her resourcefulness to have survived on her own for as long as she did. Yet another part feared they would be too late, that he would never witness her smile again or feel her in his arms. His palms tingled, but he pushed aside the thoughts, refusing to allow physical attraction to rule his actions. It had gotten him in enough trouble of late.

The Gordons rested against tree trunks and waited until they had the cover of dark and the woodland creatures settled down to sleep. When all was silent, they crept from the trees like wraiths before hiking the distance to the keep, remaining hunched and low to the ground. Using only hand gestures, Ewan positioned his men to begin their watch.

***

Allyson stood beside Lady Grey as the older woman inspected her female servants. Allyson hadn't understood what was happening until Lady Grey upbraided one woman for not being compliant enough the night prior when a guardsman sought her attention. Allyson fought the reaction to shy away in disgust as she realized Lady Grey was little more than a madam who ran a brothel in her castle. It might not have been a seedy tavern, but it was the same business. They could have knocked her over with a feather when she heard several women respond to Lady Grey with Scottish accents. Allyson cast surreptitious glances at those servants as she tried to draw closer for a better look. She feared she might recognize a woman from her own clan, since they'd suffered raids countless times while Allyson grew up. It wasn't unheard of for both men and women to be captured. The men were usually killed, and the women assaulted and killed or taken captive, then put to work. Ever since William Wallace's raid on the castle just over fifteen years earlier, tensions along this stretch of the Northumbrian border had been violent. Wallace burned a church with women and children inside, and every Scot bore the brunt of the English ire after that.

As Allyson continued to observe the scene playing out before her, a woman swept into the kitchens and stood beside Lady Grey, who took little notice of the newcomer. The younger woman was attractive, but there was a hardness about her features that made Allyson nervous. The new arrival cast a gimlet eye over Allyson as though she needed to determine if Allyson was competition. For what, Allyson didn't understand.

"Elizabeth, you're in time to welcome Sir John's newest toy before the evening meal begins."

The dark-haired, dark-eyed woman glared at Allyson, who deduced she must have been Sir John's mistress and the person who enjoyed receiving the pain he inflicted. Allyson smiled but did nothing more. She needed to assure the woman that she wasn't competition and held no interest in Sir John's twisted love play, but Allyson didn't dare speak with so many ears nearby. However, the audience didn't dissuade Elizabeth from stepping in front of Allyson and sneering.

"His new toys never last as long as his favorite," Elizabeth smirked, but Allyson still refused to respond. "Cat got your tongue? Or did my John cut it out already?"

Elizabeth's comments tempted Allyson to stick her tongue out just for the sake of taunting Elizabeth, but she wouldn't take the bait. Elizabeth Charlton was just as well-known as her lover, and Allyson didn't need to give either of them reason to practice their cruelty on her. The woman had grown up along the border much like Allyson, but where Allyson's father was a prosperous clan leader, Elizabeth's father was a notorious reiver. He'd raided her clan's lands many times and had received countless injuries for his efforts. There was a price on the man's head, but no one was interested in claiming it. Either their life would be forfeit, or they would prefer him dead.

"Elizabeth, take Lady Allyson into the Hall and assure Lord Grey and Sir John that we will serve the meal post-haste." Lady Grey didn't bother to look at either woman, turning her back to them. When they passed through the doorway and into the Great Hall, Allyson scanned the crowd, but no one appeared to pay them attention. She grasped Elizabeth's arm and dragged her into a nearby passageway. The woman spat and hissed like a trapped cat, but Allyson would have her say.

"Listen to me," Allyson snapped. "I am no more interested in Sir John than I am the pox. You can have him all to yourself. I'm not competition for his favors, so you're welcome to continue whatever it is you two get up to in that chamber."

"And if I desire to watch him tame you? What will you do then? Perhaps I want to observe as he plunders your body on that wrack, and mayhap I'll even join in the fun. Have you ever kissed a woman?"

"Do you think I have?" Allyson countered. She believed every word Elizabeth uttered, but she wouldn't allow the woman to witness her disgust. Elizabeth would feed on it.

"I don't think you've even kissed a man." She edged closer to Allyson, who shifted to keep from being cornered. "Has a man ever run his fingers along your quim, dipped them into you and made you gush?"

Allyson considered responding that she was betrothed, which was as good as married and would imply that she was more knowledgeable than was true, but she was just as unwilling to bring the Gordons into her troubles as she was the rest of her clan. Her betrothal might be moot given the mess she'd created. While she didn't want to marry Ewan, she would have appreciated his imposing stature as protection.

"I told you, I have no interest in coming between you and Sir John."

"But I may hold that interest. Would you whip me if Sir John insisted? If I insisted? Would you be the one to remove my gown and my chemise? Perhaps run your hands over me?"

In another time and another place, Allyson might have found Elizabeth's words wickedly seductive, but with her life in limbo, they only fueled the fire within Allyson to escape. She would return to her clan or court and never take for granted the safety both places afforded. She would even reconsider her opinion on marrying Ewan if it meant she left unmolested. Allyson noted Elizabeth hadn't suggested that she be on the receiving end of either Elizabeth's or Sir John's domination, and she counted that as a blessing.

Movement nearby cut their conversation short, and Allyson glided into the Great Hall as though she hadn't just experienced one of the more perverse moments of her life, and that said a great deal after four years living in a royal court where lovers changed as often as the Scottish weather.

Ewan couldn't see a thing. The rain started just as they reached the retaining wall, and it dumped in diagonal sheets of icy needles. The mud had already trailed rivulets down his neck and chest, his sodden hair plastered to his scalp and forehead. He exchanged a glance with Eoin before gesturing for his men to fall back. They would hide in the tall grass, laying on their bellies to wait out the storm. It was too dark for Ewan to determine how thick the cloud cover was. He prayed it was a mere spring shower and not a deluge. After an hour of waiting, Ewan once more gestured for them to retreat, this time to their camp.

"What happened? Why are you back so soon?" Kenneth demanded.

"If ye hadnae noticed, we've a spot of rain," Ewan grumbled, once more not bothering to smother his brogue. "We couldnae see a bluidy thing. Nae the hand in front of our faces nor the men on the battlements."

"You gave up? A little rain, and you gave up." Kenneth groused, and Ewan shouldered himself between Allyson's father and his brother. Eoin was as dirty and tired as Ewan, but his temper had frayed faster that night.

"We returned to regroup and devise another plan. The walls are too slick for any of us to climb, the mud will trap our footprints, and we're likely to freeze before we catch any sign of Allyson or what's happening." Ewan explained.

Laird Elliot remained irritated, but he didn't speak again, understanding that the young Highland warrior was correct. The men settled in for the night, Highlanders and Lowlanders alike using their plaids to shelter them against the elements. Ewan sighed, since it would be another long day of waiting until they could scout again the next night. He wished he knew how Allyson fared. He couldn't imagine the terror she must have been experiencing, alone and unprotected. A possessiveness Ewan didn't understand took root in his mind, and his natural protective nature, instilled in all Highland men from birth, demanded he storm the gates alone and pull her out if necessary.

The sun rose, and Ewan felt as though he'd only closed his eyes for five minutes. As the men moved about, Ewan looked toward the keep. He squinted, certain he'd glimpsed a bright color at the corner facing their hiding spot. He was much too far away to determine what it was, but he swore he caught green and yellow hues matching the ones Allyson had dropped to leave a trail. Ewan nudged Eoin and pointed before creeping forward on silent feet. He emerged from the trees and crouched low as he inched closer. When he reached the part of the meadow that he'd hidden in the night before, he lay on his belly and dragged himself closer. He got as close as he dared before raising his head to peek at the battlements, praying whatever he'd seen hadn't already disappeared.

His keen vision was rewarded with a view of Allyson standing alone on the wall walk. She faced the north as if she might see Scotland and her home. Her blonde hair lifted from her back and whipped around her face and shoulders. She abandoned her attempt to restrain it, choosing to tilt her face toward the sunlight. A man and a woman joined her, but Ewan didn't get the impression they were the lord and lady of the keep. He strained to see the man and noticed his gait was off, as though he limped. Ewan knew in an instant he was watching Sir John approach Allyson, even if he didn't know who the other woman was.

"Is that Sage?" Eoin whispered, and Ewan nodded his response. The brothers inched closer and watched as Allyson turned at the couple's approach. There was no way for Ewan to decipher what they discussed, but he could tell Allyson was cautious, but not cowering. She shook her head several times and leaned away when the woman reached for her hair. This made Sir John laugh while he, too, reached for Allyson's hair. He stood on the far side of Allyson, making it difficult to view all his movements, but Ewan tensed when Sir John grabbed a fistful of Allyson's hair and seemed to pin her in place while the woman appeared to nuzzle her neck. Ewan exchanged a glance with Eoin, both recognizing the body language from more than one liaison that involved multiple partners. Ewan snapped his gaze back to Allyson, who hadn't moved. She hadn't pushed either the man or the woman away, but her posture showed she didn't welcome the attention. However, she drew the line when Sir John leaned in to kiss her. Her palm contacted his chin at an angle as she shoved him away, making his head snap backwards. She tried to avoid the fist that flew toward her, but the other woman trapped Allyson in place. Ewan watched in horror as the knight's knuckles contacted Allyson's cheek. His other hand wrapped around Allyson's throat, and she appeared to grow, but Ewan understood Sir John lifted her off the ground. But just as suddenly, she fell against the wall when Sir John doubled over. Ewan was proud of Allyson for kneeing the bastard in the cods, but his fear for her life returned. Allyson didn't waste time and ran along the wall walk before disappearing.

"What do you make of that?" Eoin asked. "That was bizarre. I mean, you and I—well, two women—

it's not new to us, but Allyson doesn't seem like a woman likely to appreciate that. Not after how she reacted to your promise of infidelity."

"I didn't promise to be unfaithful," Ewan hissed.

"You didn't promise to be faithful either," Eoin tossed back.

"Never mind that for now. You're right though. It appeared as though they were attempting to seduce her rather than threaten her with violence. He tried to kiss her, lecherous bastard."

"Suddenly thinking yours should be the only kisses she receives?"

"Don't put words into my mouth, little brother," Ewan warned. Eoin was a little too close to hitting the mark, and Ewan wasn't in the mood to dissect his emotions. "We need to let the Elliot know his daughter is alive and mostly unharmed, from what we saw."

They remained until Sir John and Elizabeth left the wall walk. Ewan prayed that Allyson tucked herself away and was beyond their reach. They slipped back to the camp and explained what they saw to Allyson's father, who appeared ready to explode, but restrained his temper.

CHAPTER TWELVE

s Allyson's third day began, she remained in her chamber as long as she dared before slipping into the Great Hall. Despite the miserable visit to the dungeon, her exchange with Elizabeth when they met, and a disconcerting encounter on the wall walk with both Sir John and Elizabeth, they had left Allyson alone for the most part. She ate alone on the dais and slipped back to her chamber to gather her cloak. Lord Grey clarified that she could move about the keep freely, but if she attempted to step out to the bailey, she would find her new residence in the dungeon. She was on house arrest. The nobleman had said nothing about contacting her father or how much he would demand as a ransom. Allyson doubted he'd even attempt to contact her father. She sensed he would allow Sir John to have his fun with her until he became bored. Then Lord Grey might consider sending a missive, but the wealth visible in the keep proved they had no need for more coin.

Allyson made her way onto the wall walk as she had the previous day. She'd been searching the landscape the previous day and detected movement, but her unwelcome companions had interrupted her. She lifted her hand to her bruised cheek. She moved to the farthest corner from the guards on patrol and scanned the horizon and out to the woods near the loch that lay to the north. She swept her gaze over the meadow, certain she'd spied something the day before. Allyson squinted and shielded her eyes from the sun as she peered down, moving her head one way then another to view more. Her breath caught when she was sure she saw the grass sway as though something slithered among it, but whatever was there was far larger than a garter snake or asp. She braced her hands on the wall and leaned as far over the edge as she dared, going onto her toes.

Ewan was going to be ill. He was going to watch Allyson tip over the edge of the wall and plummet to her death. She was hanging over the wall, and he wondered if she still had her feet on the ground. He and Eoin returned to their hiding place from the day before, hoping Allyson would return to the battlements, but now he feared she would lose her balance and tumble from the battlements. His head jerked as he lifted it to get a better view, but he froze when she abruptly stood up, then waved. It wasn't a gregarious sweeping of her arm. She tucked her arm against her chest and wiggled her fingers. She'd spotted him, and the smile he caught reassured him that she recognized who lay in wait. Allyson paused, then held up one finger, as though she wanted him to wait a moment. She dashed back the way she came, and Ewan feared for a moment that she might try to make an escape.

"What's she doing?" Eoin muttered.

"I don't know, but I'll wait as long as it takes to find out."

The wait ended up longer than either expected,

but a half an hour later, Allyson reappeared. She held something in her hand, and Ewan watched her pull a loose stone from the wall. It appeared as though she tied whatever she held onto the rock with a ribbon. Allyson looked at Ewan as she dropped the rock over the side. She inched away from the wall; her reluctance obvious. She brushed her hair away from her face and looked once more toward the woods. She placed her hand over her heart as she continued to gaze at the trees. Ewan suspected she'd guessed her father waited there. Unlike the last two times she left the battlements, she walked without haste.

Allyson couldn't believe her eyes when she detected the movement, but her intuition told her it was Ewan. It surprised her to see how close to the keep he hid, but as she considered it, his presence didn't shock her as much as she'd expect. Knowing his massive frame and experienced sword arm were near comforted her. And wherever Ewan went, Eoin was sure to be at his side. She'd glimpsed the twin, but Ewan held her attention until she remembered her father. She deduced he would be with the twins, but he wouldn't be dressed for slithering through weeds. Allyson knew better than to underestimate her father. He'd been a successful border laird since he was barely out of boyhood. He wielded a sword with such force men half his age shied away from sparring with him. Atop a horse, there were few who matched the force and balance with which he fought. But he would have stuck out among the grass if he'd attempted to approach in his breeks and doublet. When Allyson focused, she noticed Ewan's plaid.

When her gaze met Ewan's, an idea sparked, and

she prayed she would find what she needed. She ran back to her chamber in search of a quill and ink, along with anything she might write on. She didn't expect to be lucky, since the chamber they had appointed her was less than sparse. Her belongings and a few drying linens were all that was in the chamber besides the bed. There was no other furniture, no looking glass, not even a grate for the fire. She'd slept in her gown and cloak the past two nights and still shivered beneath the meager covers. When her chamber proved a lost cause for finding writing tools, she slipped down the passageway and descended a flight of stairs to the family chambers. She knew at that time of day, Lord Grey would be in the lists with his men, and Lady Grey would be overseeing the kitchens or making her rounds to the various workers in the bailey. Allyson kept her back against the wall as she inched toward Lady Grey's chamber. She'd seen the woman retire to it the previous evening, and she counted on there being parchment and ink.

When she reached the woman's door, she pressed her ear against it and held her breath. When no sound traveled to her, she pressed down on the door handle and pushed it open a crack. No one and nothing stirred, so she leaned forward to peek through the crevice between the hinges. Confident the chamber was empty, she dashed inside before pushing the door closed but not shut. She had no time to waste, fearing discovery and Ewan's departure. She dashed across the floor until she reached a dressing table that held ink, quills, and parchment. More quills laid in the drawer she opened. She took one and dipped it into the ink, leaving the quills already on the table in their place. She wouldn't risk Lady Grey discovering someone had tampered with her desk in case the woman kept count of the ones on the desktop. Allyson suspected she was the type to do that. She scrawled a note and carried the wet parchment and quill with her to her chamber. Once inside her room, she tore her note apart from the blank portion of the parchment then hid that and the quill under the mattress. She blew on the damp ink until she was certain it had dried, then she dug through her satchel. She'd discovered an old ribbon at the bottom when she'd unpacked the morning she arrived. Allyson pulled her *sgian dubh* free and severed a piece before cutting it down the center. She had no idea how many opportunities she would have to convey a message to Ewan. She didn't dare waste the few supplies she had. Allyson darted up the stairs until she emerged on the wall walk. Before tying the note to the rock, she scanned its contents.

Safe for now. Untouched but tormented. Scottish women captive forced to serve. More brothel than noble home. Full garrison. Sage will torture if you're captured. E, I fear for you. Take care. A.

It was concise but conveyed what she sensed were the most urgent pieces of information. She turned her head enough to use her peripheral vision to ensure none of the guards watched her before she dropped the stone over the side. She looked at Ewan and then to the trees once more, regretful that she hadn't seen her father, but she spun on her heels and returned to the warmth of the keep's interior.

———

Ewan stifled a grumble as he abandoned his hiding place to return to camp. He couldn't approach the castle wall while it was daylight. He would have to wait to claim Allyson's message once no one could detect his presence. It was another day of waiting, but at least he'd seen Allyson and was reassured that she was in one piece.

"She looked for you, or rather toward you. I think the lass knows you're here, but she didn't seem alarmed that you weren't with us," Ewan explained to Kenneth.

"She realizes I can't approach in breeks and a doublet. If you knew to cover your face to hide the glow of your skin, then she knew my clothes would serve as a beacon. She understands your plaids help you blend in, making it possible for you to hide among the foliage. She must trust you, lad, if she risked searching for something to use for a missive."

"Aye." Ewan wasn't sure what else to say. He didn't feel like he'd done anything to gain her trust back, but she appeared so relieved when she recognized him. He assumed she was happy to see anyone who might rescue her, so he didn't consider it personal. But the last look she cast him made him wonder if she was glad he came. She hadn't looked for Eoin and barely glanced at him once she noticed he lay beside Ewan. He refused to read more into it, but his heart hammered.

"Do you believe you'll be able to retrieve it without detection?" Kenneth continued.

"I'll do what I have to, to ensure I get that missive. She risked much to get it to us."

Kenneth nodded before glancing once more at the castle, then turned away. Ewan hunted with his brother, but there wasn't enough to occupy his mind until night fell once more.

CHAPTER THIRTEEN

Just as they had done the first night they attempted to scout the castle, Ewan, Eoin, and their men slathered mud on their faces and necks. They stalked through the high grass, keeping low but not needing to slither. Ewan watched as the guards changed shifts and marked the time by the position of the moon. They waited while the new rotation of guards made their rounds of the entire battlements before settling into their stations. Ewan and Eoin divided the men and went their separate ways with Ewan creeping to the spot where Allyson dropped the rock. He pressed his back against the wall, using the structure's shadow to offer him even more concealment. He searched the ground and soon found the parchment and ribbon. He pulled them free from the stone and dropped them in his sporran before signaling for his men to follow him.

Remaining in the shadows, the men surveyed the defenses and searched for any weaknesses in the structure. Ewan didn't expect to find any, but they would investigate. From what Ewan ascertained, the only weak point in the keep's defenses was the wall built out of the loch's shoreline. The fewer guardsmen posted to that area indicated they didn't expect an attack to come from that direction. Ewan made do with the weak light of the moon and the torches overhead to feel along the wall, finding places where the centuries old mortar crumbled when he pried his fingers into it. It would take great effort and strength, but he and his men could scale the wall, making finger holds as they climbed. They had no grappling hooks to launch over the walls or rope to assist their ascent. He hoped the Elliot men were as capable as they appeared. He'd grown to respect them as their time together dragged on. They were competent warriors and dedicated to their clan. They followed their laird's directives with no hesitation and worked together as a team used to spending long days on horseback. Ewan never found fault with any of them, and they all chomped at the bit to ensure Allyson made it out safe and sound.

Once Ewan and his warriors finished scouting their section of the keep, they eased back into the meadow as Eoin's team joined them. When Ewan was confident the guards hadn't caught sight of them, he rose to his full height and sprinted back to their camp. They'd kept their cook fire small, but it burned bright enough for him to read Allyson's bold script with ease. He noted her penmanship looked more like a man's, precise and practical, as opposed to the flourishing marks most women included. He read the missive before passing it to Kenneth, who glanced back in the castle's direction before rereading it.

"What do you propose based upon what you saw?" Kenneth posed the question equally between the twins and studied their expressions as they considered their answers.

"Allyson was right aboot the garrison. From what I witnessed, there are close to a hundred men who will take up arms to defend the keep and the Greys.

We know Sage is in there, too. That butcher kills as many as fifty people a day." Ewan swept his gaze toward the castle.

"That just tells us there's a dungeon filled with people who would like to see him dead," a Gordon warrior interjected.

"Aye, Scots mostly, I presume," Eoin responded. "They've reinforced the gates to withstand a battering ram, not that we have one. And they have winches to tip oil during an attack, but they don't seem prepared for a few lone warriors to slip over their walls. The guards spend too much time milling aboot and not enough time patrolling. At least that's the case with the ones near the gatehouse. They're overly confident."

"I agree," Ewan nodded. "The guards ignore the wall that butts up against the loch. It's a closed body of water, so they assume no one will sail up to their back door. There's no patrol along there after the initial sweep when the shifts changed. We saw it's the same during the day. That's how Allyson stayed there for so long today. No one's watching." Ewan curved his fingers into claws as he gestured. "The mortar is falling apart, so you can make finger holds if you dig a bit. Climbing would be hard going with little purchase for your feet, but not impossible. Grappling hooks would help, but we have none, and I doubt any of the crofters have ones to share."

"My mon should return in the morning with another report from the village. He found a wench who took pity on a weary traveler. He should have plenty to tell us after spending two days in a tavern. I'm sending a rider back to Redheugh in the morning. I'll call for more of my warriors to join us. It's only a few hours ride each way, so they will be here before nightfall tomorrow."

"We'll wait for his report, your men, and to see if

Allyson can communicate with us again, then we'll make our move." Ewan stated.

"I hate knowing she's spending another night in Sodom and Gomorrah." Kenneth had taken to swiping his hand over his tired face more and more often as the days stretched out.

Ewan noted the concern and frustration the man experienced at his inability to charge in and rescue his daughter, but he wondered which drove Laird Elliot: the fact he was duty bound to rescue his daughter or genuine concern for Allyson. Ewan sensed it was the former because the man knew it was expected, but he rarely spoke of anything about Allyson that showed a bond. The expression on Allyson's face as she looked toward the trees and where she suspected her father waited didn't match the detachment Kenneth Elliot appeared to have for his youngest. Ewan didn't understand it, but the feeling grew stronger the longer they searched for Allyson. It was like the laird and his daughter were little more than strangers. He'd replayed Cairren's words from when she informed them of Allyson's disappearance. She said Allyson had received little attention until she arrived at court. Ewan now suspected Cairren hadn't exaggerated, and Allyson was often overlooked. He knew she was the youngest of six, but he couldn't imagine ignoring any of his children, regardless of how many he had. Yet, as the notion crossed his mind, he remembered that not long ago he felt no qualms about breeding a couple of sons with whoever he married and continuing on with his life as though marriage changed little. If he'd been so ready to leave a wife behind at his clan's keep, that would mean he'd been prepared to leave his children behind, too. Watching Kenneth was making Ewan reconsider his view on parenting and having a family.

Allyson rolled onto her side in her freezing chamber and wondered what the Gordon twins and her father were doing camped in the woods. It shocked her to find Ewan and Eoin hiding so near the keep, but she realized in an instant that they were scouting how to breach the castle's defenses. From what she could tell, and from what she put in her note, the castle appeared impregnable, which only made her confidence waiver. While Sir John hadn't forced her to visit the dungeon again, the incident on the wall walk with Elizabeth and him disconcerted her. She perceived the couple would attempt to seduce her into joining their twisted love play, and when she continued to refuse, she sensed they would take the choice away from her. It had become a question of when, not if, they would strike. Her time spent in the Great Hall taught her no one would defend her if Sir John flung her over his shoulder and dumped her on a table before having his way with her right there in front of everyone. There was nothing anyone would do if Sir John caught her behind a closed door or forced her into the dungeon. Allyson resolved to only venture out of her chamber when they were serving a meal or she was certain Sir John was in the lists. The man still trained daily, and it consumed most of the morning. For as long as she could, she would drop daily reports for Ewan. She prayed it wouldn't take more than another two or three days to get her out. Allyson doubted her freedom from being molested would last much longer than that.

She shifted again and gazed at the stars that shone through the window embrasure. She'd investigated a few more chambers that day and discovered only the lord's and lady's chambers had glass in the windows. The rest had thin hides hung to protect against the elements. The one in Allyson's room was so thin that it was pointless to use it. If she was going to lay shivering, she might as well have something to look at. She missed her chamber at Redheugh, her family's home. She couldn't see the North Sea from the battlements here at Chillingham, but she often inhaled wafts of sea air. But at her family's keep, she climbed the battlements and had a view of the rolling valley between her home and the Hermitage. A river flowed to the north of the pele tower, and Allyson had spent hours there as a child. As she continued to gaze at the stars, she wondered if anyone at Redheugh was looking upon the same stars. An unexpected question floated through her mind: would she ever discover if the stars were brighter in the real Highlands, where Ewan lived?

I'm only thinking aboot the toad because aught is better than being a captive here. Even marriage to him. If I wasn't so desperate to escape here, I'd still want to escape him. Allyson's mind paused as she rolled onto her back and stared at the ceiling. *I shouldn't be so ungrateful. We aren't truly betrothed yet, not without the contracts being signed or the ceremony, so he wasn't obligated to come with Father. Eoin definitely wasn't. They both chose to chase after me and dragged their men along, too. If I'm honest with myself, which I don't want to be, it'll be Ewan and Eoin who devise a way to free me. Father is a powerful warrior, but there is something aboot the Highlanders that makes them unstoppable, unbeatable. I suppose that's what I need right now. Warriors who will plow through aught to win what they want.*

Allyson drifted to sleep, picturing Ewan as she'd seen him that morning. She remembered how braw and handsome he'd looked when his head poked through the grass. She considered the strength and muscle she'd felt each time they'd danced over the years, and she admitted it had seemed exciting and reassuring all at the same time. He was more than just attractive, and she'd wondered several times while dancing what it would feel like to kiss him with his powerful body pressed against hers. As she lay alone in bed, she wondered if she'd have been so averse to the arrangement if they'd never met in that blasted passageway.

Morning arrived far too soon for Allyson as she trudged up the steps to the dais and slipped into her seat. As had become her routine, she kept her head lowered at all meals but observed everything and everyone she saw. That morning, she counted the number of men she was certain were knights, then counted how many were regular warriors. When she finished, she moved toward the stairs to retreat to her chamber again, but Sir John intercepted her.

"My dear, I've been remiss in my hospitality." His words might have sounded suave, but his tone threatened. Sir John linked Allyson's arm through his and pulled her in the direction of the dungeon steps. She'd noticed Elizabeth leave the table but hadn't paid attention to where the woman went. Allyson wasn't interested in anything Sir John might do to her, and she wasn't interested in raising Elizabeth's ire because the retired knight's attention returned to her. But he gave her no choice but to precede the man down the stairs. She wanted to gag at the stench, which seemed worse than the first time he'd forced her to visit the underworld. There was more noise, too. As Allyson continued down the corridor, she noticed the cells were full this time. Each one appeared to have at least three occupants. She tallied the number of doors and estimated there were at least four dozen people locked away when there had only been a handful a couple days prior.

"More border villagers who forget they live in England rather than that shite hole they call home." Sir John spat as he described Scotland. Allyson bristled and wanted to defend her homeland, but she recognized Sir John was back to his games. He only said it to bait her, so she pressed her lips together in a thin line to keep from speaking. "Fear not, the next time you're here, it should be quieter."

Allyson flinched, understanding Sir John meant the cells would be empty because their current occupants would be dead. She kept her eyes straight ahead until they reached the door to his torture chamber. She angled her body closer to the wall, so he couldn't trap her once again. She'd nearly hurled when he'd run his hand over her breast and toward her mons, and she wouldn't allow him to catch her unprepared again. Or so she assumed until the door swung open. There were lit torches in all the wall sconces and manacled to one wall was a naked Elizabeth Charlton.

CHAPTER FOURTEEN

Allyson faltered and didn't know where to look as Elizabeth licked her lips and arched her back, forcing her breasts forward.

"I asked you the last time you were here if you'd ever wondered what it would be like to watch a woman's breasts sway as her body accepted a lashing." Sir John stood behind Allyson once more and cupped her shoulders as he pressed his lengthening rod against her backside. Morbid curiosity tempted Allyson to gaze at the other woman's body. She'd seen her sisters and roommates undressed, but she'd never paid attention. She glanced at the woman and failed to see anything appealing, but as Elizabeth twisted, Allyson could see deep scars and welts along her ribs. It disturbed Allyson to imagine what type of events led to these marks, but as Sir John removed a whip from the rack, then ran the handle down the front of Elizabeth, she understood. Without warning, Sir John spun Elizabeth around, and the whip cracked through the air. The sound it elicited from Elizabeth was a mixture of pain and pleasure and made Allyson jump. She shied away when Sir John offered her the whip but forced a casual expression of disinterest. The last time she'd been to the chamber, she'd insinuated such a pastime intrigued her. She couldn't go weak in the knees now. Not if she hoped to leave without becoming Sir John's next victim.

"I shall be an observer as you suggested," she demurred.

With Elizabeth's and Sir John's backs to her, she stared at the floor as the whipping continued. The sound of the lash whizzing through the air nine more times filled her ears before there was a rustling and the sound of the manacles being released. She glanced up as Sir John carried his mistress to the rack in the center of the room, and for a moment, Allyson feared he would rip the woman apart. Instead, Sir John unlaced his breeches and climbed on top of the table and Elizabeth. Allyson inched back to the door and pulled on the handle, praying Sir John hadn't locked it. She'd never been more grateful for small mercies than when she fled the terror chamber.

Allyson ran until she reached her chamber where she dropped the bar across the door. She trembled as understanding washed over her. She'd been in too much shock earlier to process all that she'd seen or attempted not to see. Allyson had never seen a man and woman couple, but she understood the fundamentals. She'd also heard of those men and women who liked their joinings rough with spankings and restraints, but she'd never imagined anyone would want to inflict or receive such agony as foreplay. She'd never seen a man's rod before either, and she wished her first glimpse had been of the man she married. Her mind leaped to Ewan and the question of what his rod would look like skidded across her mind. She attempted to push it aside, but the curiosity of whether it would be proportionate to the rest of him took hold.

Allyson shook her head and crossed the room to

where she'd hidden the quill and parchment. She assumed their games would occupy the lovers at least long enough for her to drop another note for Ewan. She scrawled a brief update of what she'd learned at the evening meal and prayed the information would improve her chances of rescue.

Sage is depraved beyond reason. Whips mistress and she enjoys it. I saw too much and am sickened by it but remain untouched. Her father's a reiver nearby. Mayhap the one who brought me here. Lord Grey's riding out in the morn to meet the Earl of Northumberland and will be away for a fortnight. Taking Lady Grey, too. Thirty knights and sixty warriors here now. Taking three score with him. Fears ambush on the road and is serving part of his forty days as vassal. Leaving me to Sage. E, trust none here. A.

Allyson dared a longer note with more detail this time. If they discovered her missive, she was as good as dead anyway. She figured in for a penny, in for a pound. She would do whatever she could to keep her rescuers safe while they endeavored to free her. Allyson moved to the window and looked at the men in the lists. She'd assumed Sir John would go there that morning, but he'd had very different plans. While Lady Grey had intimidated her when she arrived, the woman had turned into an ally of sorts. She hadn't lied when she said she could arrange for people to treat Allyson as an honored guest or as little more than a whore. So far, she'd been an untouchable guest, at least to all the men but Sir John. The warriors and servants left her alone, and she wondered if she could sneak more freedom once the noble couple left and Sir John had the responsibility of the entire keep and Elizabeth as a distraction. The sun was overhead, and the sky was cloudless. While it was beautiful, it provided no protection or cover for Ewan if he attempted to approach the retaining wall again. She clasped her hands, careful not to crush the parchment, and bowed her head.

Heavenly Father, I realize I am to blame for all that has befallen me, my father, Ewan, and the men who accompany them. I've endangered more than my life and done far more than inconvenienced those men. They have families with whom they should share proper meals and beds in which they should sleep. I doubt I can ever make up for what I've caused, but I am remorseful for what I've done. I pray for Your forgiveness and believe I shall receive it as my heart is truly repentant, but I don't expect to receive anyone else's. I'm not sure that I deserve it. Lord God, I am but at your mercy. Amen.

Allyson sat in the window embrasure as she stared once more at the sky. A sense of calm washed over her, and a weight lifted from her shoulders. She'd always believed as a child that the peace she experienced after prayer was the Holy Spirit delivering God's forgiveness or guidance. She looked at the missive in her hand and tore a corner from it, then dipped the quill in ink she'd stolen from the steward's solar the previous afternoon.

E, I can't deny this is my fault. Fear drove me to run and now fear drives me to escape not for my sake but to get you, your brother, and your men, and my father and his men as far from here as possible. It all seems so pointless now. Our conversation, my rejection, my cowardice.

The words I'm sorry seem so inconsequential now, but the apology I wish to give you when next I speak to you will come from the depths of my heart and my conscience. I'm so sorry, A.

When the ink dried on both notes, she cut a strip of ribbon from what was left and hid everything in the pocket of her kirtle. She waited for the storm she saw coming before she donned her cloak and headed for the battlements.

Ewan paced as close to the tree line as he dared. His glance shifted to the castle each time he turned. The Elliot spy returned at daybreak with distressing news. The man's words replayed in Ewan's mind.

Sage brought in new prisoners and the dungeon now holds four score captives. The mon brought them for the sheer entertainment and satisfaction of killing them, not because of any true crimes. His mistress is as depraved as the bastard. People speak in the village of how they enjoy torturing one another, how it arouses them. The tavern wench said they make people watch and sometimes force them to join in. Never heard of such twisted shite, but it's no secret.

Ewan was apt to agree. He'd had his fair share of partners and explored various forms of pleasure, but never had he considered beating a lover. He gazed at the castle as he stopped his pacing. He wondered what they'd forced Allyson to endure. His stomach turned over as he imagined Allyson being the victim of such perversion. While the predilection wasn't unheard of, nor had he passed judgement on it in the past, the urge to protect Allyson pulsed within him. He was certain she would never be a willing participant, and that was what infuriated him when he considered her being subjected to such sights.

"Weather's rolling in," Eoin pointed to a distant thick cloud cover. It was what Ewan needed to ensure his safety when he approached the castle.

"I'm going alone," Ewan announced.

"Like bluidy hell you are. I'm coming at least."

"Nay. I'm scouting. I'll go once I see Allyson on the wall walk, and it'll only be to retrieve a missive if she drops one."

"And if she doesn't drop aught? Will you leave her to wonder if we're still here?"

"Of course not. The missive is the only reason to get that close to the keep. Otherwise, I'll remain hidden until I can signal to her, then I'll retreat."

"We will retreat. You aren't going alone."

"I am. If aught happens to me, someone must be our father's heir."

"I'll land my fist in your face if you say such rubbish again. Where one of us goes, so does the other."

Ewan recognized he was fighting a losing battle, and while he'd do anything to protect his brother, his dissent was half-hearted. He'd feel better with another set of eyes and ears guarding his back when he approached. He didn't intend to wait for nightfall again now that he'd learned more about Sage and his mistress. The additional Elliot warriors would be there by then, and he wanted a plan in place to strike that night.

Ewan and Eoin waited another hour before the heavens opened, and the sky was dark enough to offer them cover.

"Do you think she'll come out in such weather?" Ewan asked Kenneth.

"Aye. She'll understand this is the best time to contact you. The guardsmen will huddle together and not expect anyone to go for a stroll. She's hunted enough times to remember the cloud cover will disguise your approach. My lass will be there."

It surprised Ewan to hear how familiar with his daughter Kenneth sounded, but then he reasoned that anyone who lived in a keep would have seen guards taking shelter while on duty in the rain, and if she hunted, she'd be aware the weather would provide cover and also weaken her scent to her prey. He and Eoin trekked through the meadow until they reached the spot where they'd lain in wait the day before. The rain beat down on his head and back, but he barely noticed as he prayed Allyson would appear. They waited half an hour, but their patience was rewarded when a small hooded figure appeared at the edge of the wall. Allyson shifted as she pried a rock free from the wall, then shielded her eyes to search the land beyond the keep.

"Stay here," Ewan hissed to Eoin. "If the parchment falls in a puddle or remains out here, the water will destroy it." Ewan leaped to his feet and rushed toward the wall, weaving through the meadow and keeping low to the ground. He approached the wall and waited for the alarm to sound. When nothing stirred, he crept along it until he stood beneath Allyson and looked up at her. She waved and leaned forward, mouthing "be careful." Ewan nodded before mouthing the same in response. Allyson placed the notes against the rock and tied them together. She peered back at Ewan before pointing to the missives and holding up two fingers. She pointed to the rock again, but this time held up one finger and pointed to him before tapping the rock and sweeping her finger to encompass the trees and the field. Ewan nodded once more, and she dropped the rock into his hands. She watched him dash back to where she assumed Eoin waited, then she watched them return to the trees.

CHAPTER FIFTEEN

Ewan separated the missives before he stepped near the fire. Whatever Allyson had written, she'd made it clear one was only for him. He'd save it until he was alone. Once Kenneth and Eoin joined him as they all warmed themselves, he read aloud the missive Allyson intended for all of them. His fears had, in part, been justified. He wanted to rampage through the keep, tearing asunder anything and anyone he encountered until he wrapped his hands around Sage's neck and snapped it. Kenneth swore several oaths before going to stand on his own. They hadn't spoken of the betrothal since leaving Glasgow, and Ewan wondered if Kenneth feared Allyson would no longer be marriable. A sennight earlier, he would have welcomed that news, but now he wasn't so sure. Her time at Chillingham surely traumatized her, and he supposed that would be far greater punishment than anything her father meted out. Spending her life alone as a spinster seemed extreme, but her father's fears would be warranted if word got back to court. No man would want to marry her. Except for him. Ewan lost his aversion to marriage somewhere between Glasgow and discovering who held Allyson. He'd marry her and offer her his protection, but he still intended to carry on with his life. He'd reflected upon how different Allyson was from his mother, but he didn't consider himself that different from his father. He'd never keep his leman in their home, and he wouldn't flaunt his relationships at court, but he still didn't find any reason to alter course despite taking a wife.

Eoin joined some men who left to hunt, and Kenneth retreated to a solitary spot under a fir tree. Ewan used the moment of quiet to read the missive Allyson intended for him. Its contents surprised him. There was sincerity in Allyson's words, and he heard her voice as he read it. But there was also a touch of defeat, as though she held little hope that she would escape alive. That she feared for him and the others and expressed her guilt rather than plead for rescue spoke to him. Several days ago, he was convinced she was a coward and spoiled to run away because she didn't get what she wanted. But the time alone on the road, then what she must be facing in the keep, made him realize she was far from a coward. She was dangerously naïve, but she wasn't a coward. The rain made it almost impossible to see, but when he stepped to the tree line, he believed he saw her still standing on the battlements. Alone.

<hr>

It was approaching nightfall when the Elliot warriors arrived. A swollen river and bogs that threatened to suck down man and beast slowed their progress. Learning that Lord and Lady Grey were departing the next morning also forced Ewan to delay his plans, but he recognized that it would even the odds if they breached the walls either under the portcullis or through the postern gate.

The men huddled around three cook fires, having built more now that their numbers swelled. Ewan chewed on the rabbit leg but tasted little. He once more longed for a hot meal and an ale. The notion of a willing woman made his cock twitch, but the appeal wasn't there as he gave it more consideration. It wasn't exhaustion that failed to raise his sail. He wasn't sure what it was, but as tired as he should have been, nervous energy thrummed through him. It wasn't like what he felt on the eve of battle. The anticipation of freeing Allyson the next day then being underway made him fidget. He'd long ago consumed the whisky packed with his bedroll, so he had little to do as a distraction. When nature called, he stepped away from the camp and away from the light. The darkness allowed him to notice a small light that shone at the keep. It was lower than the torches on the battlements, and it appeared to flash. It shone bright then darkened, then brightened again with a steady pattern. Ewan was certain it was a beacon.

Ewan crept out of the woods and inched along the tree line until he viewed the castle with nothing obstructing his view. The light appeared to come from a chamber window, and Ewan's intuition screamed that it was Allyson trying to signal him. He pushed through the tall grass until he glimpsed a figure in the window casement. It looked like Allyson, but he couldn't see the woman's face until she held the lantern higher. Ewan recognized Allyson, and he recognized the panic on her face. He sprinted the rest of the way until he stood beneath the opening in the wall.

"Ewan?" Allyson's voice floated down to him.

"Aye, Allyson. Tis me."

"Catch." Ewan raised his hand in time to grasp a potato with a piece of linen wrapped around it. "Hurry. They'll find me soon."

Allyson lifted the light once more as if to help as he stepped away from the wall. He considered telling her to jump, but the height was still too great. If he failed to catch her, the fall might injure or knock both of them unconscious. He nodded and spun on his heel and sprinted all the way back to the camp.

"Allyson dropped another missive," Ewan announced as he came to a halt by Eoin.

"What? How?" Kenneth demanded.

"I spotted a beacon and sensed it was Allyson. She stood in a window with a torch and dropped this down to me." Ewan held up the potato before unwrapping it, then dropped the linen and potato but kept the parchment. He unfolded it and scanned its contents before looking up aghast. He looked at the others before reading aloud.

Elizabeth is dead. Sage strangled her on his wrack while coupling. Accident, he claims. Lord Grey furious. Locked Sage in chamber with body. Lord and Lady depart soon. Word spread to the village. Servants fear Elizabeth's father arrives by morn. Greys avoiding Charlton. Discovered Charlton nabbed me. Fear he'll kill me when he comes for revenge. A.

Ewan looked at the faces that shared his shock. He shook his head as he read the missive for a third time. The sound of horses galloping toward them made all the men scramble to hide among the trees, those closest to the fires kicking dirt to extinguish them. A large contingent of riders approached with Lord Thomas Grey's standard at the front of the line. Ewan watched as the knight and his lady raced away from their home and the impending retribution. None of the Scots moved until the last English rider was out of sight.

"They're tucking tail and running," Laird Elliot spat. "What type of mon besides Sage inspires such terror that a vaunted knight would run away from home? In the dead of night, at that."

Ewan couldn't believe Kenneth's genuine confusion. He bit his tongue to keep from shouting. *The type of mon who knows another is coming to avenge his daughter. A father who won't stop short of tearing everyone limb from limb for taking his lass from him.* Ewan opted for a different line of comments.

"Do we try to intercept this reiver and partner with him to storm the keep, or do we leave him to break into the keep and we follow once the gates are open?"

"You'd have us make a deal with the mon who put my daughter in danger? I'll gut Charlton before I do that." Kenneth fumed.

"You can do that after we get Allyson out alive. One way or another, the mon who took her into that cesspit will be the one who helps us get her out." Ewan narrowed his eyes as he placed his hands on his hips. He shifted his weight forward, knowing he made his threat clear without speaking aloud. He wouldn't allow Kenneth to get in the way of retrieving Allyson.

"They will raise the portcullis for him," Eoin spoke in calm tones, the voice of reason between two hotheads. "We don't need Charlton to know we're here, but we do follow him through when they open the gate. They'll allow him entry because they know him from previous visits or because they fear him just as Allyson does."

Ewan nodded, conceding his brother was correct. He dropped his hands from his hips and pulled his plaid over his head before settling against a tree trunk to wait out the night.

Allyson dashed back to her chamber once she'd extinguished her torch in the empty fireplace of the chamber she'd slipped into. She dropped the bar across her door and stoked the fire. She'd taken firewood from Lady Grey's chamber when the woman went belowstairs to ready for her journey. Allyson had already squirreled away extra peat earlier that day. She didn't know how long she'd have to remain barricaded in her chamber once Elizabeth's father arrived. She would also use a lit torch as a weapon if the reivers attacked her. She climbed into bed to catch as much sleep as possible since she suspected the next day would be very long.

———————

The sound of screams woke Allyson as the sun rose. Weak light floated through her window, but it was enough to see across the chamber. She ran to peer out at the chaos erupting in the bailey. It was easy to recognize the man who'd captured her as Charlton's stout pony screamed and reared before the reiver slashed his sword across a guardsman's belly. He attacked with indiscriminate rage as he called for Sir John to present himself. Allyson watched as a band of cutthroat cattle thieves flowed into the bailey following their leader. Allyson hadn't been able to see the man the night she arrived, but she recognized Charlton from stories she'd heard while she still lived near the border. King Edward sanctioned the man's thievery because the reiver's band of outlaws fought for the English monarch and were instrumental in beating back the Scots when they attempted to reclaim land that had once been part of their country. It wasn't long before her abductor dismounted and fought his way to the keep steps with several of his men in tow. Allyson refused to be unprepared for this attack.

CHAPTER SIXTEEN

Ewan leaped from his horse as the Gordons and Elliots charged in after the reivers. Ewan wasn't interested in avenging Allyson until he was certain she was away from the battle. He left the fighting to his brother and her father once he saw men rushing into the keep. He took the steps two at a time until he barreled through the doorway. Fighting continued in the Great Hall, and he sliced his sword through anyone who impeded his progress. He stormed up the stairs until he reached the landing, then began pushing open one door after another. He swept all the chambers, realizing he was on the floor where the lord and lady's family slept, but he wouldn't take the chance of missing Allyson. Ewan charged up the stairs to the next floor and repeated the process until he came to a locked door.

"Allyson, step back," he bellowed before running, then ramming his shoulder into the door. The wood splintered as it gave way. Ewan kicked the door open and searched for Allyson.

Allyson heard the booted feet running toward her door, so she'd pulled each of her dirks from the sheaths on her thighs. She had a torch blazing in a sconce near the fireplace, so she positioned herself within reach of it. A garbled voice came through the door before it burst open, and Ewan appeared on the other side. They stared at each for a moment before Allyson dropped her knives and ran into his open arms.

"I'm sorry. So, so sorry," she murmured against his broad chest as his arms wrapped around her. She went lax as the fight and fear drained from her, and she felt safe for the first time in days.

"I know, lass. You can make it up to me by coming with me, so we can be away from this hellhole and get you somewhere safe."

Allyson nodded as she leaned back to look at her handsome savior. She wasn't sure what possessed her; perhaps it was a relief after the constant uncertainty, but she gave in to the urge to kiss Ewan. She grasped handfuls of his leine and pulled him down to where she could wrap her arms around his neck and press her lips against his. His surprise was short-lived, then he returned her need with a need of his own. Forgotten were the hostile words exchanged and the shared resentment. There was only a consuming fire between them. Ewan swept his tongue across the seam of her lips, pressing the tip between hers when she didn't understand. She parted them enough for Ewan to invade, surging into the warm, silky cavern just as his cock wanted to do with her sheath. A voice in the back of his mind niggled that this was the least appropriate time to grow aroused, but Allyson felt and tasted better than any other woman he ever had. A few passes of his tongue across hers, and Allyson caught on, dueling her tongue with his. She thrust hers into his mouth and moaned at the decadent feeling, but noise down the passageway startled them apart.

"Go." Ewan pointed to the far side of the chamber which would put the bed between Allyson and the door. She scooped up her knives and ran to hide. She peeked around the corner and watched as two men stormed into the chamber. Ewan swung his sword from side to side in wide arcs as they attempted to trap him between them. Ewan thrust his sword into one man's ribs before withdrawing it and swiping it across the outside of the other man's thigh. Both men dropped to the ground, and while Ewan ran the second man through, Allyson crawled to the first man's side and slid her blade across his throat. Ewan spun around as the dying man sputtered. His eyes widened as he took in the sight of Allyson kneeling beside the now-dead man, his blood splattered on her kirtle and dripping from her dirk. She shrugged before rising to her feet.

"I've hunted stag before," was all Allyson offered as an explanation. Ewan nodded and reached out his hand to her. Allyson grabbed her packed satchel and placed her palm against Ewan's. Both stared as a charge passed between them, a current that pulsed as strongly as their desire had only moments earlier. They left the chamber, then the keep, in silence. Ewan steered them away from the fighting in the Great Hall, taking Allyson out through the kitchens. They dashed across the bailey to where the Gordons and Elliots gathered. Laird Elliot engulfed his daughter in a tight embrace before cupping her cheeks and dropping a kiss on her forehead. They stepped apart, but Allyson bristled when a voice carried across the bailey. She spun around and caught sight of the man who'd brought her to Chillingham. The Scots watched as the leader of the reivers dragged Sir John Sage by the hair through the bailey until Charlton shoved the man to his knees.

"Much as I would like to gut you, you worthless pile of dung, King Edward won't allow it. Not yet. I will turn you over to him for him to decide your fate.

I wouldn't make plans for a long life if I were you, Sage. You will die by my hand for what you did to my daughter." Charlton bashed Sir John's temple with the hilt of his sword.

Allyson glared at the man throughout his pronouncement, and as though he sensed her, he swung his gaze in her direction. Ewan pushed her behind him, and the men encircled her, swords raised, prepared to defend her.

"Lord Elliot, you come out the victor this day. You have your daughter while I don't have mine. I'd hoped your beautiful daughter would turn Sage's head from my Elizabeth, but alas, they were a matched pair." Charlton plowed his booted foot into the unconscious Sage's ribs. "Don't expect me to be so generous the next time we meet. If I didn't have a daughter to bury and this shite to shovel, I would challenge you here and now."

"Charlton, you've always had brass bollocks. You assume much to believe you'd survive a fight with my men and these Highlanders. You've run away from our fights too many times to count. Come to my land again, and your soul will join your daughter's. Wherever that might be." Kenneth glared at his adversary. They'd postured this way many times over the years, but both men were experienced warriors who refused to back down, so both survived the countless skirmishes inherent to life along the border.

Ewan wasn't interested in the borderers' banter. His sole interest was getting Allyson onto his horse and away from Chillingham. He took the reins from one of his men and helped Allyson onto his horse. She tried to shift to the animal's back, behind the saddle, but Ewan shook his head. He wasn't satisfied with Allyson riding pillory. He wasn't certain if he feared she might topple off the back without his arms to hold her in place or if he wanted to feel her in his arms, her body nestled against his. Ewan reasoned that it was the former, but his heart knew that it was the latter. He mounted behind her, adjusting her to offer her as much comfort as possible on a saddle not intended for two riders. Ewan nodded to his brother and their men before spurring his horse toward the portcullis and freedom.

Allyson roused when Ewan tapped her shoulder. She rubbed her eyes, unaware she'd drifted off.

"You're almost home, lass," Ewan whispered. Allyson shifted, and Ewan groaned. She looked over her shoulder, but he shook his head. He'd been in a permanent state of semi-arousal for the entire two-hour ride to Redheugh. Allyson drifted off soon after they set off, but Ewan had endured the feel of her hip rubbing against his groin with each step his steed took. He watched her face, and her expression didn't look like one of excitement or relief. "You don't look happy to return to your clan."

Allyson nodded. She was silent for a long moment before glancing at the keep in the distance, then looking into Ewan's green eyes. She noticed they were the shade of grass after a summer rainstorm. She pulled her lips in as though she weighed her words before speaking them. "Has the thought of going somewhere or being somewhere ever been more appealing than actually being there?"

Ewan unconsciously tightened his hold around Allyson. Her voice was so soft and resigned that something in his chest pinched his heart. She didn't look like a young woman eager to see her family or return to her home.

"I suppose court is like that for me. It seems exciting, but I'm always happier to ride away."

Allyson nodded, but said nothing else until they rode into the bailey. Ewan assumed she was nervous about what her father would say to explain their arrival. Ewan helped her from the saddle, and when she looked like she might collapse, he tucked her arm through his. They walked together into the Great Hall, where four similar faces turned toward them. Ewan noted Allyson's siblings bore a striking resemblance to the older woman amongst them, but there were traces of their father in their features. Allyson didn't look like any of them. Where her hair was blond and her eyes blue, all the members of her family that Ewan saw possessed brown hair and brown eyes.

"I know. I don't look like any of them. Surprising?"

"A little," Ewan admitted as they approached the woman who was clearly the matriarch. Lady Margaret Elliot smiled at Ewan, but it slipped when she turned her gaze on Allyson. Ewan felt Allyson tense, but her expression remained neutral.

"Allyson, this is a surprise. Your father's messenger arrived demanding men ride out to join him, but he said naught aboot them returning with you. What're you doing here?"

Ewan was taken aback at the curt tone and frigid reception Allyson received. He shifted, but Allyson's fingers dug into his arms. He glanced down at her, but she continued to look at her family. She knew her mother had more to say. She was certain the woman had a good idea that whatever the reason was, it had something to do with the betrothal, since that was why her father went to court and why Ewan would be accompanying them.

"Mother, I ran away from court to avoid marrying Ewan. I evaded Ewan and father for three days but the border reiver, Charlton, captured me and took me to Chillingham. I've been there for the past four days." Allyson knew there was no point in avoiding the truth. Her family would soon know once her father began his rant against her. She knew it was inevitable; she just didn't know when it would start.

"You ran away from court?" A young man chortled. "That sounds aboot par for the course with you, little sister."

Ewan noticed that the term so similar to the affectionate one he used with Eoin held no warmth coming from Angus Elliot. Ewan recognized the heir to the clan from many encounters at court over the years. They weren't friendly, but he had held no dislike for the man until he heard the way he addressed Allyson. It rankled. Lady Margaret stepped forward until she stood before Allyson and Ewan. Two out of three of Allyson's sisters and one brother watched their mother advance on their youngest sibling.

"I beg your pardon, Ewan. I've been remiss in welcoming you as our guest here at Redheugh. It's a pleasure to have you." Allyson's mother spared a glance at her before turning and stepping next to one of Allyson's sisters. Allyson was a beautiful young woman, but the woman Lady Margaret stood next to was stunning. She nudged Allyson's oldest sister forward. "Allyson, you must stay in the tower. Your nephews now sleep in your chamber since it's close to Laurel and her husband. It doesn't seem to make sense to disturb the arrangement since you won't be here long. The chamber next to Mary's is available for you, Ewan."

Ewan stiffened. He couldn't believe any of what he was hearing. Allyson was being relegated to the oldest portion of the keep. He'd seen the tower when they arrived, and it looked as hospitable as a bog. It stunned him that Lady Margaret would suggest he take a chamber next to Allyson's widowed sister, even pushing the woman toward him, while Allyson stood there. It was clear everyone knew he was to be betrothed to Allyson.

"Yes, Mother. If you'll excuse me, I shall retire and make myself more presentable."

"You'll have to wait to do that," Mary spoke up. "When I returned home a widow, we stored my belongings in your chests and armoire. We have packed yours up."

Ewan refused to look at the woman who flirted with him, offering him coy glances as she passed an assessing gaze over him. Ewan felt dirty, and it wasn't from days of being on the road and camping in the woods.

"If that is the case, perhaps you could show me the gardens, Lady Allyson. I imagine you'd like to stretch your legs after the ride." Ewan offered.

"Thank you. That would be most pleasant," Allyson murmured. They turned, but Lady Margaret's voice stopped them.

"I'll send Berta to tend to you and ensure everything is as it should be."

Allyson's neck and face flooded with color and heat. She nodded before Ewan led her toward the doors of the keep. They wandered to the gardens, and Allyson passed through the gate Ewan held open with her head ducked. She'd been able to bathe each day while at Chillingham, but her mother's few words about sending the midwife to examine her made her feel filthy.

"Allyson?" Ewan brushed hair away from her shoulder. Her hair had been in a tight braid when he entered her chamber at Chillingham, but now wisps and strands lay around her shoulders and ears. She'd been so vibrant at court, both when they danced together and went head-to-head. A few minutes with her family, and she'd retreated into an invisible shell.

"Hmm?" Allyson stared into the distance, but didn't seem to focus on anything. Her listlessness troubled Ewan, but he realized he didn't know her well enough to know what to say or do.

"Shall we walk, or would you prefer to sit in the sun, or maybe the shade?"

"Whatever you prefer." Allyson wandered toward a patch of lavender, and Ewan realized that was the scent he'd recognized when he whispered in her ear that day that their futures became entwined. He cut a stalk and handed it to her, and the smile she offered was genuine, even if a little shy. "Thank you."

"Is Berta your clan's midwife?" Ewan murmured as he shifted to block the sun from Allyson's eyes. She nodded but turned away.

"Regardless of what happened, you have grounds to break the betrothal after the way I acted. If that isn't enough, I'll have Berta say what she needs to, so you'll be free of me."

Ewan eased her around and tilted her chin up. "Ally, you made a mistake, but it's not the end of the world or your life. I believed you when you said you were untouched. And even if that weren't the case, no matter how ill-advised running away was, no woman asks to be assaulted. It wouldn't be your fault." He was uncertain where the diminutive came from—it seemed to suit her—but she didn't react. It was as though she hadn't heard it.

"Thank you, but that doesn't mean you want to marry me any more than you did in the Privy Council chamber."

"Mayhap I didn't say it, but I'm warming to the idea. I never thought you were a coward, and I don't like you thinking you are one. You withstood a test that would break a lesser woman. I can't imagine what Sage made you witness, and if ever you need someone to share that burden, you need only look to me. But you aren't damaged or ruined. No matter what your family suggests. That's not enough to turn me away."

Allyson squeezed her eyes shut to keep the tears from falling. She fought to push the lump in her throat down far enough to speak. "Thank you, Ewan, but my sister, Mary, would be a better match for you. She's beautiful and a widow. She possesses the experience you prefer."

Ewan straightened and looked over Allyson's head to ensure no one watched them before he pressed his mouth to the corner of her lips. He kissed each side before nudging her lips apart and deepening the kiss. She swayed into his embrace as he pulled her closer. He'd assumed the power of their first kiss came from the fraught situation around them, but this kiss was even more intense. Ewan felt himself fall headlong, and for once, he didn't shy away from his feelings. He trailed kisses along Allyson's jaw and neck, then back to her cheek.

"I don't want any Elliot but you." Ewan whispered against her ear.

"But she's the type of woman you prefer," Allyson reasoned before Ewan pulled away.

"How would you know what kind of woman I prefer? You saw me leaving one woman's chamber and now you understand me?"

"I may have seen you leaving Lady Bevan's chamber, but it's not as though I haven't heard of the other women attached to your name. Mary has more to offer a man of your—tastes than I do."

"I believe I was just tasting you and enjoying it."

Allyson's eyes flew wide open, and she huffed at Ewan's arrogant grin.

"You know that wasn't what I meant. It's obvious everyone else sees it, too."

"Could your mother and sister have been testing

my honor? Were they waiting to see if I took the bait?"

"Hardly." Allyson's laugh held no mirth as she shook her head. "It must have shocked my mother to learn the king intended us to wed. She wouldn't have volunteered me first when Mary still needs to re-marry and my other older sister, Alice, is still unwed."

"You have a sister named Alice?"

"Yes, she's the sibling closest in age to me, but you can see they're all quite a bit older than I am. I was an accident. My mother couldn't think of an-other name, so she accepted Allyson when someone suggested it. It's so close to one she'd already used, she said it kept her from forgetting it."

"Good God," Ewan uttered. Having rhyming names was confusing at times, but he knew neither he nor his brother received their names as an af-terthought to the other. "Ally—"

"Why do you call me that?" Allyson interrupted. "It's the second time you've done it."

So she did notice it. Ewan smiled before sneaking a kiss on her neck.

"I don't know, but it suits you. It doesn't sound like anyone else's name."

"Thank you," Allyson nodded as she looked at the ground. "I appreciate that."

Ewan wrapped his arm around her waist and guided them onto the path. They strolled through the gardens until Eoin informed them the noon meal was about to be presented.

CHAPTER SEVENTEEN

E oin overhead the Elliots speaking to Allyson and Ewan, and it stunned him how they degraded Allyson. When she and his brother stepped outside, Eoin insisted that he and Ewan use the tower chamber and Allyson remain in the keep. When Allyson left to bathe and rest for the afternoon, Eoin and Ewan slipped away to talk.

"You heard what they said to her." Ewan's words were a statement, not a question. His twin's expression mirrored his shock and disgust. "I can only imagine what they'd say if we hadn't been there. I understand what Cairren meant aboot the lack of attention, but it's more than that. It's a complete disregard for Allyson, as though she isn't even a member of their family."

"I know she's the youngest in the family, but I still can't imagine speaking to a sister or a daughter like that. I wouldn't speak to a servant like that," Eoin glanced back at the keep.

"People at court assume Allyson seeks attention, and that's why she's a flirt, but she came into her own when she arrived at court. She finally found a place where the attention wasn't always negative, so she clings to it; thrives on it."

"Aye. I went to that tower chamber, and while it might be fine for you and me, it's not fit for a lady. There are no comforts to speak of, and it'll be draughty at night."

"Have you noticed how little Allyson looks like her mother or father? How she doesn't look like the brother and sisters we met?" Ewan asked as he checked over his shoulder to ensure they didn't have an audience as they headed to the tower. "She even commented on not looking like the rest of them. Do you think there's a reason for it?"

"Do you mean, do I wonder if she's not really a member of their family?"

"Or mayhap not a full member of their family?" Ewan cocked an eyebrow. "She is several years younger than her next oldest sister from what she's said. And it appears like the rest came one after another in quick succession. Could she be illegitimate?"

"You mean, did her mother engage in an affair? There's no way she's her father's bastard. There would've been talk if a baby arrived, and Lady Elliot hadn't been expecting." Eoin shook his head in disbelief.

"If she isn't Laird Elliot's daughter, that would explain why they sent her to court and why he'd be eager to marry her off before her sisters wed." Ewan reasoned. "It would also explain Elliot's detachment from her."

"It was odd how little Kenneth seemed to know of Allyson. I noticed it, too."

"I don't know what to make of any of it, to be honest. I just know I don't like it. Before a sennight ago, I never thought ill of Allyson, and she was a happy young woman. She's wilted in the hours we've been here. She was like a different woman in the gardens. Distracted, uncertain, lost," Ewan explained.

"I'm curious to see how things play out this

evening. We still haven't met the other sister or brother."

"You mean Alice?" Ewan scowled, then nodded at Eoin's surprised expression. "Aye, Alice and Allyson. According to Allyson, she was such an afterthought that when someone suggested it, her mother accepted a name similar to one they'd already used, so she wouldn't forget it."

"She believes that?"

"She does, and from the way she said it, so flat and accepting, she's heard it plenty of times over the years."

"Could she have done something in her past that set them against her? Is there a family secret, and that's why they sent her away to court?"

"Mayhap, but I doubt it. If there was a shameful truth, the queen wouldn't have accepted her. The ladies-in-waiting might run wild once they're at court, but the queen demands a pristine reputation to accept them. I suppose we can only wait and see."

Allyson couldn't believe her misfortune. She lifted one gown after another and stared at the holes in each of them. She'd been unprepared to take the chamber next to Mary's after her mother's offer to Ewan. She'd taken a nap, then a bath and waited for her chests to arrive. When the servants set them on the floor, Allyson noticed someone hadn't shut the lids properly. Now she wanted to cry as she looked at the kirtles she'd brought with her. They were all wrinkled and needed laundering, but she had little choice if she was going to attend the evening meal without appearing in rags. She hurried to dress and brush out her hair before descending the stairs to join everyone in the Great Hall. She spotted Ewan and Eoin as soon as she entered. Women flocked around them, offering them food and drink or unabashedly flirting. Running back to her chamber before anyone caught sight of her crossed her mind, but Ewan's head turned in her direction as though he sensed her arrival. He broke away from the gaggle of women and crossed to stand with her.

"You look refreshed, my lady," Ewan smiled, but it faltered when Allyson muttered a thank you but stared at the dais. Ewan observed Margaret usher Eoin to a seat while the other family members took their places. They left two seats open; one between Allyson's sisters, Mary and the woman Ewan assumed was Alice. The other seat was at the end of the table, away from the family and among the retainers and their wives. Ewan wrapped Allyson's arm around his and escorted her to the dais, but Allyson's step faltered when Margaret rushed toward her.

"I expected you to dress properly for the evening meal, Allyson. Go and change," Margaret demanded.

"Mother, I haven't aught to change into. Whoever packed my clothes failed to shut the lids to the chest. There are moth holes in all the woolens, and mouse bites in all the other items. I found mouse droppings, too." Allyson kept her eyes down, and Ewan found it frustrating that Allyson acted as though it were her fault.

Looking much aggrieved, her mother relented, but not without a stinging retort. "You'll borrow something from your sisters, but it'll take time to take in the gowns at the bust."

"Yes, Mother." Allyson wanted to melt into the floor while Ewan's hand covered the one that rested on his forearm.

"Follow me, Ewan. Your meal awaits." Margaret led them both to the dais, but before Ewan could offer to assist Allyson into the seat between her sisters, Margaret announced that was his seat. He glanced at Allyson, but she was already moving to the seat at the end of the table. He shot his brother a scowl but quickly eased into the seat.

The meal was delicious, but Ewan was miserable. Alice and Mary vied for his attention, plying him with wine and food. If they'd been at court before he learned of the betrothal, he would have relished the attention. He would have flirted with the women and even placed his hand on Mary's thigh, letting her know he intended to visit her later that night. But as the conversation flowed around him, he watched Allyson sit in silence and push her food around her trencher. The constant chatter from Alice and Mary grated on his nerves, and he found the sisters annoying. Their disregard for their sister and his position as her future husband disgusted him even more than their mother's comments, which were intended to humiliate Allyson.

A tinkle of laughter carried to Ewan as the servants brought out dessert. He looked down the table and caught Eoin saying something that made Allyson laugh. A rosy hue flooded her cheeks as Eoin continued to speak. It was too loud to hear what Eoin said, but Allyson's reaction led him to believe his brother was flirting with her. He felt a surge of jealousy toward his brother that he hadn't experienced since they were adolescents. They'd been best friends as young children, but entered a competitive stage as they entered manhood. It ended as quickly as it began, and Ewan hadn't envied his brother anything in years. However, the longer the conversation lasted between Eoin and Allyson, the greater his anger grew. Once the servants cleared away the tables, and the musicians began to play, Ewan pushed back his seat, ignoring the women on either side and stalked down the dais. He pressed his hand on Eoin's shoulder as he made to rise and pushed him back into his seat.

"Lady Allyson, would you share the first dance with me?"

Allyson's gaze shifted between Ewan and Eoin while she bit her lip. Ewan wanted to punch his brother as he waited for Allyson's answer.

"Eoin already asked for the dance," she whispered.

"He can wait." But Ewan didn't. He took Allyson's hand and led her to where the other dancers began to move.

"He'll think I'm rude," Allyson's hushed voice barely reached Ewan over the sound of the music and the other people.

"He's rude to ask for the first dance when he's not the one betrothed to you," Ewan grumbled.

"But you're not betrothed to me either, Ewan. The documents weren't signed, and the ceremony never took place. Besides, you don't want a wife, or at least not the type of wife I want to be." Allyson looked away as her voice trailed off.

"I think you mean you don't want a husband, or at least not the type of husband I intend to be."

"Aye."

The answer felt like a blow between the eyes, but Ewan shouldn't have expected anything else when he admitted that he hadn't changed his mind on marriage, or at least how he viewed it. His conscience screamed that he should correct Allyson's misapprehension and explain the contracts had been signed. They danced the next two songs in silence before Eoin claimed his turn. Ewan retreated to a wall and glared at his brother's back, ignoring Allyson's sisters who passed by, their smiles offering more than a dance. Allyson danced with several of the young guardsmen, but they didn't stir his envy like Eoin did.

"You're a dog in a manger," Eoin announced as he came to stand beside his twin. "You don't want her, but you don't want anyone else to have her."

"I didn't say I don't want her."

"Very well, you may want to bed her, which requires you marry her, but you don't want to keep yourself only unto her. And she'll never accept you like that."

"Our fathers signed the agreements," Ewan retorted. "It doesn't matter what she will or won't accept. She doesn't have a choice."

"You'd force her down the aisle? Into your bed?"

Ewan turned on his brother and fisted his hands to keep from grabbing Eoin's collar.

"Neither of us has ever forced a woman. That you would imply, let alone say, as much hurts."

"You know I didn't mean physical force. Ewan, she's a kind lass and deserves better than anyone has offered her. I listened to her brothers and the others at the table. It's worse than we assumed. They don't intend to disparage her. They've so little regard for her, they don't even realize how dismissive they are. I don't think they realize how their words come across to an outsider."

"I noticed the same. Alice and Mary weren't casting glances at Allyson or gloating that they sat with me. It was as if they didn't have a younger sister. The only one who doesn't seem to belittle her is her sister Laurel. And I suspect that's because she's married with her own family, so she has no interest in Allyson at all."

Ewan and Eoin watched Allyson dance with a clan elder, and the face they recognized from court reappeared as the old man said something that made her laugh. Ewan's breath caught as he watched her face transform into a work of art. She'd been so disheartened since before she left Stirling that he'd almost forgotten how breathtaking she was when she truly smiled.

"She deserves to smile like that every day, Ewan. You'll break her heart worse than her family if you marry her and stray."

"But it's not as though she loves me, or I love her. She has no emotions invested in this, so it won't be betrayal. It won't hurt more than her pride, and she'll get past that soon enough."

"I'm going to beat you," Eoin hissed. "Not a betrayal? It doesn't matter whether you love each other. You're going to stand before God and her and pledge to keep yourself only unto her, then turn around and bed any woman who takes your fancy. How is that not a betrayal? How can those words mean so little to you? She's not our damn mother!"

"Keep your voice down before you attract attention," Ewan snapped.

"Then keep your bluidy plaid down. I'm telling you right now, Ewan. If you don't intend to make a real commitment to her, to have a marriage with honor and faithfulness, then step aside. I'll marry her."

Ewan spun on his brother and was prepared to swing when Allyson stepped beside him and placed her hand on his arm.

"I don't know what you're arguing aboot, but people are taking interest. They're accustomed to fights now and then, but not between two men the size of the Cairngorms. What's the matter?"

"Naught," the twins replied together, and Allyson laughed. The sound eased the tension between the brothers, but Ewan still fumed. He had no reason to be so angry at Eoin, and a sennight night ago, he would have thanked his brother and washed his hands of Allyson. Now, he looked down at the young woman whose face showed concern, and he realized he couldn't live with Allyson returning to Huntly as his brother's bride. He couldn't live in the same keep as her, watch her laugh and joke with Eoin, retire to her chamber and await his brother's company. He couldn't stomach the idea of watching her bear Eoin's children when those bairns could be his. He shot his brother a glare, catching Eoin observing him. He nodded, and Eoin stepped away. The twins had come to an understanding.

CHAPTER EIGHTEEN

The next two days passed in a blur for Allyson because she slept through most of them. The adventure finally took its toll, and her mind and body demanded time to recover after being fueled by fear and despair.

Ewan wasn't so fortunate; the days were agonizing. He spent the mornings and early afternoons in the lists with Eoin and Kenneth. Laird Elliot's strength and skill impressed him. He'd underestimated the older man, but his opinion changed when he landed on his backside in the mud after Kenneth's sword clashed against his with so much force that the impact vibrated up his arm and made his teeth clack together.

However, the time away from the lists was unpleasant at best, and downright uncomfortable at worst. Mary cornered Ewan on his way to the tower his second day there and offered to scrub his back when he bathed.

"Lady Mary, your offer is gracious, but I must refuse. That is hardly appropriate since I am to marry your sister."

"Neither you nor I believe that. Not that it's inappropriate, nor that you'll marry Allyson. Why would you after she ran away from you?"

"Because the king arranged the marriage, my lady."

"That doesn't mean you want to marry her, and it doesn't mean you will. Besides, you're not even betrothed yet. We can enjoy ourselves until then." Mary reached for his chest, but Ewan grasped her wrist and stepped away.

"I don't understand how you could offer such a thing when it's your sister you'd betray." The words he exchanged with Eoin the night before came back to him. Being propositioned by someone else, in particular Allyson's sister, seemed like a betrayal, and of the worst kind. But he saw the hypocrisy in his refusal.

"You don't want to marry her. It's obvious to everyone that's she naught but a weight around your neck." Mary once more reached for him. "A weight I could soothe away."

"Nay. You are under the wrong impression if you believe I don't want to marry Allyson, and you are most certainly under the wrong impression if you think I will dally with one of her sisters."

"Your reputation precedes you, Ewan. I've heard of your appetites, and my baby sister isn't enough."

Ewan jerked away and curled his lip in disgust as he glared at Mary. "That's where you are mistaken. Your sister is everything I could hope for and more than I deserve." Ewan turned away and slammed the door to the tower in Mary's face. The overt proposition shocked him, so he'd said whatever he could think of to dissuade Allyson's sister, but as he entered the tower chamber, he realized he'd spoken the truth about Allyson.

Ewan stripped off his filthy clothes and used the

ewer and basin to wash before sitting on the end of the bed. He considered all that had happened since the day Allyson spotted Eoin and him leaving Lady Bevan's chamber. He'd seen Allyson and Cairren and thought to tease them, to ease the discomfort of being caught. That Allyson saw him when he'd planned to ask her to dance that eve embarrassed him. He realized now what a cad that made him, wanting to dance with the young lady only hours after bedding an experienced woman. His thought-less words had more effect on her than he expected, but once he'd apologized, he believed they'd put the matter to rest. He even assumed she overreacted to the taunts.

Then his world turned upside down. He and Eoin arrived at their chamber to find their father awaiting them with news that shook Ewan to his core. Before he said anything, his father was dragging him to the Privy Council chamber where the king and Laird Elliot leaned over a table reviewing a doc-ument. Ewan realized that document was his be-trothal agreement. He tried to argue against it, but the king's stare made him fall silent. Then hell broke loose when Allyson arrived and discovered why the king had summoned them both. His ego bore the brunt of her sharp tongue, and when she moved from one dance partner to another that night, he wanted to turn the tables on her. He hadn't paid at-tention to any of the women he danced with, and while Eoin spent the night with a willing partner, he'd retired to their chamber alone, angry that Allyson had such an effect on him while he appeared to have none on her.

Guilt stabbed at him when they learned she'd run away, and Kenneth's explanation of Mary's past only made it worse, though he held little sympathy for the woman now. She'd moved on from her past torments and was a widow who intended to enjoy life, but she wouldn't enjoy it with him. He'd been angry and frustrated with Kenneth and Allyson when he was certain they would catch her in Glasgow, but she slipped away. The irritation grew as they traveled through the rain for two days; however, discovering the hoofprints and the footprints that showed a struggle tipped his world again. Suddenly, Allyson's words and deeds no longer cut so deep. He saw her for what she was: a scared young woman who felt powerless.

As Ewan glanced about the chamber Allyson's mother intended for her, he realized he'd underestimated how dire Allyson perceived the situation was when she learned everyone expected her to marry him. She'd left a family that saw no value in her and made a place for herself at court only to have that torn away from her with the threat of returning to the same life she'd escaped, except Ewan would have imposed a different humiliation upon her. The type that came from being a rejected wife, and he realized that would be even worse than a rejected sister and daughter. She had no choice about her relatives, but she clung to her choice in husbands.

He and Eoin arrived early to the evening meal, and after asking the housekeeper about the family's usual seating, he and his brother sat at the end, far from Allyson's sisters. They left a seat between them, but it remained empty when Allyson didn't appear. Ewan declined to dance, nursing a mug of ale instead.

Ewan awoke to an aching head and a churning belly. He had far too many mugs of ale to avoid having to speak to any of Allyson's sisters, but he'd stopped before becoming intoxicated. He refused to tempt fate and succumb to Alice's or Mary's wiles. He'd dragged himself to the chamber tower while Eoin continued to flirt with a serving woman. He was relieved when Eoin returned to the chamber not long after him. They hadn't been at Redheugh long enough for Eoin to be bedding any of the servants.

He walked toward the lists, but he was in no mood to swing his sword that morning, so he wandered to the kirk instead. He pushed the door open and slipped inside, making his way to a pew at the front. While Ewan and Eoin may have indulged in gluttony and lust, both men were devout in their faith. They were hardly paragons of abstinence and chastity, but he wanted to have faith that he was capable of practicing humility, patience, and kindness. All three virtues would benefit both Allyson and him. She deserved a healthy dose of kindness and remembering his arrogance before Allyson ran away made him ashamed. He needed to gain some humility if he were ever to lead his clan successfully; this seemed to be the moment he would learn it. He prayed that he and Allyson possessed enough patience for one another to work on their relationship.

Relationship? We dinna even have one. We were friendly before this began, but really little more than acquaintances. I may have come to realize a great deal aboot Allyson's character and even come to appreciate it despite the mess she got herself into, but I doubt she'd be likely to say the same aboot me.

Heavenly Father, what would Ye have me do? I confess I have erred in thought, word, and deed countless times, but I heartily repent. I wish it hadnae taken a forced betrothal and rescuing ma bride-to-be from a mad mon for me to realize how great ma transgressions have been. Ye may forgive me, but will Allyson? Will she believe me and that ma repentance is genuine?

I feel as though Ye're asking me, Lord, why, or rather how, it can be genuine. Eoin is right. As usual. She doesnae deserve duplicity and treachery from a husband. It's taken seeing her family for me to realize I dinna want to be the type of mon who can so disregard another person's feelings and wellbeing. Lord, would ma clan respect me if I did such? I dinna think so. They may have tolerated Father's infidelity because of Mother's chilling disposition, but they wouldnae forgive me once they got to ken Allyson. It would be as though I were double-crossing the entire clan and nae just ma wife. I may have spent the last several years sowing ma oats, but I've always intended to be a good leader to ma people once the time comes. How can I do that if I have nay honor? The answer to that is simple. I canna.

Lord God, guide me as Ye have all ma life. Help me to see the path Ye would have me traverse. Continue to be ma beacon when I search for a light to follow, and I pray Ye lead me to Allyson. But, Holy Father, if in the end, it's not Yer will for us to be together, I pray Ye provide Allyson with a mon who can treat her as she deserves, someone who can honor and even cherish her.

Ewan bowed his head after looking at the crucifix that hung from the wall while he prayed. He closed his eyes and recited the Lord's prayer.

Our fadir that art in heuenes, halwid be thi name; thi kingdom cumme to; be thi wille don as in heuen and in earthe. Giv to vs this day our breed ouer other substaunce; and forgeue to vs oure dettis, as we forgeue to oure dettours; and leede us nat in to temptacioun, but delyuere vs fro yuel. Amen.

Ewan sat back on the pew and returned his gaze to the crucifix. He inhaled, filling his lungs with a cleansing breath. He experienced a sense of calm wash over him, the same that came over him whenever he was certain the Lord had heard him and sent the Holy Spirit to fill him with forgiveness. It was an experience that soothed his soul and reaffirmed his faith. He felt better equipped to face Allyson and resolved to change his view on marriage. He wanted to be a man who lived by honor and virtue, and he would demonstrate that to Allyson.

CHAPTER NINETEEN

H e had greater luck the next evening, when Allyson appeared after two days of seclusion. She looked rested and better able to endure her family. She wore a gown that didn't fit her well, so Ewan realized it was one that still needed altering, but it complimented her fair coloring.

He met her at the bottom of the steps and glanced about to check that no one noticed as he guided her down a passageway he'd discovered led to the gardens but wasn't often used. When they entered the shadows, he stopped them. She tempted him to press her against the wall and swoop in for a kiss, but he didn't want to frighten her. After four years at court, he doubted he was the first man to want to steal a kiss from her, but that only seemed to make taking her by surprise even worse. When coupled with what she must have witnessed at Chillingham, Ewan didn't want to terrify her.

"Lass, you look vera bonnie this evening," he murmured as he turned to face her. A torch further down the passageway offered enough light for them to see one another.

"Bonnie?" Ewan noted that she sounded disappointed with the word.

"Aye, vera pretty."

"Thank you," Allyson whispered, but while she was polite, she still sounded unhappy.

"Lass, what is it? Do you not want me to compliment your appearance?"

"No, I'd just hoped—" Allyson trailed off and leaned back against the wall.

"Hoped what, Ally? What's troubling you?"

"It's naught, Ewan. We should go before anyone mentions we're missing. You don't need my clan to force you to the kirk because we get caught alone."

"It is something, and I'm not opposed to someone finding us."

Allyson shook her head and looked back toward the Great Hall. She whispered, "Don't."

"Ally, what is it? I don't understand what's the matter, but I want to."

"Ewan, don't do this. Don't pretend that any of this matters."

"Who said I'm pretending?" Ewan refused to wait any longer. Whatever bothered Allyson made her question his sincerity. He wrapped his arm around her waist and pulled her against his larger frame. His other hand cupped her jaw as he lowered his mouth to hers. The contact snapped his control. He inched her back against the wall as his tongue dove into her mouth. He kept the pressure light, but he was insistent. He wanted to taste her and touch her until she melted against him as she had in the garden. His hand slid along her neck until his fingers trailed over her collarbone to her breast. He groaned as his palm encompassed the supple mound. He kneaded the flesh as Allyson's tongue flicked his, luring it back into her mouth. Her hands tangled in his hair as he stooped to kiss the exposed skin above the neckline of her gown. The kirtle hung loose enough for him to push the material lower until he could lick the swell of her breast. Ewan fought to regain his self-restraint and pulled away but not before he squeezed her breast once more.

"Why—why'd you do that?" Allyson panted.

"Because I thought I wouldn't survive without it," Ewan confessed. "Because I've missed you the last two days and worried aboot you. Because you're so damn bonnie that I can't help myself."

"Bonnie? Just bonnie. Ewan, go find Mary or Alice." Allyson tried to push away, but Ewan's hands shackled her to the wall as he pinned them at her sides.

"Why the hell would I want to find either of them when I nearly spilled myself kissing you?" he demanded.

"Because they're the beautiful ones. They're the ones every mon wants."

"You're beautiful, too, Ally. And not every mon wants them. They're your sisters, but I can barely tolerate them."

"No one said you had to tolerate them to look at them. And what Mary will do for you, to you, doesn't involve her personality."

Ewan dropped Allyson's arms and lurched backward like she burned him.

"I do not want Mary, and I do not want Alice. I don't want them in my bed, and I don't want to be in them." Ewan snapped. "They aren't the ones I've kissed and been yearning to kiss."

"Yearning?" The disbelief in Allyson's voice tore through Ewan's annoyance. He reminded himself that she wasn't being awkward on purpose. Allyson was beautiful, but so were her three sisters, and she'd grown up cast in their shadows. She was aware Mary and Alice were solicitous to him, and she assumed, with his past, that he wouldn't hesitate to accept the offers.

"Ally, we don't have time for me to explain every-thing, but I will. Meet me tonight in the garden, please. But for now, rest assured I will never touch either of your sisters. Ever. Will you?"

Allyson nodded but couldn't force the words out without bursting into tears. She was unprepared for Ewan's embrace. Where the last one had been arous-ing, this one was comforting. He kissed the crown of her head as she wrapped her arms around his waist.

"I don't understand any of this," she murmured.

"I know, little one. I'll make sure you do if you'll meet me."

"Aye, I'll meet you."

Ewan led them back toward the Great Hall and urged Allyson to enter before him. He waited until she stood with her father and brothers before fol-lowing her. Eoin joined him as they approached the three Elliot men and Allyson.

"Allyson, when are you returning to court?" Angus inquired.

"I don't know. I hadn't thought that far," Allyson admitted.

"Don't you think you should leave soon?" Graeme, the younger of the two brothers, persisted. "Don't you miss your home and friends?"

"My home?" Allyson whispered before straight-ening her spine. "Court isn't my home, but it's the most appealing place I can think of, and that isn't saying much."

Allyson stepped away from her relatives, and Ewan took her arm to escort her to the dais. Eoin fol-lowed as though he were on guard, his eyes shifting to watch for anyone else who might make Allyson their target. Once seated, Ewan and Eoin shared a glance over Allyson's head. He was in a perpetual state of shock at how blatant this hostility was to Allyson. It made no sense to him, but there had to be a reason, and he intended to discover it or take Allyson back to court.

The meal passed with little disturbance, and the twins engaged Allyson in conversation throughout it. They weren't interested in speaking to anyone else, nor were they willing to allow Allyson to be ignored. When the dancing began, Ewan witnessed Allyson transform into the vibrant woman he remembered from court. It was the same as it had been her first night here. It appeared the Elliot clan didn't share the laird's family's rejection, and several young guardsmen took turns dancing with Allyson. Ewan observed as she partnered with one man after another, some young enough to be a suitor while others were old enough to be her grandfather. She laughed with each of them, light on her feet and graceful as they swung her around.

It was Shrove Tuesday, and the last day for merriment before the solemnity of Lent began. Ewan feared without the opportunity for entertainment and lightheartedness, he wouldn't see her smile for the next forty days.

"She's enjoying herself," Ewan mused. "She looks like she does at court. It amazes me, and not in the good way, that her parents and siblings can have such an effect on her personality. But I can't blame her. I think I would be the same."

"No, I'd be the same," Eoin countered. "You'd have told them all to go to hell by now."

"True. I'm ready to do that now." Ewan turned to face his twin. "I've asked her to meet me in the garden tonight. I'm going to figure out whether or not we have a future. Eoin, you should have been the older twin. You're far wiser than I am."

"I have no interest in being the older brother. You need the voice of reason, so you're lucky we came as a matched set."

"Mary propositioned me yesterday, and I realized that my betrayal, if I strayed, would be even worse than her sister's. It forced me to consider how things have unraveled in the past sennight and a half. I went from wanting to dance with Allyson that blasted day that changed all of this to dreading marriage to wanting to drag her to the kirk. I stopped to think aboot what this must be like from her position."

"But I can't imagine Mary changed your mind. She's been eying both of us since we walked in, so what really made you alter your course?"

"I told you. If I marry Allyson, which I was never averse to, and am not faithful, that's worse than her sister trying to bed me. She can't pick her relatives, but she's fighting tooth and nail to have some control over who she must marry. It terrified her and left her powerless, so she ran. You and I will never experience that. It may not have thrilled me to discover others made plans for me, and I did feel powerless, but I was never scared. We're men; we have all the power, and that keeps us from experiencing the fear women must live with when they have no control over the decisions made for them. I'm the heir to a large clan that has influence throughout not only the Highlands but all of Scotland. Besides Father and the king, who can force my hand? No one. Not really. But who can force Allyson? Everyone. She deserves a husband committed to her, and if I won't do that, then I have no business marrying her."

"But you do want to marry her?"

"I do."

"Why? Is it because she's pretty? Because you've enjoyed stealing kisses?"

"I won't deny both things are true, but I've had time to evaluate what I know aboot her. She's brave and resourceful. She's able to create a life for herself wherever she goes. She can endure more than most will face, and she's come out unscathed. She may be naïve and foolish at times, but with age and support, she'll learn the way of the world. She will make a fine lady for our clan. Even now I can tell, and that's the position she will step into. Father may still be laird, but with Mother gone, she will be Lady Gordon for all intents and purposes."

"I'm glad you see that at last."

"At last? When did you figure that out?"

"When she hissed and spat at you like a trapped wildcat."

"You might have explained this sooner, little brother."

"You had to come to these realizations on your own."

Ewan shot him a withering glance as he raised his mug of ale to his mouth, but he recognized Eoin was right. His brother had tried to make him realize it, but he'd remained stubborn.

CHAPTER TWENTY

Allyson glanced behind her as she moved toward the passageway that would take her to the gardens. She stifled a groan when she spotted Alice and Laurel approaching. She had no desire for her sisters to waylay her as she attempted to meet Ewan in the gardens. Allyson assumed everyone had retired, especially Laurel, who'd already gone abovestairs to check on her children, but both women drew closer. She strained to see past their shoulders and noticed Mary sitting before the fire, watching Alice and Laurel stalk their prey.

"Where are you going, sister?" Alice purred.

"I thought to step outside for a moment. A breath of fresh air and a moment of solitude before I retire for the night."

"Are you sure you're not meeting a mon?" Laurel narrowed her eyes as though she might read Allyson's thoughts.

"Nay. I'd prefer to be alone," Allyson countered. She needed to convince her sisters she held no interest for them.

"Alone? You didn't appear to want to be alone all eve as you danced with one mon after another. You didn't spare any mon your attention. You made a disgrace of yourself. And the way the Gordon twins passed you back and forth, it made it obvious they're both bedding you." Alice managed to look down her nose at Allyson, even though they were the same height.

"Just because that's what you might do, doesn't mean that's what I'm doing. I've met both brothers before at court, they're our guests, and I'm to be betrothed to one of them. It stands to reason that I would dance with them. One will be my husband and the other will be my brother-by-marriage." Allyson forced herself to cease speaking before she said something that she couldn't take back, something the sisters would hold against her.

"What are you implying?" Alice angled herself closer, cutting off Allyson's path to the gardens.

"I'm implying naught. I'm saying I've seen you and Mary flirting with the mon I'm to marry, and I don't appreciate it."

"Our little sister is trying to grow a backbone," Laurel laughed. "You're naught but a wee lass who doesn't understand what that mon wants or how to give it to him."

"And Alice does? She's never been married either. How would she know?" Allyson glared at her sisters as she waited for her sisters to admit Alice was no innocent.

"She's had the benefit of my and Mary's experience. We have been able to enlighten Alice to what a mon expects in his bed."

"You've turned her into a whore," Allyson shuddered and took a step back, her hand going over her heart.

Alice reached up and pinched the back of Allyson's arm as she pushed her toward the Great Hall and where Mary sat. "You would know after your time at court. There's no way that you haven't been bedded like every other whoring lady-in-waiting."

"Where do you get your information? None of you have been to court more than a handful of times, and the last time was for Father to present you before the king and queen. That was years ago. None of you have spent time there, nor are you acquainted with any other ladies-in-waiting. How would you be aware of what happens there? You have naught but made up stories."

"Mother and Father told us what goes on there." Laurel lifted her chin higher in an attempt at haughtiness, but she looked ridiculous with her head tilted back.

"Neither of them has spent much time at court since Queen Elizabeth returned. How would they know? And if they're so convinced it's a moral abyss, why did they send me to serve there?"

"To rid us of you." Alice didn't hesitate in her response. She leaned close to Allyson's ear but did little to lower her voice. "We all thought Father would find you a fat auld mon, slobbering to get a son off you."

"But that's not who the king chose, and now you and Mary are jealous that I've got a mon, a braw one, and you've got naught."

"It's not fair," Alice whined before catching herself.

"Little in life is fair. It wasn't fair that I was born into such a coldhearted family, but I'm surviving."

"We're only cold toward you," Laurel sniffed.

"Why? What did I ever do to any of you?" Allyson was certain her sisters heard the neediness in her voice because they both grinned.

"You're not one of us," Laurel hissed.

"You presume either Mother or Father took a lover."

"We're certain Father has. Several. You're one of his bastards fobbed off on Mother and us. We never wanted you," Laurel practically barked the last words.

"How can you be certain?" Allyson needed to know, needed to hear her sisters confess what they'd taunted her with for years.

"Besides you resemble none of us? We never saw Mother's waist expanding, so when we arrived home from court to find you screeching like a banshee, there was no other explanation. Mother did not bear you."

"I have as much control over how I look as I do who my parents are. Why punish me?"

"You think we could speak out against Father? Besides, you're the one we don't want. You're a disgrace, and a reminder to Mother of how horrid Father was to her. Why would any of us want a constant reminder?" Laurel crossed her arms, casting Allyson a look of utter disgust. Allyson felt like little more than refuse under her sisters' hateful heels.

"Then leave me alone. You never took an interest in me before. Don't bother now."

"But you have something I want," Alice chimed in.

"Ewan isn't a something. He's a person, and he's a person the king has already decided will marry me."

"He won't if you step aside. You ran from him to avoid marrying him. You don't want him, but you won't let anyone else have him either. You're selfish," Alice whined.

"I was scared."

"Every bride is scared." Mary joined the conversation, having grown impatient for her sisters to move closer to the fireplace. "My husband forced me on our wedding night, but I got over it. Laurel can barely tolerate the sight of her husband, but she's born his children. Who are you to decide you can avoid your duty?"

"You intend to punish me. Make me watch you two," Allyson gestured to Mary and Alice. "Attempt to seduce him. He can't marry both of you. He can't marry either of you. Like I said, the king decided this matter."

"I don't intend to marry him," Marry countered. "I just intend to bed him. A mon like that has appetites only an experienced woman can satisfy. Alice will marry him, but in the meantime, I shall enjoy him."

"You're disgusting. The bible teaches us 'flee from sexual immorality. Every other sin a person commits is outside the body, but the sexually immoral person sins against his own body.' You are covetous."

"That's laughable coming from a soiled dove who's probably bedded more men than our tavern wenches."

"You are convinced men have led me astray, yet Berta examined me when I arrived and found naught amiss. I have not been with a mon." Allyson realized she'd fallen into her sisters' trap. While she defended herself, she admitted that she hadn't the knowledge or experience a man like Ewan expected from his bed partners. She bit her tongue lest she dig herself in deeper.

"Step aside, little sister. We won't ask again," Alice sneered.

"You haven't asked for aught. All you've tried to do is bully me, but one thing I learned at court is how to survive those who would intimidate me. I have naught left to say to any of you." Allyson spun on her heels but drew up short when she spotted a large form cast in the shadows of the passageway.

She couldn't tell if it was Ewan or Eoin, but one of them had heard the disastrous conversation. The exchange with her sisters mortified her too much to meet Ewan in the gardens, so she pivoted and dashed up the stairs.

<hr>

Ewan stormed into the tower chamber, livid. He slammed the door shut as Eoin glanced up from sharpening his sword. Ewan paced across the small chamber several times, yanking at the collar of his leine as though it tried to strangle him. Finally he ripped it over his head and flung it against the wall.

"Failed to steal a kiss from Allyson? Did she smash your toes or knee you in the cods?" Eoin chuckled.

"Nay. I waited for her in the garden, but when she didn't appear, I searched for her. I found her in an argument with her sisters. It started with Alice and Laurel, but then Mary joined in. They told her she's illegitimate and that none of them ever wanted her. They called her a whore for her time at court and told her she would never be what I want. How the devil would they know what I want? Even if my reputation precedes me, which I'm now certain it does, or even if those bitches just made an accurate assessment of my past, that doesn't mean I don't want to marry Allyson. I chased her across God's creation."

"And until this evening, you intended to bed any woman you fancied regardless of being married. It seems they had a similar line of thought as you did."

"But to say it to Allyson's face?"

"You did. You did it not only in front of me but our father, her father, and the king. I don't know which is a worse humiliation."

"Bugger it. I've never wanted to strike someone as badly as I did her sisters. And they're women!"

"You stood there and listened? You didn't come to her defense?"

"At first, I was too stunned to say aught. When I gathered my wits, Allyson was already defending herself. I was in two minds whether to step in, but I didn't want her sisters to think Allyson's weak. If I intervened, they would never respect her."

"That's laughable, brother. You think they'll ever respect her?"

"As though calling her a whore wasn't bad enough, they taunted her, claiming she could never satisfy me. They went back and forth from every side, cutting Allyson down to the quick. Then Mary and Alice confessed they've decided Mary will be my mistress until Alice marries me! Bluidy bleeding hell! Can you believe that? Who says that to their sister?"

"Women can be conniving and manipulative, but this takes it to the extreme. It's one thing when the women are competing at court. It's political as much as it's personal, but they usually aren't sisters. They're not even from the same clan most of the time." Eoin paused as he shook his head before asking the pivotal question. "What are you going to do?"

"Since I can't wring their scrawny necks, I will avoid them when I can. I want to spend time with Allyson, anyway."

"I'll do aught that I can to help you." Eoin grinned.

"Don't you dare bed any of Allyson's sisters, or I'll throttle you." Ewan warned as Eoin threw his hands up in surrender and laughed.

"I'm not bedding any of her relatives. Maybe a wench or two at the tavern, but I have no interest in any of the Elliot sisters."

"Eoin, she saw me." Ewan came to stand before

his brother, and it surprised Eoin to see how embarrassed, even ashamed, Ewan looked. "You asked why I didn't step in. She must be asking herself the same question. I'm certain she couldn't tell whether it was you or me, but I know she saw someone. What do I say?"

"If she asks, explain it to her the same way you did to me. It made sense to me."

"I don't know that she'll see it that way. She defended me when Alice called me 'something.' If I'm to be Ally's husband, then I should protect her."

"But she's also a woman who wants to prove she can stand on her own two feet, one who doesn't cower behind a mon."

"I hope she sees it that way."

"Don't bring it up unless she does. Then she might assume it was me rather than you eavesdropping."

"I wasn't eavesdropping!"

"I think you were. I think that's exactly what eavesdropping is."

"I don't know that I can avoid it. Silence is as good as a lie in this case."

Eoin shrugged and returned to sharpening his blade. Ewan stood by the arrow slit and stared at the sky, wishing he could be anywhere but at Redheugh, but only if he could take Allyson with him.

CHAPTER TWENTY-ONE

The following fortnight took on a pattern that filled Ewan's day, but he was certain it left Allyson alone for most of it. He awoke, then he and Eoin made their way to the lists. They spent the morning and early afternoon training with their men and the Elliot warriors. He'd find Allyson alone in the gardens, reading or weeding. Other times she visited the various workshops in the bailey, and a few times he found her having just returned from the village. They walked together in the bailey or sat in the garden, some days enjoying companionable silence, but other days they talked of Allyson's life at court and Ewan's life with his clan in the Highlands. Ewan discovered when Allyson was away from her family, she returned to the lighthearted woman he knew from court. She shared the latest gossip and laughed at Ewan's impersonations of the Lowland courtiers who flocked to King Robert's side. Allyson had Ewan laughing so hard he held his side when she attempted a Highland burr.

It didn't take long for them to become comfortable with one another's company, and Ewan realized he enjoyed having Allyson nearby. He wasn't in a rush to return to court when he had so much time to get acquainted with Allyson. He would never be able to spend time alone with her if they returned to Stirling. He looked forward to leaving the lists in pursuit of her and their afternoons together. He avoided her sisters and ensured he was never alone. He felt guilty at times abandoning Eoin in favor of Allyson, but his brother supported him and was happy to fill his time in the barracks with their men, gaming and talking. Ewan would never admit it, but the men were just as notorious gossipers as any women he knew. Eoin endeavored to not be alone anywhere where he might encounter Mary or Alice. He slipped out to the village some nights, but not until he was certain Ewan made it safely to their chamber. Eoin teased Ewan about needing a protector, but both men knew it wasn't far from the truth. While Ewan was mostly content with his routine, he sensed Allyson didn't feel the same about hers.

Allyson felt like time was mired in sludge each day until Ewan came looking for her. The hours between rising and meeting with Ewan seemed endless. She remained secluded in her chamber for most of the morning, reading or sewing. She only sewed when her eyes grew too weary from the dim morning light in her chamber. She disliked sewing, but she was good at it. She'd learned that Laurel was expecting again, so she began a set of baby clothes, but her heart wasn't in it. Allyson had only taken on the project because it seemed like the right thing to do for her sister. She ventured to the gardens or the village most afternoons just for a change of scenery, but she did everything possible to avoid her sisters.

Allyson discovered she enjoyed her time with Ewan, and it surprised her to learn he had a rich baritone and often hummed when they sat together in the garden. The more she got to know him, the less daunting the prospect of marrying him became.

However, the niggling fear that disappointment would crush her when he returned to his roguish ways made her guarded. Fear of when the betrothal documents would arrive made her stomach churn, but as one day passed into another, and no messenger arrived from Stirling, fear of why the king hadn't sent them took over. She found herself jumpy and on edge throughout the day and evening and only calmed when Ewan's company distracted her. She was at ease enough to be herself, a woman much like she was at court but without the pretense.

"Ally?" Ewan asked as they walked through the bailey at the end of their first sennight at Redheugh. She looked up at Ewan, but he sensed her mind wasn't on him. He'd sensed Allyson suffered from constant worry about their situation. He wished to reassure her, but every encounter he had with her sisters seemed to set him back. Margaret appeared to encourage her older daughters and turned a blind eye to the inappropriate advances while Kenneth was oblivious to the women in his family. Whenever possible, if Ewan wasn't with Allyson or in the lists, he engaged Kenneth in conversation. He tried to move the conversations in a direction that would shed light on why Allyson was the black sheep of the family, but he never succeeded. After the fourth or fifth time, he gave up and spent the time talking about clan business and politics. The Elliots and Gordons were staunch supporters of King Robert, so politics was fairly safe when they stuck to the topic of the border. Ewan realized he treaded dangerous ground when they spoke about politics that pertained to the Highlands and clan relations. He nudged Allyson's arm. "You seem distracted today?"

He could tell something troubled her.

"Oh? I'm sorry. I don't mean to be, but I was thinking aboot one of the aulder women in the village. She doesn't have any children to care for her, and she was poorly before we arrived. I visited her yesterday, but I fear she isn't long for this world. I just wish there was more I could do." Allyson looked up at Ewan, who offered her a compassionate smile and a pat on the hand that rested on his forearm. He led them into the garden and to the shade of an apple tree.

"Is there aught you can do? Can the healer visit her?"

"There's naught for me to do, but the healer visits daily. She's just frail, and I think she wants to reunite with her family in heaven. She's outlived her husband and six children. She's seventy if she's a day. I wish there was more I could do to make her comfortable."

"I'm certain your visits offer her comfort."

"I hope so, but lately, she doesn't seem to know if I'm there or not. I tidy up her home and make sure she has a hot meal each day. The healer's convinced her she doesn't need to fast this Lent, that it's weakening her too much, so I bake fresh bannocks and make a pottage every couple of days."

"You can cook?" Ewan failed to hide his surprise.

"Aye. I learned when I was younger." Allyson's tone warned Ewan that it wasn't a topic she wanted to elaborate upon, so he let it drop. Instead, he lifted her hand to his mouth and kissed each knuckle before turning it over and kissing her palm, then the inside of her wrist. When there was no sign of resistance, Ewan wrapped his arm around her waist and pulled her close.

"You are a fine woman, Ally. One day you will make an excellent Lady Gordon. You have a huge heart, and you care for your people. Ministering to the sick isn't a task all people are made for, but you sound as though you understand it's a duty that the laird's family shouldn't overlook. I'd venture a guess that other members of your family don't see it as such, but rather a burden."

"No, my sisters don't visit the elderly or the infirm. My mother does when she has time. My sisters fulfill their duties, but Mother never gave each of them many. With three of them to assist Mother, only Mary has ever had the full weight of being chatelaine on her shoulders. Then again, I suppose I'm no different. I've carried the lightest burden, I suppose, since they never wanted my help."

"Mayhap, but I suspect your duties were the least desirable and the hardest to perform."

Allyson shrugged, but Ewan wasn't far off. "I helped tend the sick and the elderly. When they died, I helped prepare them for burial. You've seen I work in the gardens, and I oversaw the sheep shearing and wool spinning. Not particularly glamorous, but they are jobs that needed doing."

Ewan used his other hand to tilt Allyson's chin before he lowered his lips to hers. It began as a soft brushing of skin, but it was only a heartbeat later that passion sparked between them. Allyson opened to Ewan's questing tongue as he tilted his head to gain better access. He swiped it along hers before they tangled and dueled. Ewan was unprepared for the ferocity of his need, but he didn't want to hold back. He'd stolen kisses from Allyson throughout the week, but they hadn't given into desire like they did now. He backed them further into the shade, using his broad back to shield Allyson from anyone who might see. Her slim fingers slid beneath the neckline of his leine as she stroked them over his shoulders and neck. She rose onto her toes, trying to draw Ewan closer. Only the memory that they were in public kept Ewan from lifting Allyson to wrap her legs around his waist. He pushed his sporran out of the way and gripped her backside, grinding his pelvis into hers. Her moan set off his need all over again. He pulled away long enough to glance around the garden until he spotted a corner where no one would see them unless they stood where Allyson and Ewan were now. Ewan grasped her hand as they trotted further into the shadows before he spun her around, pressing her back against the wall. His large hand pinned her wrists over her head as he devoured her neck before attacking her mouth. Allyson's surrender was complete and without resistance as she arched to press her body more fully against his.

"You taste delicious," Ewan murmured as he returned to her neck, laving the corded muscles before swirling his tongue in the dip between her collarbones. "I shall feast upon you one of these days."

Allyson suspected Ewan meant more than just kissing her neck. She'd heard that men and women used their mouths in other ways to pleasure one another, but she didn't entirely understand how. She realized she wanted Ewan to show her, to teach her how.

"Kiss me, please," she pleaded and sighed when Ewan offered what she craved. She widened her stance when Ewan pressed his thigh between hers. His hands on her bottom guided her as she rocked against the hard planes of his body. An intensity, an urgency, built within her core, creating an ache that was almost painful. It was as though she couldn't get close enough to Ewan, and with the clothes in the way, she knew she couldn't. She'd never once wanted to strip bare before a man or see him in the buff, but Ewan made her throw away all regard for decency and propriety. When air swirled around her ankles, then calves, she understood Ewan was lifting her skirts. She didn't stop him, too curious to learn what came next.

"I'm going to touch you, Ally. Touch you in a way no other mon ever will. I'm going to explore the treasure between your thighs until you can barely contain your need to scream my name. I will show you pleasure unlike any you've ever imagined, so you crave my touch over and over."

"I already do. Why can't I stop you? I know I should, but I don't want to." Allyson's breathy response spurred Ewan on as his hands traveled further up her legs. He fisted her skirts in one hand as the other caressed the bare skin of her backside. She was much slimmer than Ewan realized, and he had a momentary pang of fear that he might crush her when he finally made love to her. His large hand cupped most of her bottom as he dipped his finger into her sheath. He groaned when he discovered the dew already gathered between the folds. He was certain his cock would leak as his mind and body yearned for his sword to thrust into her sheath. His finger trailed back and forth until he pressed it into her, making her tense.

"Shh, Ally. I don't want you to fear me or this. I won't do aught to break your barrier. I'll leave you a maiden just as I found you." Allyson relaxed and dropped her forehead against his chest, allowing herself to enjoy the sensations Ewan's touch created. He continued to probe, adding a second finger, stretching her as her hips responded with a rhythm her mind didn't recognize but her body knew. When he withdrew his hand, she whimpered, but he soon had her moaning again when he brought it around to rest against her mound. He lifted one leg higher on his thigh, lifting her foot off the ground. She wobbled and grasped his leine to steady herself, but Ewan feared her knees might give out when he plunged his fingers back into her, his thumb seeking the pearl that emerged as she grew more aroused.

"Do you feel this, *mo aingeal?* This is how a mon brings a woman to climax, by rubbing this bud until she writhes and is flooded with pleasure. I would do this for you every day for the rest of our lives. Would you like that?"

"Can't you tell? Must I admit it?"

"Yes, Ally. I want to hear it. I want to hear my name from your lips as my fingers stroke you."

"I want you, Ewan. I want this. I would have this over and over." Allyson looked up at Ewan, but despite her words of yearning, he feared for a moment that she would push him away. Her expression was conflicted, and he realized that he was pushing her too far too fast. She might desire coupling with him, but she hadn't decided if she wanted to marry him. He was putting her in an untenable position that threatened to ruin the moment.

"Then enjoy this right now. Don't worry aboot what will happen next. *Mo aingeal,* I want to take care of you." Ewan said no more, but Allyson sensed that his offer extended beyond their current intimacy. She suspected he meant in a larger, more permanent sense, and she realized she didn't oppose the thought. She nodded before her mouth sought his. He continued to work her sensitive flesh, and he wanted to crow with pride as Allyson responded to his touch by exploring his body. She pulled his leine loose from his belt and trailed her hands over the scorching skin of his chest and back. Once she was certain she'd touched every inch, her fingers hooked into his belt and pulled him closer, and his responding growl made her sigh with satisfaction. Allyson intuited her body was creeping toward a precipice, and she was willing to tumble over the edge headfirst.

Ewan froze, his body taut and ready to react. His hands pulled away from Allyson with such suddenness that she tipped backward against the wall. She opened her eyes to discover Ewan pushing his leine into his belt with one hand while the other rested on the hilt of his sword. Her body pulsed with unspent lust as he placed a finger against his lips before he finished tucking his shirt back in. Allyson glanced down at her gown, straightening the bodice and brushing her hands down her skirts. She breathed a sigh of relief that she wore her hair down, so there was little chance anyone would think it more mussed than the slight breeze would do. She tried to peer around Ewan, but his warning was clear even without a word. Allyson shrank back and waited as Ewan turned, using his superior height to peer toward the gate. He darted a look over his shoulder at Allyson and shook his head. Whoever approached was not someone they wanted to discover them. Allyson held her breath, waiting to learn who entered the garden, so she might anticipate how great the fallout would be from someone catching her alone with Ewan.

Frustrated at the situation, Ewan forced himself to take several deep breaths as Angus approached. Ewan hadn't known the man well before arriving at Redheugh, but he'd spent more time with him in the lists than Ewan liked. He didn't care for the man's smugness or dirty fighting. He'd taken a smashing blow to his ribs the day before from a sword that wasn't nearly as dull as it should have been for training. The man often kicked dust at his opponents while they sparred. This might be an acceptable tactic during real combat, but it was unnecessary for training. Eoin had spent ten minutes that morning flushing his eyes with water to get the last grains of grit out. Ewan had been ready to smash Angus's face in the dirt.

Allyson wanted to sink into a hole when she recognized Angus. There was no chance this encounter would go unmentioned. He had always been a tattle-tail when he was a child, and he had changed little over the years. He took a perverse pleasure in being the barer of bad news. She squared her shoulders and notched up her chin, prepared to go into battle with her brother, but Ewan reached his hand behind him until he found hers. He squeezed her fingers in reassurance before releasing them, so Angus wouldn't see.

"What do we have here?" Angus's supercilious tone set Ewan on edge all over again.

"Allyson and I were walking in the garden but stopped when a pebble landed in her slipper," Ewan explained.

"In the furthest, darkest corner of the garden?" Angus leaned to catch sight of Allyson around Ewan's shoulder.

"Aye. I wanted to look at the primrose. It only grows in the shade, so it's back here in the corner. I like the color," Allyson reasoned, not looking away as Angus's face morphed into a mocking expression.

"You like the color," he mocked.

"That's what I said. I like purple."

Ewan considered what Allyson revealed and realized he'd often seen her in gowns of various shades of purple. She also threaded purple ribbons through her hair in the evenings at court. He tucked away that newfound piece of knowledge for another day. He turned his attention back to the siblings as Angus took a step forward. Ewan perceived the menace in his posture and shifted to block Allyson. He held up his hand, but Angus turned his look of disgust toward Ewan. This led to Ewan tightening his hand on the hilt of his sword. Allyson recognized the situation was spiraling out of hand.

"I think you enjoy being groped in dark corners. Is that what you learned at court?"

Allyson refused to allow her expression to show her shock and disdain. She kept it relaxed and neutral. "I don't like dark corners. I'd rather be with my friends and the music." She infused as much innocence into her voice as she could, fearing the tartness he tempted her to hurl at him would slip through. "I wanted to pick some primrose for my chamber, and Ewan was polite enough to accompany me and wait."

"That's not what it seems."

"And what does it seem?" Ewan interrupted. He placed one hand on his hip while the other appeared to rest lazily on his sword, but Allyson recognized Ewan was prepared to draw it with little warning. Allyson watched as the two men, both heirs to large and powerful clans, squared off. She realized it had little to do with her now as Angus sized up Ewan. Angus seized upon an opportunity he'd been hoping for, and it was becoming a pissing match between the two of them, but Allyson feared Ewan would break Angus in half. She'd seen her brother in the lists and heard tales from the raids he took part in, but he didn't appear to be an even match to Ewan's greater size and calmer demeanor. He looked like a lad who wanted attention from a man.

"It seems like you were pawing at my wee baby sister. It looks like you were compromising her honor, whatever might be left of it," Angus taunted.

"Now you're concerned? You didn't sound at all concerned when you learned of what befell her at Chillingham," Ewan narrowed his eyes as he spat each word.

"Befell her? She brought that upon herself. She got what she deserved for being so flighty and selfish."

Allyson curled her toes in her slippers and clenched her jaw to keep from crying. Angus spoke what she thought countless times since returning to Redheugh.

"No woman deserves what your sister survived," Ewan quiet tone belied the steel edge. "Why do you suddenly care what your sister does? What does it matter to you if we are in the garden?"

"Because you're not married, not even betrothed, yet. You'd have her trap you and force to the kirk steps?" Angus grinned, but there was no humor in the expression. Ewan saw the malice and took a step forward.

"It would be hard to force a mon my size to do aught I don't want to. When I stand on those steps with Allyson beside me, it's because I want to be there. As far as I'm concerned, that day won't come soon enough."

"You don't have to marry the chit to bed her," Angus offered in a conspiratorial tone as he stepped closer to Ewan.

"We're not speaking of your other sisters. We're speaking of Allyson."

"So, you're bedding Mary? Or is it Alice? Or is both of them? I hear you like to share your women with your brother. Do you like women to share you, too?"

Ewan lunged forward. Anger at what Angus insinuated about Allyson and how he touched on the truth led Ewan to draw his fist back, but a weight tugged on his arm. He looked down to see Allyson's frantic expression. Her hands had turned to ice, and he could feel the cold through his sleeve.

"Count yourself lucky Allyson is here, or you'd be flat on your arse right now. Speak of her like that again, and I will do more than punch you. Your sister won't save you again."

"Save me? Ha," Angus chortled. "You're just trying to make yourself feel better after I hit a little too close to the truth. Your past is no secret with me. Lady Bevan and I are well acquainted. Even your aunt is a close companion when I'm at court."

Ewan's lips curled in disgust. He didn't care for his aunt-by-marriage, but he knew she was no worse than him when it came to hopping from one bed to another at court. That Angus would mention his liaison with the very woman involved in the incident that sparked the contention between Allyson and him set his temper off. With Allyson's hands still on his arm, he used his other hand to grab a fistful of Angus's leine. He tugged hard enough for the other man to stumble. They came to stand nose-to-nose before Ewan leaned to the side and whispered, "Try this again in front of your sister, speak ill of her again, and it'll be Graeme who's named the next laird. Dead men don't lead clans." Ewan shoved him away, then wrapped his arm around Allyson and steered her past her brother, who seethed but said nothing more.

Neither Allyson nor Ewan spoke until they stood before the door of the tower. It was nearing the evening meal, and Allyson needed to change her gown if she wanted to avoid more comments from her mother about her appearance. Ewan would secure his sword in his chamber before entering the main keep and Great Hall.

"That didn't go well," Allyson muttered.

"It was going perfectly until Angus showed up," Ewan tried to lighten the tension that had grown between them. He coiled a lock of hair around his finger and tugged until Allyson giggled.

"That's not what I meant, and I'm certain you know that."

"I do, but he's ruined enough of our afternoon. I won't let it all go to pot."

Allyson's cheeks heated as she dipped her head

and closed her eyes but failed to keep the edges of her mouth from lifting. "It was a nice afternoon."

Ewan used his finger to nudge her chin up before he placed a gentle kiss on her sculpted cheekbone. "One of the best I've ever spent, but that seems to be the case any afternoon I spend with you."

"Thank you, Ewan. Thank you for defending me, for keeping me company—for everything," Allyson stumbled over her words at the end. She backed away, but cast one last smile over her shoulder as she walked toward the keep.

CHAPTER TWENTY-TWO

T hree nights after the encounter with Angus, Allyson slipped into the garden an hour after her family retired for the night. She wandered toward the spot where she and Ewan had kissed, but she was positive her heart stopped when she spied a couple. She couldn't believe her eyes as she watched Ewan locked in a passionate embrace with Mary. He had his hand somewhere beneath her skirts, and the bodice of her kirtle sagged about her shoulders. Allyson was certain she would be ill as her world crumbled around her all over again. She lifted her skirts and ran, ran directly into a broad chest that was so like Ewan's but couldn't be because he was kissing her sister. She pushed past him and ran toward the postern gate.

"Allyson? Allyson, wait! Allyson," Ewan called as he chased after her. He'd seen his brother and wanted to bash his head in. He also understood Allyson assumed Eoin was him and that it was Eoin chasing her. "Ally, stop! Ally!"

He was the only person to call her Ally, and that permeated her hazy mind as she rested her hands and forehead against the gate.

Ewan caught her and turned her, but she swatted

him away. He grasped her hand and brought her finger to his lip and ran it over the scar that sliced it. He was aware she used it to tell them apart, and he was certain she felt it when they kissed.

"It's me, Ewan, Ally," he whispered as she collapsed against him, heaving sobs shaking her slender frame. "I'm sure you assumed it was me, but it's Eoin."

He held her, but the longer she trembled, the more concerned he became. Ewan realized she had reached her breaking point, and his arse of a brother pushed her over it. He scooped her into his arms and carried her back to the garden. He would sort this mess out, possibly murder his brother and her sister, and then comfort her until she understood that he'd not hurt her for all the treasures in the world.

"No. Don't make me go back there. No, please. Ewan, no." Allyson whimpered in his arms as she attempted to burrow further into his chest.

"Wheest, *aingeal*." Angel. The idea made Allyson hiccup as she laughed. She remembered he'd called her his angel before.

"I'm hardly that. I'd think you'd rather call me *diabhal* or *deamhan*."

"You are neither the devil nor a demon, though I'd call my brother that. I'm ready to relegate him to hell."

"No. Leave it alone. I know it's not you. That's all that matters to me."

"It means a hell of a lot more to me. I'm not having your nasty sister spreading tales that it was me, and I know Eoin. He has a reason for this. I doubt I'll agree with it, but it exists."

Ewan lowered Allyson to her feet before storming over to his brother, who hovered over Mary's reclined body on a bench. He grabbed a handful of Eoin's leine and ripped him away. He plowed his fist into the underside of Eoin's chin, making his twin's head snap backwards.

"Cover yourself," Ewan hissed at Mary before turning back to Eoin. "Explain now. You knew I was meeting Ally here. Why?"

"Wait?" Mary bleated. "You're not Ewan? You're the other one?"

"Aye, lass. I'm 'the other one.' You were hoping to get swived by your own sister's betrothed. He may not be available, but there's no reason I shouldn't have some fun."

"I don't want you," Mary hissed.

"You couldn't tell the difference," Eoin shrugged.

"I can tell you're not the one who will inherit the lairdship. I'm the oldest. I should be marrying a laird or his heir, not my bastard sister."

Allyson staggered backwards as she listened to Mary. Allyson turned to escape, but Ewan held her against his side.

"Eoin, you still need to explain, and unless you want me to be an only child, you'll do it now."

"I wanted to discover why Allyson's family treats her as they do. Mary assumed I was you, and before I realized it, she was kissing me. I decided to test just how far she was willing to go, but I wouldn't have tupped her. I do intend to tell Laird and Lady Elliot though." Eoin cast a look of revulsion at Mary, who seethed as though she were the wounded party. Eoin turned toward Allyson. "I regret you saw that, my lady. That was not part of my plan. I found Mary out here, and she said she'd overheard Ewan saying he intended to meet you here. She wanted to find him first, hoping you'd catch her with Ewan. She assumed I was Ewan and wasted no time throwing herself at me. Now we understand your sister is so jealous, she'd sin to get what she wants. And we know that at least one of your siblings believes you don't share the same parents as her."

"But I still don't understand why anyone believes that." Allyson looked at Ewan, pleading for someone to make sense of the nightmare she couldn't wake from. "Mary, you're old enough to remember when I was born. You must have been here when Mother labored with me. I didn't just turn up. Are you saying Mother had an affair? That's not what was said the other night."

"I wasn't here. None of us were. We were at the Hermitage with Father. Mother didn't join us because she'd been ill. Just like Alice said the other night, we never saw Mother increasing. We returned to discover we had a new sister. One with blonde hair and blue eyes."

"All babies have blue eyes," Allyson reasoned.

"But not a one of us has blonde hair."

"You believe Mother has been lying all this time aboot me being her daughter?"

"Yes. I still believe Father sired you, and your whoring mother dumped you on us."

"Is that what everyone in this clan believes? Hasn't Mother denied it?"

"And admit her husband was unfaithful? Hardly. Besides, why bother when it's obvious."

"I want to go inside," Allyson murmured as she swayed on her feet. Ewan lifted her into his arms as he cast his brother a scathing glare.

"Lady Allyson, I truly am sorry. This was not how the scene played out in my head," Eoin stepped forward and bowed. When he stood, Allyson noticed the remorse, but she wasn't prepared to forgive him yet.

"It might not have been. But after she kissed you once, that should have been enough. You enjoyed yourself. I suspect you'd be swiving my sister if we hadn't found you. That would be a slight against your brother, and for that, I'm not sure I'm ready to forgive you. Ewan has been trying to make things right, and you nearly destroyed it all. He might accept your apology, but I need to decide if I will."

Ewan turned toward the keep and carried Allyson through the side door. He prepared to carry Allyson up the stairs to her chamber, but she stopped him.

"I can make it on my own. I'm well now, and no one can see you outside my door."

"We still haven't had the conversation I intended, and I believe we need to."

Allyson cast him a long stare before nodding her head. "Put me down, and I will take you somewhere no one will know to look."

CHAPTER TWENTY-THREE

Allyson turned away from Ewan but reached back to offer him her hand before leading them to the stairs. They climbed to the fourth floor, and Ewan assumed they headed to the wall walk. He doubted it was as private as Allyson claimed, not with a sentry posted every ten feet. Unlike Chillingham, Kenneth was determined that no side of his keep should be unguarded. It surprised him when Allyson opened a door, and he found himself in the attic. She led the way after he closed the door behind them. She skirted around barrels and old furniture covered in large linens. She guided Ewan to a space where there was a child's set of dolls and toy soldiers on a small table, a tapestry laid on the floor, and stacks of books strewn about. He had a sickening feeling Allyson would explain this was where she spent much of her spare time as a child. He picked up a piece of vellum that had a drawing of a castle with a city surrounding it, and he recognized it as Stirling. Outside the city gates was a couple mounted on a single horse. The woman had blonde hair and was smiling at the man seated behind her. The man's face wasn't visible, but the woman was Allyson. Ewan wondered if there was another man Allyson had wished to marry.

"He isn't real," Allyson murmured. "I mean, there isn't a real mon that I drew." She shrugged her shoulders as she lifted a shawl from the back of a chair. She wrapped it around her shoulders before moving aside to make room for Ewan on the tapestry she'd laid on the floor as a rug many years ago. She sat with her knees curled and her arms wrapped around them. Ewan thought she looked so small and defenseless, even her body language said she wanted to guard herself.

"But this is what you dreamed of? A mon who would take you away from Stirling, away from court? Maybe away from here?"

"That, or someone who makes these places bearable." Allyson refused to meet his eyes as his seemed to penetrate any defense she had left. She was too tired to hide any longer. Mary's words, ones she had heard whispered her entire life but were never said before someone outside her clan, cut her to the quick. Ewan put the drawing aside and eased onto the rug next to Allyson. He wrapped his arms around her and tucked her head under his chin as tears poured down her cheeks. "I don't want to cry every time you embrace me, but that seems to be all I can do this eve."

"You don't need to hide from me, Ally. Let me be the shoulder you lean on. I didn't understand any of this until recently. But I do now. I understand why you ran, or at least I think I do. You may have felt powerless like I did, but you were the one who truly was powerless. I'll be laird one day, and I'll govern my clan as I see fit, but no one other than the king will tell me how to lead my life. Everyone seems to be able to dictate how you lead yours. You felt trapped, and you feared not just that I might mistreat your body, but you had a real reason to worry I would mistreat your soul. Less than a moon ago, I was too selfish to understand or care how being a philandering husband would matter to a wife who would have a keep and children to fill her days. Or so I thought. I assumed I would marry, and expected the king or my father, or even I would arrange it, but I also assumed my bride would enter the marriage under the same circumstances and would view it as a business arrangement as much as I did. Perhaps another woman would. But I understand something now, two things really, that I didn't then. I know you'll never see a marriage that way, and I know I don't want to marry anyone but you."

"What're you saying? That after everything I put you through, you're willing to be shackled to me? That you'll take a shrew home to your people at Huntley?"

"We both said things that day we shouldn't. I know I did, and I've had time to realize how regrettable they were."

"You've had time to pity me," Allyson attempted to pull away, but Ewan lifted her into his lap. He left his hands resting lightly on her back and thigh, showing her that she could leave if she wanted. Instead, she leaned against him, and he tightened his hold.

"I don't pity you, Ally. I feel badly aboot how things began. I feel guilty for my role in this. But when I removed myself from this and tried to see things as you do, I'm amazed by your courage. You might be naïve at times, and perhaps need protecting from yourself, but you're nobody's fool. The qualities that led you to run are the ones that will make you a fine lady to a clan, my clan. You're resourceful, determined, brave, not easily cowed by anyone, and you can experience remorse when you choose poorly.

That's what I want and need in the woman who will lead alongside me."

"But you said you didn't need anyone to lead with you."

"I said no one would tell me how to lead my life. Your family won't convince me to set you aside. The king and our fathers won't be forcing me to marry you when that's what I want."

"But you barely know me. You witnessed the worst sides of me. I'm self-centered, impetuous, I disregard others' safety to put my whims ahead of others, and—and—I'm a flirt."

"And I still want you."

"You desire me. That's not the type of want that makes for a happy marriage. You want me now until you bed me, then you'll want something else. You've said as much."

"I won't deny I'm attracted to you. I have been since the first time I caught a glimpse of you. That's why I've danced with you every night I've been at court." Ewan closed his eyes and tilted back his head before meeting her gaze and confessing. "I'd intended to ask you to dance before I even went to Lady Bevan's chamber. I'd hoped to steal a kiss that night. It embarrassed me when you caught me, and I attempted to play it off. I wasn't better than a young lad. I'm certain Eoin felt the same and followed my lead. He appreciates Cairren's sense of humor and kindness when they partner, and I'm certain it didn't thrill him to have her catch us, too. I'm aware it makes me a cad, but all I can say is it was the way Eoin and I chose to pass the time. None of us looked at it as more than that."

"That still doesn't mean it isn't just desire making you willing to marry me."

"Will you deny you were attracted to me, too? Would you have rejected me if I tried to kiss you?"

Allyson offered him a rueful expression before shaking her head. "I admit I've always found you attractive, and no, I wouldn't have rejected you."

"Ally, do you feel that way aboot Eoin, too?" Ewan held his breath, praying she said she didn't.

"Mayhap then I did. I couldn't always tell you apart. I wasn't sure in the passageway that day, but I don't anymore. I can tell you apart now. And no, it isn't the scar that gives it away. It may have helped tonight in the dark, but I can tell the difference in how you stand, how you walk, but your expressions give it away the most. Eoin doesn't have the same brooding intensity you do."

"He has always been the more easygoing of the two of us."

"There's also the way you look at me."

"And how's that?" Ewan asked.

"Speculative at times, lustful at others."

"That sounds right. But don't forget admiration."

"I haven't displayed many admirable traits lately."

"But you have; I told you already." Ewan kissed Allyson's temple and tucked hair behind her ear before continuing. "I don't know that I could've managed a childhood such as yours. Our mother wasn't loving, and our father isn't the best example for a husband, but I had a happy upbringing. Eoin and I have always had each other, and that made up for most things. You've had no one, at least not until you arrived at court. It breaks my heart to watch a woman who's charming and engaging at court withdraw into a shell when she's at home. I—I —don't want this to be your home anymore. I want to take you away from here."

"You might return me to court. You don't have to marry me to do that."

"Ally, why're you fighting me on this? Do you believe I'll return to being a rogue? Do you believe I don't mean what I say?"

Allyson tucked her chin and looked at her lap, then nodded. "I fear you will spin this tale and convince me all will be well, then you'll abandon me to people I don't know. I'll have to make friends all over again and hope people will like me, though once this story makes its way to your clan, I don't see how that's possible. And I'll have to do it all on my own, just like when I arrived at court. Do you think I always want to be charming and engaging at court? Don't you realize it's fake most of the time? We're all fake. We're all pretending for the sake of appearances."

Ewan's heart broke as he listened to the pain that resonated in Allyson's voice. He held her closer as he stroked her hair.

"I'm tired, Ewan. I'm tired of pretending the rumors here don't hurt. I'm tired of being forced to smile and chatter and dance when much of the time I want to be left alone. There are only a few people at court, a few who visit, where what you see is genuine. Part of why I balked at marrying you is because you're one of those people who I was genuine with. It felt wasted, knowing you would disappoint me in the future. I'm not under any false impressions aboot your past, and it didn't matter when it had naught to do with my future. But who you are beyond being my dance partner scares me."

"*Aingeal,* I never want to scare you. That was never my intention, but I seem to have done it far too many times for you to trust me, and that's crushing."

"Why do you call me that? What's angelic besides my blonde hair and blue eyes?"

Ewan's face took on a sheepish expression as he glanced away. "I'm fairly certain you won't appreciate the truth."

"How bad could it be?" Allyson shifted with unease.

"You remind me of two of the archangels," Ewan chuckled at Allyson's expression. She didn't appear to appreciate the comparison. "I realize they're all male, but the Archangel Raphael is supposedly a healing force, and I'm certain God sent you to heal me of my selfishness and gluttony. The Archangel Uriel is God's messenger of destiny, and I think, be it God or King Robert, one of them decided you are my future."

Allyson sat in stunned silence. The depth of significance in Ewan's explanation shocked her. He surprised her by being so introspective after always coming across as carefree. She didn't sense he would lie about something so serious as God and faith, so she resolved that he was telling the truth. She raised her head and pressed a soft kiss against his mouth. His reaction was slow, as though he gave her a chance to pull away, but when she didn't, he deepened the kiss, pressing his open mouth to hers, inviting her in. She swept her tongue across his as she released the tension that kept distance between their bodies. She gave in to the kiss and gave in to him. When they finally broke apart, she ran her fingers over the stubble on his jaw, enjoying the bristles while he stroked the hair that hung down her back.

"Ally, I want to get to know more aboot you. I've seen the two extremes, but who are you really?"

"I don't even know. There's never been anyone but the extremes." She gestured to what lay around them. "I suppose this is me. This is who I am when I'm not trying to please my family, and this is who I am when I'm not trying to please the queen."

"I want to discover that with you. What's your saint's day? What's your favorite color? What's your favorite dance? There's naught I don't want to know aboot you." Ewan's earnestness made Allyson smile.

"My favorite color is violet, and my favorite dance is the Strathprey."

"You like the lively dances. I've witnessed as much. You always look to be enjoying yourself. But you still haven't told me your saint's day."

Allyson's smile dropped, and she turned her head away. "I don't have one. Or rather I share mine with Alice, but since my name isn't Alice, just a close version, they didn't include me in the celebration."

"What? I mean, I realize your name is similar to your sister's, but the saint's name was Aleydis. Alice and Allyson are our versions."

Allyson shrugged. It was impossible for her to change the past, no matter what she might want. "June fifteenth."

"That's your saint's day? We will be away from here, and I will be certain we celebrate."

"Ewan, that's three months from now. You'll be at Huntley, and I'll be—wherever."

"You're that opposed to marrying me?"

"No, but I'm being realistic."

"Would you allow me to court you? There's still more than a moon before the end of Lent. We can't marry until after Easter, so will you give me that time? If, at the end, you don't wish to marry me, then I will insist the king release you. If you need more time, then I will convince our fathers and the king. If you do want to marry me, then we'll go to Huntley and be wed there."

Allyson mulled over what Ewan said. She desperately wanted to believe him. If he forgave her what she'd done, it was a step in the right direction, but she was scared to trust him. She accepted she didn't want him to leave Redheugh as long as she had to remain, and she'd rather he court her away from Stirling Castle. With some hesitation, she nodded.

"I'd like us to court, Ewan. I can't make any promises yet, but I'm willing to discover if we suit. If you're willing to continue to get to know me after you've seen me at my worst, then I'm willing to continue to get to know you, too."

Ewan pressed a soft kiss to Allyson's lips. He wanted to lay her on the tapestry and make love to her, but it was hardly the right time to do that when she'd just consented to consider marrying him despite her fears that he only lusted after her. He accepted the short kiss as a pledge to at least try to move forward.

"Are you tired, *aingeal*? I'll escort you to your chamber."

"I'm tired, but I won't sleep. Not after earlier. You should find your bed and rest, but I'm going to stay and read."

"Alone? All night?" Ewan looked about the attic, and while Allyson had added a shawl over her kirtle, it was hardly warm enough to remain there without a blanket since there was no fireplace. "You'll freeze."

"I'll be all right. I've spent many nights up here, and I'm yet to turn into an icicle."

Ewan shook his head as he unpinned the extra length of plaid from his shoulder. "Choose the book, Ally and sit next to me." He maneuvered himself to lean against a wall, and when Allyson settled next to him, he wrapped her in the extra length, then wrapped his arm around her. She leaned against his chest and stifled a yawn. Perhaps she was more tired than she realized, but she was reluctant to give up the warmth and comfort Ewan offered. The sensations were unlike anything she'd experienced before. Neither of her parents offered her comfort, and the embraces she received at court were either perfunctory or from men attempting to kiss her. Ewan rested his head against the wall with his eyes closed.

"You don't have to sleep sitting here. Ewan, really I'm quite content to be on my own."

"Is that what you'd prefer?" He opened his eyes and peered down at her. She shook her head slowly, so he pulled her closer and dropped a kiss on her forehead. "Read, Ally."

Allyson settled once more and opened her favorite book. Ewan opened one eye a crack and glanced at what Allyson chose. It surprised him when she'd picked a book on Greek astronomers. He supposed he expected her to read something like *Tristan and Isolde*, or another tale of courtly love.

CHAPTER TWENTY-FOUR

E wan came awake to the feel of a woman curled beside him. He'd woken that way many times over the years, but he was often disoriented and had to jog his memory to recall where he was and who he was with. He was certain the instant his mind came back to the land of the living that he lay with Allyson pressed against him. Nothing had ever felt righter than the feel of her as she slumbered next to him. Sometime in the middle of the night, he must have moved them once they were both asleep. He didn't recall it happening, but his back was still against the wall except he was horizontal, and Allyson's behind was rubbing against his groin. His cock woke before he did, and his bollocks ached for him to be inside her. He trailed his hand over her ribs and hip to her backside and closed his eyes once more.

Allyson stirred when she felt a hand rest on her bottom. She froze as she tried to remember where she was and how someone much larger than her was asleep behind her. The memory of bringing Ewan to the attic and settling next to him to read flooded her mind. She kept her eyes closed as she absorbed the heat Ewan produced as she lay with his arm under her head and his body cocooned around hers. She couldn't remember ever feeling so protected and comfortable as she did in that moment. She chided herself for enjoying a man's body next to her when she wasn't married to him, but she wouldn't deny that she didn't want to move.

As long as I remain still, perhaps he won't notice that I'm awake, and we can stay like this forever.

Allyson relaxed against Ewan's body but was unprepared for the hand that rested on her backside to slide around her waist and pull her tighter. She gasped before rolling to face him.

"Good morn, Ally. Did you sleep well?" Ewan's voice was deeper and raspier than normal, telling Allyson he hadn't been awake long either. "I'm sure I've never slept better."

Allyson tried to draw away, but the effort was halfhearted. Ewan brushed away hair tangled around her neck and pressed a kiss to her cheek. She sucked in a shallow breath before nodding. Ewan's smile melted her heart. It wasn't the roguish one she'd seen so many times at court, nor was it the condescending one she'd received while they argued in the Privy Council chamber. This one was warm, as though it was just for her, but a thought invaded her mind and had her scrambling to back away. Her senses, including suspicions, returned now that she wasn't overwrought like the night before.

"What's the matter? I promise I haven't been untoward. I didn't even realize you'd fallen asleep until just a moment ago." Ewan raised the hand that had held Allyson against him to show he didn't intend to trap her.

"You needn't offer me that charming smile. Save it for your other women. I didn't mean to fall asleep." Allyson rolled away before sitting up.

"What charming smile?" Allyson's comments baffled Ewan.

"That one." She waved her hand toward his face. "I'm not your mistress, and you're not my lover. You don't need to do that."

"I never considered taking you as my mistress, but I wouldn't be opposed to being your lover. And your husband. But I don't know what smile you're talking aboot. Honest."

"Stay there. Don't move. Don't change your expression." Allyson scrambled to her feet and moved between several large pieces of furniture before struggling to carry one back to Ewan. She ripped off the sheet that covered the looking glass before pointing to his reflection. "That one. The one that's meant to make women take off their clothes."

Ewan sat up, allowing his plaid to show his bare knee as he bent it and rested his arm on it. "Is that what it does to you?"

"I said women, not me."

"You are a woman."

"Aye, that's why I understand your intentions."

Ewan stood and lifted the looking glass from Allyson's hands and set it aside. He wrapped an arm around her waist and pulled her against his chest. "Allyson, I don't look at myself that often, but I can tell you, this smile is not one I've offered any other woman. I've never woken up to a woman beside me who I just wanted to hold. I've never woken up and wished to fall asleep just to do it all over again, so I might enjoy that moment I realized you were beside me."

"Who did you assume was there?" Allyson pushed her arms between them and crossed them.

"I didn't think of anyone else. I knew it was you. I knew that it can only ever be you from now on."

"I don't believe you."

"And why should you? I wouldn't if I was you and knew my reputation. But I still want to prove to you I'm earnest aboot my intention to court you."

"You're going to have to figure out how to do that without trying to seduce me. You won't be sleeping near me again."

"Ally, I wasn't trying to seduce you." Ewan's hands cupped Allyson's elbows. "I enjoyed talking to you last night, and I've never slept as well as I did last night, despite being on the floor. It's because you were here. That's the only explanation."

Allyson dropped her arms and sighed. She wasn't in the mood to argue with Ewan, and she wouldn't lie to either of them about enjoying their time together. "I did sleep well, but I got jealous when I imagined every other woman who's been on the receiving end of that groggy voice and handsome smile."

"Handsome smile?" Ewan chuckled.

"You and modesty are not likely friends. Don't bother trying."

"Others may have called me that before, but I find it only matters coming from you."

"Aye, because there's no one else here to do it." Allyson's was a rueful frown, but she lifted onto her toes and pressed a kiss to his cheek. "I hope I'm the only one from now on calling you handsome when you awake."

"You can be sure of that." Ewan brushed his lips against Allyson's, and she opened to him. It was a slow kiss as they built trust and tenderness between them. Allyson arched her back, pressing her breasts against Ewan's broad chest as he cupped her backside. His sporran kept him from feeling the full length of her, so he pushed it aside. Allyson gasped when his sword rubbed against her sheath, but it soon turned into a moan as Ewan's grip on her bottom tightened.

She inched her hips closer until there was no space between them.

"I want to be the only woman," Allyson murmured.

"I promise you, Ally, you are."

Allyson wasn't inclined to question him about that pledge when she'd rather enjoy the last few minutes they would share alone before returning to her family and the real world. When their kisses ended, she rested her head against his chest, the rhythmic thud of his heart giving her strength to face another day at Redheugh.

"We have to go. If we stay much longer, people will notice we're both missing. They'll assume the worst of me."

"Aye, and I need to find Eoin. I still haven't forgiven him for his stunt last night."

"Let it go. I'm not angry anymore, and I realize he intended well. The fault lays primarily at Mary's feet, even if he didn't stop her."

"I need to learn whether Mary said aught else after we left and what Eoin intends to tell your father." Ewan glanced toward the stairs. Allyson sighed and shook a weary head, but she wasn't in the mood to argue with either twin about talking to her father. She could predict how it would go, and if Eoin wasn't careful, he'd end up married to Mary before Ewan could get Allyson down the aisle. "You go first, and I'll follow you down when I'm certain no one will realize I was up here with you. I'll meet you belowstairs. Would you like to go for a walk?"

"Aye, I'd like that. I'd like to show you the river if the weather is fair." Allyson turned toward the stairs but stopped. She spun around and went onto her toes to give Ewan a hard kiss, but when she went to pull away, Ewan backed her against the wall. Their kiss combusted into a roaring inferno as their hands sought every inch they could reach. Ewan cupped her breast, and Allyson's moan signaled she appreciated the sensation. She covered his hand with hers and increased the pressure as he kneaded the mound. His fingers trailed along the neckline before dipping beneath. His fingers brushed her pebbled nipple as Allyson's head fell back. Ewan nuzzled her neck with soft kisses and swept his tongue along her collarbone until Allyson's hands found the firm contours of his backside. The sensation of her hands on him unleashed a beast that wanted to consume her.

"What're you doing to me, Ally? Why can't I stop?" Ewan muttered as her hands gathered the length of plaid that hung to the back of his knees. Her cool, smooth hands against his skin made Ewan groan as he pinned her against the wall. "Tell me to stop. You're not my wife yet. I can't take you."

"You've never married before, and that hasn't stopped you in the past." Allyson panted as Ewan continued his onslaught at her neck and the exposed portion of her chest above her kirtle.

"You're not a woman to tup and walk away from, Ally. Once you're mine, I won't ever let go. I won't share you with another mon, and I won't allow another mon to take you from me."

"I never imagined you to be the possessive type, Ewan. Easy come, easy go."

"There is naught easy aboot how I feel. It's not easy for me to understand, and it's not easy for me to describe. But I can promise you that when, not if, you marry me, you will never doubt where I spend my nights because I will spend every one of them with you. Don't doubt where I spend my days because I won't be out of your reach."

Allyson tried to laugh, but the press of Ewan's lips against her pulse point made her breath catch.

"Will you quit going to the lists, or will you expect me to come with you?"

Ewan growled as his mouth sought hers once more. The kiss was equally passionate and possessive for them both. While they both wanted to dominate, both wanted to submit. It created an urgency neither could ignore.

"Tell them you overslept." Ewan grunted as he guided Allyson to the floor. He settled beside her, but she rolled onto her side to continue kissing him. He drew up her skirts before lifting her leg over his hip. His fingers found their way to the crevice of her bottom before sliding along the slick seam that begged for him to enter. He ran his fingertips over the plump nether lips until Allyson's hips rocked unbidden. He drew his hand away to her whimpers of complaint, only to return it once his hand slid between them. "Has any mon every touched you like this, Allyson?"

She struggled to understand what he asked through the fog of passion and need. "No. Only you."

"No mon has kissed your quim like I'm going to?"

"No. No mon has kissed any part of me like you have."

"Ally, are you saying that you've never tasted another mon's tongue in your mouth?"

"Never. You're the only one."

"I'm aware you've been kissed before." Ewan pulled back to look at Allyson's glazed eyes and flushed cheeks. He was convinced she was a virgin, but he hadn't considered she was without any experience.

"A few quick kisses, but my mouth was always closed." Allyson blinked her eyes several times and looked up at Ewan. "Are you disappointed that I don't know what I'm doing? I can learn whatever you want to teach me."

"Don't say things like that." Ewan's voice came out strangled as his fingers sunk into her sheath. "You are an innocent; otherwise, you'd be aware of how seductive those words are. Do you feel what my fingers are doing to you? I want my cock to do that, and soon my tongue will."

"You can't be serious, Ewan. Your tongue?"

"Aye, and I will ensure you like it so much you expect me to do it to you morn, noon, and eve."

Allyson gave in to temptation. She'd spent her life doing what everyone expected of her, but ever since that afternoon at Stirling Castle, she'd claimed control over her life. She wanted to discover the passion Ewan offered, and she understood she only wanted to explore it with Ewan. Even the thought of Eoin, the mirror image of the man who held her, did nothing for her. It was Ewan. It was his scent, his taste, his everything that drew Allyson in, and she refused to deny herself. She reasoned that no one else would offer her the opportunity to feel wanted and cherished, so she would grasp what Ewan offered with two hands. Two hands that currently grasped his chest muscles.

"Do you trust me, Ally? I won't take your maidenhead, but I'll bring you release. Do you understand what I mean?" Ewan's voice was patient as he waited for Allyson to decide.

"I do. I haven't—but I understand what you're talking aboot. I've heard of it." Allyson took a deep breath. "I trust you, Ewan. Only you." Allyson gazed into Ewan's emerald orbs as though she might drown in their depths.

"I won't do aught to destroy that trust. I know I'm still earning it, and I know it's not unbreakable."

"Shh." She pressed her finger to his lips. "Show me."

Ewan pressed a hot kiss to her lips before inching his way down her chest as he pushed her skirts to her waist. He alternated blowing warm and cool air over her tender flesh, the swollen lips of her sheath ached as his attention became riveted on them. Ewan watched Allyson's eyes drift closed and her face relax before his thumbs spread her open, and he feasted his eyes on a part of Allyson he'd never imagined he might see, let alone taste. His thumb rubbed her bud until it emerged from its surrounding petals, then he drew the flat of his tongue along her seam, in no hurry. When she twitched and tried to shy away, Ewan feathered kisses along the inside of her thighs until she settled. He looked up to find her watching him. He smiled, and she laid back, trusting him once more. Ewan settled his attention on Allyson and worked her flesh with his tongue and his fingers until she writhed underneath him.

Allyson feared her body would shatter into thousands of tiny pieces, never to be put back together again. It felt as though she were breaking apart, and Ewan was the only way to be made whole again. Tension built low in her belly as she squirmed, unsure if she wanted to pull away or get closer. The sensations of Ewan's ministrations would surely send her up in flames, but she refused to miss a moment by keeping her eyes shut. She opened them and leaned forward to watch, noting that he appeared to delight in his task. Their eyes caught as Ewan thrust two fingers inside her as his tongue flicked her nub. The pressure became too much to bear; a tightening in her core unfurled into pleasure pulsating throughout her body and into her limbs, her toes curling within her slippers.

"Was that—" Allyson fought to catch her breath. "What was that?"

"That was your release. It's what I hoped to offer you, and it was a sight that was more beautiful than aught else I have ever seen." Ewan shifted to lie beside her as he pushed her skirts down. Allyson's spent body didn't resist Ewan tucking her smaller frame into the warmth and comfort of his larger one. He brushed hair from her temples and neck, proffering a kiss on her nose and forehead as she drifted off to sleep. Ewan realized, catching sight of the dark shadows under Allyson's eyes, that she had slept far less than he had that night. Awake, he enjoyed the experience of lying beside a woman without having sought his own satisfaction. He couldn't remember the last time he pleasured a woman solely for her enjoyment. It was always a prelude to his own or in reciprocation. He'd slept beside more women than he wanted to remember, but he'd never watched a woman sleep. Allyson's breathing slowed, and her face relaxed as she settled into a more comfortable position. With the most tender care, he caressed her head and shoulder, admiring the freckles he was certain no one noticed unless they were this close. The irrational possessiveness returned, and he wanted to be the only man ever close enough to notice.

Nae even a moon ago, I couldnae have cared less whether Allyson or any woman had freckles. I was angry that she should order ma wings clipped, but now imaging another mon courting Ally, wooing her, touching her, marrying her, makes me want to scream like a caged beast. She objected to the notion of an unfaithful husband, and that was with nay real sentiment toward me. It was the principle, if nae the practice, that mattered to her. I would have demanded fidelity from her too, but nae for the same reason. I didna want to fear a bastard inheriting ma father's legacy, and I didna want to share what I believed should belong to me. That was selfishness that drove me.

Honor and integrity drove Allyson. I should have seen that sooner. Maybe I would have kept ma gob shut. Ma feelings are growing, and I pray hers are, too, because I dinna think I can return to the way things were before Chillingham, before last night.

CHAPTER TWENTY-FIVE

Allyson woke once more with a furnace at her back. She didn't want to move lest the comfort disappear and reality return with its normal vengeance. She absorbed the rhythmic breathing that came from the man holding her, knowing he was awake. A moment of self-consciousness surged forth when she imagined Ewan watching her sleep. Did she snore? Did she twitch while she slept? God forbid something worse.

"You are an angel at rest when you sleep. I was right to call you *'mo aingeal'*." As though Ewan read her mind, he reassured her silent worries. "I fear that your family will question where we are. It must be early afternoon. We're fortunate that it's Lent, and there is no morning or midday meal."

"As you said, I'll tell them I overslept. After spending the first two days here sleeping, hopefully it won't be a stretch that I slept another day away. But I must hurry to my chamber to change, or I will have a hard time explaining. No one knows I come up here, and I'd like it to remain that way."

"Afraid your siblings will ruin your sanctuary?" Ewan grinned, but it fell with Allyson's succinct response.

"Yes."

"I won't share your secret, Ally."

Allyson nodded before climbing to her feet, just as she had several hours ago. This time she was determined to leave, but she turned to face Ewan.

"Do you still want to go for that walk, or will you go to the lists?"

"The walk. The lists will be there for another day. I think I can survive missing a day here and there." Ewan flexed his chest as he crossed his arms and flexed those.

"You don't need to convince me of how braw you are. I already know." Allyson failed to keep the grin from her face as her eyes swept over Ewan's towering frame. She recalled having it pressed against her, and heat crept its way from her sheath to rest in her belly. Ewan kissed her forehead and spun her around with his hands on her shoulders. He gave her a gentle push before tapping her backside.

"You'd best leave now, or you won't leave at all, and I will have to summon a priest here. Then there'll be no secrets left."

Allyson smiled and took the stairs down before Ewan heard the soft click of the door. He moved to return the looking glass to where he'd seen Allyson find it. As he adjusted it against a stack of paintings, the drop cloth of one shifted. A hint of blond hair showed in the still-covered image, and Ewan wondered if her parents had commissioned a painting of Allyson when she was younger. He moved the looking glass aside once more and uncovered the painting. He stood aghast as he took in the image before him. The resemblance was immediate as Ewan looked at a couple standing side-by-side with their hands clasped on their wedding day. Beside the couple were two older couples. It was obvious they were the bride's and groom's parents. What struck

Ewan the most was the bride's mother had blond hair, and Allyson was the spitting image of the groom's mother. It was impossible to doubt that Allyson belonged to the laird's family just as much as her siblings. She might not have shared the same features as her brothers and sisters, who looked more like Lady Margaret than Laird Kenneth, but it was clear she was as much the couple's child as any of the others.

If anything, she was the only one who proved her parentage. She looked like both of her grandmothers, while the rest of the brood only bore a resemblance to their mother and grandfather. They looked little like the laird's side of the family. Just enough for no one to have questioned them in the past.

Ewan pulled covers off half a dozen other paintings that depicted both sides of Allyson's family. Each one bore testimony to how much Allyson shared features from both her mother's and father's relatives. While Ewan realized there was a possibility that the laird and lady might not have been familiar with the older images from Kenneth's lineage, someone brought the paintings of Margaret's family. There was no explanation for how they arrived at Redheugh without the lady knowing and ordering them stored here. At the very least, the laird and lady were aware of the painting from their wedding day. They were aware proof existed to put the rumors aside, and yet, they'd kept them hidden amongst pieces of old furniture and tapestries. Ewan felt his temper rising to a point that threatened to boil over. The only thing to temper the urge to smash everything before him was the need to vindicate Allyson by placing the proof under her family's nose. He put the covers back in place over the evidence, then hefted three paintings, carrying them to his chamber. He chose two small images and the large wedding painting. He would save these until he could ensure the entire clan witnessed the laird and lady explain their atrocious behavior, when there was no doubt they had the power to allay suspicion years ago.

———————

Allyson slipped into the kitchens and gathered a basket full of smoked fish, two loaves of bread, fresh tarts, and apples, along with two jugs of ale. She found leftover neeps and tatties, which she disliked, but she'd seen Ewan eat two servings of the night before. With no meal to break their fast or a nooning, Allyson assumed Ewan would be hungry, but she was uncertain how much food he would need to compensate for the fasting. He'd been content with the small portions while they traveled, but so had everyone else that day. Since arriving at Redheugh, she'd noticed he and Eoin had healthy appetites, which came as no surprise given their size. Her father's warriors were large men whose size often intimidated her, but they looked barely out of boyhood compared to the two Highlanders, and yet neither Ewan nor Eoin ever intimidated her. She felt comfortable around Eoin, but Ewan made her feel safe and protected for the first time in her life. She'd never doubted her father would protect her if the need arose, but it felt as though he begrudged her the duty.

She entered the Great Hall and scanned the people milling about, but Ewan wasn't present. She recognized Eoin speaking to her brothers, but her mother and sisters ignored everyone else as they sat before the fire sewing. Allyson accepted they wouldn't invite her to join them, so she didn't worry that they'd call her away from her walk with Ewan. She spied Mary casting surreptitious looks at her and at Eoin, but she turned her back on Mary when her older sister smirked. Allyson held a sneaking suspicion that Mary assumed no one would go to their father to report the incident from the night before. She watched Eoin, but he appeared to take no notice of Mary despite her constant glances in his direction. They were part wary and part hungry. It was clear to Allyson that Mary lusted after Eoin as much as she did Ewan; she was interested in the latter for his position, but would accept the former for pure sport.

"Are you ready, lass?" Ewan's voice startled Allyson, and she squeaked. Her face flamed red to have Ewan hear her making such a high-pitched sound, but his warm smile had her grinning in return. "I didn't mean to spook you, *aingeal*."

Ewan lifted the basket from Allyson's arms and playfully hefted it several times before offering his arm to her. They left the keep and strolled through the bailey, where Allyson pointed out various people who smiled and waved. It reassured Ewan to see Allyson received a warm welcome from most of her clan, despite her familial relationships. Ewan had seen many of the people at work when he'd ventured out to the lists, but no one had introduced him. They paused to greet the blacksmith and farrier, who spoke of their interest in the Gordon horses. Ewan was proud of their mounts and might have spoken about their lineage and strengths for ages, but he was mindful of Allyson standing next to him. She remained patient and hospitable as one person after another drew them into conversation, and it was close to an hour later before they passed through the postern gate. Allyson led them down the path to the river that flowed near the keep. Ewan's eyes darted across the landscape as they moved further from the keep and the protection of the guardsmen. Allyson seemed oblivious to her surroundings until she spoke up as Ewan glanced once again over his shoulder.

"The guards on the southern portion of the battlements will see us until we pass under that oak," Allyson explained as she pointed to a gnarled oak tree. "Once we arrive at the river, my father has guards posted every two leagues to ensure no one sails up to attack. Both of my grandfathers fought in the Battle of Largs, and the stories impacted my father. He refuses to allow anyone to use the waterway to gain the upper hand. You'll see them once we're on the other side of the tree."

As they passed under the boughs of the massive tree, Allyson pointed to dots in the distance that Ewan realized were men on patrol. He would have noticed them, but not as quickly as Allyson did. He supposed she was familiar with where to look, but it impressed him that she was more aware than he realized. They found a spot along the riverbank. Allyson lifted the plaid she'd brought with her from the top of the basket, and Ewan helped her spread it out. Then they sat and unpacked the food. Ewan's eyebrows shot up when he realized how much food she'd packed. He hadn't considered how much food must have been under the plaid, despite the basket's weight.

"I wasn't sure how hungry you would be since we can't eat in the morning. I wanted to be sure I had too much rather than too little. I'm afraid the options are a bit limited with no meat or eggs or cheese."

"This is wonderful, and you're very thoughtful." Ewan lifted a cheesecloth and grinned as he discovered the neeps and tatties. "I love these."

"I noticed you preferred them last eve, so I brought them with us."

"You noticed?"

"You did take two servings, and each one was three times more than anyone else. Everyone other than Eoin, I should say." Allyson elbowed Ewan in the ribs as he raised the dish to his nose. Even cold, he loved the mashed dish of potatoes and turnips. He broke off a hunk of bread and used it to scoop a large bite, but smiled ruefully around the mouthful of food as Allyson watched. He hurried to chew and spluttered until Allyson clapped him on the back and handed him a jug of ale.

"I suppose I should have offered you some first."

"No. I don't care for them, so you don't need to race to get your share. You can have them all. They're for you."

Ewan rested the crockery in his lap and leaned over to kiss Allyson's cheek. He brushed the back of his fingers along her jaw. "That was very thoughtful. I don't remember the last time someone considered my favorite foods and made sure I had them. Thank you, Ally."

Allyson nodded, then looked away, embarrassed by Ewan's penetrating stare. She felt as though he was looking inside her mind, even inside her soul. She bit into an apple and licked the corner of her mouth as juice dribbled toward her chin. She glanced over and caught the look of hunger in Ewan's eyes and understood it had nothing to do with the food before them. Her cheeks heated even more before he swiped the pad of his thumb over her chin. She was certain she would go up in flames when he pressed the tip of his thumb between her lips. Her tongue flicked out and licked the trace of juice from the digit. Ewan was on her in a moment, and Allyson responded in equal measure.

They forgot the meal as Ewan eased her back onto the blanket and followed her, covering half her body with his. Their lips fused together as Ewan cupped her jaw, and Allyson tangled her fingers in his hair. Ewan's other hand trailed down her neck until his fingertips grazed the bare skin of her chest.

Allyson's heart sped as the sensation shot a shiver along her spine, and she pulled Ewan closer. She was aware the men on patrol would see them, but she didn't care. She had no reputation to protect. She remembered from the last time she visited her clan that her sisters spread a rumor about what must go on at court and how her innocence was in question. Half the people who lived in and around Redheugh doubted her virginity, so she felt unconcerned about trying to convince them otherwise. She wanted to enjoy these moments with Ewan.

Ewan was lost to the pleasure of Allyson's mouth as his tongue dove into the silken depths, but he stopped himself before his hand roamed to her breast. He still recalled they were in public and that anyone might stumble upon them. It was that memory that brought Ewan to a stop. He eased away as he kissed her jaw, then temple, and finally the tip of her nose before sitting up. He sat up and assisted Allyson, but he couldn't take his eyes off her disheveled hair and rosy cheeks. They ate in companionable silence, but once they cleared away the empty containers, Allyson laid back down and stared up at the clouds.

"When I was a young girl, I would lie out here and watch the clouds float by. I would pick out shapes and tell myself stories based upon what I spotted. I would be out here for hours."

"Did your guards enjoy your stories, or did you keep them to yourself?"

"Guards? I didn't bring any."

"You came out here alone? How old were you?"

Allyson shrugged as she continued to stare up at the sky. "I don't know. I suppose I started coming out here when I was six or seven, and continued until just before I left for court."

Ewan clenched his jaw to keep from speaking. It

stunned him to learn that Laird and Lady Elliot allowed Allyson to roam unsupervised beyond the walls. He wouldn't allow any child or beautiful young woman outside the gates of the Gordon keep without someone to defend them, let alone the laird's daughter. Regardless of what anyone thought or said about Allyson's parentage, the laird and lady claimed her as their own. That made her a target.

"Ally, that's not all right. As the laird's daughter, you would be the perfect hostage held for ransom, and as a beautiful young woman, it terrifies me to imagine what some nefarious mon might do to you. Promise me, Ally, if we wed that you'll always take at least one guard with you any time you leave the walls. I will never stop you from going where and when you want, but I can't stomach you being unprotected. Especially not after what happened at Chillingham. Please." Ewan was practically begging by the end of his entreaty, and Allyson saw how seriously Ewan viewed the situation. She nodded and reached forward to brush hair over his shoulder before leaning in and kissing his cheek.

"I wanted to escape the keep and all who were there, so when no one ever stopped me, I came down here. I was aware I was within sight of the guards, but I also understood that wouldn't matter. No one would reach me if someone came on horseback or by boat."

"It seems like there has been a lot in this life you wish you could escape," Ewan mused in a hushed tone. "You'd rather risk the unknown than continue with what you grew up with."

"Aye." Allyson laid back down, finding it easier to admit her feelings when she didn't have to look directly at Ewan. "As much as the cutting remarks still hurt, being ignored as a child was far worse. When I was alone out here, it didn't feel like I was being over-looked. It felt like freedom. It felt like my choice."

"That's why you ran. When the king, our fathers, and I threatened the little freedom and choice you found at court with people who paid attention, you ran."

"Among other things, yes. It felt like I was being suffocated as I stood in the Privy Council listening to everyone deciding for me again." Allyson glanced at Ewan before continuing. "If we're being honest, I don't think I would have reacted as I did if it was someone else."

"Oh?" Ewan couldn't think of anything else to say, or at least not anything polite.

Allyson rolled onto her side, bending her elbow and resting her head on her hand. "You're a handsome mon and will always be a handsome mon. Women will always flock to you, and as you said at court, you didn't plan to turn them away. I was certain of it before you even spoke the words. Those two things together crushed me. I couldn't face being forgotten and rejected again and again. If the king and my father presented a mon who wanted to be faithful, I wouldn't have run. Even a mon who might ignore me but not stray would have been satisfactory. But to live my life being pushed aside for someone else, over and over? Well, I could just stay here for that."

Ewan reclined and pulled Allyson flush to his body before feathering a kiss on her lips. "I understand now that I've seen you here. You're a different person, and I detest it. The Allyson I know is full of vim and vigor. You laugh and enjoy life at court, or at least look like you do. Here you retreat. It's disconcerting, to say the least. I want to see you jesting and teasing like I'm used to. And I want it to be for real. I understand much of it is for show at court, but you seem lighter and less troubled when you're there."

"I suppose it's true. For all the machinations and deceptions that go on at court, for all the times I had to force a smile, I was able to be myself. But even then, pretending to want to be around people constantly was exhausting. I just want somewhere where I can be myself and not have to perform."

"I want to offer that to you."

"Why? I still don't understand what made you change so drastically, so suddenly. It doesn't make sense, Ewan. It makes it hard to trust you." Allyson ducked her head and blinked several times to keep the tears at bay.

"I prayed. I talked to God and—" Ewan paused as Allyson glanced around frantically to ensure no one heard Ewan. He realized she feared someone would pronounce him a heretic for claiming to speak with God. "I mean I didn't speak with a priest to make my confession, but I prayed for forgiveness after considering my many transgressions. Ally, I've always considered myself a mon of honor and duty, but there would be no honor in being unfaithful after pledging myself before God, you, and witnesses then turning around and throwing it all to the wind. If I'm to lead my clan one day, I must do it by example. And that's the one way in which my father failed."

"Your father? Was he not faithful to your mother?"

"Hardly. My mother was not a warm woman, and she detested being a wife and found no enjoyment in being a mother."

"Were your parents not attentive to you and Eoin?"

Ewan shook his head slowly. He wished he could empathize with Allyson, but he'd had a happy childhood. Despite his parents' faults and the damage they each did to their marriage, they hadn't neglected their sons. "They were. My mother wanted to be a nun, but her father refused to consider it and arranged a marriage to my father. She didn't want him or any mon in her bed, so when she delivered twin lads, she fulfilled her duty. She refused to allow my father near her and encouraged him in word and deed to take mistresses. I can see now how he erred. He put his own pleasures ahead of honor. While my mother lived, he never should have bedded another woman." Ewan took Allyson's hand in his and entwined their fingers. "I don't know that we'll get along once we wed. I don't know if any lasting affection will grow, but if you should decide you no longer want to share a bed with me, I will not take another woman to mine. Pleasures of the flesh shouldn't come before a vow to God or to my wife. I don't know that my clan thinks any less of my father for his choices. In fact, I'm certain many sympathize and even support it, but the past fortnight has given me reason to question that. I don't want my people to accept me as a hypocrite. It's also taken this unexpected turn to make me realize not all wives will be like my mother."

"You assumed your wife would be like your mother?" Allyson wrinkled her nose, but Ewan saw the twinkle in her eye and realized she was trying to lighten the solemn mood that overtook him.

"When Eoin and I were aboot five or six, Mother grew cold and no longer treated us with affection. I think she believed we outgrew the need for it. But despite that, she was attentive. She argued Father should spare the expense and allow her to tutor us. She'd benefited from an education provided by the nuns at the abbey near her clan's home, so she was knowledgeable enough to teach us our numbers and to read and write in Gaelic, English, French, and

Latin. She drilled everything into us, and Eoin and I are better for it. She loved to be outdoors and took us on long walks where she taught us aboot all sorts of flora and fauna. She might not have been warm with other people, but she had a way with animals. Woodland creatures chattered aboot her feet and followed her. She taught us to respect nature and God's creatures, but she warned us never to touch them. She'd learned that they carried diseases and were unlikely to be as trusting of us as we might be of them."

Ewan paused as he stared into the distance where the river babbled. A smile twitched at the corner of his mouth, and Allyson knew he was reminiscing. He turned back to her before continuing his story.

"When we grew old enough to join Father in the lists, she assumed she'd finished her duties as a mother, so she focused all of her attention on prayer and running the keep. By that time, she'd engrained her faith into me and Eoin, and I still find solace in going to church and praying. But she'd ended any relationship she had with Father. They were barely civil to one another, and Father did naught to disguise his relationships with other women."

"And up until a couple of sennights ago, you didn't see any issues with your father's choices. He's a strong laird and respected mon. I suppose I can understand how you'd grow up assuming that an arranged marriage didn't have to keep you from enjoying your life, that it was a business agreement more than aught else."

"But I should have also seen how miserable it made both of them. And I shouldn't have assumed all noble wives would be like Mother."

"And I realize that not all men are like your father or mine."

"You think your father—?"

"I believe so. I'm not certain, but I've suspected it

over the years. You've heard my sisters. It seems like everyone knows. My parents were close when my brothers and sisters were young, but they had some falling out. They barely spoke to one another and still talk as little as possible. They only spend time together at meals where they're cordial but not as loving as I heard they once were."

"When's your birthday? Not your saint's day, but when were you born?" Ewan had a sneaking suspicion that he understood why Allyson's parents were cold to her, and rage boiled within. It was the only explanation fathomable for why a couple that had once been happy and welcomed their children went so long without another and held no affection for their youngest.

"Autumn. Why?"

"Were you conceived around Hogmanay?" Allyson's cheeks turned flaming red, but she nodded. "Ally, do you think your parents, or perhaps your father, imbibed too much, and nine moons later you were born?"

"You think I resulted from a drunken night together? That mayhap my father forced my mother?" It was as though all the blood leached from her body and left her freezing. She shivered as her world tilted on its axis, but as confusing as the notion was, it suddenly made sense of her life. Her mother resented the memory, and her father regretted it. Allyson looked up at Ewan as tears tumbled down her cheeks. "I think you're right. I never once considered that."

"It would explain a great deal, don't you think?"

"Aye. It does." Even if they'd discovered the reason for Allyson's treatment, it did little to ease the years of pain and neglect. It only served to make her feel worse. She really was unwanted.

"They shouldn't have taken that out on you.

Those were their choices, not a bairn's or a wean's. You had no more say in which family you were born into than anyone else."

A thought crossed Allyson's mind that made her stomach turn over, but she had to know. "Do you have any unwanted children?"

Ewan shook his head. "No. I've always been careful. Besides the fact that our father would geld me and Eoin if we ever were so careless, no child should ever be unwanted and bear the stigma of bastardry. That should be the burden of the parents, but it's always passed onto the child." Ewan's vehemence made Allyson wonder if someone important in his life suffered that fate. Another fear crossed Allyson's mind that she couldn't resist asking about.

"Is there a woman you wished to marry, a woman you love, who is unsuitable because of that?"

"No. Why would you ask that? I've never been in love, and I certainly never considered marriage."

"You just seem so adamant that I figured someone close to you might bear that stigma."

"Aye. My cousin. My mother's sister made an error in judgment when she was young and anticipated her wedding. When she discovered she was with child, her intended groom called it off, arguing if she was willing to bed him before marriage, he'd never be certain she wasn't with other men too. He claimed it would be impossible to be certain the bairn was his. My cousin came out looking just like her father, but he still wouldn't marry my aunt. I fear my cousin will never be able to marry because of that. She's a sweet lass, but her parents' sordid history precedes her."

"That's wretched. With the rumors that swirled around here for years, I feared I would never marry. I'm the fourth daughter. The chances of me marrying outside the clan weren't that strong to begin with, so finding a mon here who would want me seemed unlikely. Serving as a lady-in-waiting seemed like my only opportunity since the talk of my past never reached there."

"Do you think that's why your parents sent you to court?"

"Yes. Without a doubt. I expected my father to arrive any day to say he'd arranged a marriage, so he might foist me onto someone else. Or my parents would have allowed me to languish at court until the end of days."

"Then it shouldn't have come as a surprise when they summoned you to inform you of our marriage."

"It wasn't marriage that put me off. It was the groom." Allyson saw no point in sugarcoating the truth they both knew.

"And now?" Ewan held his breath.

"Now the groom seems a far sight better than he did at court. Maybe it's the fresh air." Allyson pulled a handful of grass and tossed it at Ewan. He rolled onto Allyson and took her mouth in a searing kiss she returned wholeheartedly. She opened to him, and his tongue slid into the warm cavern, a groan escaping Ewan when Allyson drew his tongue in further. Ewan's hand slipped beneath her back and traveled to her backside, tilting her hips toward him. Allyson twisted to press her body against the full length of Ewan's and moaned as he squeezed the globe within his hand. Her hand slid into the open neckline of his leine, her fingers scorched by the heat his smooth, muscular chest exuded. Her other hand roamed over the lean figure, discovering every taut muscle as they bunched with his movement.

"I won't allow what happened to my aunt to happen to you, Ally. I intend to marry you and refuse to accept anyone who would stand in the way, but I won't take what isn't mine to have. Without pledging to marry you during the betrothal ceremony, I won't do more than I did this morning. It might kill me, but I'll gladly wait if it means you'll share my bed until we depart this life."

"You make my whole body ache for something it hasn't experienced but somehow knows. I want more of this morning, and I want to learn to reciprocate. I realized that it's you I want. It wasn't just the pleasure, because the thought of being with someone else doesn't appeal to me. It's because it was you. I don't understand why, but something changed in me when you rescued me from Chillingham. The fact that you chased me scared me at first, but that you were the one to storm into that chamber, that you fought your way to me, it made me realize that you are a good mon. A mon I didn't give a fair chance is what I'm learning every time we talk." Allyson stroked Ewan's cheek as they gazed at one another for a long moment. Something passed between them, and Allyson discovered that not only did she want to trust Ewan, she did. "I trust you, Ewan. Please don't ever break that. I'm not sure how I would survive."

"Ally, you are too special to ever hurt intentionally. I pledge here and now, no matter what happens, you will always have my protection. If not in name, then always in deed. I never want to destroy that trust, and I want you to know you can depend on me no matter what our futures hold."

"You swear to be *mo ghaisgeach*." My hero. Ewan's chest swelled with pride as he brushed his lips against hers.

"Always. I'd hoped to speak to your father aboot the betrothal documents. We left them behind at court, so I wanted to find out if he would send a messenger to retrieve them." Ewan wasn't telling a complete falsehood. He'd been thinking about them since the night before and had become more determined while they laid near the river.

"Will the king allow that? Won't your father have to be here to sign as well?"

"Nay. Ally, your father or I should have told you that the contracts were signed in the Privy Council chamber after you left. You can sign them, but it's not required."

Allyson sat silently for a long moment while she digested the news that the documents had already been signed. She'd suspected as much before she left Stirling, but she'd ignored it as she took time to get to know Ewan.

"Ally, are you angry that it's taken me so long to tell you?"

"No one told me, but I assumed as much. I'm not pleased that you didn't speak up aboot it, but I had opportunities to ask and chose not to." Allyson looked over at Ewan, whose worried expression made her realize that he hadn't withheld the truth to manipulate her. "Would you allow me time to read it before I sign? I would be familiar with what provisions Father made for me should I end up a young widow. I don't believe what happened to Mary would happen to me with your clan, but I need to be certain." Allyson left unsaid that she needed to be reassured of where she would live, since she doubted the Elliots would welcome her back and she wouldn't return to court. She needed to be certain she would have a roof over her head for herself and any daughters she might bear.

"I will ensure you have the opportunity, but lass, I already made certain my clan provides for you no matter what happens once we wed. Whether or not you bear a son, you will have a home with the Gordons."

"You can't be sure of that. If something happened to Eoin too, and we don't have a son, then there would be no reason to keep me."

"Keep you? You're not a dog or a horse. You'll be a member of the clan as soon as the priest pronounces us married. That won't end with my death, Ally."

Allyson nodded, but she was far from convinced. Even if her sister hadn't had a disastrous experience, she was aware of what happened to unwanted widows. Even in the best of circumstances, clans rarely welcomed them home with open arms. The alliance would end, and an extra mouth to feed would return to the table. She prayed a convent wasn't in her future. She would take a croft on a plot of land before making a life at an abbey, but she suspected that the latter would be her father's solution.

"I can't picture my father will be patient enough to wait for me to read it." Allyson worried her lower lip, and Ewan exercised all his restraint not to touch her mouth and free her lip. He wanted to continue their conversation, and if he touched her, the temptation to kiss her would be too much.

"Technically, we aren't required to have your signature to complete the agreement. However, our fathers' and my signature made it binding, which means you're as good as my wife even before the betrothal ceremony. Your guardianship passed to me, which means I can insist we give you as much time as you want to read them. I'm afraid seeing the documents beforehand wouldn't make any difference if there's something you disagree with."

"I know. I just wish to prepare."

"I'd ask you to handfast with me now if I thought it would offer you more protection, if it meant we could begin our lives together sooner." Ewan's brow furrowed as he realized he was saying he would marry Allyson that very moment if he could.

"It's Lent. Whether either of us wants to hand-fast doesn't matter. Any agreement you and I come to could be overturned while it's made during the holy season.

Ewan considered the situation before nodding his head. He believed he had a resolution. "I will send the message with one of my men and direct my father to send them to me rather than your father. Once I'm in possession of them, we can read them together. If there is a term you want changed, I can propose an amendment."

"If you suggest aught, my father'll realize it's because of me. He might refuse it and refuse you."

"He won't. I, at least, know the bride price my clan will pay is a hundred head of sheep. I'm aware the English killed most of your flock during a raid last summer. Your clan needs the livestock too much for your father to turn me away." Allyson swallowed the lump in her throat as she closed her eyes to keep the tears from falling. She nodded but wouldn't look at Ewan. "Ally?"

"I'm worth a flock of sheep." Allyson's voice trembled as she forced out the words. Ewan pulled Allyson into his arms and tucked her head against his chest. He held her as though he had the power to shield her from the rest of the world.

"*Mo aingeal*, you are worth a great deal more than sheep. I would pay all the gold in the world to make you my bride."

"It still means I'm being sold."

"It seems that way, and I suppose you're right. But I'd rather see it as securing the privilege of being your husband."

Allyson offered a watery smile. "Thank you for trying to make me feel better. I appreciate it."

They broke apart and spent the rest of the afternoon gazing at the clouds, pointing to what they saw and making up silly stories just as Allyson had done as a child. This time she wasn't alone.

———

Despite passing a glorious afternoon with Allyson beside the river, he still needed to address what happened in the garden the previous night. He wasn't able to confront his brother until after the evening meal when they returned to their chamber.

"What were ye thinking allowing that wench to kiss ye?" Ewan demanded, his burr taking over his speech. "Didna ye think aboot Ally finding ye? Or any other bluidy person? What if someone discovered ye and didna wait to investigate if it was ye or me? They could have me betrothed to that bitch right now. What then? Would ye marry Ally? Is that what ye were hoping?"

"Nay. I dinna want to marry Allyson." Eoin abandoned the pretense of a Lowland accent too.

"Why nae? What's wrong with her?"

"Bluidy bleeding hell, Ewan. Ye ken I dinna think aught is wrong with her. I was the one trying to get ye to see that."

"But ye said ye'd marry her."

"Only if ye left her with nay choices. It was the honorable thing to do. But ye stepped up, and if I didna ken better, I might think ye're soft on her."

Ewan shrugged, then nodded. He never lied to his brother, and he wasn't about to begin. "Ye ken I wasna here last eve. I didna do aught that would dishonor either of us, well naught that took her innocence. We had time to talk a tad, but when I woke this morn, it was the first time I ever awoke to a woman next to me and kenned exactly where I was and who I was with. It felt right." He shrugged again before running his hand through his hair. "We spent all afternoon together, and we talked aboot a great deal of things. We continued telling each other more aboot our childhoods and our interests. We watched the clouds pass by and jested as we pointed out shapes, then told tales aboot what we saw. It was the best afternoon I've spent since we were weans. Every time I have the chance to learn more aboot her, I like what I discover."

"And ye want me to believe ye arenae keen on her?" Eoin smirked.

"Aye, I suppose I am." Ewan stopped himself before he shrugged once more. He ambled to the window and looked out what was little more than an arrow slit and stared at the stars and moon, wondering if Allyson might do the same thing. She'd admitted she enjoyed looking for the patterns and figures the ancient Greeks described just as much as she enjoyed looking at cloud shapes.

CHAPTER TWENTY-SIX

A week later, a thunderstorm swept across the Lowlands and dumped rain for three days. The deluge was so persistent that none of the men trained in the lists, and it forced Allyson to remain within the bailey walls. On the last day of the storm, she attempted to visit the older members of her clan to ensure they were warm and dry, but took a nasty tumble down the keep steps when she slipped. Ewan was on his way to the keep to look for Allyson, intending to keep her company in the laird's solar while they read. A commotion caught his attention, and despite being unable to see Allyson, his stomach dropped. He was certain something happened to her. He pushed through the milling crowd until he discovered Allyson lying in a puddle of mud at the bottom of the steps, a nasty graze on her cheek. He growled as people stood about watching, but few offered to help her up. Elbowing his way to the front, Ewan didn't hesitate to lift Allyson into his arms, but instead of making his way to the Great Hall, he turned toward the tower and his chamber. Eoin met them at the door of the chamber and stood in shocked silence as a soaking and bedraggled Allyson shivered against Ewan's chest.

"Go to the keep and find a maid who will give you dry clothes for Ally. Bring them here and leave them outside the door," Ewan spoke in hushed tones. "Then make yourself scarce."

"You can't be in here alone with her, Ewan. Her father will murder you when he learns of this."

"She needs to be warm and dry, and that's not happening with you in here to watch."

"You need a chaperone."

"Because another mon would make it better. Please, Eoin, go." Eoin relented when he heard the plea in his older brother's voice.

Ewan was in a constant state of worry and unease these days as Allyson retreated further into her shell while trapped in the keep. They spent hours together in the Great Hall while they read and played games, and Ewan sneaked up to the attic every night to sleep alongside Allyson. Both were stiff from spending so many nights sleeping on the floor, but the time alone allowed them to explore their growing passion and to take comfort in one another's embrace.

Ewan lowered Allyson to the floor and peeled off her sodden arisaid. Mud coated the Elliot plaid, tempting Ewan to toss the filthy piece of wool in the fire. There was little more that would make him happier than to never see Allyson in anything that bore the Elliot pattern. As her teeth chattered, and she shivered, he unlaced her kirtle but turned his back when he finished. He listened to Allyson struggle with the material that clung to her like a second skin. He smiled as she huffed and puffed, but when she whimpered out of frustration and fatigue, he spun around to help. Ewan's mouth went dry at the sight of the sagging neckline which displayed a creamy expanse of skin while the material plastered across Allyson's breasts revealed puckered nipples that pointed at him. Her tangled skirts were pasted to her hips and legs, making it difficult for her to move.

"I can't get the damn thing off me," Allyson puffed in frustration.

Ewan noticed the defeat in her voice and expression. He stepped closer, and when Allyson didn't rebuff him, he helped ease the bodice down her arms, pushing it to her waist. Her soaked chemise hid nothing. Once more, Ewan's mouth was still dry as a desert, but he hungered for a taste of what remained covered. Allyson pushed the gown to the floor, and Ewan took her hand to steady her as she stepped out of it. Decency never seemed so overrated as when he turned away a second time, crossing the chamber to retrieve a Gordon plaid. When he returned to Allyson's side, she'd kicked off her boots and rolled down her stockings. Her white toes peeked out from beneath the hem as Ewan unfolded the plaid. He wrapped it around Allyson's shoulders, and once she held it closed, she shuffled some more as she untied the ribbons to her chemise, and it fell to the floor beside her kirtle. Ewan reached for her, but a knock at the door stopped him. He glanced down at Allyson before opening the door a crack.

Eoin stood on the other side with five servants who bore a tub and steaming buckets of water. Eoin cocked an eyebrow and shrugged. Ewan understood his brother was being thoughtful, but there was no way for them to enter without seeing Allyson. Even if she were clothed, it was the knowledge that servants would see her in their chamber that had kept Ewan from suggesting the bath. Ewan waved Allyson to stand behind him, and she scurried to move into the corner behind Ewan and the door. Once he opened it to the team of servants, Ewan blocked Allyson from their view, and Eoin moved to stand beside him, effectively creating a wall between Allyson and those who would see her in a state of *déshabillé*. Eoin kept his eyes averted and left with the servants.

Allyson watched the steam rise from the freshly poured bath and waited with impatience as the servants finished preparing her bath. A woman arrived as the men finished and laid a fresh set of clothes on one of the beds. While Allyson was certain no one saw past Ewan and Eoin, it was obvious they hid a woman, and the clothes confirmed it. She wondered which Elliot sister the servants would name. If she hadn't already decided to marry Ewan, word of her being undressed in his chamber would have made the choice for her. She prayed one of her sisters didn't claim to be the one here. Once Ewan and Allyson were alone, Ewan moved aside to make room for Allyson to walk to the tub. He glanced at her before stepping toward the open door.

"Don't go."

Ewan spun around and gawked at Allyson for a long moment before slamming the door shut and turning the key in the lock. He came to stand beside Allyson but didn't touch her.

"Ally?"

Allyson feared she couldn't go through with allowing Ewan to see her undressed. The feel of his hands as he helped her remove her kirtle and the needy look in his eyes had sparked heat within Allyson's belly, but now that they stood alone, modesty and desire battled. She forced her fingers to relax their grip on the plaid as she peered down at the Gordon plaid that covered her from shoulder to toes. She'd seen it draped over her before, but it seemed different this time. It was the only thing she wore, and it covered all of her.

"I like wearing your plaid." She couldn't think of anything else to say, and it embarrassed her to sound so lame to her own ears. But the fierce pride that shone from Ewan's face made her realize she'd said the right thing.

"I want to see you in it every day, Ally. I don't want you to wear any other."

"I'm not a Gordon yet."

"You are to me. You're wearing my plaid, Ally. You're in my chamber. You've consented to marry me. As far as I'm concerned, we are betrothed. The documents are signed even if we haven't had the formal ceremony. You're entitled to wear it, and I'd like little more than for you to do that."

Allyson studied Ewan and realized he didn't exaggerate his thoughts. He was welcoming her into his family and his clan, and she realized there was little more that she wanted than to become Ewan's wife. She loosened her grip until the plaid fell around her shoulders. Ewan lifted the hair free trapped beneath the plaid and spread it across her shoulders.

"I don't need any more time to decide whether I'll marry you, Ew. My father won't have to force me to the kirk the day after Easter. I may be the one dragging you there. I—I wish I could marry you today."

"Ally," Ewan's voice broke as emotions swirled through him like a Highland thunderstorm. She'd never used a diminutive of his name before, and despite the other terms of affection they now shared, the shortening of his name felt intensely intimate. "Don't make your decision based on physical desire." Ewan thought the words might kill him, but he recognized it was the right thing to say. She was still less experienced than he, and he understood that desire often led to regretful decision making.

"This isn't just aboot desire. I lay in a heap of sopping wet skirts with people watching but no one offering me help. You were by my side in an instant and never hesitated. You brought me here, not intending to seduce me, but so you might tend to me. I know it was Eoin's idea for the bath, but I also understand you didn't suggest it because you were protecting me. I know you have my best interests at heart, and I know I can depend on you. You've proven over and over that you're a good mon, Ew. No one has ever tried to take care of me before, and I've never considered letting anyone, but damn it, I want you to. But only because I've realized I want to take care of you, too. I want to be the one you can turn to just as I now turn to you. I want to be the one you depend upon, your shelter from the storm. I want to be by your side."

Ewan's heart swelled as he gazed into her cornflower blue eyes, detecting no falsehood or exaggeration. Rather, there was a solemnity that made Ewan confident there was a future between them that might include love and devotion. Allyson stood rooted in place as Ewan assessed her, and she prayed he'd find what he searched for. When his arms eased around her, and instead of kissing her, his forehead rested against her shoulder, she knew they'd reached a point where their intimacy went beyond just the physical. She wrapped her arms around Ewan and rested her cheek against his chest. They embraced until Ewan pulled back and checked over his shoulder to see if steam still rose from the water.

"You'd better take your bath. You're cold, and the water soon will be, too." Ewan stepped away, prepared to stand by the arrow slit, but Allyson dropped the plaid. Ewan gawked as his hands fisted and unfisted at his side, temptation ripping him apart inside. Before he had an opportunity to speak, Allyson took his hand and led him to the tub. She stepped in and lowered herself until she could draw her knees in to her chest. The invitation was clear as she left as much room as she could. "*Mo aingeal,* if I climb into that bath with you, you will not leave an innocent."

"No, I won't, but I will leave as your wife."

Ewan clenched his eyes shut and shook his head with such regret Allyson feared he might cry. "You said yourself that the church might overturn a handfast during Lent. I will marry you, and there is naught anyone can do to stop me, but I won't destroy your reputation in the process. You will enter our marriage just as everyone intended."

"And if I don't want to wait? If I want to make this choice myself?"

"Ally, I'm not trying to take it away from you. I'm scared."

"Scared? Of what? That I might bite?"

Ewan's nose flared, and Allyson realized her comment was more potent than she realized. She patted the water in front of her, but Ewan shook his head again.

"Allyson, the greatest revelation to come out of this, besides your affection, is rediscovering my honor. You made me confront my self-centeredness and how it affects others, particularly you. I can't go back on it. I can't fail you."

"Your honor is becoming overrated. I doubt you gave your coupling this much consideration in the past," Allyson grumbled.

"Because that was fucking, and I want to make love to you." Ewan's frustration got the better of him, and the moment the vulgar word left his mouth, shame filled him. Allyson was a lady, not a tavern wench. Ewan turned his head away, too ashamed to look at Allyson. He'd been trying to be a gentleman and instead sounded little better than a dockhand.

"Do you believe I've never heard that word before?"

"Mayhap you have, but not directed at you."

Allyson's laughter filled the chamber, and Ewan glared at her. "What do you think men at court offered? Some might have attempted to seduce me with flowery words, but most were forthright in what they wanted. That word is rather versatile. It encompasses a great deal."

"Allyson, it doesn't mean I should use it around you. So much for honorable behavior."

Once more Allyson laughed. "Are you worried you'll corrupt me? Teach me naughty habits? I'm two-and-twenty. You're not suddenly going to lead me astray. I survived hearing it before, and I haven't dissolved into tears because of it." Allyson reached for the soap and lathered it between her hands, then began to wash her hair but paused. "I'd hoped you'd help me with this."

Ewan pulled the lone stool in the chamber to the side of the tub and ran his hands through her hair, taking over the task of washing the long blond locks.

"Allyson, you are a test of my patience and willpower." Ewan dropped a kiss where Allyson's shoulder met her neck. "You made me want to become a better mon, one I can respect. Even if you're the one to try to knock me off the straight and narrow path, I want to show you I can withstand temptation. I want you to respect me for that too."

"I suppose I'd be rather horrid if I kept pushing you. But to be clear, I respect you and trust you, Ewan. I've seen the changes in you. You were prepared to fight my brother to defend my honor. A lesser man would have skirted the issue. A lesser man wouldn't have accepted sleeping alongside me on the cold floor night after night without coupling when you have a bed," Allyson waved toward his cot. "Or found enjoyment in another woman's arms. But you didn't. You're the one who wants to wait, and I don't think you're urging us to wait because you're easing your need elsewhere. I think you're sacrificing for me."

"Ally, there is no enjoyment to be found in another woman's arms. And it's not a sacrifice to wait if it means I'll be your husband."

"Ew, you are a test of my patience and willpower." Allyson turned his words around on him as she leaned her head back into his hands as he continued to scrub her hair. Her eyes drifted closed as she marveled at his gentle touch. He cradled her scalp as he poured fresh water over her hair, then lathered soap on a linen square. He ran the cloth over her neck and shoulders before sweeping it up and down each arm. When he moved to Allyson's breasts, he abandoned the cloth and lathered the soap onto his hands before kneading the mounds. It was the first time he held them unencumbered by clothing. They were small but high, making it easy to reach as Allyson's head rested back on his chest. He circled her nipples with his thumbs until they tightened into pebbles he rolled between his fingers, tugging and lengthening before repeating his movements.

Allyson's moan had his bollocks aching for release. His cock throbbed as he drove himself toward madness, touching and feasting his eyes on a body he longed to join his with. Allyson shifted restlessly in the water, sloshing it against the sides. She reached back and pulled his head close enough to press her mouth to his, her tongue demanding entry into his mouth. Ewan shifted around the side of the tub, making it easier for Allyson to deepen the kiss. One hand cupped her head while the other wandered between her breasts, down her belly, until it reached the thatch of hair that covered her mound. Allyson let her knees drop wide, pushing her hips up to meet Ewan's questing fingers. When he slid a digit into her entrance, she drew his tongue into her mouth, mimicking an action she'd heard of at court. Each time they'd been alone, Ewan had been attentive to her needs and pleasure, and Allyson not only felt guilty but grew impatient to lavish the same attention on Ewan.

"Ew, I want to touch you and taste you," Allyson panted. "I need to know what you feel like in my hand, against me. Please." She wasn't above begging.

"Let me tend to you first then you may do as you like to me." When Ewan caught the mischievous gleam in Allyson's eyes, he added a caveat. "Except taking me into you."

"That assumes I'm only thinking of your cock in my quim. I'm aware I can take you into my mouth," Allyson purred. Ewan jerked back and nearly fell over, he was so stunned by her comment. "I heard Lady Bevan, Lady MacAdams, and your aunt talking aboot it one day. I was on a walk with the queen and the other ladies, but I stopped because my hem snagged a nettle. While I attempted to untangle it without touching the itchy plant, I heard the three of them speaking on the other side of a hedge. I admit I listened. I'd never imagined such a thing, and I couldn't help my curiosity. Until now, I never thought I'd want to do something that seemed so—so—indelicate, but—" Allyson trailed off as her eyes lowered to where Ewan's sporran hid his painful arousal. "I want you to teach me. If it's aught as good as what you've done with your mouth, I desperately want to give you that pleasure."

Allyson didn't wait for Ewan's response. She stood and wrapped a drying linen around her before grabbing one to wrap around her hair. Ewan's hands went around her waist as he lifted her out of the tub. He pulled the linen from her body and hurriedly ran it over her, rubbing her skin until it was a rosy red. As Allyson toweled her hair, Ewan rushed to stoke the fire, adding a cheery heat to the usually draughty chamber. She stood aside as he pulled the bed before the fire. Leaving the linens on the stool, Allyson floated across the chamber until she stood beside Ewan and the bed. She dropped to her knees and unlaced the boots that encased his calves. He toed them off before she rolled down his stocking, marveling at the feel of the muscles in his calves as she ran her hands over them. When she reached for the hem of his plaid, he scooped her up and laid her on the bed.

She had no time to object before Ewan settled between her legs, his thumbs separating her nether lips. His tongue delved into her like a thirsty man searching for succor. Allyson could do little more than grip the bedsheets as her hips undulated to the rhythm Ewan created as he sucked on her bud. Need drove them both. Allyson recognized the muscles in her core drawing tight as the wave of release built, then crashed over her. Need drove Ewan to push Allyson over the edge as he continued his onslaught, never taking his eyes off Allyson as he watched her expressions shift with each sensation he built within her.

Ewan was unprepared for how quickly Allyson would pounce once he raised his body over hers. She wrapped her arms and legs around him and twisted, throwing all of her weight onto him. She lay stretched on top of him, and his hands flew to her backside, cupping and squeezing the bare flesh. She shifted to straddle him as she unbuckled his belt, pulling it from under him.

"Take off," she demanded as she flung the belt and sporran to the floor. She slowed her movements when she unfastened the broach that held the long swatch of plaid to Ewan's leine. He sat up as she pushed and tugged until he was free of the shirt, and her hands caressed his suntanned skin. "Do you train often without your leine?"

"Aye. While I believe it's important to train with it on, despite how tight and cumbersome it can become when it's plastered to me with sweat, at times, it is too annoying to ignore."

Allyson ran her hands through the golden curls that covered the deep valley between his chest muscles. She'd seen men training shirtless both at Redheugh and Stirling, but no man had resembled Ewan. His broad shoulders nearly stretched the width of the bed. The chiseled muscles of his abdomen flexed and rippled with each breath, and she'd nearly drooled when they bunched together as he pulled his leine over his head. An idea flashed into her mind. She leaned forward and ran the flat of her tongue over his nipple, eliciting a laugh that morphed into a deep groan when she bit it. She was careful not to make it painful, but Ewan's reaction was immediate. He rolled them until Allyson lay beneath him, his strength proving that he'd allowed her to position them with her on top. Her fingers traced the dips and sinews of his shoulders as they strained while Ewan held his body away from Allyson's.

"I believe I like this view the best," Allyson murmured.

"View?"

"Aye, the way you look right now. The way the muscles in your shoulders move fascinates me. There is such power there that it's impressive, and yet, I never fear you'd use that strength against me. I can see the muscles in your chest straining as your arms and shoulders bear your weight, and your stomach makes me want to trail my fingers over every groove." Allyson did just that before moving down to grip his backside, discovering notches in his hips where her hands fit perfectly. "Besides, I like being able to reach."

When Allyson raised her chin for a kiss, Ewan gladly accepted the invitation. He eased his weight onto one forearm while his free hand brushed the backs of his fingers over her breasts before gliding his fingers over her ribs to her hips, then slipping beneath her to grasp her bottom. He pressed his arousal against her, and their sounds of need echoed in the chamber. Ewan rocked his hips as Allyson squeezed her thighs against them, using her heels to give her leverage to meet each thrust.

Their movements were slow as their eyes locked, their intense gazes conveying more than words would. Allyson was certain his rod lengthened and thickened as they continued to press his sword and her sheath together. Ewan reached back for one of her hands, drawing it under his plaid until he guided her fingers around his cock. When Allyson attempted to pull his plaid free, Ewan grasped her wrist.

"If we're both naked, there is little chance either of us will stop before I'm buried to the hilt inside you."

"I still don't think that's such a bad thing, but you've said no. I won't take advantage of you." Allyson winked but released her hold on his plaid, preferring to rest her hand on his shoulder. "Teach me."

Ewan rolled onto his side, and Allyson followed. "Cup my rod as you are and stroke up and down without letting go." Ewan's head fell back as he clenched his jaw. The need to thrust and spill swept over him with a speed that hadn't happened since he first began palming himself as an adolescent. He drew deep breaths in through his nose as his body calmed after the initial drive to climax subsided. Allyson experimented with speed and tightness, watching Ewan's reaction and noticing what made his cock harden and twitch. It wasn't long before she was confident in her newfound skill. Ewan's insistent kisses and massages of her breasts also confirmed that he enjoyed her touch. When she noticed the tip of his rod grow slick, she spread the liquid over the taut skin but released him. His groan sounded more like agony than enjoyment, but he growled as he watched her lick her thumb. He rolled them once again, shifting to the center of the bed. It was Allyson's turn to shimmy down Ewan's body until she kneeled between his legs.

"I want my turn," was all Allyson said before she flipped his plaid back and swiped her tongue from the base of his rod to the top, swirling it around the tip then lapping up more of the viscous cream that appeared. Allyson held her hair back before lowering her mouth and taking as much in as she dared. She'd watched Ewan's expression when she ran her tongue over him, but now her eyes drifted closed as she reveled in the sensation, both new and exciting. Ewan couldn't take his eyes off the sight of Allyson sucking his cock with such abandonment that he believed she enjoyed what she was doing. He'd experienced this pleasure countless times before, but he knew some women viewed it as a burden and did it for their livelihood. Others enjoyed it, but that came from a satisfaction of knowing it brought a man to his knees. Allyson's interest was genuine and unassuming. Watching her explore his body and how it reacted to her touch made it a new experience, one unlike anything that existed before Allyson.

"Ally, I canna last much longer," Ewan whispered as he attempted to pull away, but Allyson swatted at his hands. When she looked up, her expression was one of determination and warning. She returned her focus to Ewan's rod as she noticed it tighten before a tangy fluid filled her mouth. She didn't care for the taste, but she rejoiced in a rush of success, knowing she caused his release. She kneeled upright, licking her lips as she watched Ewan's heaving chest, noticing the sweat that had broken out on his brow. "Praise the saints and all angels, that was divine. If I didna ken, I'd think ye'd done that before. I—I—St. Columba's bones, I canna think straight."

Allyson grinned as Ewan's labored breathing continued, and he mumbled to himself in Gaelic and forgot about his burr. When he held his arms out to her, she flipped his plaid down and nestled against his side.

"You really enjoyed it that much?"

"I've surely died and gone to heaven."

"You are such a Highlander. You exaggerate."

"I may be a Highlander, lass, but I dinna lie aboot this. I didna ken aught could feel so good. I may expire once I'm inside ye. I can only imagine how exquisite that will feel if this was any hint." Ewan's fingertips drew lazy circles on Allyson's shoulder before his hand skimmed over her back. The sensation made her shiver but was soothing at the same time. Ewan peered down at Allyson, who watched the flames flicker and dance. He wanted nothing more after such intimacy than to cover them with a blanket and fall into a deep sleep with Allyson pressed against him, but he recognized they'd sequestered themselves away too long. The sun had shifted and inched toward the western horizon, and Ewan suspected Eoin had taken up residence at the base of the tower to ensure no one would intrude upon his time with Allyson. It explained why no one knocked to clear away the bath. He refused to take Allyson's maidenhood to protect her reputation, but he would irreparably destroy it if anyone learned of what they'd done that afternoon, and Ewan feared that being out of sight for so long would lead Alice or Mary to claim he'd been tucked away in a love nest with one of them. "Ally, I dinna want to move, but we must. If we stay much longer, people will ken what we've been up to. Everyone in the bailey saw me carry ye in here, and nay one has seen hide nor hair of us since. Even if we didna go all the way, people will say we did."

"That ship has sailed and sunk. There's no chance that people aren't already talking aboot you bringing me in here. There's naught in this tower but empty chambers. Servants carried a bath and steaming buckets in here. No one needed to guess who they were for. Even if Eoin pretended to be both of you, no one has seen me for hours, and no one will have seen the two of you together. That's un-usual in of itself. They will assume the worst. We may as well have coupled."

"That may be what everyone assumes, but we ken we didna. If yer mother insists Berta examine ye again, there'll be nay denying the truth."

"I'd rather not. When Berta examines me, it's in-trusive and humiliating. It couldn't be further from what it feels like when you make my toes curl and my eyes roll back."

"I make yer toes curl, lass?"

"And my eyes roll back," Allyson grinned. She stretched to drop a kiss on his nose before moving to the other bed where the servant left her fresh clothes. He hurried to put his leine back on and secure his plaid with his belt and sporran. She halted when she looked at the clothes for the first time. "These are Mary's."

Allyson looked back at Ewan. Anger, distrust, frustration, and sadness warred within her. He came to stand behind her and placed his hands on her shoulders. Tension that hadn't existed minutes ago radiated from her. Ewan recognized her suspicion, and while it hurt that her trust wavered so easily, it hurt him more that anyone in Allyson's clan assumed he'd chosen one of her sisters and assumed he'd brought either Alice or Mary to his chamber. She picked up the kirtle and ran her thumb over the embroidery before dropping it on the bed. Her shoulders sagged as she leaned back against Ewan's chest. While he was relieved her suspicion was fleeting, it still hurt him to see her so resigned to being marginalized.

"They assumed you chose Mary. I know this speaks more to her unchasteness than your trustworthiness, but it hurts so much. Despite a crowd of people watching you carry me in here, people still believe you're tupping Mary. None can fathom that you would pick me."

"Ally, I canna standby and keep watching this. Beside the fact that I want naught to do with ma name linked to hers or Alice's, I abhor how everyone treats ye. I think this is just as bad, if nae worse, than tossing insults in yer face. It's more underhanded, but that makes it even more insidious. I ken ye prefer to ignore it and nae give it any attention, but I willna stand for it. I willna turn a blind eye and remain silent any longer. Ye're to be ma wife, and I willna accept anyone hurting ye any longer. What kind of mon allows the vulnerable to be abused? Nae the kind who deserves to be yer husband."

Allyson turned in Ewan's embrace and wrapped her arms around his middle, the sound of his heartbeat both soothing and bolstering. She absorbed the strength and steadfastness that seemed to radiate from Ewan's body. When she was sure she was strong enough to stand on her own, she nodded.

"It's time my family realizes I'm not a kitten to keep kicking. I may not hiss and spit, but I have claws. They're all in for a surprise when I arrive at the evening meal on your arm and in Mary's clothes."

"That's ma lass." Ewan helped Allyson into the kirtle, tying the laces behind her while she folded his plaid into an arisaid she pulled around her. She glanced at the pile of soiled clothes and the sopping wet Elliot plaid. She grimaced, knowing she had to take them to her chamber before joining the evening meal.

"I'll meet you by the Great Hall, but I must take these to my chamber first." Ewan was hesitant to agree to Allyson going anywhere on her own where she might encounter her family, but he wouldn't dictate her coming and going. "I'll be all right, *mo leannan*. It'll take me but a few minutes."

She slipped around him and scooped up the wad of wet clothes and moved to the door. She squared her shoulders and straightened her spine. She shot Ewan a smile before leaving the chamber.

CHAPTER TWENTY-SEVEN

Ewan froze when the door opened, but he sensed immediately that it was Eoin. He supposed it was twin intuition.

"She wore a bonnie smile when she reached the bottom of the stairs," Eoin grinned, not bothering to hide his burr while speaking to his brother. "And if that wasna enough to make people look sideways, she's wearing yer plaid. I dinna think it's possible for ye to make a louder announcement than that."

"Aye, we can. The maid brought Mary's clothes instead of Ally's. She's wearing them to the evening meal."

"Ye canna be serious." Eoin's expression was aghast as he stared at this brother. "Nay one's ceased clishmaclavering aboot how chivalrous ye were to help Allyson, but they're also wondering what ye've been on aboot up here. How could any of them believe Mary is here instead?"

"Because they think the worst of me and dinna place any value on Ally."

"I canna say that I'm surprised that they sent Mary's clothes," Eoin agreed. "After the way she threw herself at me in the garden, assuming I was you. She would have had me toss her skirts right there and then. I was just lucky you and Allyson found us rather than someone else.

Ewan and Eoin made their way to the Great Hall. The twins went to the base of the stairs, and Ewan beamed at Allyson as she descended. She'd combed her hair, and it lay across her back and shoulders like a glimmering halo, the candlelight illuminating the blond strands. When she reached the brothers, Ewan brought her hand to his lips and brushed a kiss against the back.

"Ye're the most beautiful woman I've ever seen, and a Gordon plaid has never looked better, *mo aingeal*. Ye look like one."

"I don't feel like one, unless it's an avenging angel." The trio turned to watch Lady Margaret approach. Ewan wrapped his arm around Allyson's waist after she adjusted the arisaid to display the kirtle she wore beneath. She steeled herself for whatever her mother had to say, knowing it would likely humiliate her in front of Ewan. She felt his arm tense around her and realized he was preparing for the inevitable too.

"Where have you been?" While Margaret kept her tone low, there was no missing the demand in her words. "Ewan, why is my daughter wearing your plaid? Has something transpired while I've been busy?"

"A great deal has trans—" Ewan didn't finish before Mary cut him off.

"Why're you wearing my gown?" Mary demanded.

Allyson didn't flinch as she answered. "When Eoin requested a maid deliver dry clothes to Ewan in their chamber, the maid assumed it must have been for you. Your reputation made your clothes seem like an obvious choice. It's not as though I could walk around naked once I left the chamber, so I had no choice but to put on your gown once we finished my bath. I wanted to wear Ewan's plaid."

Ewan waited for her mother to sound the alarm after she left little to anyone's imagination.

"For hours? Unlikely. I can imagine what you've been up to." Margaret's sneer set Ewan's nerves on edge. "I shall send Berta to see you this very night," Margaret's lip curled in disgust.

"Do as you must. But does it matter? Either I'm just as I was when I arrived, and there is naught to fash over, or I'm not and I must marry Ewan. One way or another, he and I will stand before the kirk in a few sennights."

Ewan pushed Allyson behind him and put his hands on his hips.

"Are you questioning my honor, Lady Elliot?" Ewan's ominous tone had Allyson pulling on his arm, but he didn't budge.

"Not yours. My daughter's. She seduced you."

"You have the wrong lass. That was Mary who tried not Allyson. We talked. That's all." Eoin was the only person he would admit to that he'd done far more with Allyson than talk.

"Mary? Very well, Laird Elliot will amend the documents when they arrive from court," Margaret gloated.

"I said tried. She offered herself to me more than once and even accosted Eoin, thinking he was me. Not very discriminating in her tastes." Ewan leaned forward, his own sneer clear on his face. "I wouldn't have any of your other daughters even if the king paid me. That you'd so gladly put Allyson aside only drives me to remove her from this keep and your family as soon as possible. The documents have already been signed. You can't undo what the king decreed."

"You'd rather take a fourth daughter of questionable morals than the oldest daughter who was married to a laird."

"What is questionable aboot Allyson? She has a pristine reputation at court. Unlike two of your other daughters, she doesn't offer herself to strangers. What if I prefer a virgin? Allyson's the only one in the family who would pass." Ewan didn't wait for Margaret's response.

He spun on his heels and practically dragged Allyson back outside. As though Mother Nature understood his need to get away, the rain ceased and the sun appeared. He stormed across the bailey to the stables with her in tow. Once they were inside, he came to a stop so abruptly that Allyson crashed into his side, and he had to catch her before she fell. "Wait a moment."

Ewan offered no other explanation before striding to his horse's stall and rapidly saddling his mount. He led the animal to Allyson and lifted her into the saddle once they were outside. He swung up behind her and spurred the steed toward the gate. Neither of them spoke until they were once more outside the keep's wall. Ewan wrapped his arm around Allyson's middle, holding her tightly against him as he spurred the horse into a gallop. He wasn't sure where he would take them, but he headed west. After ten minutes of hard riding, he considered taking them to the Hermitage and Robert Bruce, the king's son. He'd seen a priest there, and it tempted him to elope. He seethed at Margaret's vulgar accusation. He might have been tempted to couple with Allyson, and she might have been a flirt at court, but he'd never questioned her virtue. That her mother would do so once again, and in front of anyone, let alone her daughter's potential groom, was so outrageous that Ewan had to leave before he struck something or someone. He refused to leave Allyson behind to face her mother's wrath, of which she would undoubtedly be the recipient. He'd caused the situation by keeping her in the tower for so long, and he'd only made it worse by losing his temper. After a wonderful afternoon with Allyson, her mother's viperous tongue was more than he could overlook. He shifted Allyson's hand that held a hank of mane, and placed it against her belly, then covered it with his own. He wove his fingers between hers as they continued to ride.

Allyson remained silent for as long as she could, but as the minutes dragged on, she feared Ewan might ride away with her for good. "Are you taking me all the way back to court?" She tried to infuse humor into her voice, but she suspected she failed.

"Nay, but I am considering the priest at the Hermitage."

"What? Nay!"

"Have you decided then? You won't marry me?"

"I won't marry you without your brother there."

"What does Eoin have to do with aught? Why do you want him there? Hoping the wrong one of us will await you at the kirk's steps?" Ewan was aware his comments were uncalled for, but he had bile to spew, and he was being an arse for doing it at Allyson. She pushed his hand away before pulling on the reins, bringing the horse to a halt. She swung her leg over the saddle and turned to look at Ewan. She had a fleeting urge to slap him, but she refrained.

"No, I don't want Eoin. And it angers me as much as my mother's words angered you that you would even suggest such a thing. I was thinking of

you. I'm positive you'd regret it for the rest of time if
he wasn't there. I don't want you to live with regret
for marrying me." She glared at Ewan as she ground
her teeth. "You do more than just insult me. I expect
this from my mother. I don't expect it from you."

"Ally—"

"Don't call me that."

"Don't you like it?"

"Not when I'm this angry with you. It's pa-
tronizing."

"I didn't mean it to be. It was supposed to be
apologetic. I have no idea what came over me to say
something so hateful."

"Is that how you usually react when you're angry? Do you always lash out?"

"No. Never." His mother had done that and said
things she could never take back. She'd done it a few
times to the twins, but both brothers had heard their
mother's acerbic comments to their father. "I was furious, and to hear you mention my brother at the
same time as considering a marriage, it pushed me
too far. It was illogical and jealous, and I don't know
why I said it. The words seemed to tumble out before
I could stop them. I'm no better than your mother.
I'm sorry, Allyson."

"Ally. I prefer it when you call me Ally." She relented when she heard the anguish in Ewan's
voice. "And I understand. She has a tendency to push
me too far, too. But I don't want her to come between us. I feel like we made such progress in the
past fortnight. I don't want that ruined."

"Me neither, *mo aingeal*. I should be thanking you
for once again being so thoughtful rather than me
being so hateful. You often put consideration into
what you do for me. First my favorite food on the
picnic the other day, and then my favorite brother."

"He's your only brother," Allyson chuckled.

"That's why he's my favorite even when I'm miffed with him."

The horse shifted restlessly beneath them, so Ewan dismounted, then lifted Allyson down. With the reins in one hand and Allyson's in the other, he led them further along the path to where the river ran alongside it. Allyson guided them to the river bank where the horse drank while Ewan wrapped his arm around Allyson, and she rested her head against his shoulder.

"We can't go to the Hermitage unchaperoned. There is little chance my parents won't balk at the king's illegitimate son being our host. We won't marry there without Eoin, so that means sending one of Lord Robert's men back to Redheugh. That'll inform my mother of where we've gone, and she's likely to send my father after us. I'm certain he hasn't forgiven me for having to chase me the first time. He might throttle me if I do it a second time."

"I didn't give you much choice. I kidnapped you."

"It's hardly a kidnapping when I put up no fight."

"Ally, let's return to court. If I can't take you home to Huntley yet, and I don't want you to remain here, that's the only place for us to go."

"I know. I'd rather be there than here any day of the week and twice on Sundays. But we can't wed for another three sennights. Even if you'd found the priest at the Hermitage, he wouldn't have married us. Not until Easter." Allyson bit her bottom lip as she wrestled with nervousness and jealousy. "I don't know if I want to spend nearly a moon at court with you."

"Why not?"

"I'd rather move on with life than treading water, which is what we would do at court."

"There's more to it than that. I can tell. What's eating at you, *aingeal*?"

"I want to believe everything you've promised since we arrived here, especially all that passed between us today. All those sennights at court where temptation is at every table and in every chamber, well, it scares me."

"Afraid you'll find a mon more handsome than me?" Ewan wrapped his other arm around Allyson and lifted her off the ground, so they looked at each other eye-to-eye. "I should be the one who's worried, Ally. I've pledged myself to you, and I will keep it. But you've made no promises to me. I won't pressure you either. I told you, you have until Easter to decide what you want to do. I haven't changed my mind, but you might find someone you prefer in that time."

"But I'm not likely to bed them," Allyson snapped before her eyes opened wide. Being at eye level with Ewan made her uncomfortable after her comment. She hadn't intended to reveal her fears in so many words.

"I understand why you're worried, and you have every right to be with what you know aboot my past. All I can do is prove to you that I won't disappoint you."

"Ewan, you said that with the papers signed, even without the betrothal ceremony, we are betrothed before the eyes of the law."

"Aye. We must state before witnesses our pledge to marry in the future, but a priest doesn't have to oversee it."

"Could we exchange our pledges tonight with Eoin as our witness?"

"We could, but why tonight?"

"I would have the betrothal completed. Then no one can force an end to it."

"I will speak to Eoin as soon as I can, but I still intend for us to return to court as soon as we can."

Allyson was slow to nod, but finally she relented and agreed that they should return to court before they mounted and turned back to Allyson's home. A place Ewan swore would no longer be her home within a sennight.

CHAPTER TWENTY-EIGHT

Ewan and Allyson returned to Redheugh in time to see her brothers and fathers ride out for a three-day sortie. Ewan scowled. After what happened with Margaret and Mary, he'd planned to reveal the truth of Allyson's parentage that evening. But now he knew he would have to keep the paintings in his chamber until the men returned. He wouldn't reveal his discovery until all of Allyson's family could be present. He also knew they wouldn't be able to leave for court until after Kenneth's return. His face remained grim until he glanced down and saw Allyson staring up at him, a question in her eyes. He relaxed his face and wound her arm through his.

They entered the keep together for a second time, but the atmosphere was palpably different. Five angry faces turned toward them. Allyson's mother, sisters, and her brother-by-marriage glared at them as they approached. If it had been up to Ewan, he would have found them seats at a lower table, but that was impossible with so many watching. Ewan could only imagine what Margaret told her daughters and son-by-marriage, but whatever it was, it wasn't enough to discourage Mary's and Alice's looks of interest as they neared the dais. Ewan guided Allyson to a seat that placed her between Eoin and him. His brother gave him a rueful glance, telling Ewan that his twin was aware of what transpired and more than likely had heard whatever garbage Margaret spewed. Except he knew it might not be entirely garbage since he'd been rude to his hostess and elder, but he felt no remorse for defending Allyson. It was time someone did.

Eoin looked over Allyson's head and shook his before leaning back and canting his head to whisper to Ewan. "*Rinn thu dìnnear cù ceart a-mach às an fhear seo. Bha am boireannach a 'hopadh às a rian agus a' cagnadh mo asail a-mach a 'smaoineachadh gur e mise a bh' annad. Dh 'fhaodadh tu a bhith air leum ann am meall de chonnadh agus a thighinn a-mach nas glaine.*" Ye made a right dog's dinner out of this one. The woman's hopping mad and chewed ma arse out thinking I was ye. Yecould've jumped in a pile of shite and come out cleaner.

"*Chaill mi an temper agam nuair a thuirt i gun do mheall Allyson mi agus thuirt i nach robh Allyson na maighdeann às deidh a bhith sa chùirt. Tha mi tinn gu bàs a 'cluinntinn sin.*" I lost ma temper when she said Allyson seduced me and claimed Allyson wasna a virgin after being at court. I'm sick unto death of hearing that.

Allyson went rigid as she listened to the two men discuss her as though she weren't there. They assumed that in the Lowlands no one spoke Gaelic. They weren't entirely wrong. No one in her clan did because they spoke Scots, and her family spoke both Scots and French. But they were wrong to assume that she didn't speak Gaelic. She'd learned from the former cook who'd grown up in the Highlands. The old woman, Morgana, had been one of the few to take pity on the lonely child. She welcomed Allyson into the kitchens and not only taught her Gaelic but also to cook and bake. That was why a croft on her own, if Ewan or any other man left her a widow, wasn't intimidating. She knew she could keep herself from starving. She listened as the brothers continued to speak.

"*Bha i a 'bruidhinn mu dheidhinn gum biodh sinn a' cadal anns na stàballan leis na h-eich. Ged nach biodh sin mòran na bu mhiosa na an tùr fuilteach sin. Ghluais i air adhart agus air adhart mu mar a dh 'fheumas tu a bhith a' sniff suas a sgiortaichean gus a togail thairis air a peathraichean. Chan eil i a 'tuigsinn carson nach biodh tu ag iarraidh boireannach nas fheàrr ri do thaobh agus anns an leabaidh agad.*" She was talking aboot having us sleep in the stables with the horses. Though that wouldnae be much worse than that bluidy tower. She raved on and on aboot how ye must be sniffing up her skirts to pick her over her sisters. She doesnae understand why ye wouldnae want a prettier woman at yer side and in yer bed.

"*Chan eil boireannach nas fheàrr na Allyson.*" There is nay woman prettier than Allyson.

Allyson couldn't bear to listen to them speak around her any longer, and she felt guilty, as though she eavesdropped on a private conversation. "*Gabhaidh i fois ach cha toir i mathanas dhut Eòghann. Chan ann mura h-aontaich thu Alice no Màiri a phòsadh. Bhiodh e na b 'fheàrr nam fàgadh an dithis agaibh.*" She'll calm down, but she won't forgive you, Ewan. Not unless you agree to marry Alice or Mary. It would be best if you both left.

The twins froze as realization set in that not only did Allyson understand their conversation, her advice was for them to leave her behind. Ewan glanced down at her before glancing at Eoin then settling his gaze on her. He shook his head before leaning close to Allyson. "The only way I'm leaving is with ye. If ye are convinced that Eoin and I must depart, then ye're coming with us. I dinna care that yer da is away, and I dinna care that we havenae received the betrothal documents. I'm bluidy well nae leaving ye here." Ewan did nothing to hide his brogue; he saw little point if Allyson understood their conversation, and he was too angry. "If she willna let ye leave as ma betrothed, then we'll handfast. We dinna need a priest for that. Ye'll be ma wife, and God help anyone who tries to keep me from ye."

Allyson sat stunned as the talk spiraled beyond her control. She'd expected to sit down to pottage and idle chatter. Instead, she was listening to her future being planned without her once more. She stared at Ewan, but no words formed in her mind, or rather plenty formed, but she couldn't make sense of them enough to speak. She shook her head as her hands gripped the edge of the table. She feared she might be ill.

"Ewan, we can't do that. The king would be irate if he thought you stole me away. He could invalidate the handfast and dissolve the betrothal. Then where would I be? Unmarried and ruined. You'd go on with your life, and I'd be left with naught. I wouldn't be allowed at court. I wouldn't be welcome here. I wouldn't have a widow's portion or dower lands."

"Ye have so little faith in me that ye assumed I would allow any of that to happen?"

"How would you stop it if the king has you locked in the pit? There isn't much you can do withering away in a dungeon."

"The king willna put me in any dungeon."

"How can you be so certain? He sent his own godson, Magnus Sinclair, to the Stirling dungeon."

"Nay. Magnus was supposed to be under lock and key, but nae in the dungeon. Besides, after that debacle, none of the Highland lairds would stand for the king locking away another one of their lads, especially a laird's heir. The king relies too much on our clans to fight on his behalf to alienate us all."

"You have far too much confidence in your position. No one should underestimate King Robert. He didn't find himself on that throne without a fight. Do you want to start a war with the crown? Do you think your father wouldn't defend you? Do you want your clan dragged into this?"

"You're assuming the worst, Ally, and none of it has come to pass. Don't beg for trouble where it doesn't exist." Ewan reverted to his courtly accent, and Allyson wasn't sure she liked it as much as his brogue. The burr suited him. She hoped he would abandon the clipped and flat speech once they returned to the Highlands.

"I still don't think I can leave with you. It's Lent. The church would uphold no marriage, not even a handfasting."

Ewan sat back in his chair as he considered Allyson's arguments. He cast his gaze on his brother, who remained silent during his exchange with Allyson. He raised a brow at Eoin, who shrugged. He leaned forward once more and covered Allyson's hand with his.

"We aren't leaving, Ally. Eoin and I will keep to ourselves as much as we can. We'll continue to go to the lists in the morning, and I'll spend what time I can with you in the afternoon just like we've been doing, but we'll take our meals with our men."

Allyson shook her head, but Ewan saw the resignation on her face. "You can't eat with your men. It would cause too many chins to wag if you went from sitting on the dais to a table below the salt."

"Your father and brothers will return in a few days, and then we will resolve all of this. In the meantime, I'm sending a messenger to court for the betrothal agreement. When the meal ends, we'll slip into the gardens and make our pledge with Eoin as our witness."

The rest of the meal passed with little talking among the three despite the conversation flowing around them. Allyson excused herself as soon as she could, claiming fatigue but made her way to the gardens as they agreed. Ewan and Eoin were already waiting.

"Ally, I've never wanted aught more than I want to make this commitment to you." Ewan's sincerity and eagerness were clear in his words and his gesture when he kissed the back of Allyson's hand. Allyson and Ewan turned to face one another once Ewan unfastened the length of plaid from his shoulder. Eoin wrapped the material around their wrists as they joined hands. Ewan took a deep breath before making a pledge he never imagined would have such significance as it did in that moment. "I, Ewan Andrew Gordon, will take you as my wife upon the date we pledge our troth before God and priest."

"I, Allyson Elliot, will take you as my husband upon the date we pledge our troth before God and priest."

Ewan and Allyson stared at one another for several heartbeats before both of their faces broke into wide smiles. Ewan bussed a kiss on Allyson's cheek before pressing a brief one to her lips. The brothers retired to their chamber, where Ewan and Eoin discussed what they would do until they could ride away from Redheugh with Allyson and put her past behind them.

———

Ewan turned to climb into bed that was little more than a cot, when someone pounded on the door. He drew his dirk and checked to see that Eoin was armed before creeping to the door. Enemies rarely announced their arrival, but neither man was willing to be unprepared now that they were unwelcome guests. Ewan drew the door open to find a Gordon retainer on the other side.

"A messenger in the king's livery just arrived with this for ye." The man held out a rolled parchment and nodded when Ewan took it from him. Ewan turned to look at Eoin after he closed the door. He crossed the chamber and sat on Eoin's bed next to him. He slid the ribbon off and unfurled the document. A smaller piece of vellum lay on top of the larger one. Both men recognized their father's handwriting.

I pray this finds you well, sons. Laird Elliot sent word that you've recovered your runaway bride, Ewan, and that you've stopped at Redheugh. The king is eager to resolve the matter of your betrothal. Laird Elliot informed the king that Allyson would be before a priest the day after Easter, regardless of her feelings on the matter. He assures she's past her fit of temper and will cause no problems as a dutiful wife. You need only marry her and bring her to Huntley, then get the flock to her father. You can do as you choose while you're away, and if it should take a little longer to return, she'll surely be none the wiser. Get her with child, and she'll have little time to cause trouble. Her dowry will pay for the additions to the keep, so be certain to secure the coin before you depart. Godspeed.

Ewan clenched the parchment so tightly that it vibrated between his hands. Eoin eased the document and the missive from his brother's hands lest Ewan crumple it.

"And ye wonder why I thought what I did aboot marriage. Father condones me being unfaithful and even encourages it," Ewan growled. He pushed away from the bed and stalked back to the window, where he scrubbed his hands over his face before leaning toward the narrow opening. He stood thinking in silence, Eoin giving him space, until he decided on how to proceed. "As soon as Kenneth returns, we depart. We're taking Ally back to court. If Father is there, ye must speak to him before he has a chance to speak to Ally. Lord only kens what he might say to her. If he's nae there, go to Huntley. Tell him how things have changed, how I've changed. Eoin, if he lets on that I should keep a leman, he'll devastate Allyson, and I dinna ken that she'll ever trust me again."

"But ye've already explained to her that yer view on marriage has changed, that it doesnae match Father's anymore."

"Aye, but who's kenned me longer? She'll believe aught Father says, assuming he kens me better. The last thing I need is for her to bolt again or lock herself away. Allyson is the one person who could make me come to blows with Father. I will protect her nay matter what, Eoin. I'm warning ye now, I will choose her." He spun around and glared at his brother, daring Eoin to mock him.

"Ye're in love with her," Eoin mused quietly. His comment made Ewan stop short as Ewan moved toward his bed. He wanted to shake his head, deny Eoin's accusation, but he realized Eoin would never condemn him for loving Allyson. He had suspected he was falling in love with her, but his reaction to her mother that day confirmed it. His need to defend her had bordered on the pathological.

"I believe I do, and I dinna ken what to do," Ewan confessed.

"What to do? Make the marriage to the lass real, have a passel of bairns, and live a happy life together."

"It'll never be that simple."

"Then make it that way. Explain what's happening. Confess what Father wrote and warn her that

Father doesnae ken that ye've chosen a different view on marriage than he holds. Then face the future together." Eoin strode to his brother's side, placing his hand on Ewan's shoulder and squeezing. "It doesnae have to be any harder than that. The lass loves ye, too."

Ewan looked at Eoin for a long moment before nodding. They sat together once more and studied the betrothal agreement, pointing out portions that concerned them. He had barely scanned it when he saw it the first time, too enraged to care. He recalled most of it favored Allyson in the event he left her a widow, but he was dissatisfied with her options to return to Redheugh or retire to a convent. Her widow's portion was enough to provide for her even if he died within the next few years, or it would be a hefty dowry to an abbey. He pointed to the line and turned to Eoin. He couldn't accept Allyson being forced to leave their home.

"If I die before ye, ye must make certain she can remain with us. If ye're laird, ye must make certain that nay one will force her out upon yer death," Ewan's grave voice made Eoin nod several times.

"She's to be ma sister. I always wanted one. After all, I've always been stuck with yer ugly mug."

"Ugly? Ye shouldnae be so hard on yerself." Ewan grinned and appreciated his brother's attempt to add some levity. "Ye'll see to her wellbeing if I'm gone?"

"Of course. I would have regardless, but I can see how much she's come to mean to ye. Ewan, ye have a lifetime of responsibility and duty ahead of ye. I'll always do everything I can to support ye, but I'll never be the lady of the clan. If ye've found a woman who ye love and who'll be a good addition to our clan, then I will endeavor to ensure she's always protected, just as ye would do yerself. Besides, ye're nae so ugly now that I think aboot it."

"Thank ye, brother," Ewan murmured. The brothers embraced and clapped one another on the back. "Do I wait till morning?"

"Ye'd dare go to her chamber at this time of night? When it's next door to Mary's? I damn well wouldnae go there alone."

"Good thing ye're coming with me."

"What? This isnae a good idea, Ewan."

"Just come with me to her door. Then ye can go, and I'll be out before morn."

"Before morn? Ye're going to risk spending another night with her? Ye're a bluidy bampot, and I'm one too to be considering this. Ye already tested yer luck arguing with Lady Elliot."

"Aye. I am. I need to see her, and I willna have yer big ears listening outside the door, nor am I going to be traipsing aboot in the dark for someone to catch me and claim I've compromised Mary or Alice."

Eoin's mouth flattened into a thin line, but he crossed the room and held the door open for his twin.

CHAPTER TWENTY-NINE

Ewan and Eoin crept into the Great Hall and past the sleeping men and women until they reached the stairs that led to the family chambers. Years of hunting and fighting taught them to tread silently as they climbed to the second floor. Ewan pointed to a door on the right, and they eased their way along the passageway until Ewan knocked softly. He waited, but there was no answer. He tried again, but Allyson still didn't answer, so he pressed down on the handle, cringing when the metal creaked. He poked his head in but immediately realized she wasn't in her chamber. He scanned the surfaces and caught sight of the kirtle she wore to the evening meal along with her hair combs on a table next to a pitcher and ewer. He suspected he knew where she was.

"She's nae here," he whispered to Eoin. "Go back to our chamber. I ken where she is."

When Eoin shook his head, he pointed above them and mouthed "attic." He noted Eoin's confusion, but he wouldn't spill Allyson's secret, and certainly not in the middle of the passageway in the middle of the night. They walked back to the stairs, and Ewan waited for a moment as Eoin descended and looked back once before crossing the Great Hall. Ewan continued on to the door that led to the stairs that would take him to the attic and hopefully Allyson.

Allyson scrambled to hide the book she read when she heard someone open the attic door. She scurried behind a large trunk and waited. It was too late to blow out the candle she'd brought with her. Whoever approached would have seen the light upon opening the door. She preferred to have it lit to identify the intruder. She sighed when she recognized Ewan's head as it appeared at the top of the stairs.

"Ally?" his whisper wasn't very quiet.

"Aye, Ewan. I'm here." She stepped around the chest, but realized she wore only her chemise and robe. The previous times they'd been in the attic, she'd been fully clothed, not that it had mattered once her skirts were around her waist. Despite Ewan seeing her completely naked earlier that day, somehow Ewan spying her in her bedclothes seemed intimate in a way the other times didn't. She clutched her robe at the throat and waited for Ewan to cross the distance between them. "What're you doing here?"

"I went to yer chamber, but when I discovered ye werenae there, I figured ye'd be here."

"You went to my chamber. What if someone saw you?"

"Eoin and I were careful nae to be seen." Ewan didn't notice that his brogue continued, even though he spoke to Allyson instead of his brother.

"Eoin? You were both wandering aboot! Are you trying to rip my reputation to tatters? Angus told people aboot you, Eoin, and Lady Bevan. They'll assume you were up to your old tricks if they find you at my door in the middle of the night. Riding off with you for the afternoon did little to improve matters after everything Mother accused me of. People overheard. Good God, Alice or Mary could claim you were visiting them." Allyson made to step around Ewan, but his hands gripped her upper arms.

"Dinna panic, *mo ghaol*." Ewan leaned down to gaze into her eyes.

"What did you call me?" Allyson croaked.

"Ma love." Ewan watched as Allyson's eyes shuttered, and he suspected she believed it was a trite cliché, not the beginning of his promise of devotion. He swept her into his arms and carried her to the place they'd slept the previous nights. "Ally, I'm nae tossing that phrase aboot lightly. I've never called a woman that. I said it because I mean it. I'm in love with ye, Allyson."

"You are?" she breathed.

"Aye, *mo ghaol*, I am." He brushed hair from her temple and pressed a soft kiss. "I didna imagine I would be. I didna plan to be, but I realized how strong ma feelings are when yer mother spoke to ye this afternoon. Ma need to get ye away from her, from here, nearly overwhelmed any sense of reason. All I focused on was protecting ye."

"That doesn't mean you're in love with me. You feel obligated because you intend to marry me. You may even be fond of me, or you've seemed to be of late."

"This has naught to do with obligation, Allyson. It has everything to do with a feeling that's in every inch of me. I've had Eoin at ma side every day of our lives, and I never imagined I'd need another person. But I need ye. I need to see yer smile. I need to hear yer voice. I need to have ye at ma side. I trust ye just as I do ma brother, and that's because I've gotten to ken ye. The woman I kenned at court wasna the whole woman I now ken ye to be. There is so much more than anyone else sees, and I'm the only person ye allow to glimpse these parts of yer character, yer soul. Ye wouldnae do that if ye didna return ma feelings."

Allyson looked down at her hands that rested in his much larger palm. His fingers were curled around the back of hers while he wrapped his other arm around her with his hand resting on her hip. Her back leaned against his shoulder, and she laid her head against his chest. She absorbed the comfort he offered and realized she'd never been as content as she was when she was in Ewan's company. Sitting against him in the shelter of his arms seemed right. She couldn't imagine ever being this at ease with another man. She twisted so she could gaze into his emerald depths.

"I return your feelings, *mo chridhe*."

"I'm yer heart?"

"Aye. As unlikely as it is, I won't lie and deny I'm in love with you, too. You're not the mon I assumed from what I saw at court. I jumped to conclusions based on my own fears and past. I didn't give you a chance. This afternoon, all that you said, it confirmed what I've discovered since we've been here."

"I dinna think we would have gotten to ken one another past our preconceived impressions had we remained at court. Neither of us would have been so unguarded, and I'm certain I wouldnae have curbed ma excesses. Chillingham excepted, running away from court was the best that could have happened for us. It's given us an opportunity to see who we are away from court."

"What you say is true. If we'd spent this time at court, I would have despised you and never forgiven you for what I assumed were your flaws. Even if we married and retired to the Highlands, I doubt I would have opened my mind to appreciate what you're like away from court. Or it would've taken me much, much longer. By then it might've been too late. I would have driven you into any open arms."

"The only open arms I want are yers, and I hope they close around me."

"As much as I can reach," Allyson giggled before bringing her lips to his. She ran her hand up his chest to his neck and tunneled her fingers into the hair at his nape, her thumb running over the bristle. He used both hands to cup her jaw as they poured their feelings into the kiss. It wasn't like any of the ones they shared before.

Ewan knew it was time to show Allyson the contracts and his father's missive. He gave her one last lingering kiss. When they broke apart, Ewan shifted and pulled the parchments from his sporran. Allyson saw Ewan's unease and guessed what he would show her. "The contracts?"

"Aye, but that's nae all that arrived. My father sent Eoin and me a missive." Allyson canted her head and furrowed her brow as she attempted to read Ewan's troubled expression. "It pains me to share this with ye, but I fear what ma father might say to ye before I can convince him he and I nay longer see marriage through the same eyes."

Allyson glanced down when Ewan unrolled the vellum. She watched his expression as he handed her the smaller of the parchments. She saw his nervousness, and she perceived his tension as it pulsed through him. She scanned the contents of the missive and nodded once, slowly.

"Does your father believe it's possible to love one woman and to be faithful to her?"

"I dinna ken. Perhaps once he did, but I dinna ken if his experiences have jaded him too much for him to see nae every marriage has to be like his."

"But most marriages he knows of are like his was.

The king has a slew of bastards. I'm my father's bastard."

"Dinna say that, Allyson. You are nae."

"You heard my siblings. You've seen how my parents treat me."

Ewan inhaled until air filled his lungs to bursting before setting Allyson aside. He stood and helped her to her feet, then led her to the paintings. He uncovered the ones he'd discovered that that first morning. When Allyson gasped, he let go of them and reached for her as she stumbled backward, her fingers covering her mouth and her eyes wide as saucers. She shook her head as tears poured forth as Ewan pulled her into his embrace. She pointed past him before clenching her hand into a fist that laid against his chest. She trembled as she buried her face in the swath of plaid that crossed his chest and shoulder. She clung to him as she sobbed. Ewan knew she'd recognized the resemblance as quickly as he had. It only took Allyson seconds to realize all the hateful things said to her over the years had been entirely false, and to make matters worse, neither of her parents did anything but perpetuate the suspicions.

"Why?" She sobbed. "It must have been as you supposed. My father forced my mother, and neither of them want me as a reminder. Dear God, am I the result of my father assaulting my mother? Like Mary's husband did her?"

"I dinna ken, *mo aingeal*. I dinna have an honest answer for that, and we willna ken unless we ask. But I hope ye ken it's nae like that between every husband and wife. I willna ever force ye. Ye can tell me nay, and I will always respect that and respect ye." Ewan ran his hand over Allyson's back as he offered all the comfort he could. His soft tones and burr helped her to relax her shoulders so they no longer sat at her earlobes.

"And if I turn you away, who will you go to instead? Perhaps my mother gave in to my father because she tired of his infidelity."

"That isnae how our marriage will ever work. Yer body is yer own and always will be. Ye may be ma wife, but ye will never be ma broodmare. If ye dinna want to couple with me, I will never abuse ma strength and take from ye what ye dinna offer. I told ye before, if ye decide ye dinna want me in yer bed, then I will live with that. I willna turn to another woman."

"I find that hard to believe. A mon who's enjoyed as many women as you have doesn't seem likely to embrace abstinence."

"Believe it or nae, I do ken there is more to life than rutting. I would hope that I'm a good enough lover that ye will always want ma attention. But if I fail to be a good enough husband, and the coupling isnae enough, then I will accept yer decision. I willna set ye aside. Allyson, it's nae as enjoyable, but both men and women can bring themselves pleasure without having a partner. Do ye ken aught of that?"

"Aye, the church says it's a sin, one of the worst." Allyson's fear was clear before she spoke her next words. "For someone so devout, how could you suggest such a thing?"

"I do have a deep faith, but I'm a healthy mon and ye're a healthy woman. Our bodies have wants, and if the Lord didna accept us doing such things, He wouldnae have made it possible."

"There is much we can do, but that doesn't make it right. We can murder, but we know not to do that. That's what free will is. God may have granted it to us, but we control it."

"Do ye still find me an unrepentant sinner now that ye ken?" Ewan waited for Allyson, his discomfort growing with every heartbeat that passed before Allyson shook her head.

"No. I'm selfish though. I can accept it if it means you choose that instead of another woman."

Ewan exhaled the breath he'd held, then swallowed. "But what aboot when I must be away on patrol, or if I'm called away to visit another clan? Ye've discovered the beginning of what a mon and woman can share. What if ye dinna want to go without once ye learn the pleasure that comes with coupling?"

"You fear I would be unfaithful because my lust would overcome me?" Allyson stifled the laugh that threatened to burble forth. She knew Ewan was serious in his questioning.

"Aye."

"You're the only mon I've ever lusted for. I've made it to two-and-twenty without being overcome before, despite offers made at court. I'm not suddenly going to lose control. At least not with someone other than you."

"But that was before ye kenned. Ye may decide differently now that ye've enjoyed yer release."

"And you fear I would find another mon to help me if you weren't available the moment I become aroused?"

"If I'm nae there, who'd be arousing ye but another mon?"

"Mayhap I'd be picturing the braw mon who usually tends to me," Allyson purred as she smiled with a seductiveness that years at court taught her. Ewan pounced and ravaged a kiss from her as he lifted her off her feet, guiding her legs around his waist. He walked them to a wall and pressed Allyson against it.

"I better be that mon, Ally. I'll kill any other who comes near ye. I'd rather ken ye're fingering yerself and sinning that way than discovering ye've committed adultery."

"Don't you think I'd want to kill any woman who comes near ye? Teach me then."

"What?" Ewan murmured against her neck as he laved his tongue along her salty skin.

"Teach me. Show me how to tend to myself. But Ewan, even if you don't, I won't find another mon just because I can't be with you the moment the mood takes me. It has naught to do with whether or not I can pleasure myself. It's because I don't want anyone but you. Who do you imagine would be on my mind while I take care of myself? If you'd be tending to yourself, would it be because you miss me? Or would it be because you couldn't take another woman to your bed, so you settled for that?"

"Because I canna be with ye. Who do ye think has been on ma mind every time I've taken maself in hand since we arrived here?"

"You've been—?" Ewan pulled back, and Allyson huffed when she spotted his Cheshire grin. "You are unrepentant. You picture me?"

"Aye. Over and over. I picture what I've seen of ye when ye ride and imagine it's me ye're straddling. I imagine all that I want to do with ye and to ye, all the ways I want to make ye scream ma name."

"Has coupling been on your mind that much?" Allyson wondered aloud. "Do you usually think aboot it that much?"

Ewan chuckled. "I thought aboot it a fair amount before, but now I think aboot making love to ye incessantly."

"You think aboot it incessantly, or you plan to make love to me incessantly?"

"Both," Ewan growled as he captured her mouth in a searing kiss Allyson was eager to return. It wasn't until they were both breathless and gasping that they broke apart, then attempted to continue their conversation. "Ally, I could have snuck out to the village or convinced one of the servants to keep the secret, and I could have bedded women every night since I arrived. I dinna want anyone but ye, *mo aingeal.* I would rather take maself in ma hand over and over than touch a woman who isnae ye."

"Can you believe I feel the same way aboot you?" Allyson cupped Ewan jaw in her small hands as she gazed into his emerald orbs.

"I can. If ye feel for me what I feel for ye, then aye." Ewan kissed her cheek before lowering her to the ground. "Ally, our conversation has jumped aboot quite a bit. I want to be sure ye understand the most important thing. I willna ever force ye. Never."

"I know, *mo chridhe.* You've never struck me as the type who would. Before, it was because I assumed no woman would ever turn you away. That still crosses my mind, but now I understand it's not in your nature to abuse women."

"Do ye ken that aught we do, alone or together, isnae an egregious sin? What happens between a mon and a woman is between them and God's eyes. If He doesnae smite them, then there is naught to confess. I amnae going to allow a mon who's never been with a woman to condemn me for something he has nay knowledge of."

"Shh. First, you tell me you talk to God directly. Now you're rejecting God's emissaries on earth. Perhaps I shouldn't stand too close, or His lightning bolt might strike me, too." Allyson grinned before kissing Ewan playfully on the tip of his nose.

"Ally, on our ride home and this evening in ma chamber, I gave a lot of consideration to how things stand. We dinna have to handfast or have a wedding at the kirk to be married."

"How can—" Allyson's eyes widened before a

smile emerged. "Consummation would make the betrothal binding. It would mean we are wed regardless of any ceremonies."

"*Mo aingeal,* our situation keeps changing so rapidly, it's hard to keep up. I meant what I said this afternoon, that I wouldnae make love to ye until ye're ma wife. But all that yer mother said and what Eoin told us, changes things yet again. I want to be sure ye have the protection of ma name nae just ma sword."

"Are you saying that we make our betrothal a real marriage?"

"I think we ken it's inevitable. But I dinna want ye to fear I'm suggesting this as a practicality. I love ye, Allyson, and I want to make love to ye. I want ye to be my wife in all ways."

"You know I already welcome the idea of coupling, but it does mean more that we've confessed our feelings are stronger than just fondness. Whether or not joining with you provides me security as your wife, I want to show you how I feel, Ewan."

"I want the same, Ally. I want ye to ken just how deeply I care aboot ye."

Ewan met Allyson halfway as their mouths fused together, their kiss passionate and urgent. Allyson fumbled to unpin the broach at Ewan's shoulder, forcing them to pull apart long enough for Ewan to drop the pin into his sporran before unfastening his belt. His plaid fell away as Allyson shed her robe. Her mouth fell open at the sight of Ewan's bare body once he stripped off his leine.

"I thought—I mean, I imagined—I—holy Mary, Mother of God, you are like a Greek statue," Allyson babbled. She reached out her hands and ran them over the expanse of his chest, and when she finished exploring, Ewan untied the ribbons of her chemise. It was his turn to ogle.

"Ye are a goddess come to life, Allyson. I should

have said so earlier. I promise to make love to ye all night, but I fear ye may nae enjoy the moment our bodies join. I will do all that I can to make it good for ye." Ewan's concern made Allyson's heart melt. She pressed her much smaller body against his, enjoying the feeling she'd discovered earlier that day.

"I know you'll be gentle. I don't want to keep waiting. Not now that there's no reason."

Ewan eased Allyson onto the tapestry and came down beside her. He caressed the valley between her breasts before brushing his fingers over her nipples. When he took one into his mouth, Allyson couldn't contain her moan. Her hand sought Ewan's length, and when she found it, she wrapped her hand around it, stroking until Ewan released his own growl. Ewan alternated breasts, licking, sucking, and nipping as Allyson arched her back in offering. His hand skimmed over her belly until his finger delved into her entrance. He marveled at how wet she already was, her dew soaking her nether lips and the inside of her thighs.

"Yer body is telling me it's ready for mine, but nae yet." Ewan whispered as he sank two fingers into Allyson's sheath. The sensation only made her ache for more, knowing that his cock was far thicker and longer than his fingers. He inched his way down her body, leaving a trail of kisses in his wake until his mouth fastened on her bud. He worked the bundle of nerves until Allyson was overwhelmed with need, her mewling cries telling him she drew closer to release. When her muscles clenched and spasmed around his fingers, he shifted his body over hers and lined up his cock with her entrance. The moment he saw her relax, but before the euphoria wore off, he plunged into her. Allyson gasped, her muscles tensing around Ewan's rod. He feared he would spill himself with how tight her sheath was around his rod. If he'd thought her mouth on him earlier had been divine, he had no words to express the feeling of being inside his bride. She whimpered as she adjusted to the receding pain and the invasion.

"*Mo ghaol*, breathe. I will wait until the pain fades." *Even if it kills me.*

"It's fading. It just feels odd, or I should say different. You being inside me somehow soothes one need while inflaming another. I don't ache as I did while you readied me, but now I need to move, to feel you move. Is that what's supposed to happen?"

"Aye," Ewan panted. Allyson's comments were testing the last shreds of his restraint. And when Allyson shifted, raising her hips and flexing, Ewan looked to her for permission. She nodded once and Ewan began to move. He rocked his hips, giving her a chance to become accustomed to the sensation. When she gripped his backside, pulling him toward her, he withdrew most of the way and surged into her.

"Yes," she murmured. "I want you so damn much."

"Ye have me. All of me, Ally. I'm all yers forever."

They moved together over and over, thrusting and rocking as they found a rhythm that drove them both over the edge. They stifled their screams of ecstasy with a deep kiss before Ewan settled his weight onto his forearms, fearing he would squash Allyson if he pressed all his weight against her. But Allyson wanted no space between them, wrapping her arms and legs around him, encouraging him to rest against him. When he relented, Allyson knew he still bore much of his weight, but their bodies melded together from stem to stern. They lay like that until Ewan noticed Allyson's breathing became more labored. He rolled them, so he was on the bottom and Allyson lay strewn across his chest. Her hair tumbling over her shoulders and his chest. His hand stroked her backside as they exchanged small kisses.

"That was different, wasn't it?" Allyson whispered. She'd heard the matrons and widows who took lovers talk about coupling, and nothing they'd described resembled anything Allyson just experienced.

"It was. I never guessed aught would be so intimate as what I shared with ye." Ewan glanced up at Allyson, who looked down at him. "I gave ye a piece of ma soul."

"In exchange for a piece of mine."

"Ally, I love ye. There can be nay doubt in ma mind now. Nae after that. I never imagined a physical act would have such a cataclysmic effect on ma emotions. I'm yer husband now, and I have never been happier."

"I love you, too, Ewan. And I assumed it would be good after the other things we've done, but I hadn't a clue it would be like that. I understand why they keep virgins ignorant, or at least try to. Can we do it again?"

Ewan chuckled as he kissed the top of her head. "Aye. Many, many times."

"Tonight?"

Ewan didn't answer with words that time. He rolled them over and showed Allyson that they could do it several more times that night. Once they were sated but not yet sleepy, Ewan knew there was an issue they still needed to discuss. Ewan was glad they'd resolved two topics, but he dreaded revisiting the one that caused Allyson to sob earlier. But they couldn't leave the attic without addressing what launched them into the conversation that led to them making love. "Ally, what aboot the paintings? What aboot what ye fear of yer father's and mother's past?"

Allyson's hand that was drawing lazy patterns on his back dropped, and she seemed to shrink before his eyes. He wanted to kick himself for pressing the issue. She looked tiny and vulnerable as she stared in the paintings' direction. But she shook her head resolutely before looking back at him. She rose and went to stand beside the stack of paintings, Ewan following her until he slipped his arms around her waist, pulling her back flush against his chest. He nuzzled her neck as she relaxed in his embrace.

"That is their cross to bear. Whatever happened between them is not my fault. If my father abused my mother, there is naught I can do to change it. If my mother allowed him into her bed then regretted it, then that's her choice to live with."

"But what aboot the rumors and how yer brothers and sisters treat ye? Even how yer mother treats ye?" Allyson turned to look at Ewan, and he released her.

"I wish I could fix that, but we'll leave soon, and perhaps I won't look back."

Ewan pulled Allyson back into his embrace, and she burrowed closer as she absorbed his heat, his re-assuring strength bolstering her fading resilience to face her family. They moved to the spot where they slept each night they spent in the attic, and like the previous times, Ewan wrapped his plaid around Allyson. Ewan's arm rested on Allyson's waist as her back pressed against his chest.

"Sleep well, *mo ghaol*," Ewan whispered.

"Goodnight, *mo chridhe*," Allyson murmured, then yawned. They were both asleep in the space of a few breaths.

CHAPTER THIRTY

The next ten days passed in uncomfortable isolation for the Gordon twins and Allyson. Foul weather delayed Kenneth's and his sons' return. Flooding upriver forced them to stay in one of the clan's villages to help the locals. There was little left of their reputations to protect after Ewan and Allyson rode out of the bailey, so they continued to spend their days together. Margaret hadn't forgiven Ewan or, by extension, Eoin. She tolerated their presence, but made it clear they were unwelcome. She ceased her campaign to push Alice and Mary toward Ewan, but she didn't cease her disdain for Allyson. While Ewan and Eoin preferred Margaret ignoring them, it pained them to see how her mother's indifference toward her still cut Allyson so deeply. Mary, Laurel, and Alice gloated at Allyson's shame, and the unwed sisters did little to curtail their pursuit of both Ewan and Eoin during the evening meal, now treating them as interchangeable.

While her family paid little attention to them, Allyson, Ewan, and Eoin spent time in the Great Hall playing nine-men's morris, knucklebones, and fox and geese. Ewan discovered Allyson was an expert chess player, and he teased that she would become Clan Gordon's chief tactician and logistician. After the evening meal, Eoin disappeared to the tower chamber while Allyson and Ewan spent their nights in the attic. One such night, Allyson shared her selection of books that she'd hidden away over the years. It made Ewan chuckle to see tales of courtly love and chivalry when he knew the royal court was far from the lavish tales spun by bards. He teased that she'd spent too much time living near the English if she believed such stories, and Allyson accused him of being jealous. They dissolved into laughter as he tickled her ribs, but it only took a moment and a glance for the mood to shift. Ewan swooped in for a kiss, and Allyson welcomed his tongue into her mouth. They struggled out of their clothes; the endeavor made more difficult when they didn't want to let go of one another.

Once they were undressed, Ewan guided Allyson to straddle his hips. She looked dubiously at Ewan's hard length, but when he guided her to take it into her, she settled with a low moan. The feeling was different from when Ewan was on top. He encouraged her to set their pace; the position drawing him in deeper. She experimented just as she had the afternoon in his chamber when she learned how to take him in her mouth. It wasn't long before the sounds of their bodies moving against one another filled the attic. Allyson didn't fear anyone hearing them, as there was an entire floor of empty guest chambers between the attic and the family chambers. They held little back as Ewan pulled Allyson down for a kiss that left her feeling drunk.

Another night, Allyson posed Ewan as she drew him with a charcoal pencil and a piece of parchment. Ewan hummed to them as Allyson sketched.

When she twisted away to find a quill and ink in a nearby chest, Ewan pulled the bow loose from her laces. Allyson pretended not to notice as he loosened the ribbons that held her kirtle closed. When she returned to her seat, she pretended the loose bodice frustrated her and resolved the problem by stripping her arms and pushing it down around her waist. Ewan toyed with her breasts and nipples as she worked while Allyson studiously ignored him, or at least pretended to. When she could no longer withstand the torment, she tossed her art aside and launched herself into Ewan's arms.

It was only a matter of moments before they were both undressed. Ewan lifted her into his arms, and she wrapped her legs around his waist. He backed them against a wall, slipping inside Allyson as she rocked her hips forward to accept him. Ewan had feared their second night together that Allyson would be too sore to make love again, but she'd demonstrated each night that she was both willing and able to join with him. As he took her against the wall, she scored her nails along his back, inciting an urgency within him that she gladly met. His fingers bit into her hips as he lost control.

"More, more," Allyson encouraged him. "You won't break me. Harder, Ew."

He was more than happy to accommodate her requests, slamming into her over and over. When she cried out her release, he lowered her to the floor and guided her to bend over a chair covered in a dust cloth. He entered her as she arched and threw back her head. He grasped her hair in a ponytail and held it as he kissed her back and shoulders. She met each thrust as she pushed her hips back against him. Ewan had never seen anything more erotic than the picture Allyson made as she turned her head to the side, but her eyes drifted closed. He pistoned his cock into her until she once more shattered, the muscles of her core milking him as he exploded within her. He supported Allyson's body against his as they stood, panting and still fused together.

"I love you, Allyson Gordon. More than life itself." Ewan confessed, unready to let go.

"I love you, Ewan Gordon, and heaven help the person who tries to get between us."

Allyson and Ewan knew Kenneth and her brothers would return soon, despite the delay the weather caused. They laid together on Ewan's bed, having retreated to the privacy of the tower while Eoin visited the tavern in the village. Allyson floated in a state of half-wakefulness as Ewan sang. She learned that his rich baritone wasn't just suited for humming. He sang hymns his mother taught him as a child, and his voice soothed the anxiety and dread that filled Allyson each day as her father's return approached.

"Part of me wishes Father would stay away longer, then we could continue as we have. But another part of me wants him to hurry, so we can be done with it all and be on our way to court. I hate skulking around. I just want everything out in the open."

"I know, lass. I wish the same. I'm not ashamed of the choices we made, but it feels as though I should be when we're hiding."

"When Father returns, we'll request an audience and explain what we've done. He wanted this marriage in the first place, so he can hardly be upset that we decided not to wait for Lent to end."

Ewan opened his mouth, but the tinkling of bells

announcing the laird's return interrupted him. Allyson and Ewan moved to the arrow slit, his superior height allowing them to look out the window together. Their moment of reckoning was about to happen.

CHAPTER THIRTY-ONE

Allyson left to change for the evening meal, which would be held earlier with the arrival of men who'd been cold and wet for several days. Ewan moved to the other bed and pulled the paintings from beneath it. He and Eoin agreed that it was best to hide them, not wanting any of the servants to report that they had them. He waited for his brother to return for dry clothes.

"The laird has returned, and the family is reunited once more. That's why I'm taking a stand this eve. I'll be sure everyone sees these paintings. There can be nay doubt that Ally is part of the laird's family once they see them. And all the better that the laird is finally home." Ewan laid the art on the bed and examined the three pieces. He'd been impatient to confront Margaret, but he'd forced himself to wait until Kenneth returned. He had no reason to wait any longer. When Allyson wore Mary's gown and his plaid, it hadn't been the vindication he'd wished for Allyson's sake. "Let's be on our way. I want to have these ready before everyone enters the Great Hall."

"Does Allyson ken ye have them?"

"Nay. Ma mind wasna on them earlier, but when

the bells rang to announce the laird's arrival, I remembered."

"Do ye think she'd want ye to do this? I dinna ken if this is such a good idea as ye think. Ye may want to warn her first."

"She kens of them," Ewan shrugged. "She intends to ask her parents aboot them."

"There is a vast difference between planning to ask and displaying them for all and sundry. I'm telling ye, brother, I dinna think this is wise. I dinna think Allyson will appreciate the surprise."

"Eoin, we're leaving in the morn. I'm nae staying a day longer now that I can tell Kenneth we made the betrothal a marriage. I'm getting Ally away from here, even if it means going to court."

"I canna say this comes too soon, but did ye discuss that with her?"

"Nay. Ye must have seen her come down the tower stairs just after Kenneth, Angus, and Graeme arrived. There wasna time to discuss our departure being tomorrow. But she and I already agreed we'd leave as soon as possible. She kens of Father's missive, and we've discussed changes to the agreement that would make her more comfortable before marrying."

"And ye agree with them all?"

"Aye. Her concern is the same as mine. She wants to be sure she has a roof over her head that isnae a convent's if I should die first. She isnae willing to accept the Gordons will welcome her to stay on, so I'm adding a provision for a croft either in our village at Huntley or one on our land. She also wants her father to provide more in the case we have daughters, and I die before they wed. She fears she'd be presuming too much to rely on ye, if ye become laird. She doesnae ever want to feel like a burden again." Ewan walked to the door and waited for Eoin to open it before they headed to the Great Hall. "If these changes will make her happy and ease her constant worry, then they are a wee act that will make a big difference. I love her, Eoin. I'll do aught to make her life better than it has been."

"I ken ye do. How others dinna see it is beyond me. I will stand beside ye in this just as I do everything. But I still think ye should have discussed the paintings with her first. And I wouldnae hold yer breath that Kenneth will agree to the amendments."

"All will be well, little brother."

"And pride goeth before the fall, big brother. Dinna assume ye ken it all."

Their conversation ended when they arrived at the Great Hall. They'd skirted the crowd in the bailey that milled about, welcoming Kenneth and his sons. He'd glimpsed Margaret and her daughters, but Allyson wasn't present. Ewan and Eoin approached the dais as the servants finished laying the table. Ewan waited for Eoin to pull out the seat Allyson now claimed each evening. Ewan propped the largest image on the chair, then placed a smaller one on his seat and the other on Eoin's. Voices floated from the entrance as people entered the gathering hall.

They left the dais and waited for the others to arrive. Allyson joined them, wearing her Gordon plaid instead of her Elliot. For the sake of keeping the peace, she'd reverted to wearing her Elliot plaid while her father was gone. Conversations halted when, one after another, people noticed Allyson standing with Ewan's plaid wrapped around her. She noticed that many people pointed behind her, so she turned to look at the dais. She felt her temper rise as she took in the sight of the three images of her family resting on chairs for all of her clan to stare at. She clenched her jaw as she looked up at Ewan, and she was certain he read her murderous intent. She was livid. "You shouldn't have done that," she hissed.

Allyson's family gathered near the dais, but Alice's face turned a shade of fuchsia when she saw Allyson in Ewan's plaid. She pointed an accusatory finger and stepped up to Allyson's face.

"You slattern," Alice hissed. "He was supposed to be mine."

"She may wear his plaid, but that's only because he has to marry her. She isn't who he wants," Mary purred. She smiled coyly as Ewan, and it made his stomach turn.

"I've been no one's but Ally's. You may continue to throw yourself at me and my brother, but neither of us will accept you," Ewan glared at Alice.

"Don't put words in my mouth, brother. I don't want either of them near me." Eoin shook his head and threw up his hands. He looked at Kenneth. "I'll tell you now, Laird Elliot, I won't marry any of your daughters. I need to know my wife isn't the type to bed any mon who looks in her direction."

"Enough!" Kenneth roared. "You will not speak of my daughters in such a degrading manner."

"We won't?" Ewan pushed Allyson behind him and took a step forward. His temper was just as heated at Kenneth. "How aboot the way your family speaks aboot Allyson? You didn't stop Alice from lobbing disparaging names at Allyson. You'd do well to pay more attention to how you run your family and your clan. There'll be no more whispers aboot Allyson's parentage. She's the only Elliot offspring who looks like both sides of the family. If aught, it's suspicious that none of the others bare more than a passing resemblance to you and only look like Lady Elliot's side of the family."

As one, the laird's family turned to stare at the paintings Ewan pointed toward.

"How did you get in the attic?" Margaret demanded. She pushed Ewan's shoulder as though she could make him move aside, so she could reach Allyson. The younger woman refused to hide behind Ewan and stepped forward. But Ewan's hand flew up to catch Margaret's wrist as she made to slap Allyson.

"She's mine now. Touch her, and you will pay." Ewan's hushed tones were more menacing than if he'd bellowed like Kenneth had moments ago.

"She's not yours," Margaret argued as she tugged her hand free.

"She spent the entire afternoon alone with me in my chamber." Ewan cocked an eyebrow. "Why don't you explain your reason for allowing your clan to gossip that Allyson's a bastard when proof has existed her entire life?"

"Because I didn't want her," Margaret blurted. She drew back, surprised by her own vehemence. She cast her glare on her husband, who looked surprised at the admission. "When she came out looking like Kenneth's mother, I knew she was his."

"Who else's child would I have been, Mother?" Allyson's lower lip trembled.

Margaret didn't shift her gaze from Kenneth as the dirty family secret spilled forth. "I never wanted to marry your father, but we made do for many years. That was until he discovered I had a lover."

"My bluidy brother," Kenneth seethed.

"Your stepbrother," Margaret corrected. "That any of the first five bear a resemblance to the Elliots is a coincidence. You couldn't be rid of him, so you kept sending him on one patrol after another. Too many mugs of mead on Hogmanay and too many nights alone, I made the mistake of letting you back into my bed. I've been regretting it for two-and-twenty years. The mon I love died before she was born, and all I was left with was a brat I didn't want reminding me of you."

"I'm not my father's son?" Angus pushed forward. "You mean to tell me that not only am I illegitimate and not my father's true heir, the only one who is his heir is the sister we've ostracized her entire life."

"You were the ones I wanted," Margaret justified.

"That doesn't matter, Mother," Graeme stood next to his brother. "This changes everything."

"It changes naught." Margaret refused to accept that the earth-shattering news should alter anything about their lives.

"It does!" Graeme protested. "Allyson is Laird Elliot's heir, and we are naught but bastards. How could you do this to us, Mother?"

"I didn't do aught. It's his fault." Margaret pointed toward Ewan. "What business did he have in the attic? Only one person could have taken him there. She did this on purpose to tear apart our family."

"Family, Mother?" Laurel squawked. She stepped toward Margaret, so no one outside their group could hear. She scanned the crowd, but did not see her husband. "What family? If my husband discovers I'm a bastard, he could have our marriage annulled. Then where will I be with three weans and a bairn on the way?"

"None of you are bastards," Kenneth intervened. "You were all born while I've been married to your mother. You are legitimate because of that, even if I didn't sire you. Angus is still my heir."

Allyson never suspected her mother would spill such a horrible secret when she and Ewan discovered the paintings. She was angry at Ewan for threatening the secret that she spent time in the attic, but this turn of events shocked her. She'd hoped to be accepted into the family, not destroy it. Her hand fumbled against Ewan's as she tried to hold his. He entwined their fingers and squeezed her hand. Margaret ignored Laurel, keeping her attention on Allyson and Ewan.

"You still haven't answered my question. What were you doing in the attic?"

Panic pushed bile up the back of Allyson's throat as she feared her family would discover her secret hideaway. Ewan refused to speak unless Allyson gave him a cue, so when she remained silent, he did the same. Ewan glanced at Kenneth and witnessed the devastation on his face. The man had known about his wife's affair all along, but it appeared he had struggled with the secret that five of his six children weren't actually his. Ewan had watched Kenneth's expression when they discussed Allyson. The laird appeared completely mystified. A long silence ensued until Allyson turned toward Kenneth.

"Father, you must have known I was yours. I look like your mother, even if I have blond hair from Mother's family. Why didn't you ever defend me? Why didn't you ever set people straight and end the rumors?"

"What rumors, Allyson? You've always been my child, just as your brothers and sisters have been."

"No." Allyson shook her head. "You've claimed them as your own despite not siring them, but the one child you sired, you've never defended, never protected."

"What do you mean never defended, never protected? I bluidy well chased you all the way to England."

"Once, Laird Elliot. That doesn't make up for Allyson's entire life where you've turned a blind eye and deaf ear to how the clan's treated her." Ewan stated.

"What the hell are you talking aboot?" Kenneth demanded.

"You've never noticed how we treated Allyson?" Angus looked incredulous. "We've been under the impression she was your bastard all these years. We pitied Mother, assuming you'd forced her to raise a child you got on some whore." Angus spun around to glare once more at Margaret. "We followed your lead. We felt sorry for the burden we believed Allyson was to you. You didn't want her, so none of the rest of us did either. My God, Mother, you tried to break up a betrothal the king decreed because you claimed Allyson didn't deserve to marry before Mary and Alice, nor did she deserve a noble husband."

Allyson cowered when Angus stepped before her. Once again, Ewan pushed Allyson behind him. He didn't carry his sword in the keep, but his hand went to the dirk sheathed at his waist. Angus nodded at Ewan, regret painting a deep frown on his face.

"Allyson, I don't know what to say. I have been horrible to you your entire life. I've spoken ill of you and to you. I doubt you will ever call Redheugh your home once you leave here, but if I become the next laird, you will always be welcome here as my sister, equal to all the rest." Angus bowed before stepping back. Allyson watched him swallow several times as he looked toward the dais. She noticed he blinked several times as he composed himself.

"Allyson, I followed the lead of others, never considering I should think for myself," Graeme made to step closer, but a glance at Ewan made him freeze. "It was easier, and it just seemed natural. When Angus is laird, I suppose I shall be his second." Graeme paused and frowned. "Regardless, you will have the protection I've failed to offer you until now.

I understand it's little consolation, but it's all I can offer."

Allyson nodded and looked at her father. "I still don't understand why you never stopped all of this."

"You're a lass. I figured you were your Mother's responsibility. I didn't want to interfere."

"Interfere? Bluidy bleeding hell, Father! This entire clan assumes you either raped my mother or fucked a whore!" The color leeched from Allyson's face, and she turned so ghostly white Ewan feared she'd collapse. He pulled her into his arms, his expression daring anyone to speak against him.

"No one has ever made such an accusation within my hearing. I thought you preferred to be alone and chose to do things on your own. You were always my most independent child. That's why I agreed when the queen requested you serve her as a lady-in-waiting. I refused her requests for your sisters. I never trusted them as I did you, and the queen understood once you began your service. She realized the error it would have been to send Mary, Laurel, or Alice. Allyson, my neglect wasn't intentional. Your sisters are close in age, so they always had one another and seemed fine without me being very present. I believed my duty was to raise my sons while your mother raised you lasses."

"I only believe parts of that, Father. You've seen and heard how Mother treats me. You never wondered why? You never considered it over the top? Beyond the pale?"

"Your mother and I haven't gotten on in years. We agreed long ago not to interfere in each other's realms. I manage the clan business and warriors, along with training Angus and Graeme. Your mother oversaw all things in the keep, which included the four of you." Kenneth gestured toward the four young women. "Allyson, I'm sorry I've failed you. I care aboot all my children, but I've known all along you were the only one I sired, and yet you are the one I've most disappointed and taken for granted."

Ewan watched the women's faces as Agnus and Graeme apologized, and Kenneth attempted to rationalize his dereliction. All three of Allyson's sisters stood around Margaret, not a remorseful face among them. He understood none of the women would ever welcome Allyson. The hatred Margaret held toward Allyson was too embedded in her daughters for them ever to reconsider their beliefs. They were too jealous and covetous to ever forgive what they believed were Allyson's sins to bear.

"This is quite the spectacle you've created, Ewan. Are you proud to have aired our family's dirty laundry? Got a little more than you bargained for, didn't you? And you, Allyson, what were you doing rummaging through things that don't belong to you? If you hadn't been in the attic, doing God only knows what, you wouldn't have found those." Margaret jerked her thumb over her shoulder. A speculative look crossed the older woman's face. "That's where you go to hide, isn't it? That's where you sneak off to when you wish you were anywhere but here. When we wish you could be anyone but yourself."

Margaret signaled two maids and whispered to them when they came to stand before her. They hesitated but nodded before turning toward the stairs. They rushed up them, and Allyson pushed away from Ewan when she realized the women headed toward the stairs that led to the attic.

"No!" Allyson lifted her skirts and dashed after them. By the time she reached the landing, the women were out of sight. She ran up the next flight of stairs and down the passageway to the attic door. She rattled the doorknob, but they'd locked it. She didn't have her key with her. Allyson pounded on the door, but the maids refused to answer. She ran back down to her chamber and retrieved the key, making it back to the attic door as her mother unlocked it with her own key and disappeared through the doorway. She elbowed past the twins and her brothers, but her mother and sisters were already in the attic by the time she reached the bottom of the steps. She heard her mother's voice, filling her with dread.

"All of it," Margaret ordered.

Allyson stared in horror as the maids ripped apart precious books and her sisters shredded drawings she'd made as a child. She recognized the one of her on a horse with a faceless man, the one Ewan had seen. She snatched it from Laurel's hands, holding it against her breasts.

"Why?" She begged.

"You are not welcome here. Your noseying around destroyed our family," Margaret snapped.

"I thought it was your infidelity, Margaret," Kenneth wrapped his hand around his wife's wrist and squeezed until she dropped the figurines she held. He pulled her away, his face florid with rage he barely contained. Graeme and Angus rushed to stop their sisters, barking orders at the maids to leave. But the damage was done. Allyson's possessions lay strewn across the floor, wooden figures smashed to smithereens, parchment torn, and books barely hanging on with bindings in tatters. Ewan feared Allyson might collapse as she swayed beside him. He eased her against him, encircling her in his embrace, tucking her head against his chest as though he could shut out the world around her and keep her from seeing the devastation.

"I'm so sorry, Ally," Ewan murmured. "I never in my wildest dreams imagined they would do something like this. I didn't think I'd be giving away your secret." Ewan felt tears fall along his cheeks, the first he'd shed in nearly a score of years. Allyson looked up to see the regret and heartbreak on his face, but all she could do was nod.

Eoin stepped forward, then squatted on the tapestry where Ewan and Allyson spent several nights. He examined what remained, moving salvageable items to the side. The pile was small. He rolled the tapestry, hiding the rest. The twins looked at one another, a message passing between them. They would ride at dawn, but not before Ewan had the contract amended. No one in the Elliot clan would ever dictate where Allyson lived again.

"Ally, we're going to your father's solar right now to explain what's happened while he was gone, then you're coming back to the tower with me. We ride first thing in the morning. Is there aught you need from your chamber?" Ewan whispered.

Allyson shook her head, her mind too clouded to fully make sense of Ewan's words. Ewan looked over her head at Kenneth, who still held his wife's arm. Their contempt and disgust for each other was plain for everyone to see.

"I'm going to do what I should have done the first time you bore me a bastard. You will retire to a convent. You are too great a disgrace to be seen. I will petition the king and the Pope to sever our marriage." Kenneth growled, and Ewan feared for a moment that he might strike Margaret. He shifted his gaze to Laurel, Mary, and Alice, who stood in silence, awaiting their fate for their contribution to the ugly scene. "Laurel, you and your husband will move your family into a croft. If you can show remorse for your actions in the coming the years, I will consider allowing your family to return to the keep. Alice and Mary, choose a convent or I will find you husbands forthwith. Naught changes for Angus and Graeme, except you two will join me for hours in the chapel

on our knees, atoning for our misdeeds. You all remain my children as you always have been, but this
family changes as of today. Ewan, please join me in
my solar to complete our business."

Ewan moved to guide Allyson toward the stairs,
but she shook her head. She cast a sweeping glance
around the attic, her heart broken and in need of solace. "Go. You said you don't require my signature. I
need some time alone. I'll find you in a little while."

"No. I won't leave you alone. I don't trust your
mother or your sisters. I'm scared you're no longer
safe here. Your mother isn't a well woman, and the
hate she's instilled in your sisters won't disappear just
because you've confronted them. Please, come to the
solar with me. When we finish, I'll bring you back
here. I'll guard the door, and you can have as much
time as you need."

Allyson capitulated and nodded. Ewan felt the
fight go out of her as she leaned heavily against him.
They followed Kenneth and Angus to the laird's solar. Eoin stood outside the door, guarding the discus-
sions while Graeme corralled the women to the
Great Hall where they ate in silence. The conversation swirled around Allyson as numbness settled over
her. She'd taken a seat next to Ewan, his hand
holding hers, but when she shivered, he lifted her
into his lap, cradling her against his large chest. She
absorbed the heat Ewan radiated, and her eyes
drifted closed. Ewan felt the moment Allyson drifted
off, her body going lax against his. He hadn't noticed
he stroked her head until it was time to wake Allyson.
Ewan explained what transpired with Mary and Eoin
in the garden, what happened while Kenneth was on
patrol, and how he and Allyson intended to return to
court to inform the king that they were duly wed.
When Kenneth's initial bluster blew over, he accepted that after what he witnessed that evening,

Ewan had done the right thing to protect Allyson. Ewan shook Allyson's shoulder until she woke.

"*Mo aingeal*, do you want to return to the attic, go to your chamber, or settle for the night in mine?"

"I don't know." Allyson's thready voice worried Ewan. The color hadn't returned to her face, and her hands were like icicles. "Whatever you want, Ew."

What Ewan wanted was to order the Gordon horses saddled and to ride out that night. He recognized that would needlessly endanger Allyson, and they all needed the benefit of a good night's sleep before setting off. They faced two days of hard riding, which meant at least one night under the stars. Ewan feared Allyson might fall ill from the strain.

"We'll stick to the original plan. I'll take you to the attic, then your chamber. Gather aught you want to take with you, then we'll go to my chamber."

"Nay. We can stay in my chamber. I'd rather be alone, but I know you won't agree to that, so we can sleep there."

"If that's what you prefer, then that's what we shall do."

Ewan and Allyson left the laird's solar and made a stop in the attic. Allyson lifted the lid on a dusty chest and pulled out a stack of parchment, each covered in drawings that demonstrated Allyson's artistic gifts. Ewan recognized how her talent improved over the years. She rolled them tightly before securing them with a ribbon that held her hair back. She found a small sack that she filled with the items Eoin set aside. They made their way to Allyson's chamber, where she hurried to pack a satchel with two fresh chemises and two kirtles she'd mended. Once she added stockings, her combs and a bar of soap, she had all the belongings she intended to take from the place she'd called home for most of her life. Ewan helped her undress and offered to sleep on the floor by the locked and barred door, but Allyson shook her head and wordlessly patted the bed beside her. It was narrow and forced them to lie on their sides. Allyson fell back to sleep as soon as Ewan's arm wrapped around her middle. Ewan watched Allyson sleep for a long time before exhaustion overtook him. He wished he could spend every night for the rest of his life as they were now, but he wasn't sure that would be possible once they returned to court. Even if they were legally married, the king and the bishop would likely force them to wait out the rest of Lent to share a chamber, insisting they sleep apart until they were sacramentally wed.

CHAPTER THIRTY-TWO

The Gordons, Allyson, and Kenneth set off at dawn the next day with little fanfare or send off. Angus and Graeme wished them well, but none of the women in the laird's family made an appearance. It was just as well. Allyson didn't have the fortitude for another confrontation. She mounted and followed Ewan through the gates of Redheugh, praying she need never return. They rode hard the next two days, making camp only when the road became too dangerous to navigate in the dark. Kenneth appeared tempted to intervene when Ewan spread his bedroll next to Allyson's, but a glare from Ewan and a possessive arm wrapped around Allyson's waist reminded him that she was now Ewan's responsibility. They hadn't announced before departing that their betrothal was now a marriage, but Ewan intended to request an audience with the king to inform him that the wedding would need to take place immediately. They'd been away from Stirling for a month, and they had little more than a week to wait for Lent to end.

They rode into Stirling early the morning of their third day of travel. Ewan was proud of Allyson's resilience. She had shown no discomfort while on horseback for hours at a time, and she tended to her horse herself. She helped prepare their meals, cooking the animals caught and making bannocks each morning. Eoin teased that they'd make a real Highlander of her yet. Ewan's heart thudded as Allyson beamed at the praise. The time it took to return to Stirling had a rejuvenating effect, and Allyson emerged from her shell once more. Her relationship with her father was strained, but neither appeared to hold any animosity toward one another.

As they dismounted in the bailey, Allyson experienced a wave of trepidation. Her return would force her to accept the consequences of her decision to run away. She stared at the facade and wondered what rumors circulated among the ladies-in-waiting. While at Redheugh, she had the distraction of her family and Ewan. While nothing good had come of her time with her family, the extended time with Ewan had fostered a growing love between them. Had they not been able to spend so much time together, isolated from the interfering courtiers or Ewan's duties at home, Allyson doubted they would have grown close. They might not even tolerate one another. Instead, she'd found a best friend, a partner, and a man she adored.

"Are you ready, *mo ghaol*?" Ewan whispered as he came to stand beside her.

"I suppose, though, it wouldn't matter if I weren't. I fear the king shall be angry with me and the queen disappointed."

"We won't know until we enter." Ewan laced his fingers between hers and squeezed. Allyson's eyes dropped to the sight of their hands joined. Ewan intended for them to enter as equals and to display his support from the onset. They followed Kenneth into the castle, with Eoin bringing up the rear. Guards divested the men of their weapons before they entered the passageway leading to King Robert's Privy Council chamber. They found Laird Andrew Gordon pacing in the corridor. The chamberlain bade them to wait, and it felt like an eternity before he returned to open the door and ordered them to enter. Allyson glanced around the large gathering chamber, noticing that several men gathered around a center table, discussing parchments laid across the surface. Other courtiers milled about the periphery of the chamber, but all conversations halted when Allyson and Ewan entered. Curious faces and smirks aimed at Allyson made her want to shift nervously, but she employed every skill she'd learned at court to maintain a neutral mien and proper posture. They approached the king, the men bowing and Allyson curtseying. Then they waited again, Ewan rubbing his thumb over the back of Allyson's hand. When the king finally shifted his attention to them, his gaze was riveted on their hands, and a smile tugged at his mouth before he stifled it.

"It seems you resolved the earlier issues," King Robert boomed, and Allyson wanted to shrink into the floor as everyone in the chamber looked in their direction. "It appears not only have you made amends, but you've developed a fondness for one another."

"Your assessment is correct, Your Grace," Ewan responded. "Much has happened in the past moon, but the time away from the distractions of court life gave Lady Allyson and me the opportunity to get better acquainted with one another."

"Distractions? I believe you mean temptations." The Bruce studied Ewan, then shifted his gaze to Allyson. "There is a difference aboot you both. Ewan, you appear a wee humbler, and Lady Allyson, you appear more at ease than I have ever seen you."

"I am, Your Majesty," Allyson spoke clearly but

softly. She'd never felt comfortable during audiences with the king. She much preferred the time she spent with Queen Elizabeth. While still an imposing figure, the queen didn't strike fear within Allyson.

"Your Grace, before aught else is said, I must inform you that Lady Allyson and I are legally married. We will have the sacramental wedding during Eastertide."

"A betrothal ceremony is the same as a wedding. No priest will conduct the service." The king shook his head. A look of genuine regret crossed his face as he studied the couple once more, noting Allyson's stricken expression.

"Your Majesty?" Allyson waited for the king to acknowledge her, holding her breath, fearing King Robert's reaction to her addressing him rather than waiting to be spoken to. When King Robert nodded, she proceeded. "If I might clarify, You Majesty. A betrothal isn't sacramental. It doesn't have to include a priest because it's a promise to marry in the future which means it doesn't violate canon law. We, um, already ensured that we're legally married. We made our promise to marry in the future, and Eoin witnessed it. And since then, we, um—" Alyson couldn't finish, her cheeks on fire with embarrassment.

King Robert paused as he considered Allyson's announcement; he was slow to respond but eventually nodded his head. "It seems I will need to inform the bishop that there will be a wedding during Eastertide."

"Thank you, Your Grace."

The king returned to the center table and his advisors. While Eoin and Allyson talked quietly, Laird Gordon looked between his older son and his new wife.

"That went far more smoothly than I imagined," Andrew spoke up. He had remained silent since they entered the Privy Council chamber. He'd barely acknowledged their arrival in the passageway. Ewan grimaced, fearing what his father would say next. The words made Ewan cringe. "I believe a tavern and a wench are in order to bid farewell to your bachelorhood."

"Nay, Father. Those are part of my past. I have no interest in any woman other than Allyson."

"Come now, you aren't really married until the church ceremony. You made your position clear before this disaster. You don't intend to alter your lifestyle. You have at least a sennight, if not a moon or more, before you'll marry before God. Until then, we've got the contracts secured, and we can go on aboot our lives. Laird Elliot and I will set a date for the marriage. Until then, we'll return to Huntley while Lady Allyson remains here or returns to Redheugh. It matters little to us."

Allyson went rigid as Andrew's words drifted to her. Eoin broke off mid-sentence as he looked past Allyson to his father and brother. He glanced down at Allyson before placing his hand on her arm in reassurance. Ewan's irritated voice spoke over Andrew's, and his words calmed Allyson's moment of panic.

"That is not what will happen, Father. I will not be leaving Allyson anywhere. You heard Allyson, and I'm certain you understood her. We are already married, and the church service will be in ten days. If we can't marry before a priest the day after Easter, then I will remain at court or Allyson will come home with us, but I am not going anywhere without her. She absolutely will not return to Redheugh. That is unacceptable." Ewan pushed his shoulders back and lifted his chin in challenge to his father. "I am more than just betrothed to Allyson, and I am responsible for her wellbeing. And let me be very clear aboot something, Father. I love Allyson. Much has happened in the past moon, which I'll explain at a better time. But make no mistake, I will be faithful to Allyson until I draw my last breath. She and I will have a very different marriage than you and Mother or Allyson's parents. I will honor my vows from today until the end."

Andrew watched his son, noting his son's conviction and a hint of defiance as he defended his bride and his marriage. It was the most honorable act he had seen Ewan commit, and it filled him with pride.

"I wish you a happier marriage than I had with your mother. If you love Allyson, as you say you do, then you're already on the right path. Your commitment and integrity reassure me that one day you will lead our clan with honor." Andrew clapped his son on the shoulder before sticking out his hand. Father and son grasped forearms in a warriors' handshake. Andrew turned to Allyson and smiled, waving her over. "I owe you an apology for those uncouth words you must have overheard. I understand that circumstances have changed much while you were away. I welcome you to Clan Gordon, lass. I hope you find your new home and family welcoming because we look forward to your arrival at Huntley."

"Thank you, Laird Gordon. You are correct that much has transpired since we last stood in this chamber. I've come to know both of your sons, and I count Eoin as a friend I can trust in all things. But it's Ewan who I love. I will do all that I can to be a good wife to him and a good lady of the clan to your people. I appreciate your welcome, and I hope you can forgive the inordinate amount of trouble I have caused."

"It's Andrew, lass. We are as good as kin now. And it would seem that the time away from court has made this marriage possible. You don't look ready to murder my son in his sleep. And he is certainly a better mon for it."

"I won't be doing that, I promise." Allyson smiled as Ewan wrapped his arm around her and kissed her crown.

"Lady Allyson, the queen will be happy that you've returned." King Robert had remained silent as he observed the couple along with the father and son. He noticed that Kenneth seemed to float on the outskirts, saying nothing but watching his daughter like a hawk. He wondered what transpired to change the dynamics of these relationships. Allyson swallowed, dreading having to appear before the queen. She didn't want to avoid the queen so much as she wanted to avoid the other ladies-in-waiting. The king observed her trepidation. "Perhaps you would benefit from some time to refresh yourself. The evening meal should be soon enough to reunite with your friends and for you to greet the queen."

Allyson curtseyed while the men bowed and left the Privy Council chamber. Allyson looked about and felt suddenly lost, unsure of whether she should retire to her chamber or if she could slip out to the gardens. She assumed Ewan would have business to discuss with his father, and she doubted her father intended to spend time with her. She wasn't surprised when Kenneth excused himself and left to make arrangements for his return to Redheugh.

"Come, Father." Eoin wrapped his arm around Andrew's shoulders, guiding him away from the couple. "I will explain all that happened, and we must plan for delivering the sheep to the Elliots."

Allyson and Ewan stood watching the two men move further down the passageway before they looked at one another, broad grins breaking across their faces once more. Ewan pulled Allyson closer, whispering in her ear. "Eoin will keep Father occupied until the evening meal, then he will make himself scarce for the night."

"Oh?" Allyson glanced at the men's retreating backs.

"Ally, you're my wife now. We have time to make up for from when we traveled with a retinue."

"That's only possible if we——"

"Aye, *mo aingeal.* I recall you have roommates, so we are going to the Gordon suite."

Allyson glanced around, fearful someone overheard them. As far as anyone was aware at court, they weren't yet married. She didn't doubt that word was already circulating about their return, but she didn't want rumors spreading that not only had she run away, she was allowing Ewan to bed her. She wasn't certain who was aware that both lairds and Ewan had already signed the contracts.

"Are you sure that's wise?" Allyson bit her lower lip. She wanted to retire with Ewan and spend the next week and a half in their chamber, not leaving it until the church service. But she feared the consequences of going with him when everyone at court thought they were only betrothed and loathed one another.

"Ally, regardless of whether people are aware of what happened, there will be speculation. Wouldn't you rather we appear as a happy couple in love than have people gossip that our fathers forced the marriage?"

"I would. I just fear we're being indiscreet."

"If you'd rather go to your chamber and I go to mine, then I'll take you there."

Allyson shook her head. "No, I want to go to yours."

"Good, but Ally, that makes it our chamber. I don't want his and her chambers; I want our chamber."

"Truly? I assumed you would keep your space, and one day you would move into the laird's chamber, and I would move into the lady's chamber. Until then, I figured you'd give me a chamber when I arrive at Huntley, and you would visit when you wanted us to couple."

Ewan's deep laugh made Allyson shift nervously as she continued to peer around the passageway. "What would be the point of that? I'd be visiting your chamber morn, noon, and eve, and sleeping there each night. I'd much rather we have the space my chamber provides, and when the day comes, we will move again. The laird's chamber will be ours, and the lady's chamber can become your solar, if you like."

Allyson nodded, then grinned. Her gaze slid over Ewan, and a hunger came into her eyes that Ewan shared. They hurried through the passageway toward the Gordon suite. But Allyson drew to an abrupt halt when she spotted Lady Bevan in the distance. Ewan had been looking down at Allyson as they talked, so he was unprepared for her to stop.

"Ally?"

Allyson said nothing. The only suite at that end of the passageway was the Gordons'. The only reason for Lady Bevan to be standing there was if she intended to visit one of the Gordon men. Ewan shifted to follow Allyson's glare. He wanted to sink through the floor when he spotted the woman who sparked the fight that drew them into such a whirlwind month. He squeezed Allyson's hand as they continued on, Lady Bevan not moving from where she stood at the door to the chambers.

"Ewan, I've been wondering when you would return." Lady Bevan's smile was pure seduction as she stepped toward Ewan. She cast a withering glance at Allyson. "I wasn't sure if it was you or Eoin, but I see you have your betrothed clinging to you. I've missed you and your brother."

"Good morning, Lady Bevan. My brother and father are together, probably in the lists. My wife and I are headed to our chamber. Excuse us." Ewan wrapped his arm around Allyson and moved to step around the beautiful widow, but she wasn't willing to give up.

"Wife? Last we heard, she ran away, and now you claim she's your wife. Did I miss an entire liturgical season?" Lady Bevan reached out to trail her fingers over Ewan, but he stepped back. She leaned to whisper none too quietly in his ear. "You know where to find me once you're free of her. I look forward to reminding you of what I can do with my tongue and your cock."

Allyson had heard enough. She stepped between them as Ewan took another step away and opened his mouth to speak. He never got the chance. "My husband's cock is already being polished. By me. Find Eoin, find Laird Gordon, find anyone, but make such an offer to my husband again, and the only thing your tongue will do is lie on the floor. After I cut it off."

"Look! The kitten's got claws," Lady Bevan chuckled, but there was no mirth in her voice.

"Better than the pox you had during winter." Allyson smirked. "Did you think no one knew aboot that? Everyone knew. It wasn't until you bedded Laird MacLeod that anyone was sure you weren't still infected."

"You little bitch."

"Aye, and you can call me all the names you want while you stand out here. My husband and I have something more—ahem—pressing to tend to."

Ewan led Allyson to their door and rushed to unlock it. He pushed Allyson into the chamber before locking and barring the door behind them. He turned to find Allyson gazing at the large bed in the center of the chamber. She looked nervous, and he wasn't sure if she feared his reaction to her comments, the bed, or both.

"Ally?"

"Are you angry with me?"

"Nay. Not in the least. She had it coming, and while I might not have said quite what you did, she should understand that I'm not interested." He took Allyson's hand and led her toward the bed, but she stopped a few feet short. "If you'd rather retire to your chamber and rest, I know it was a long two days in the saddle."

"Hmm?" Allyson looked at Ewan and shook her head. "No. I don't want to go there."

"Then what is it? Why do you look so uneasy?"

"It's naught." Allyson tried to avoid explaining, but Ewan's questioning expression gave way to one of concern. "It's just that at Redheugh, I was confident you hadn't coupled with anyone where we made love. Here—well, after running into Lady Bevan when she made it clear she intended for you to make love to her here, it just is a wee uncomfortable."

Ewan led Allyson away from the bed and toward the fireplace. He took a seat and pulled her into his lap. He stroked the hair off her shoulders, glad that she hadn't begun wearing it up like she would once it became known she was no longer a maiden. He twirled a lock around his finger as he took her hand in his.

"My father has kept mistresses in this suite when he's spent extended time at court, but Eoin and I never brought women back here. We had an unspoken agreement that our family chambers were just for family. We preferred having somewhere to retire to that was private. You're the only woman I've ever brought in here, and Eoin has never brought a woman here. I know what it looks like with a woman waiting outside my chamber, but I promise you, she's never been inside. Even if I weren't married, or if I still held my old opinions on marriage, I wouldn't have welcomed her inside." Allyson smiled and nodded, and Ewan saw the relief on her face. He also guessed what she would wonder next, and as her expression grew solemn once more, he spoke up. "No, I haven't taken a woman to my bed at home either. I like my privacy, as does Eoin. As twins, we didn't have much of it growing up. And I'm certain that sounds ridiculous given what you saw all those sennights ago, but he and I both like to retire to our own space. That said, I won't lie. I'm eager to get you home and into our bed. I like the idea that my privacy now includes you, naked, and ready to make love."

"You're incorrigible."

"Would you have me any other way?"

"I'd have you on that bed, right now." Allyson hopped off Ewan's lap and danced away as he playfully reached for her. She backed away as she unfastened her Gordon arisaid and reached down to pull off her riding boots. Ewan watched her with eagle eyes while he stripped off his own boots and stockings. He was undressed before she finished unlacing her kirtle. He twirled her around and ripped the laces from the eyelets before he practically ripped the gown from her. They fell onto the bed, their laughter soon turning into moans as Ewan slid inside Allyson.

"I love you, and I want no other, Ally. Never doubt that. Especially not while we're here."

"The past is the past," she responded. "I may have bedded none of the men here, but I flirted with my fair share. I suspect you will see how I just felt when we join the evening meal."

"I intend to leave such a lasting impression on ye, lass, that ye'll never look at one of those Lowlanders again." Ewan was aware Allyson preferred his brogue, and she reacted instantly. She pulled him in for a fierce kiss as she wrapped her legs over his calves, her arms holding him tightly against her. "I canna get enough of ye, *mo ghaol*. I want to make ye scream ma name."

Ewan thought he would go cross-eyed from the sensation of being buried to the hilt within Allyson. The feel of her soft body beneath him, the taste of her mouth as they kissed, and the way her channel held him in place, he struggled not to spill too soon. He pistoned his hips over and over as she rose to meet each thrust.

"Keep talking to me with that burr, and it won't take but a minute," Allyson purred.

"But I want to make this last."

Those were the last words spoken as they writhed together until they screamed one another's name. Sated and exhausted, they fell asleep wrapped in one another's embrace, Allyson's head resting on Ewan's chest. They remained locked in their chamber for the rest of the day, making love throughout the afternoon and early evening. They summoned a tray midafternoon when they knew the rest of court would gather, but they refused to emerge until there was no avoiding the evening meal.

CHAPTER THIRTY-THREE

Allyson scanned the courtiers gathered in the Great Hall awaiting the evening meal. She spotted the table where her closest friends sat, along with the tables with the other ladies-in-waiting she didn't care to see. She swept her eyes across the large chamber to where Andrew and Eoin sat with their men. Ewan squeezed her hand and nudged her forward. She'd had one of her court gowns sent to their chamber, and Ewan requested servants to draw a bath. They'd enjoyed soaking in the hot water and making love before helping one another bathe. Allyson wore her hair up for the first time besides when she tended the sick or helped in the Redheugh kitchens. It signaled to one and all that she was a married woman. If that didn't announce her change in status, entering the Great Hall holding hands with Ewan and wearing a swath of Gordon plaid certainly did. They made their way to the Gordon table, where the men rose as Allyson approached. She slid into a spot between Ewan and Eoin, comfortably wedged between the massive Highlanders. It took a while, but Allyson eased into the conversation with her brother-by-marriage, father-by-marriage, and their retainers. Ewan remained quiet, encouraging Allyson to be part of the clan. She discovered she enjoyed Andrew's sense of humor and understood where the twins got many of their mannerisms.

When the meal ended, a page approached and whispered in Allyson's ear that the queen wanted to speak with her. Allyson excused herself, prepared to make the walk on her own, but Ewan wrapped her arm around his and rested her hand on his forearm. When they neared the royal table, the queen surprised Allyson with a welcoming smile.

"Lady Allyson, you look well this eve," Queen Elizabeth stated as a greeting.

"Thank you, Your Grace. I'm very well." Allyson responded.

"The king informed me that not only have you both come to accept the prospect of marriage, you've decided not to wait for Easter to enter wedded bliss, taking it upon yourselves to speed things along."

"It is as you say, Your Grace," Allyson demurred.

"Then I offer you my felicitations. I'm pleased to see Ewan rose to the occasion and has earned your hand in marriage."

Allyson's fingers pressed against Ewan's arm as she thought of exactly how he'd risen to the occasion —several times.

"Thank you, Your Grace," Ewan spoke up when he suspected Allyson struggled not to giggle. "We look forward to our church ceremony, but I won't deny that I am enjoying a state of wedded bliss. Your Majesty," Ewan turned his attention toward King Robert. "I can only offer my heartfelt gratitude that you chose me to marry Allyson. I don't know your reasons, but I will always be grateful for your decision. Thank you, Your Majesty."

Ewan and Allyson backed away once the king

and queen accepted their thanks, and they returned to the Gordons.

"Lady Allyson," a masculine voice carried from over Allyson's shoulder, and she wanted to squirm when she recognized it. "It is a relief to see you safely returned to court. We have missed you and been deeply concerned."

Allyson turned to greet Allistair MacDonald, a young man she'd danced with on several occasions and kissed more than once. He was tall and ruggedly handsome, with jet-black hair and deep blue eyes. She'd once considered him the handsomest man ever to visit court. She now realized she hadn't given Ewan enough consideration. There was no man more handsome than her husband. She sensed Ewan tense as the man approached and reached out his hand. Allyson had little choice but to place hers on his, but she pulled it away as soon as he finished proffering a light kiss over the back of it.

"Allistair, thank you for your kind words. This is but a brief stop and not really a return to court. I'm eager to make my way home to Huntley and Gordon territory."

"Home to Huntley? I thought you just returned from your home, your real home." Allistair sounded confused on purpose, and Ewan wanted to choke the man.

"My real home is Huntley, or rather wherever Ewan is."

"How quaint," Allistair's smile looked painful, as though he fought not to curl his nose in disgust.

"Thank you for stopping to say hello. I hope you enjoy the rest of your evening." Allyson nodded and turned her back to Allistair.

Ewan was forced to sit through four more similar exchanges as men approached Allyson, one going so far as to request a dance the day after Easter. Allyson tittered and explained that would be impossible, since she'd already saved every dance for Ewan. Allyson was charming, but she was clear that she had no interest in continuing any flirtations with men from her past. Ewan ground his teeth and forced himself not to lash out at the men who he felt were leering at Allyson. He had never been possessive, having shared everything with Eoin their entire lives, but he found that Allyson brought that side out of him. His snarl kept women from approaching, and he was relieved not to have any more specters from his past appear while he was with Allyson. He suspected, just as Allyson wasn't fond of reminders from his past, he would never grow accustomed to men flirting with his wife.

When the meal ended, Allyson found herself swallowed in a gaggle of ladies-in-waiting who peppered her with questions and false concern. She knew they merely wanted information to turn into gossip. Her father, Ewan, Eoin, and she had agreed they would not speak of what happened at Chillingham to anyone, not even the king unless pressed to. So Allyson steered the conversation toward the time she and Ewan were at Redheugh, gliding over her mad dash to Culcreuch and Glasgow. She spoke of their walks and the time spent reading together, playing games, and dancing. She knew news that there had been dancing so close to the beginning of Lent would be enough to distract many of them. That it had only been a few nights just before Shrove Tuesday wasn't what the women focused upon. Allyson slipped free and embraced Cairren Kennedy, delighted to see her best friend.

"You seem much happier than you were the last time I saw you," Cairren whispered.

"I am. Cairren, he's not at all what I thought. It took me a while to trust he could be anyone other than the rogue we were used to, but he is so much more. He's changed a great deal."

"And why do you think that is? Is he that much in love with you?"

"God, if you'll believe it. He said he prayed and felt God guiding him toward a different path. He said God's light drew him to the path that only held me and a lifetime of fidelity. He's proven he told the truth time and again."

"You love him, don't you?"

"Absolutely."

"And he loves you?"

"Yes. I didn't think it was possible, but he truly does."

"He looked fit to be tied when those men came to your table."

"I feared he'd beat them senseless, but he managed with restrain himself," Allyson chuckled. "He's a better person than I am. If any women had approached, I might've ended up in the castle's dungeon. We had a run in with Lady Bevan earlier. I may not have been as polite as I should have been. In fact, I was quite vulgar, and I don't regret it in the least."

"Good. I heard the king has arranged a marriage for her, too."

"To whom?" Allyson couldn't help herself; she wanted to know this piece of gossip.

"To auld Laird Farquharson."

"Good gracious, he's old enough to be my father's father. He's got to be close to seventy."

"Aye, and word is, he's still as randy as an old goat."

"What on earth did she do to deserve that?"

"She had some unkind words aboot you while you were gone, bragging that Ewan and Eoin would return to her bed once you were back. But her gravest sin was trying to seduce the king when she didn't realize the queen could see and hear her. You know the king prefers discretion, so it forced him to send her away. I overheard that the queen selected the groom."

"That is a shocking turn of events."

"Rather. The queen intends for her to leave two days after Easter."

"So she can watch the wedding," the two women said together before dissolving into laughter.

They clung to one another's arm until Ewan came to retrieve his bride. Allyson promised to visit with Cairren for longer in the days to come, as she had a sense that something else happened while she was gone. As Ewan suspected, Eoin was nowhere in sight when he led Allyson to the exit. He'd seen his brother speaking to Cairstine Grant, but he didn't see either of them as he and Allyson left. They retired to their chamber, where they spent most of their time over the coming week. Eoin shared a chamber with his father, allowing the newlyweds their space. Ewan left to train in the lists in the morning, and Allyson joined the queen and other ladies-in-waiting for their morning walk, but they spent their afternoons together. They joined the court for the evening meal, an expectation they couldn't avoid. When they weren't distracted with one another, Allyson drew and read; Ewan often serenaded her. The days between their return to court and their wedding slid past in a flurry of lovemaking and cuddling.

Allyson took one last glance at herself in the looking glass. It felt surreal to be in a gown she'd sewn four years ago but had kept stored in her chest. She'd sewn the gown when she learned she was being sent to court, understanding her parents hoped she would find a husband there. She'd wanted to be prepared, but as the years dragged on, she'd doubted when she would wear it. But she'd been resolute and saved it for this special day. Cairren helped style her hair, which she wore down but with a ribbon woven through a thick braid that coiled around her head. She'd never felt more beautiful than she did in that moment. She prayed Ewan would think she looked bonnie, too. She remembered their encounter in the dark passageway all those weeks earlier when he'd called her bonnie, and it had hurt her feelings to think he saw her as merely pretty when she knew her sisters were beautiful. She'd learned since then that bonnie meant more than just "pretty" to Highlanders. Now she enjoyed Ewan complimenting her appearance when he allowed his burr to color his words. It made her spine tingle.

"You're stunning, Allyson. Ewan won't know what to do having to wait through the entire ceremony," Cairren teased.

"I'm glad the king convinced the bishop that we could shorten the vows outside the kirk and move directly to the wedding Mass. Seemed a little too late for a lengthy exchange. Ewan and I have already made our promises to one another."

"I suppose, but it would have been wonderful to see you standing there with your braw Highlander. They are so different from the men in the Lowlands. It's rather exciting when they come to court."

"Perhaps, one day you'll have your own," Allyson teased, but when Cairren didn't join her laughter she sent her maid away. She sat beside Cairren and took her friend's hands in her. "What is it?"

"My father sent word that he's arranging a marriage for me, but I don't know to whom."

"Perhaps it'll be a braw Highlander after all."

"The Lowlanders at court are snooty enough, but I hear that Highlanders detest outsiders. I couldn't be more of one. I mean, look at me." Cairren placed her hands on her sun-darkened cheeks before holding out her arms, pushing back her sleeves. Her olive skin shone in the candlelight.

"I am looking at you. You're one of the most attractive women at court. What mon wouldn't want you?"

"Want to bed me, maybe, but marry me? Hardly. I won't resemble any of the Scottish roses in the Highlands. I'll stick out because I take after my mother's people."

"And the Scots have a history with the French. You're worrying aboot something that hasn't happened yet. If anyone has learned the futility of that, it's me."

"I suppose," Cairren agreed. She smiled with warmth as she stood and walked to the door with Allyson.

"You can always come to Huntley. Ewan and I will never turn you away."

"One runaway bride at court is more than enough. I shall just have to wait to see what happens."

The women left Allyson's old chamber together and made their way to the chapel. A crowd already gathered near the entrance to the kirk, but they parted like the Red Sea to allow Allyson to make her way to where Ewan waited. He wore a fresh leine and his formal plaid. He had never looked more breathtaking to Allyson, and the people watching fell away as her attention focused solely on Ewan. His smile dazzled her as she watched him take in her appearance. The look in his eyes was a mixture of appreciation and hunger, lust and love. They joined hands as once more the Gordon plaid was wrapped around them.

"I, Ewan Andrew Gordon, take you, Allyson Elliot Gordon, to be my wife. I plight thee my troth." Ewan beamed at Allyson, squeezing her hands beneath the checkered wool.

"I, Allyson Elliot Gordon, take you, Ewan Andrew Gordon, to by my husband. I plight thee my troth." Allyson blinked several times as she struggled to keep the happy tears from falling. She refused to have anyone doubt her desire to marry Ewan. He pulled her against him, dipping his head for a kiss, uncaring that it was too soon in the service for that. The bishop cleared his throat but soon gave up, ordering everyone into the kirk for the Mass. If asked, neither remembered much of the Mass. It went on around them, but they had eyes for no one and nothing but each other. When the service was over, Ewan lifted Allyson off her feet and held her, kissing her in a manner that left no one in question that he loved his bride. He refused to rush, and it was only when Allyson tapped his shoulder that he eased her to the ground.

"Need to breathe," she panted. Ewan chuckled, then swept her into his arms. He carried her to the Great Hall, where the feast celebrating their marriage and the beginning of Eastertide commenced. The king and queen offered Ewan and Allyson special seats at the high table, but the honor was lost on them as they fed one another and shared a chalice. They spent much of the meal whispering to one another, smiling at their shared secrets. They remained for three dances, then escaped to the quiet and privacy of their chamber. Once they were both free of their wedding finery, Ewan helped Allyson take down her hair. He enjoyed brushing the golden strands as they flowed down her back. Allyson was content to relax as Ewan's gentle touch made her body come alive.

"Wife, I think it's time we retire to that bed. We have a second wedding night to celebrate."

"Husband, if one is good, then two is better."

Ewan and Allyson climbed into bed, but laid on their sides looking at one another for a long time, only their hands touching. Slowly, they reached out, letting their hands roam over one another before Ewan rolled toward Allyson. He trailed kisses down her body until his lips brushed her curls. He laved her seam over and over as Allyson gripped his shoulders. Her knees fell wide as he ministered to her heated flesh, lapping up the cream that gathered in anticipation.

"I want to touch you too, Ew," Allyson begged. Ewan slid his body over hers until he nuzzled her neck, and she wrapped her hand around his cock. Only a few strokes later, Ewan seized her wrist, bringing her hand to his mouth. He kissed each fingertip before placing her hand on his shoulder. He thrust into her as she raised her hips to meet him. Ewan was determined not to rush this coupling. They took their time, building anticipation until the torment and need for release was too great to endure. They broke apart in one another's arms. Just like every other night since they made love for the first time, they alternated between bouts of lovemaking and sleep until they could no longer shut out the outside world. It was midmorning when a knock came to their door.

"That'll be Eoin," Ewan pulled his plaid around him and waited until Allyson covered herself with her robe. Ewan opened the door to find his twin on the other side. "We ken we need to be on the road. We'll be in the bailey in a quarter hour."

Allyson couldn't hear what else the twins said to

one another, having discovered they didn't always speak in complete sentences and often communicated more with looks than words. When Ewan shut the door, Allyson bounded out of bed and rushed toward the clothes she'd laid out the day before.

"You don't have to look quite so excited to escape our bed," Ewan chuckled as he pulled Allyson's robe off.

"You said we'd be down in a quarter hour."

"Aye, that'll leaves us ten minutes. I dinna need that long," Ewan teased as he cupped Allyson's backside and pulled her against him. Allyson scanned their chamber. Ewan arranged for her belongings to be sent to Huntley the day after they arrived at court. They'd each packed their satchels the morning prior, so there was little for them to do but get dressed. Allyson shrugged, then grinned.

"And I thought you'd only take five minutes."

"Cheeky lass." Ewan followed Allyson to the end of the bed and growled at the lusty smile she cast him over her shoulder. Twenty minutes later and still a bit breathless, Ewan and Allyson joined Eoin and Andrew in the bailey. The king and queen appeared to bid them farewell, wishing them safe travels until they should see them again. Allyson rode in center of the riding party, with Ewan and Eoin flanking her and Andrew in the lead. It was three days of hard riding along the eastern coast and into the Highlands, but as they traveled inland, the Cairngorm Mountains took her breath away. She glanced at Ewan and remembered how she'd once compared the twin Highlanders' size to the majestic peaks in the distance. Her home was now in the Highlands, far from the bitter memories of life along the border. Her future was with the Highlander who rode at her side, and she couldn't ask for more.

EPILOGUE

Ewan watched as Allyson folded the missive that arrived that morning before easing their sleeping son from her breast. The bairn cooed and blew bubbles as Allyson wiped his plump lips and pulled her hair free of his tiny fingers. As if she sensed Ewan observing her, she looked over at her husband, who sat on the floor with their two older sons. Allyson had discovered she was carrying their oldest son, Torquil, soon after they arrived at Huntley. She cast up her accounts one morning, and Ewan forbade her to leave their bed until the healer examined her. When the midwife slipped past him to go up to the chamber where the healer remained with Allyson, Ewan's legs buckled underneath him. Eoin suggested a dram of whisky, but Ewan was already taking the stairs two at a time. That was nearly five years ago. When, two years later, Allyson summoned the midwife again, Ewan was better prepared for news of their middle son's impending arrival. Leith sat beside his older brother as they passed carved wooden soldiers back and forth. Allyson rose and carried their youngest son, Teague, to his cradle. At a year old, he was nearly too large for the infant's bed. All three of their sons took after their father in size and build. Ewan had feared for Allyson during each delivery as he watched her push three large bairns out of her tiny body. He knew then that his wife was invincible.

"Angus's written to say Mother's dead," Allyson whispered as she took Ewan's hand as he led them back to the chair she'd just left. He sat and pulled her onto his lap. "It's been five years since I last saw her, and I can't say that I feel aught at the news that she's gone."

"She wasna a well woman, *mo ghaol*. We kenned that. Yer father was right to send her to the convent. The nuns were able to tend to her." Ewan gave up his courtly Lowland speech once they returned to Huntley, and Allyson was glad for it.

Margaret Elliot spent the last five years of her life at an abbey near Redheugh, but she slipped into madness when she learned that Mary and Alice both got with child from men in their village and wouldn't be marrying noblemen. The two sisters turned out to be content with their husbands, neither man tolerating their prima donna antics. Kenneth Elliot petitioned the king and Pope for an annulment which the Pope granted him, but he fell ill with the ague and died before he'd been able to seek a new bride. Angus took on the lairdship, and the Elliot clan thrived with a laird who kept himself informed of all things happening inside and out of the keep. Graeme proved to be a wise advisor to his older brother, and in the years since Allyson and Ewan married, the two clans strengthened their alliance by trading regularly. Allyson had put the past behind her and accepted her brothers for the men they became. But she hadn't returned to Redheugh since the day she and Ewan rode away, and he promised she would never have to.

"I know. It was better for everyone, but I feel as

though I should be sad or even guilty that I don't feel sad. There's just naught. I was at least a little saddened by the news of my father's passing. He made an effort once Mother went to the abbey, and he did get to meet Torquil. Does that make me a bad person?" Allyson picked up the missive again, but couldn't bring herself to open it. She handed it to Ewan, but he put it aside, wrapping his arms around Allyson as she leaned into the comfort of his chest. Five years had deepened their abiding love. Ewan was a model husband, while Allyson did all she could to make him happy and to serve the clan that welcomed her with open arms.

"Ye're nae a bad person, *mo aingeal*. Ye are completely normal to feel as ye do. Neither Eoin nor I was as saddened by Mother's death as I'm sure we will be when Father passes. Neither of our mothers were the type ye are." Allyson nodded as she looked at the family they'd made together. She'd sworn the moment she learned she was expecting Torquil that she would love her children equally and never let a day go by that they didn't know she loved them all. Allyson kissed Ewan neck as he stroked her hair. She loved the life they created together and the family they were raising. She had more than she'd ever imagined.

"*Mo chridhe*, do you think Eoin will have time to carve another wee bed for Teague? I will need that cradle again in six moons."

Ewan froze as he absorbed Allyson's words, and when he was certain he'd understood, he leaned away. "A bairn?" He whispered.

"Aye." Allyson and Ewan kissed until their children became restless and demanded their attention. Allyson tucked hair behind Ewan's ear before whispering, "And that's how we ended up with four bairns in five years."

THANK YOU FOR READING A ROGUE AT THE HIGHLAND COURT

Celeste Barclay, a nom de plume, lives near the Southern California coast with her husband and sons. Growing up in the Midwest, Celeste enjoyed spending as much time in and on the water as she could. Now she lives near the beach. She's an avid swimmer, a hopeful future surfer, and a former rower. When she's not writing, she's working or being a mom.

Visit Celeste's website, www.celestebarclay.com, for regular updates on works in progress, new releases, and her blog where she features posts about her experiences as an author and recommendations of her favorite reads.

Are you an author who would like to guest blog or be featured in her recommendations? Visit her website for an opportunity to share your insights and experiences.

Have you read *Their Highland Beginning, The Clan*

Sinclair Prequel? Learn how the saga begins! This FREE novella is available to all new subscribers to Celeste's monthly newsletter. Subscribe on her website.

www.celestebarclay.com

Join the fun and get exclusive insider giveaways, sneak peeks, and new release announcements in

Celeste Barclay's Facebook Ladies of Yore Group

THE HIGHLAND LADIES

A Spinster at the Highland Court

BOOK 1 SNEAK PEEK

Elizabeth Fraser looked around the royal chapel within Stirling Castle. The ornate candlestick holders on the altar glistened and reflected the light from the ones in the wall sconces as the priest intoned the holy prayers of the Advent season. Elizabeth kept her head bowed as though in prayer, but her green eyes swept the congregation. She watched the other ladies-in-waiting, many of whom were doing the same thing. She caught the eye of Allyson Elliott. Elizabeth raised one eyebrow as Allyson's lips twitched. Both women had been there enough times to accept they'd be kneeling for at least the next hour as the Latin service carried on. Elizabeth understood the Mass thanks to her cousin Deirdre Fraser, or rather now Deirdre Sinclair. Elizabeth's mind flashed to the recent struggle her cousin faced as she reunited with her husband Magnus after a seven-year separation. Her aunt and uncle's choice to keep Deirdre hidden from her husband simply because they didn't think the Sinclairs were an advantageous enough match, and the resulting scandal, still humiliated the other Fraser clan members at court. She admired Deirdre's husband Magnus's pledge to remain faithful despite not knowing if he'd ever see Deirdre again.

Elizabeth suddenly snapped her attention; while everyone else intoned the twelfth—or was it thirteenth—amen of the Mass, the hairs on the back of her neck stood up. She had the strongest feeling that someone was watching her. Her eyes scanned to her right, where her parents sat further down the pew. Her mother and father had their heads bowed and eyes closed. While she was convinced her mother was in devout prayer, she wondered if her father had fallen asleep during the Mass. Again. With nothing seeming out of the ordinary and no one visibly paying attention to her, her eyes swung to the left. She took in the king and queen as they kneeled together at their prie-dieu. The queen's lips moved as she recited the liturgy in silence. The king was as still as a statue. Years of leading warriors showed, both in his stature and his ability to control his body into absolute stillness. Elizabeth peered past the royal couple and found herself looking into the astute hazel eyes of Edward Bruce, Lord of Badenoch and Lochaber. His gaze gave her the sense that he peered into her thoughts, as though he were assessing her. She tried to keep her face neutral as heat surged up her neck. She prayed her face didn't redden as much as her neck must have, but at a twenty-one, she still hadn't mastered how to control her blushing. Her nape burned like it was on fire. She canted her head slightly before looking up at the crucifix hanging over the altar. She closed her eyes and tried to invoke the image of the Lord that usually centered her when her mind wandered during Mass.

Elizabeth sensed Edward's gaze remained on her. She didn't understand how she was so sure that he was looking at her. She didn't have any special gifts of perception or sight, but her intuition screamed that he was still looking.

A Spy at the Highland Court **BOOK 2**

A Wallflower at the Highland Court **BOOK 3**

A Rogue at the Highland Court **BOOK 4**

A Rake at the Highland Court **BOOK 5**

An Enemy at the Highland Court **BOOK 6**

A Saint at the Highland Court **BOOK 7**

A Beauty at the Highland Court **BOOK 8**

A Sinner at the Highland Court **BOOK 9**

A Hellion at the Highland Court **BOOK 10**

An Angel at the Highland Court **BOOK 11**

A Harlot at the Highland Court **BOOK 12**

His Highland Lass **BOOK 1 SNEAK PEEK**

She entered the great hall like a strong spring storm in the northern most Highlands. Tristan Mackay felt like he had been blown hither and yon. As the storm settled, she left him with the sweet scents of heather and lavender wafting towards him as she approached. She was not a classic beauty, tall and willowy like the women at court. Her face and form were not what legends were made of. But she held a unique appeal unlike any he had seen before. He could not take his eyes off of her long chestnut hair that had strands of fire and burnt copper running through them. Unlike the waves or curls he was used to, her hair was unusually straight and fine. It looked like a waterfall cascading down her back. While she was not tall, neither was she short. She had a figure that was meant for a man to grasp and hold onto, whether from the front or from behind. She had an aura of confidence and charm, but not arrogance or conceit like many good looking women he had met. She did not seem to know her own appeal. He could tell that she was many things, but one thing she was not was his.

His Bonnie Highland Temptation **BOOK 2**

His Highland Prize **BOOK 3**

His Highland Pledge **BOOK 4**

His Highland Surprise **BOOK 5**

Their Highland Beginning **BOOK 6**

The Blond Devil of the Sea **BOOK 1 SNEAK PEEK**

Caragh lifted her torch into the air as she made her way down the precarious Cornish cliffside. She made out the hulking shape of a ship, but the dead of night made it impossible to see who was there. She and the fishermen of Bedruthan Steps weren't expecting any shipments that night. But her younger brother Eddie, who stood watch at the entrance to their hiding place, had spotted the ship and signaled up to the village watchman, who alerted Caragh.

As her boot slid along the dirt and sand, she cursed having to carry the torch and wished she could have sunlight to guide her. She knew these cliffs well, and it was for that reason it was better that she moved slowly than stop moving once and for all. Caragh feared the light from her torch would carry out to the boat. Despite her efforts to keep the flame small, the solitary light would be a beacon.

When Caragh came to the final twist in the path before the sand, she snuffed out her torch and started to run to the cave where the main source of the village's income lay in hiding. She heard movement along the trail above her head and knew the local fishermen would soon join her on the beach. These men, both young and old, were strong from days spent pulling in the full trawling nets and hoisting the larger catches onto their boats. However, these men weren't well-trained swordsmen, and the fear of pirate raids was ever-present. Caragh feared that was who the villagers would face that night.

The Dark Heart of the Sea **BOOK 2**

The Red Drifter of the Sea **BOOK3**

The Scarlet Blade of the Sea **BOOK 4**

Leif **BOOK 1 SNEAK PEEK**

Leif looked around his chambers within his father's longhouse and breathed a sigh of relief. He noticed the large fur rugs spread throughout the chamber. His two favorites placed strategically before the fire and the bedside he preferred. He looked at his shield that hung on the wall near the door in a symbolic position but waiting at the ready. The chests that held his clothes and some of his finer acquisitions from voyages near and far sat beside his bed and along the far wall. And in the center was his most favorite possession. His oversized bed was one of the few that could accommodate his long and broad frame. He shook his head at his longing to climb under the pile of furs and on the stuffed mattress that beckoned him. He took in the chair placed before the fire where he longed to sit now with a cup of warm mead. It had been two months since he slept in his own bed, and he looked forward to nothing more than pulling the furs over his head and sleeping until he could no longer ignore his hunger. Alas, he would not be crawling into his bed again for several more hours. A feast awaited him to celebrate his and his crew's return from their latest expedition to explore the isle of Britannia. He bathed and wore fresh clothes, so he had no excuse for lingering other than a bone weariness that set in during the last storm at sea. He was eager to spend time at home no matter how much he loved sailing. Their last expedition had been profitable with several raids of monasteries that yielded jewels and both silver and gold, but he was ready for respite.

Leif left his chambers and knocked on the door next to his. He heard movement on the other side, but it was only moments before his sister, Freya, opened her door. She, too, looked tired but clean. A few pieces of jewelry she confiscated from the holy houses that allegedly swore to a life of poverty and deprivation adorned her trim frame.

"That armband suits you well. It compliments your muscles," Leif smirked and dodged a strike from one of those muscular arms.

Only a year younger than he, his sister was a well-known and feared shield maiden. Her lithe form was strong and agile making her a ferocious and competent opponent to any man. Freya's beauty was stunning, but Leif had taken every opportunity since they were children to tease her about her unusual strength even among the female warriors.

"At least one of us inherited our father's prowess. Such a shame it wasn't you."

Freya **BOOK 2**

Tyra & Bjorn **BOOK 3**

Strian **VIKING GLORY BOOK 4**

Lena & Ivar **VIKING GLORY BOOK 5**

www.ingramcontent.com/pod-product-compliance
Lightning Source LLC
Chambersburg PA
CBHW011931050726
47590CB00011B/3229